F COLOMA

Tonkin, Peter.

Killer

OCT 3 1979	DATE	
OCT. 12 1979	FEB. 3 1982	
OCT. 29 1979	FEB 6 1985	
NOV. 16 1979	MAY 23 1986	
NOV. 28 1979	JUL 6 1991	
FEB. 25 1980	JUL 15 1991	
MAR 25 1980		
APR. 23 1980	DE 14 07	
MAY 22 1980		
JUN. 28 1980		
DEC. 22 1980	MY 02 6	
AUG. 22 1981		

© THE BAKER & TAYLOR CO.

KILLER

KILLER

PETER TONKIN

Coward, McCann & Geoghegan, Inc.
New York

First American edition 1979

Libraray of Congress Cataloging in Publication Data

Tonkin, Peter.
  Killer.

  I. Title.
PZ4.T66Ki   1979   [PR6070.0498]   823'.9'14
ISBN 0-698-10974-0   79-1482

Printed in the United States of America

For
all the family and friends,
without whom . . .
especially for
my parents,
Simon, Michael and Carolyn
Jill, Joy and Richard
and all the staff and girls
of Collingwood school
with thanks.

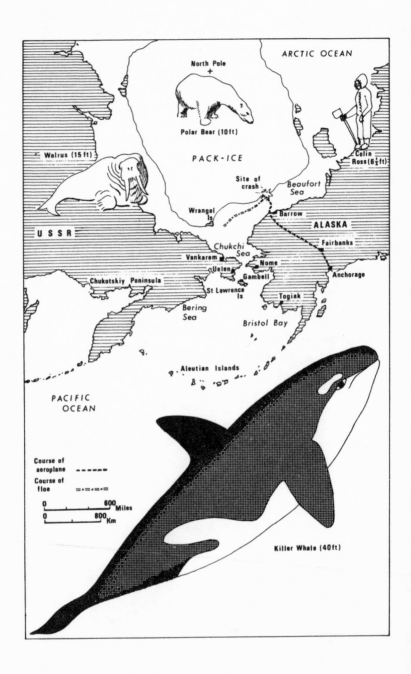

ARCTIC OCEAN

North Pole
+

Polar Bear (10 ft)

PACK-ICE

Site of
crash

Beaufort
Sea

Colin
Ross (6½ ft)

Walrus (15 ft)

Wrangel
Is

Barrow

ALASKA

U S S R

Chukchi
Sea

Vankarem

Fairbanks

Uelen

Nome

Chukotskiy Peninsula

Gambell

Anchorage

St Lawrence
Is

Togiak

Bering
Sea

Bristol Bay

Aleutian Islands

PACIFIC
OCEAN

Course of
aeroplane

Course of
floe

0   600 Miles

0   800 Km

Killer Whale (40 ft)

THE LURE OF THE DOLPHIN, FIRST BROADCAST ON BRITISH T.V. 1975

Showed film of experiments performed by the U.S. Navy concerning the training of dolphins, narwhals and killer-whales in techniques of underwater recovery.

Various authorities on the behaviour and training of these creatures revealed they were also being trained in anti-personnel work, and being taught to kill divers.

DAILY MAIL, NOVEMBER 1977

[Wild dolphins have been] trained by the U.S. Navy to patrol Vietnam's ports against enemy frogmen despatching them with bayonets strapped to their blunt noses.

DAILY EXPRESS, DECEMBER 1, 1977

Squads of dolphins trained to kill enemy divers with gas guns, have already been used to defend American naval bases.

TESTIMONY TO THE SENATE COMMITTEE ON INTELLIGENCE ACTIVITIES, NOVEMBER, 1977

(i) James Fitzgerald, former Chief of the Office of Dolphin Research, Central Intelligence Agency:
"With their built-in sonar the dolphins detected enemy demolition divers on sabotage missions. They impaled them with hypodermic needles connected to carbon-dioxide cartridges. The frogmen just blew up and exploded."

(ii) Spokesman for the Office of Naval Research:
"Some sixty North Vietnamese frogmen were nullified by our dolphins."

(iii) James Mullen, ex-trainer:
"One weakness of the dolphin is its strong love for humans. So when they kill, they are killing for those they have learned to love."

Prelude

EVERYTHING IN THE AIM Facility in Oregon shone with the same deep shine, from the back of the killer whale to the boots of the sentry who checked Admiral Hope's pass. Commander Harper had returned like a whirlwind from his grilling at the Pentagon, and the scientists and enlisted men had listened, totally bemused, to the endless stream of orders which had come from their usually preoccupied and easy-going CO. He needed more money. And if he was to get it he must impress the Navy. And if he was to impress the Navy then he must first impress Admiral Hope. And Admiral Hope had given fair warning that he wasn't a man to be easily impressed.

For the first time in two years the sergeant's bellow had echoed above the regular thump of marching feet over the placid waters of the anchorage. Teams of men had re-painted the old hulks down to water-line, had gone through the laboratories disturbing dust and notes with equal ferocity, cleaning computers, shining video-equipment. Professors seconded from half a dozen universities began saluting everything that moved. White lines appeared on the ground, stars and stripes in the air – after the flagpole had been re-painted. For thirteen days there was bedlam; and on the fourteenth, absolute quiet.

"Well," said Admiral Hope, as Harper escorted him up the white steps to the main Administration Building, "you run a tight ship, Commander, I'll say that for you."

The sentry at the door crashed to attention. The commander's hand rose fractionally ahead of the admiral's to return the rigid salute.

The Alternative Intelligences Marine Facility was centred on the bay of the anchorage. The long arms of land almost met a thousand yards out from the mainland, and, as they swept back from the sea, they gained stature until they met in a cliff almost two hundred feet high looking out over the Pacific. The back wall of the main Administration Building extended this cliff by another fifty feet, before sloping into a red roof. On either side of the Administration Building were the laboratories. In front of the Administration Building was the parade-ground, with the sleeping quarters, the recreation hall, the Facility's gymnasium, cinema and shops arranged around it. It was not a big base, but in the mid-morning sunshine it looked functional and impressive.

The admiral saw it all, from the incredibly tidy laboratories to the surprisingly clean mess-hall. They did not talk business until they were settled in Harper's office after the inspection and the formal lunch were over.

"Now," said the admiral mildly, "I've seen what the place looks like. Now you have to show me precisely what it does that is so all-fired important."

Commander Harper's hand went to sweep back his hair before he remembered he had had it cut short. He adjusted his tie instead.

"We have seven of the leading members of the genus Delphinidae here, sir," he began. "First there is the common dolphin, measuring eight to ten feet; second, the bottlenosed dolphin, slightly larger at nine to twelve feet average; third, the white beluga, ten to twelve feet; the narwhal, twelve to eighteen feet, which has only one tooth, six feet long like a unicorn's horn; next we have the pilot whale, eighteen to twenty-two feet; the bottle-nosed whale which is like a huge bottlenosed dolphin measuring up to thirty-six feet; and lastly, the star of our show, the killer whale or grampus."

Admiral Hope's hand slammed on to the top of his desk with a report like a pistol. "For the love of God, man, get to the point." Three weeks earlier, Hope's doctor had told him that if he didn't stop smoking immediately, he would die. The admiral had smoked nothing since, and it was reducing his normally threadbare temper to tatters.

Commander Harper hesitated, staring at the admiral's fat, belligerent form. "You will be aware, sir, that dolphins are mammals, that is that they have a constant temperature generated by body-heat and not governed by the temperature of their surroundings; they have been, and to a microscopic extent still are, covered with fur; and they give birth to, and suckle their young. They were once land-dwelling animals, and their frame is that of a land-dweller re-adapted to marine life. And, of course, they breathe air." The commander's light blue eyes met the admiral's red ones. The pause never really became a silence.

"Even so," Harper went on hurriedly, "they are able to empty their lungs of more than eighty per cent of their air in less than a second, and re-fill them again almost as quickly; when they dive, the oxygen supply to all parts of the body except the heart and brain is cut off, a fact which allows lengths of dive to vary from fifteen minutes in the smaller species, to an hour and fifteen minutes in the larger. Their muscles are able to store their own supplies of oxygen, which means that no matter how deep they dive, or how fast they surface, they never get the bends."

"When in hell's name are you going to come to the point?" asked Admiral Hope.

Commander Harper cleared his throat and proceeded. "Sonar. The sonar of the dolphin family is incredibly advanced. In an element where clear sight is denied it, the dolphin literally sees with its ears. Not only can it detect objects by this method, but also, by moving its head slightly from side to side thus using both ears, it can judge size and distance precisely as we do with our eyes. At rest, a dolphin will emit a series of low clicks every fifteen seconds or so. These reflect back off objects and are picked up by the dolphin's jaw and ears. If it gets an interesting reading, it raises the pitch of the noises until a precise and uncluttered picture of the object appears, together with precise measurements of its size and distance."

Admiral Hope looked at him with narrowed eyes.

Harper wondered if he should be using slides to keep the admiral's interest. He cleared his throat again. "Intelligence. With the possible exception of Man, the family Delphinidae is the most intelligent species on earth. In consequence they are easy to train. Also, they enjoy play for its own sake, and the element of fun can be introduced into training so that they literally enjoy what they are being trained to do. Furthermore,

11

there seems to be a degree of reasoning ability. The dolphin clearly has the ability to improvise outside the set parameters of its training; to remember orders and extend them outside the training scenarios; in short, to think for itself."

There was silence as the admiral digested this.

"A clear example of this in the case of the common dolphin, in its natural environment, is the number of thoroughly documented cases of dolphins saving drowing men by supporting them in the water. Now this is how the dolphin has learned to help other dolphins in its family group, and when it helps the swimmer, it is simply applying this knowledge outside normal parameters. There is very little likelihood that they confuse the swimmer with another dolphin. No, they are being literally thoughtful."

Admiral Hope drummed his fingers. "I understood I was here to evaluate the killer whale. Not to hear about the philanthropic activities of dolphins."

There was a little silence. "That is so, sir." Harper tried to collect his thoughts. "We are all aware, I think, sir, of the military uses to which dolphins have been put in Vietnam . . . indeed, the common dolphin has proved most effective in groups. But the killer works at maximum efficiency alone, and we believe it to be an anti-personnel weapon of far more formidable force . . . to begin with, since it works alone this means that a more complex schedule of training can be instituted. A killer can be taught, for instance, to attack all but a certain colour of diving-suit. Furthermore, the killer is, in nature, such a formidable creature that there is no need for any armaments – bayonets, gas guns and such. Thus the killer needs no maintenance, no re-loading. In short, once it has been trained and released, a single killer is capable of doing the job done in Vietnam by whole schools of dolphins more efficiently, with less fuss and with very much less cost."

Harper glanced at Admiral Hope, then quickly pressed on.

"At our Facility here, we have one male killer whale obtained by the Navy as a calf seven years ago in Antarctica. As part of our experiments we fed it a carefully selected diet, and have given it a body-weight in excess of seven tons, with an overall body-length of thirty-nine feet eight and one-half inches. This is ten feet in excess of the norm, but no larger than some killers observed in the wild. This killer we have trained fully in anti-personnel work. It is instantly aware of any invasion of the anchorage which it guards. It is able to pinpoint any invader, and shadow him, keeping out of sight. If immediate action is called for, it will decide upon the type of action and upon its own role in this action. The ultimate trigger to anti-personnel action is the simple reaching out of an arm towards the hull of one of the ships, as though to place a mine."

Harper stood up. He found he was sweating slightly. It had been touch and go, whether this admiral would stay with him. But a certain basic minimum of information had to be got over – even if it had meant boring the pants off his listener.

"And now, sir, if you'd like to follow me, we'll go down to the anchorage."

They went through the main hall of the Administration Building to the back of the lower floor. A gleaming sentry checked their passes, pressed a button, and escorted them into a steel-lined lift. He stood at attention between them and the doors.

"I'd like to show you the dolphins we have here, first, admiral. We keep them in pens at one side of the anchorage. They are all in there now, except the killer, which is outside somewhere."

"Outside?"

"In the anchorage, but free to go where he wants. He becomes moody if kept penned up for too long, and if we're not careful he becomes unco-operative."

"Dangerous?"

"Not actively so, sir, no. But we are dealing with an animal here that is as big as three elephants standing nose-to-tail: he doesn't have to do much to let you know he's not happy."

"I see."

"And furthermore, sir, he has been carefully trained by a system of rewards to derive the maximum enjoyment out of patrolling this anchorage, occasionally killing an invader. We use dummies for this. Radio-controlled. Very expensive."

Outside, the sun was strong, but it didn't really warm the Admiral. He saw the dolphins, but his mind was totally preoccupied with what the commander had said about the killer. After what seemed like an interminable time, Harper said, "If

13

you will follow me now, Admiral, we'll go up to the monitoring room and see the killer go through his paces."

"Couldn't we see it from here?"

"Not very clearly, sir. If you want a closer look, we can come down again later."

Hope had to be content with that. With one long look over the water which saw none of the perfectly painted ships, he followed the commander into yet another lift. Above everything else he wanted a cigarette.

There were six monitor screens linked to more than twenty cameras above and below the anchorage. Harper took over an intercom, and sat near the controls.

"Can you pick it up?" asked Hope. Harper had to think for a minute before he realised the admiral meant could he pick up the killer on the monitor.

"Doubt it, sir. He's very good at hiding. If you'll just watch Monitor One . . ."

He spoke into the intercom. Monitor One showed a concrete slipway shelving steeply into the water. A man in a white coat walked on to the slipway and waved towards the camera. "Just testing, sir," said Harper, and into the intercom, "All right, we see you. Call him in now, please."

The man in the white coat took a long pipe from a sailor behind him, half in picture, knelt, and blew down it into the water. Immediately there was a flurry of movement on Monitor Six, repeated formlessly, at second intervals on the others, until there was a still dark shape in the water by the scientist on One.

"He was watching us back," observed Harper. "He knows which monitors are on, because the cameras have red lights." Into the intercom he said, "Bring him up."

The scientist moved. A great black head broke water without even a ripple beside him. The head alone was twice as broad as the man. The size of the killer was masked by the water. The huge mouth came open.

"He has a bite-width of three feet seven and a quarter inches," said Harper, as the scientist put his hand into the killer's mouth and rubbed the pink shovel of its tongue. "Clearance between jaws three feet one inch. Fifty-six interlocking teeth between six and eight inches long."

A voice, drowned in static, came over the intercom.

14

"Very good," said the commander, "begin One."

The scientist moved. The head was gone.

"Monitor Six, sir." The picture on Six changed to show a raft moored behind one of the ships, glinting white on the blue sea. On the raft was a black box of about nine cubic feet.

Even as the admiral adjusted to the picture, the killer's head rose out of the water, so abruptly that he jumped. Harper pretended not to notice. "He's thirty-nine feet long and weighs seven tons. His fin is six feet high. His flippers six feet each. Tip to tip over his back he measures nearly eighteen feet. His flukes . . . One again, sir . . ." The whale lifted the box on to the slipway. The scientist caressed the huge tongue again, and fed the killer a slab of bright red meat.

The intercom hissed. "Right," said the commander. "Go Two. The flukes measure a little in excess of twelve feet. The flukes are his tail, sir." The scientist gestured again. The whale vanished.

"On Five, sir." Monitor Five abruptly showed a cannister deep on the ocean bed. "He can swim at a top speed of twenty-five point eight knots, that's nearly thirty miles an hour, but he prefers to cruise around eighteen knots." The killer's black hulk loomed over the distant cannister, paused, lifted, and was gone. Seconds later it was back on Monitor One, lifting the cannister on to the slipway, the scientist going through the reward ritual.

The intercom crackled. "What? Right. Go on AP One. Monitor Four, sir." Four showed the hull of a boat from under the water. "As an added precaution we have taught him to home in on small engines and investigate, sir." The hulk of the whale appeared, dwarfing the boat. A body splashed down under the boat. The whale stopped, and watched. The body began to sink. It did not move. The whale nudged it. It still did not move. The whale left it, and followed the boat. Three bodies hit the water, and began to swim.

"They are dummies?"

"Almost exclusively, sir."

"Where do you get them?"

"We . . . developed them."

"I see."

The whale abruptly vanished. Moments later a bell began to

15

ring, and a red light to flash. "He's given the alarm," said the commander.

The whale was back on Monitor Four, but the dummies were still circling the boat. The intercom crackled. "Right. Come in now."

The commander got up. "That's all, sir. If the dummies approached one of the boats on the anchorage they would be attacked. We have only three dummies left now, and we don't like taking them to destruction. As I said, sir, they are extremely expensive." The lighting came up. The monitors went off. "Would you like to go down and see him closer, sir?"

The admiral nodded. He had come to the Facility ready to tear it to shreds, and had been impressed in spite of himself. He looked at the commander with new respect. "Yeah. I should like to see the star of your show close-to. I can't really get to grips with its size, though. How big is thirty-nine feet?"

The commander fished around for an analogy. He had read the highly edited file on Admiral Hope which had been made available to him, and he knew the man's ruling passion was Second World War aircraft. "He's six feet longer than a Spitfire; the same length as the two-seater Defiant. Twice the length of your Cadillac. As I said earlier, the length of three elephants."

They went down again in the lift. The commander took the opportunity to give the admiral a little advice. "Please be careful, sir, how you stand. Do not reach out your arms anywhere near the water. Do not go near the water unaccompanied. Please remember that down there I am the expert, I know the dangers; you must do as I say, sir, irrespective of rank."

The admiral nodded. "Does it actually eat the dummies?" he asked.

"No, sir. We made sure that the dummies tasted unpleasant: we didn't want him hurting his insides with bits of metal. In a real situation, however, he will very soon find out that real human flesh tastes much more pleasant. Under those circumstances he would eat anyone he attacked."

The lift doors opened. They went out into the mid-afternoon sun. Beside the slipway he had seen on Monitor One, the admiral noticed a platform, high·above the water. It was like a short diving-board surrounded with a chest-high rail. The commander gestured towards it. "You'll see everything more clearly from the pulpit, sir." They climbed the steps up to the stubby platform, and the admiral went out along it first, until his chest was against the rail and he was gazing out over the placid blue of the anchorage. He found he was really quite excited; that sick sort of excitement he had felt as a boy doing something forbidden and dangerous.

"Longer than a Spitfire," he said, and shook his head.

"Call him in now," called the commander down to the seaman and the scientist still on the slipway. The admiral shaded his eyes, and searched the sparkling surface.

There! A distant flash of movement, by one of the ships.

"There he is." He half turned to the commander, right hand on the rail, left hand pointing . . .

And the killer beneath the pulpit saw a reaching arm . . .

"SIR!" cried the commander . . .

But the killer was out of the water now, soaring up with careless ease: ten feet, twenty . . .

The admiral's body was reacting to the roar of the killer's leap before he even realised he had heard it, jerking body back, arm in . . .

Hope felt the rough tongue, the heat of the mouth: a great force whipped him over the rail, but he did not fall; there was a shrill hissing which filled his head and he could not straighten his back. His last feeling was one of immense frustration: over three weeks without a cigarette just so he would live longer . . .

He never really knew what happened, but the commander saw.

The killer jerked its head away from the admiral as its teeth closed on his arm, tearing it out of its socket. The arm came free, falling with the killer while the admiral remained hanging from the pulpit, held by his right hand gripped on the rail. From the crater of his left side arterial blood pulsed like steam out of a kettle in an arc ten feet away from the body. The admiral's legs were working by instinct, trying to run away, pedalling in the air.

The commander knew what was going to happen then, and he knew he could do nothing to help, but he ran forward in any case, and he actually managed three steps before his legs gave, and he fell, striking his head upon the rough concrete. Everything went very bright for a moment, and there was a distant roaring. When he got up, the admiral was gone.

He pointed to the water, quite hysterical. "Kill it!" he yelled at the sentry. He staggered down to the slipway where it was fed. He knew it would be there, waiting for its reward. And it was. Its flippers hooked over the edge of the cement as it held itself and waited expectantly, its huge black and white harlequin's face at rest.

Harper, his knees still weak, stumbled down the steps, dragging out the .38 Colt revolver he habitually wore with his best uniform. He took it in a two-handed grip, and even though it was wavering hopelessly, he fired three shots at the killer. One missed. The second made a small wound high on its nose. The third opened a great gash from the corner of its mouth, behind its eye, up the side of its face.

The killer screamed . . .

The commander and the sailors, horrified by the sound, stood still . . . and it was gone.

Trailing blood from its wounded face, the killer, terribly confused and in a blind panic, dived deep and made for the open sea. In just over forty seconds it was at the net, its sonar reading the echoes from the strands as from a solid wall. It dived down the net's length until the hard rock bottom came up out of the dark; then up, straight up, trailing ropes of bubbles and blood, straight up to the surface, wild with hurt and panic, until its long black and white body tore out of the water at nearly thirty miles an hour, curved in a graceful arc to crash against the top of the net forty feet in the air, give one last gargantuan heave, fell free, into the open sea, and away.

"We perceived a low carriage, fixed on a sledge and drawn by dogs, pass on towards the north, at the distance of half a mile; a being which had the shape of a man, but apparently of gigantic stature, sat in the sledge and guided the dogs . . .

Over him hung a form which I cannot find words to describe – gigantic in stature, yet uncouth and distorted in its proportions. As he hung over the coffin, his face was concealed by locks of ragged hair; but one vast hand was extended, in colour and apparent texture like that of a mummy . . .

He sprang from the cabin window as he said this, upon the ice raft which lay close to the vessel. He was soon borne away by the waves and lost in the darkness and distance."

Mary Shelley, *Frankenstein*

*   *   *

"A great soul, any sincere soul, knows not *what* he is . . . What others take him for, and what he guesses he might be; these two items strangely act on one another, help to determine one another."

Thomas Carlyle, *On Heroes and Hero-Worship*
Lecture 1: "The Hero As Divinity"

ONE

i

As the distant note of the engines dropped, Kate looked drowsily out of the window at New York, but most of the city was hidden by a huge arm of cloud reaching in from the sea. She settled back in her seat, hoping that she would sleep, but doubting it: flying frightened her, and her heart was beating too rapidly, busily pumping adrenalin through her body, preparing brain and muscles for galvanic action. And she was too tired to talk herself out of this childishness and simply go to sleep.

It was done now, she thought. Oxford, where the duplicity had seemed so adventurous, was far away, and Anchorage was coming ten miles closer every minute. Alaska, where she would meet the man whose assistant she would become, the man who thought she was called Elizabeth Edwards because that was how she had signed her letters to him, a man she loved but whom she hardly knew; a man whose every book she knew almost by heart; whose glowing career she had followed with eager eyes but from a series of great distances; a man she had not seen for nearly ten years: her father.

She stirred restlessly, her golden hair, tied severely back, catching the late sunlight and flaming into life. The heavy book on her lap fell open at the title-page, and the stewardess, glancing down inquisitively on her way past, stopped for nearly a minute simply to read the title, and then moved on, still not understanding it:

FOOD IN THE ARCTIC

Observations upon some aspects of the cryobiology of Phytoplanktons in

21

certain areas of the High Arctic – with special reference to the varying productivity of the genus Cosindodisus *in the shallow coastal waters of the larger land-masses contingent thereupon. Lectures to the Royal Society, Summer 1970.*

By C. J. Warren.

Memories of him washed over her. She had a habit of observing herself as clinically as she observed any plant-specimen, and she knew and accepted how important he had been to her, and for all the wrong reasons.

The last time she had seen him, not counting television, was ten years ago, at her mother's funeral. She had been called home from school just before the exams, which all of her friends had thought was the most super luck, to find her mother bedridden, almost mindless, and so wasted that her great beauty was lost forever. In her mind, Kate could see herself as though she were watching a film of someone else's life, the colours too bright to be real, the emotions too vivid. She could see her mother's huge cavernous room, its high ceiling crossed with beams, the long olive velvet curtains which reached to the floor, the deep red carpet, the beautiful, dark, indistinct paintings on the walls, a tall mahogany chiffonier full of leather-bound books, the great marble-framed fireplace, fire blazing, making everything golden, its crisp comforting crackling covering the sound of the wind against the windows. And against the wall, opposite the fire, the huge antique bed with the tiny figure of her mother lying in it, strangely immobile like a doll waiting in a child's bed for the child to come and hold it. Kate could see the girl who was herself, tall for her age, willow-straight, hands clasped tightly before her, head high, golden hair loose and gleaming in the firelight, moving across the room, as though through a church. She had worn her green tartan kilt that day. What else, she was not sure; but she remembered the kilt quite clearly, and the big silver kilt-pin caught the firelight and gleamed in her memory. She saw herself, eyes full of tears, going over to the huge bed.

There was a smell, for some reason, of lavender; it had made her feel ill. Her mother had looked terrible; her face like a skull. It had given her nightmares for years, that face. She had kissed it but her mother hadn't woken or even stirred, so Kate had gone out of the room again. She had existed, stunned, through the next week, under the forbidding wing of her mother's elder sister who had come to run the house until Mother recovered, and who now found herself arranging a funeral instead.

She had expected it to rain the day Mother was buried, but it had been sunny and hot and she had been standing roasting in a heavy black coat by the graveside, feeling positively wretched, and wondering whether to cry, when her father had arrived. Although Aunt Jane was forever telling her that being fourteen meant that you were a grown-up and should act like one, she had torn away from the little congregation of mourners and run to him, throwing herself into his arms, crying at last. Even then, it seemed to her, he had been bald. The circle of hair, fluffy and white now, covering his ears, had been dark and slicked back. His face had been thinner too, and his glasses, the lenses hugely thick, had been those ghastly National Health type. Even at fourteen, she had been almost as tall as he was, though her slim figure had been completely lost against the breadth of his chest, the girth of his stomach. He had been wearing his baggy green Donegal-tweed jacket with leather elbows and cuffs. There had been a black band on his right arm. He had hesitated when he saw her coming towards him, and later realised he had not recognised her; but he hugged her and petted her, had tea with her – and tucked her up in bed before going away. She hadn't seen him since.

Oh, there had been letters, birthday cards, an occasional present; but always only Aunt Jane at Parents' Evenings and Prize-Givings, at the concerts and the plays. On her sixteenth birthday he had been in the Amazon studying fungi; he had sent her a letter from Rio full of words she hadn't understood, names she couldn't find even in her new botany book, and a piece of dried fern – which he wrote was very rare indeed – which had crumbled to dust as she took it out of the envelope. When she had played Cleopatra in the school play he had been in Italy studying lichens on volcanic rocks. She had sent him the review of her performance (really quite flattering) from the local paper – five column inches of it, and he had replied by sending her the whole of a five page article in the London *Times* devoted to his work. She already had a copy neatly folded in her scrap-book. When she was awarded her scholarship to Oxford,

23

he was in the Antarctic. She had written and told him, of course, but he probably never received the letter, the post being what it is in the Antarctic – certainly he had never replied. When she had graduated with honours and marks rivalled only by his own marks twenty years earlier, he was in Iceland, and didn't even realise his own daughter had learned his own subject in his old college every bit as well as he.

Now she was the most brilliant postgraduate student in the Faculty of Science, and the darling of the whole staff. The gawky, bony, ugly-duckling girl had become a beautiful woman. A beautiful woman who made nothing of her beauty – why should she? Her mother had been far more lovely and Father had still gone away – a student with a tireless thirst for knowledge, a true genius for assimilating facts about plants and structuring them into lucid, controlled arguments; always patient, unassuming, self-effacing in all but her work; ready to pitch in and help, able and more than willing to go on the most gruelling field-trips, cheerful, steady, useful to have around. But she had always kept men at a distance. No, that wasn't quite so. She always kept young men at a distance. She got on perfectly well with men of her father's generation – Professor Brownlow, the head of the Faculty of Science at her college, who had in fact been an undergraduate there with her father: Jon Thompson, her tutor and friend, another lifelong friend of her father's; others, senior men in half a dozen leading faculties of science all over the world, all known to her, all caring for her, all friends of her father's. No friends of her own age – no husband-figures; only father-figures.

Kate shifted in her seat. The stewardess, passing again, paused and looked at her for a moment. The golden hair looked real enough, she thought enviously, although the brows and lashes were quite dark. The nose was quite long, as was the upper lip – an English beauty, though there was nothing of the horse about her face. A round chin, broad cheekbones, the corners of her wide mouth turning up. A complexion the stewardess would have given her eye-teeth for. A little pale though, some sign of strain around the eyes.

A light flashed commandingly. The stewardess hurried on, thinking, what would a girl who looked like that be going to Alaska for?

24

Kate was going to Alaska in answer to an advertisement in *The Times*. Her tutor, Jon Thompson, had seen it weeks ago, very plain and unassuming at the bottom of a compact column:

Wanted, assistant to botanist working in Arctic Alaska. Suitable for post-grad. student. Reply as soon as possible with curriculum vitae and references.
Box no . . .

He had swept into her laboratory in the middle of the afternoon waving it delightedly above his head, ruining an experiment, unrepentant even when she snapped at him.

"Hang the experiment, Kate. Look at this." He stood about the same height as she did, and his hair was still dark. He looked like a schoolboy on a lark, brown eyes twinkling, broad fingers drumming excitedly on the august page.

"What is it, Jon?"

"This ad. Just the job for you!" The grin was just too broad, the argument just too convincing. "I mean it's your speciality, isn't it? The experiment I've just ruined is to test the effect of extreme cold on Protococcales isn't it?"

"Of course it is. You know . . ."

"Well then. This chap's doing it in the field. Much better than all this." He gestured, knocking over a stack of computer programme cards.

"Jon! Be careful!"

"Hang it all Kate, you've got to apply!"

"But why?"

Again, smiling evasion. "Well, it'll be such good experience for you . . ."

"Jon. I smell a rat somewhere here. What are you up to?"

"Well . . ."

"Jon . . ."

And he had told her. The botanist in question was her father.

At first it had completely taken her breath away, and numbed her in the strangest way. Then, suddenly, there was an excitement in her which would not be controlled. Adventure. She had felt her face flushing, her scalp and spine prickling with it. And Jon outlined his plan.

She would apply for the job under the pseudonym of

Elizabeth Edwards. Only the name would be false: the facts of her life and education, the recommendations by himself and Professor Brownlow would be real. She would get the job. She could not fail to get the job. And she would see her father, would work – actually work! – with that shadowy figure she had worshipped from afar and sought to impress for so long.

In a haze of excitement she had written a plain letter and appended to it recommendations from Jon and the professor which had brought a blush to her cheeks. With only a little trepidation she had sailed through an interview, charming three crusty old company scientists out of the full realisation that she knew far more than they did about the answers to the questions they asked.

And finally, beginning to be really frightened at last, she had packed her practical suitcase full of sensible clothes while Jon sat on the end of her bed and tried to calm her fears. The questions then were the same as those now. What if he doesn't want me? What if he's angry? What if there's no one to meet me? What if there is?

Her mouth was dry. She shifted uneasily. The book slid unnoticed to the floor. A wing of hair slipped free of her severe style and shyly revealed a wave.

What I shall do, she decided, as sleep finally claimed her, will be to run across the disembarkation hall to him as though it were the graveyard and I were still fourteen. And hope he recognises me this time.

ii

At first she thought they were part of a dream, the giant and the dwarf. They loomed beside her in the gloom of her semiconsciousness and spoke with familiar accents.

"OK Job?" asked the giant. He pronounced it to rhyme with robe.

And Job the dwarf said, "OK."

Kate stirred a little and sighed. The giant said, "Shhh. You'll wake her." He crouched at her side for a moment, and she felt something moving on her lap.

"Hey . . ." she said, and sat up straight. Even though he was kneeling beside her, the giant's eyes were a little above her own. They were green, she noticed. Her hands flew to her lap, and struck against her book.

"It had fallen on to the floor," said the giant. His voice was very deep. He spoke with an English accent.

"Oh," she said, confused, still not properly awake. "Thank you."

Then the stewardess bustled up, all blue uniform, lacquered hair and brisk efficiency. "Would you take your seat please, sir? We're about to take off."

The giant stood up, stooping slightly as though his head were near the roof, and went just behind her. Out of the corner of her eye she saw the dwarf Job put down the three bags he had been carrying, and reach up to help the English giant out of his overcoat. Her lip curled. A man that size needing to be helped out of his overcoat. Too important to carry his own bag. Probably worried about spoiling his expensive black kid gloves.

The 'plane gave a slight lurch, and Kate realised it had been stationary. This must have been Washington. The 'plane went from New York to Washington to Chicago, and to Anchorage. The engines whined, the plane picked up speed, began to lift.

Behind her, the dwarf Job's voice began to whisper. She strained to hear. "I heard a voice from Heaven, saying unto me, 'From henceforth write blessed are the dead which die in the Lord: even so saith the Spirit; for they rest from their labours!'" There were elements in his accent she could not place. He spoke with fervour and absolute belief. The words sounded like a piece out of the Bible, but not like a prayer. She wondered why he had said them, and a tickle of fear ran in her as the big 747 banked away over Washington.

Kate opened the well-thumbed book and began to re-read her father's lucid descriptions of what happens to single-cell plants under Arctic ice. As always, she become engrossed in it quickly, and time ceased to exist until suddenly some corner of her mind alerted her to the quiet conversation behind her.

"Are you sure you're ready for this? You're not too rusty?"

"Job, Job. If I didn't think I was ready I wouldn't have taken it."

"Yes, but to be out there again . . .'

"It won't be that bad. It's only for a while. A few weeks. I'm letting myself in easy. There'll be no mistakes this time. And even if there are, no one will . . ."

"Die," said Job. "This time no one will die."

"Not so loud for heaven's sake," hissed the giant. "No need for the whole world to know."

"Need for one or two to know," said Job. "Does Warren know?"

Kate's heart gave a terrible lurch at the sound of her father's name. She felt sick.

Job repeated, "Does Warren know?"

"Warren knows," said the giant.

"About all of them?"

"He'll have been given a full report."

"Perhaps," said Job. "And what if he's passed it around?"

"I can take care of it. I can take care of Warren, and whoever else knows."

They lapsed into silence. The stewardess came by and they ordered drinks. Kate listened avidly, but they didn't mention her father's name again.

After a while she wiped her palms on her skirt and they stayed dry. Her heart stopped thumping. Her breathing returned to normal.

Nobody got on at Chicago, and as they rose above the Windy City, everyone seemed to settle back at once for the long night flight to Anchorage. There was a movie, but Kate didn't watch it. Her mind was a confusion of thoughts, emotions and fears. What would her father say? Would he send her back? Where was his camp? Who else would be there? What were the two men behind her talking about? Who had died? What did the giant want with her father? Her hopes and fears went round and round until they became soporific. Just before she fell asleep, she heard the voice of the dwarf Job as he composed himself for sleep. He said:

"God be in my head And in my understanding;
God be in my eyes And in my looking;
God be in my mouth And in my speaking;
God be in my heart And in my thinking;
God be at mine end And at my departing."

28

And the cabin lights went dim, as though God had heard that the strange little man was ready for sleep, and had acted accordingly. The dusk quietened voices; the other passengers set their seats far back, took blankets from the stewardesses, and allowed the blue gloom to wash over them like a drug. The whine of the engines grew a little louder, reassuring, battling gravity on their behalf.

Over in one corner, lights burned over a table where four figures sat hunched over the sounds of plastic-coated playing cards, the rustle of paper money, the tinkle of glasses and ice; while above them rose the blue-grey haze of cigarette smoke, and a fund of dirty stories which had all of the neighbouring passengers turning their heads, half of them forward to hear more, the rest away, in case they heard too much . . .

"GET UP YOU SON OF A BITCH. GET UP AND WALK OR I'LL LEAVE YOU HERE, I SWEAR I WILL . . ."

Kate sprung awake. It was the giant's voice, hoarse with emotion. "UP YOU LAZY BLEEDER, UP. YOUR EYEBALLS'LL BE AS HARD AS MARBLES . . ."

Suddenly, horribly, he reared out of his seat, and began to walk down the 'plane. He walked all hunched over, his right shoulder high, his right arm half curled over his closed eyes; his massive body straining as though fighting a terrible wind. He went to his knees, and the whole aircraft seemed to shake.

The four men at the card table watched, horrified, silent; the stewardess ran for a steward. Then the dwarf was beside him, whispering urgently, "Ross. Ross. It's all right. You're out now. It's all right. Ross, wake up."

The giant's head came up, and his huge body relaxed. "Oh hell," he said.

"You had a dream, Colin," said Job.

"God," said the giant, "but my hand hurts, Job, my left . . ."

"Of course it does," said Job soothingly. He took Ross by his stiff arm and lifted him awkwardly to his feet. He led the giant back towards his seat. The steward and the stewardess came in at a run; they both came over.

"You all right?" asked the steward, suspiciously.

"Fine now, thank you," said the giant, but he stumbled. Job grunted as he took the full weight, and suddenly Kate found herself out of her seat and at Ross's right hand, helping them. For some reason she noticed he was still wearing his black kid gloves.

"Get him a whisky, please," she told the steward, and he vanished. She looked up into the big man's face and saw his eyes were on her. He had a long face, with an impossibly determined chin jutting below a deeply etched mouth; but it was his eyes which claimed her. Job was talking to her but she wasn't listening: his eyes were incredibly deep, still clouded by the pain of his dream, but cold in their depths, diamond hard and unforgiving. They tugged at something deep inside her, quickened her pulse, almost brought colour to her cheeks. Then she and Job were lowering him into his seat, and his deep rich voice was washing over her sleep-fuddled senses.

"Thank you very much, miss. I . . ." The heavy black brows moved over the beak of his nose.

They were so close that she might have kissed him without difficulty.

"That's quite all right," said Kate, her voice a whisper. His eyes were clear now, gazing into hers. He drew breath to say something.

"Your whisky, sir," said the steward behind her.

Kate straightened, her mind in a turmoil. She went back and sat down. She found she was shaking. Ross, his name was: Colin Ross. But what had he done that made him dream so?

iii

The sound of the engines died away. The ground was suddenly there, close enough to touch, rushing past the 'plane's belly. One wing went down slightly. Kate's heart thudded once in her breast: all this way, only to crash now, she thought as the 747 curtseyed across the runway.

Thump. Leap. THUMP.

They were down on the ground.

Kate sat back in her chair, really frightened now about what her father would say. Oxford was half a world away. What if he didn't want her, what if he just took one look and sent her to where she had always been — as far away as possible? No, he couldn't do that. There were the letters from Jon Thompson and Professor Brownlow. They would support her. They would make him see. He couldn't send her away again. Not today. After all, it was her . . . Kate realised then that it was her birthday. Today, June 21st, she was twenty-five. She leaned her head back against the headrest and closed her eyes. It somehow made everything worse, today being her birthday. She felt tears on her cheeks.

"Are you all right, miss?" The deep English voice of her giant, Colin Ross. She looked up at him. Today he didn't look so huge. His face was white and strained, but his eyes were concerned. His right hand was pulling restlessly at a black glove on his left. She nodded, feeling foolish.

Ross frowned. "I'd like to thank you for your help last night," he said. His voice was so deep it gave her goosepimples.

"It was all right. It was nothing," she said.

"Look, I'd like to help if I can . . ."

"No. Really. It's nothing . . ." Abruptly, she wanted him away. He was confusing her. She didn't want his help, she didn't want anything to do with him. Then the dwarf was behind him with his coat. Job looked bigger now. She began to wonder if everything she had heard last night was a dream. She closed her eyes and turned away.

The doors opened.

When she looked again, they were gone; and she was pleased and disappointed both at once. She quickly put to rights the minimal ravages the night had made on her severe hairstyle and basic makeup, gave herself a long hard stare in her compact mirror, treated herself to a thorough mental dressing-down, walked last through the empty 'plane, smiled at the perfect hostess and got off with an aplomb she was still far from feeling.

She walked purposefully across to the crowded concourse, back straight, head high, heart throbbing almost painfully, through the tall swing doors and into the arrivals lounge. Her father was nowhere to be seen. She looked around. There were crowds of people, none looking even faintly like him, none waiting for any more arrivals. No one even slightly interested in her. She was alone. No one here, no one to help. Now that the worst had happened, and she was alone ten thousand miles

31

away from home, her panic left her, and her mind began to function with some of the logic and clarity which had earned her her First Class Honours degree. She made her way to the information desk. There were no messages for Elizabeth Edwards.

If there were no messages, then there must be someone waiting for her. She spoke quietly and with authority, and seconds later the Tannoy boomed out, "Will Doctor C. J. Warren, Doctor C. J. Warren, or anyone meeting Elizabeth Edwards, passenger arriving on North West Orient Airlines flight 283 from Chicago, Washington and New York, please attend the information desk in the Main Concourse . . ."

The last of Kate's usually considerable composure returned as the message was repeated; returned only to slip treacherously away as she saw him shoving his way through the crowd with the belligerent energy of a tug in high seas. The puff of grey hair was exactly as it had been in her most recent picture of him: from the front of *Time* magazine; the pebble glasses not quite masking the piercing blue eyes she had inherited from him, the horrible pipe, the shapeless jacket, all as she remembered them. Only he was shorter than she, even allowing for her medium-high eminently sensible heels. There was a lump in her throat which became painful at the first whiff of his foul tobacco.

His eyes swept over her and on down the information desk. There was no one else near it, so he came towards her. As his hand went up to remove his pipe, her reserve broke and she threw her arms around his neck.

"Daddy!"

He stiffened, pulled away, his face a mask of surprise, then he gave a great whoop of joy which turned every head in the airport, and hugged her like a bear.

"Katherine, Katherine, where did you spring from? Well now, just you wait here for a moment, I've another woman to find. I could swear she just tannoyed me. Edwards, that was it. Edwards. Now where in the world can she have gone?"

"Daddy . . ."

"Tannoyed me. Just heard it. Told me to come here. Perhaps there's a message, perhaps that's it. Miss? MISS?" To the girl behind the information desk.

"Daddy, I must speak to you, I . . ."

32

"Yes, yes, dear. Lord, I hope nothing's happened to her. MISS? Best set of references I've ever seen. Jon Thompson and old Brownlow fairly foaming at the mouth. Probably got a face like a coal bucket. MISS!"

"DADDY! WILL you pay attention! I'm the one you're here to meet."

He looked at her in genuine horror. "Oh my God! If I'm here to meet you now, when was I supposed to meet this Edwards woman?"

Kate almost screamed. Instead she took a deep breath. "Daddy; now listen. Are you listening?"

"Yes."

"Good. You are here to meet me because I am Elizabeth Edwards. NO! Do not say a word. The references you have had from Jon Thompson and Professor Brownlow are about me. They wrote the references because they thought I should get the job, and we made up the name Elizabeth Edwards because we thought you wouldn't give the job to your own daughter. They have both written to you explaining. I have the letters."

"But why? I don't understand . . ."

"Partly for my thesis which is on the effects of extreme cold on certain of the simpler algae, but mostly to see you."

"But I need an assistant, not a daughter! The work on fast-breeding phytoplankton must be completed before the winter sets in, and I have to get back to the laboratory. Kate, go back to England at once, and send over this Elizabeth Edwards, even if she has got a face like a coal-scuttle. She sounds like just what I need!"

"What precisely is your work on, Daddy?"

"What? Oh, my basic brief is alternative foodstuffs, and I've come up with some interesting protein and productivity readings on simple phytoplanktons."

"The Chlorophyceae?"

"Oh yes, some of them . . ."

"Protococcales."

"Yes, that's right . . ."

"And Ulvales."

"Yes! Precisely! I have a reading of more than 0.3 per cent on some of the larger flagellata! But wait a minute, how did you . . ."

"Because as it says in my application under my name Elizabeth Edwards, I have been researching protein levels in diatoms in general and phytoplanktons in particular myself, in my lab. in Oxford."

The doctor lit his pipe. It took him several moments. Then he said, "So it was you who got eighty-seven in your Final Botany paper?"

"No, Daddy, that was you. I got eighty-six. Your record still stands. Moreover," she linked her arm through his, "only one other person has come within five marks of us for more than ten years."

"Where are the letters from those so-called friends of mine?" he asked gruffly. "They've landed me right in it. I wish you did have a face like a coal-hole. My God, some of those men up at Barrow haven't seen a woman since Christmas!"

"I can take care of myself."

"I hope so; I really do. Now, if I accept that the academic references are accurate, what about the other stuff?"

"Field trips to Norway and Greenland? Quite correct."

"You," he said, "are too good to be true."

"Oh Daddy! Ever since I can remember I have been working as hard as I could especially so that one day you would think I was too good to be true!"

"Me? But why? Never mind. Here's someone I want you to meet."

As they talked, they had been crossing the concourse to the baggage handling area. Now they stopped, and when Kate looked up, they were standing by Colin Ross. Her heart lurched. Her father was saying, "This is Colin Ross. Ross, my daughter Katherine, alias Elizabeth Edwards; probably known as Liz the Whiz to the criminal fraternity in the botany department of my old college. Kate, Colin is one of the best cold-weather men in the business, and my bosses have tempted him out from behind some desk in Washington to come and do a logistical survey of my camp, among other things."

"Yes, Doctor. We met unofficially on the 'plane. Miss Warren, how do you do?" Kate found her hand lost in the huge but gentle grip. He was big, but not a giant after all. Six feet six or seven. The top of her head was almost level with his chin.

Nor, when she turned and was suddenly facing him, was Job

a dwarf. The top of his head was level with her eyes, which made him five-seven or so, but his shoulders were so wide, and his stomach so large that he gave the impression of being shorter than he was, and beside Colin Ross he looked quite squat. "How do you do, Job," she said as her father performed another circumlocutory introduction. When he smiled, she noticed for the first time that he was an Eskimo.

"Now," said her father, "to work. Colin, you take Katherine for a cup of coffee. Job and I will help Simon load the 'plane."

"Right. They sell coffee over here, Miss Warren . . ."

"No, really, I . . ."

"Go with him, Kate. Which is your case? The black? See it. Job and I'll be OK. Go on. Don't be too long, mind. Colin, call her Kate: if they think she's with you at Barrow, there'll be no trouble at all. Go on away both of you."

Ross took her by the elbow, and steered her through the crowd.

Behind them Doctor Warren bellowed at Job, "Good idea that, making them think she's with Ross. I mean he's so big. Bit worried when I first saw her. Brilliant references, but she used another name: didn't know it was going to be my daughter. Puts me in a position: I have trouble enough keeping female assistants up there with all those frustrated snowmen, even the ugly ones get more offers of one sort or another; but my own daughter. And she's quite a beauty too. Did you notice? Got that from her mother. Got her brain from me, thank God . . ."

"If you would like to sit here," said Ross, "I won't be a moment."

She sat bemused, watching the bustle of the busy airport. Passengers, laughing, quiet, in groups and alone, came and went. Over the hubbub they made, the Tannoy announced the inevitable round of arrivals and departures: from Magrath and Bethel; Skwetna, Kena, Valdez and Cordova; to Fairbanks, Nome, Old Harbour and the Aleutians, Seattle, Tokyo and to Europe over the Pole.

Then Ross was back with two coffees on a tray, held in his huge right hand. He had taken the gloves off at last. Kate's eyes flicked to his left hand held stiffly by his side. No, the black glove was still there. Affectation, she thought, like a gunman in

35

a western. He set the tray down carefully, and sat opposite her as though he did not fully trust the chair.

"I didn't know the doctor had a daughter," he said.

"Neither did the doctor really. I've been at boarding schools, et cetera."

"Oh. Well, he's been pretty busy."

"Yes."

"And now you've come to help him."

"That's right."

"And you've never been up to Barrow?"

"No," she said, and quite suddenly she was angry at them all: angry with her father for his offhand welcome, angry with Ross because he confused her, angry with herself for coming, for expecting more, for being a little disappointed, lost-childish. "And speaking of that," she continued, "there will be no need for you to protect me in Barrow. I am quite capable of looking after myself."

She said it more angrily than she had meant, and she saw in his eyes a more confused reaction than she would have expected.

Someone's hurt him, she thought; and, who could hurt someone so gentle? and, well, I just did, for one, and for no reason.

She drew in breath to apologise, but never said the words. Job came puffing up, a worried frown incongruous on his face. "Colin, we have trouble: Simon Quick is there."

Ross swung round tense, like an animal. "Where?"

"At the 'plane."

All of Kate's unreasoning fear of the night before flooded back. These two were hiding something terrible, and it might touch her father.

"I'll go on," she said, but they weren't listening.

At their new, smaller 'plane, which was to take them north to Barrow, the same scene was being played in a slightly different manner by her father and a stranger.

"Why didn't you tell me who it was going to be?" asked the stranger, his voice under tight control.

"I didn't think . . ."

"Right!"

"I didn't think it was important, Simon . . ."

36

"Not important! Christ. He killed them all: Robin, Jeremiah, Smith, McCann, the rescue team, eleven men in all, and you don't think . . ."

"Five years, Simon, more! Can't you forget?"

"Would you forget *your* brother?"

"No, but . . ."

"You should have told me, Doc."

Warren's eyes hunted round for something to break the round of increasing hysteria. They lit on his tall, golden daughter: perfect.

"Simon, I want you to meet my daughter Katherine. Katherine, Simon Quick, my camp director. Simon, Katherine is going to be my assistant."

Kate saw a man of middle height, fine-boned, almost bird-like, but giving off an aura of power and energy which verged on the frenetic. Even in practical jeans and anorak, he was neat, nearly dapper. His face was thin, precisely put together, almost beautiful, but marked now with white strain, black rings under the eyes, a blood-crusted bruise on the left cheek. The hand he held out was bandaged.

"Mr. Quick, how do you do?"

"Please call me Simon, Miss Warren. I am as you see me: battered but unbowed. In a spot of bother." Another English accent. The voice was calmer now.

"You really need a bandage on that bruise, Simon," she told him.

"First aid too? You will be a treasure. Yes. The doctor said I needed looking after. No, not your father; he doesn't care if the whole world needs looking after as long as his floating flowers are OK." He paused to shake his head, then grinned ruefully: "But of course, you'll be the same! Here I am talking as though you're a normal human-being, and you're really here to aid and abet this marine lunacy!"

"You disagree with my father's theories?"

"Good heavens no! I don't know anything about your father's theories. Can't tell a plankton from a poppy; but anything that has me out to sea in rubber boats fetching green goo in a milk-bottle from out among the summer floes in a high wind, that's lunacy."

She shivered. "Is there always a high wind?"

37

He grinned again. "Not always, no. And we don't really use a milk-bottle."

Her father's hand came down on his shoulder. "Simon . . ."

The thin body stiffened, the laughter draining out of his eyes. Ross and Job came slowly across from the airport building. Quick remained calm, but he shook with the effort of doing so.

Ross held out his hand. "They didn't tell me you were camp director, Simon."

Quick waited until the hand dropped. "They didn't tell me it would be you working on the winterisation," he said, his voice shaking, full of loathing. He held out his hand to Job. "How are you, Job?"

"I'm fine, Simon. But you look terrible. Trouble up at the camp?"

"A little. That's what I'm doing down here."

There was silence.

Ross and Quick looked at each other like a couple of animals preparing to fight.

"Look," said Warren, his voice suddenly commanding, "Can you two get on? Can you bury the past? Work together?"

Silence.

"For Heaven's sake." He started again. "I've got almost no choice in this. I have my orders too, and they," his hand made a vague gesture towards some far distant head office, "they want both of you on this project. In the field you're each the best we've got. That's all they know. They don't care about per-sonalities." He paused again, took a deep breath. "Look." His voice was hard, his tone absolute, "if you can work together we'll forget this. I don't want you to love each other, I want you to work together. If you can, OK. If not, I'll have to get on to New York, and have one of you taken back."

"I can . . ." said Ross.

"Simon? If anyone's going back, it'll be you. Colin has to get that camp set up fully for the winter work. If you can't manage it, say now, and you needn't come back up with us. Colin can be camp director until they send up a replacement."

"No," said Simon Quick. "I can do it."

"Good. It's time this thing was forgotten."

Quick made a guttural noise in his throat. "I'll never forget. Eleven men he killed."

"Ten," said Job.

It took the wind out of Quick for a moment. But his rage was too great to be controlled at that moment, even by the Eskimo's massive calm. "You mean to tell me Jeremiah's still alive, then?"

"Jeremiah's dead, Simon, you know that; but Colin bears no guilt for it."

"No guilt? He's guilty all right. For all four of them. And for those seven poor bastards that had to go out and look for them and never came back. He's guilty for all of them. And Charlie? What about Charlie? Not guilty again?" His white face worked, eyes blazing. "I'll work with you Ross, but I won't forgive you. . . . That's my whole family you killed. My whole damned family."

He turned, and began to walk towards the 'plane. "Simon!" snapped Warren. "You will work together. Make up your mind to that now, or you go straight into Anchorage and wait for the next 'plane South." Simon's head nodded. He did not turn back. Ross watched him, his face a wilderness. Warren shrugged. He didn't want to send Simon back because it would do untold damage to his career, but he really had no time for all this now. He decided to think the whole thing over. If Simon continued to carry on like this, he could always come back down when the 'plane returned from Barrow.

Kate turned to Job. "This Charlie," she whispered, "was he another of Ross's friends?"

And Job turned to her, his face expressionless, his eyes distant. "No," he said, "Charlie was his wife."

iv

The 'plane levelled out over Fairbanks on its way north from Anchorage. The whine of the twin jets died as the throttles eased back from climb to cruise power. Unseen beneath the cabin floor the orders given by the levers passed along conduits and wires in the 'plane's belly to the harnessed fires in her engines; information passed back to the dials and gauges of the lighted instrument display-panel. The co-pilot was doing the flying, and now they had reached cruise altitude he was adjusting the trim by turning a small wheel on his right. He looked at what his instruments told him, and his instruments told him all was well, so he watched the artificial horizon roll and settle with the actual horizon as the plane turned on to its course to Barrow field.

The pilot, like most of his kind, had the ability to do many things at once. At the moment he was chewing gum, smoking a cigarette and whistling.

They could have been father and son, such was the difference in their age and experience; indeed this was the relationship upon which they had modelled their own, the pilot teaching and ageing, the co-pilot learning and maturing. The older man's name was Ed. He had taught the younger how to fly and the younger man had learned well. Ed had passed on the knowledge culled from flying more types of 'plane than the younger knew of, and in more varied conditions than the other could imagine. He had flown all over the world during the Second World War, had been a captain in his own right immediately it had finished, boosted up the ladder by the demise of so many of his generation. He had been a captain ever since, for one airline or another; but the big jets taxed him more than he could ever admit now, so he had moved over to flying smaller ones. As pilots of his generation were notoriously nostalgic this move in no way undermined his great reputation, so that whenever his name was mentioned among senior captains and aircrew there would be a sober shaking of heads and someone would say, "Now there is a *flyer*."

Hiram was the co-pilot's name. Hiram Preston. He was a man approaching thirty who had somehow missed out on his twenties. He was fairly senior but still young; maturing but immature. He still thought of himself as the All American Boy because he had yet to find out that he wasn't. He checked the instruments which told him all was well. He looked out at the clear blue sky and his eyes, with nothing to fasten upon, focussed a little more than two feet in front of him. Like the pilot, he was whistling a tune, but he was neither chewing nor smoking.

The five passengers sat in the cabin which was a little under twenty-eight feet long, and which contained three rows of six

40

seats – two rows on the left of the 'plane, one row on the right. Most of their baggage was piled in the empty seats at the back.

Kate found the steady drone of the engines soporific. Her sleep the night before had after all been troubled, and travelling is a notoriously tiring occupation. However, although she closed her eyes and leaned back comfortably into the soft depths of her seat, her mind would not stop sifting the varied mass of new information it had received lately, from the pointless minutiae of the refuelling stop at Fairbanks Airport, bleak even in mid-summer, the buildings of the terminal glistening distantly in the vivid sunlight as the aged fuel-tankers laboured up the runway towards them, to the scale of the chasm which divided Simon Quick from Colin Ross.

In a tight, obviously restrained, very English silence they had loaded their bags into the 'plane at Anchorage. Because the hold was full, they had placed them neatly on the empty seats at the back of the cabin. The pilot had spoken urgently with her father and with Simon Quick while the co-pilot, an angular, freckle-faced, pleasant young man had helped herself, Job and Ross into their seats. The words spoken distantly between the three senior men became so heated as to be audible but not understandable before the pilot had made a theatrical gesture of resignation and come aboard.

He was about fifty, she supposed, with thin red hair and big inelegant hands, the backs of which were lightly freckled. He had exchanged a few terse words with the co-pilot, and had snapped on the intercom to tell them to strap in, while the co-pilot had made the luggage secure. There was surprisingly little luggage. Her own small case, the three small bags that Job had carried, with one suitcase he and Ross obviously shared. Her father and Simon Quick had only a weekend-bag each.

She thought of Job. He was one of those people you seemed to know instantly and completely. His face always cheerful, his narrow eyes twinkling, his strange, lilting accent. He was just how she had imagined an Eskimo would be. Perhaps, she thought, that was why she seemed to know him so well so soon: he was on the surface the personification of some childhood dream and she therefore assumed that his depths and personality also fitted in with how she supposed Eskimos were.

And her father. She wondered, with a tingle half of excitement, half of the old fear which now seemed so silly, whether she was also filling out his character with dreams. He seemed so perfectly the way she remembered him. Good-hearted, cheerful, vague and vivid. The great mind humming away on levels far removed from humdrum reality. Accepting the new situation she had presented him with, seemingly without a second thought, far too consumed with his experiments and theories to be bothered for long with reality.

But the other two, what was she to make of them? They seemed to be opposites in every way. Colin, tall, dark, silent; Simon, smaller, blond, garrulous, sparking with nervous energy and drive, endlessly trying to prove that if not as tall, he was still as good as everyone else. It had been Simon, of course, who had held her attention between Anchorage and Fairbanks with his clipped, precise, dangerously tempting version of the cause of their quarrel.

They had all grown up together, he had said, Robin, Charlie, Ross and himself. Ross, Robin and he had gone to the same school. Ross and Robin had gone to Oxford together, and had split up only when Ross had gone into the business world and Robin in the army. Ross and Charlie had married young but there had been no family, partly because Ross had at that time started to build up his reputation as an Arctic expert and was rarely at home, and partly because Charlie always said that a husband and two brothers were family enough for her anyway. So they had remained a tight-knit, happy little group until that summer five years ago when Ross had been asked to lead a commemorative run to the South Pole following the same route as Scott's ill-fated expedition in 1912. He had agreed. The army, not to be outdone, had added to the expedition their own team, led by Captain Robin Quick.

The final assault team had been Ross, Robin, two other army men named Smith and McCann, and Job's brother Jeremiah. Only Ross had come out alive.

At the Enquiry, it had been implied that he had left the others to die so that he could steal their rations to ensure his own survival, and indeed, various of Robin's possessions had been found on him. But he was exonerated, and given an important job with the big consortium which now employed them all, which had interests in and near Polar areas, and which needed an expert to advise them. While his wife Charlie, unable to endure the death of her brother, had shut herself away, taken to sleeping tablets, drugs, and finally killed herself.

So for five years he had hidden behind a desk in Washington earning the money while other men did the work.

Kate had noticed her father listening closely to Simon Quick's harsh words and guessed that he knew less about the affair than he had led her to think. Through it all, though, Colin Ross had said nothing; had appeared not even to be listening. Through it all he had sat, the black wings of his brows gathered in a frown, staring distractedly out of the window, tugging at the black glove on his left hand. Instinct told Kate that there was in all probability another side to the story, one that Ross, from what little she knew of him, was too proud to tell. This seemed to her mysteriously satisfying; so she had listened without comment until the 'plane's descent into Fairbanks field.

At Fairbanks they had eaten without leaving the 'plane. The strange old petrol-truck which had laboured up the long runway to re-fuel them had been followed by another, more modern, with coffee and sandwiches. Unused as she was to flying, it had not occurred to her to wonder why the 'plane had been parked so far from the buildings at both Anchorage and at this airport. Had she asked the pilot, he would have told her in no uncertain terms, and also have given her a heated lecture upon the nature of some of their cargo. But she did not ask, and consequently sat in blissful ignorance as the jet lifted off again.

Some unexplained change in the engine-note disturbed her train of thought now, and her mind shifted away from considerations of Colin Ross to her present situation. She turned a little towards her father, who sat across the gangway from her, lost in silent abstraction.

"What's the camp like, Daddy?"

"Well, at the moment it's a complete shambles. About a week ago we had a terrible storm. You know, I wouldn't be at all surprised if winter's setting in early. Couple of huts blown down, nothing to worry about at first, then one of the generators burnt out. Nasty business. Nothing worse in the middle of an arctic storm than uncontrolled fire. Anyway, this generator went up and set one of the storage huts alight. Proper inferno it was. One man killed, not one of my scientists, thank

43

God – though most of *them* would be no loss – and a couple more people hurt. Badly hurt that is; most of us got little burns and bruises like Simon. Anyway, by morning it was a terrible mess, never seen the like. Stuff everywhere, most of it frozen solid. Help arrived almost at once of course – well, it's pretty heavily populated up there at this time of year, but this is the first chance Simon and I have had to come for replacement supplies – and a right old lot it is too . . . ."

"Tents," said Simon Quick, as though reading from a list, "collapsible canoes, sleeping-bags, blankets, cold-weather clothing, rifles, ammunition, scientific equipment, portable toilets, rope, harpoon-gun, harpoons, net, dynamite. Food: tins of meat, vegetables, fish, fruit, fruit-juice; bottles of seasonings; packets of cereals; beverages. Nearly two tons. Last less than a week at Barrow, but time enough."

"It all got us this jet anyhow," said her father, looking proudly round the slim interior with its twenty-four seats, shining grey plastic, deep blue carpet. "You don't think we ride around like this all the time? Usually we have to beg lifts from all and sundry, but the Corporation in their infinite wisdom lent us one of their executive jets to play around with until we get back on our feet. The Board of Directors would have a fit if they knew we were ferrying dynamite around in it. Pilot did."

"No, Daddy, I meant what's the camp like to work in? How's it run?"

"Oh, of course. You've never been in one, have you? Well, ours is really two camps, so it's pretty big. Basically it's for scientific research, so there are a lot of scientists; and they've given us some cold-weather men to nursemaid us, and to do the dirty work. I'm in charge of the scientists, such as they are; and Simon's chief cold-weather man. See?"

"Yes, of course. It all seems quite logical. But what's Mr. Ross going to do?"

"Ah, well; that is a question. The answer seems to go like this. One of their pet scientists," his tone made it clear that he himself was nobody's pet scientist, "has come up with a series of experiments he wants to do during the winter. Silly idea. Still, rather than give this man a completely new camp, the Board have decided it would be more economic to give him one, like ours, that was scheduled to close for the winter, from

44

November to May. Now, if they do this, a certain amount of re-structuring will have to be done. Some of the huts, for instance, could do with a little draught-proofing and perhaps some insulation. And Ross, as their chief cold-weather man, has to design these improvements. He could do it quite adequately on his desk, if you ask me, but he wants to do it on the spot. Well, if you'd lived in Washington for five years, I dare say you'd understand that."

After he had delivered himself of this speech, Kate's father lapsed into an abstracted silence. Kate knew better than to distract him, and when, after a couple of minutes he took out a pocket calculator and a note-pad she gave up all hope of communication, and looked out of the window.

For more than an hour she gazed at the monotony of the tundra, too far below to present a spectacular view, even in all its summer finery, but suddenly, as the 'plane turned to make its descent into Barrow, she found herself looking away over the Arctic Ocean. The sun was impossibly high in the clear sky, and it shone off the surface of the water, concealing its depths. Kate allowed her eyes to wander up toward the horizon, and suddenly there was a blaze of light. She blinked, and it remained constant, its hues shifting and changing only as the jet continued to turn. It was as though some unimaginable giant had set a crown of sapphires and emeralds on top of the world.

"What is that?" breathed Kate, overcome by the beauty of it; the greens shading from the deepest sea-green to the lightest crystal, the blues from the palest glimmer of a clear winter sky to the violets and indigos of a calm summer's night, all a dancing flame set in the finest filigree of gold.

"It is the pack," said Ross, suddenly behind her.

"It's your birthday!" cried her father. "Katherine, why didn't you remind me?"

"I want to see it properly, Daddy," she pleaded, the little girl again.

"What? Oh. Yes. I suppose so. Yes. Of course you can. Certainly. Go and tell the pilot. Say I said it was all right."

Kate dragged herself away from the window and went towards the cockpit. At the head of the aisle there was a blue curtain over a narrow doorway opening into the tiny entrance foyer. On her left was the door of the aircraft. On her right the toilet. In front, the cockpit door. She knocked, slid the door open, and entered. The little room was full of smoke. The pilot .had a cigarette hanging from the left side of his mouth, and his eyes were slitted as he controlled the descent, one hand on the control lever, the other on the throttles. The co-pilot was talking to Barrow field and preparing to lower the flaps and landing-gear.

"Excuse me," said Kate, utterly at a loss: so much seemed to be going on. The cockpit canted slightly. The pack, magnificently visible through the windscreen, angled and began to slide away.

"Can we help you?" asked the co-pilot.

"Yes. Can we have a closer look at the pack, please?"

The pilot's eyes flicked up from the instruments for a second, seeing what Kate saw as if for the first time. Without hesitation he said "OK. Tell Barrow, Hiram. Would you like to stay up here Miss Warren? You'll get a much better view."

"Thank you very much. Yes, I would love to."

She leaned lightly against the bulkhead. The pack swung back until it was an acceptable horizon and began to draw nearer as the quiet jets thrust forward.

The aeroplane sped through the lower sky at a speed in excess of four hundred knots, its passage aided by a warm, humid wind blowing steadily from the south.

Kate watched the green-blue fire as it drew nearer. After a while it began to fade, and the ice was revealed like great blobs of cottonwool half-floating in the sea, and the pack itself, its surface a wild jumble of ice blocks thrust hundreds of feet into the air. But she was not deterred. She was gripped by an excitement which reached right back to her schooldays. An excitement she had first felt in a vague and distant geography lesson when her imagination had suddenly made the dry facts about arctic climates take life. Deep within her the romance of the ice still lingered; not the hurried, tiring life she knew from her field trips to Norway and Iceland, but life in tents and igloos, hunting seal and polar bear, fishing from kyaks or leaping from floe to floe. The Eskimo: the flat-faced, cheerful, stoical people her imagination had conjured from her text books. The sea-lion, the walrus, the whale.

All this was contained in the pack as it swept majestically towards them. Suddenly, away to the right, at the very edge of the pack, rose a glittering cloud of spray.

"There she blows," cried Ross in the cabin behind her.

"Can we follow it?" Kate asked the pilot.

"OK," he said, "Hiram, you take her down." The 'plane angled, the horizon vanished for a moment and the sea drew nearer, golden and black, suddenly thrust churning aside by the monstrous back of the whale, slate-blue and streaming.

"That's the biggest blue whale I've ever seen!" cried Ross.

"Over a hundred feet, over a hundred tons," said Job.

Disaster struck just at that moment, but none of them noticed.

The co-pilot felt a slight change in the handling of the 'plane. Ice crystals brushed over the perspex at the front of the cockpit. The pilot was turned towards Kate, speaking. They had over-flown the whale. The co-pilot began to turn.

The airspeed indicator swung up unaccountably. The co-pilot glancing at it, and seeing it high but steady, lowered the landing-gear and put the flaps in full landing attitude. The 'plane slowed to just above stalling speed as it flew low over the blue whale for the second time. As the throttles were eased back the flow of fuel to the engines was cut. Less fuel flowed through the filter systems between the throttle-valves and the jets.

Disaster was a fierce north wind blowing down off the pack, laden with ice-crystals many degrees below freezing.

The pilot looked away from Kate and down at the whale, suddenly aware of some niggling doubt eating at the back of his mind. Although he had had no hesitation in telling Hiram to take them down in the seemingly safe manoeuvre, something in the attitude of the aircraft now unconsciously set his palms to tingling, telling him to take control back from the boy at once. It was not until he looked out of the cockpit window that he realised how deep they had slipped into trouble.

In the seconds – not more than thirty – between now and the last time he had looked out through it, the window had become starred with ice-crystals.

"Christ! We're icing up." He slewed round and looked back down the outside of the fuselage. The leading-edges of the

47

wings were already heavy with ice, the engine intakes fat and slick.

"Hiram. Take her up . . ." The pilot was not in a panic. Ice here was hardly unexpected. It was dangerous, but not fatal. "Go and sit down now please," he said. "There's nothing to worry about. Hiram, the flaps in, please. Undercarriage up . . ."

Kate turned, went back into the cabin, and flopped into the outer of the two seats at the front on the left. She was uneasy. Her father looked across the aisle at her.

"What happened?"

"I don't know. It's all right now . . ." The engines coughed.

The 'plane did not shudder or break in any way its smooth progress; only the steady note of the twin jets broke briefly and distinctly, each jet coughing individually, modestly, as though clearing its throat before an audience. Then the 'plane began to gain height in a smooth, shallow curve.

The intercom crackled across the silence in the cabin like a nail squealing on a board.

"Sorry about that, lady and gentlemen: a little trouble with the . . ."

The engines coughed again, more persistently, as though trying to gain attention.

"Anti-icing," snapped the pilot, not bothering to switch off the intercom. "Give her to me."

Preston released his control column, his hands shaking slightly. "Fuel filter anti-icing on. Intake icing on."

Beneath the engines, in the area between the throttle controls and the jets themselves, were the fuel filters. In these, the fuel was passed through an extremely fine-mesh filter element. The filters were warmed by oil. This warmth was enough to keep the fuel flowing freely under all but the most bizarre circumstances. These circumstances now obtained.

"I see ice building on the intakes, Ed," the co-pilot said, "but the system seems to be coping OK."

Around the filter the oil circulated, warming the fuel as it passed through the fine mesh. In the wings, full of fuel, and in the inch-wide pipes beneath the sealed envelope of the cabin, the fuel moved steadily, like blood. In the fuel, however, through a chain of circumstances stretching far back in time,

48

there was water. Unavoidably, in all fuel, a tiny amount of water was found, and this collected in the bottom of the fuel tank. The tank should have been drained regularly, or the water would accumulate in dangerous quantities. Possibly this had not been done.

Furthermore, at Fairbanks they had not been allowed up to the loading-bays because they were carrying dynamite. They were therefore re-fuelled by barrels brought out to them, and there may have been water in the fuel in those barrels. Either way, for one reason or another, or perhaps both, there was now water in the 'plane's fuel system. And under the deadly influence of the freezing north wind, this water was turning to tiny grains of ice. The grains of ice were being tumbled through the system to clog up the filters far beyond the capability of the warm oil to melt and disperse them. Against the fine mesh they built like blood clots, cutting off fuel to the jets, waiting to give the engines their final seizure.

The coughing persisted, openly mocking now.

"Passengers, please fasten your seat-belts. No smoking. Remove spectacles and sharp objects from the clothing. Be prepared to lean forward, foreheads on arms crossed on knees. Hiram – get me Barrow, then try to help me keep her up."

The co-pilot was speaking into the radio now, his voice rising with concern at some hissing reply to his message, as he passed it on to the pilot. "Ed! Barrow's blacked out, visibility below minimum and still falling. Christ! How did that happen?" The engines continued to choke.

The passengers numbly prepared themselves as directed. Kate put her practical handbag on the ground and leaned forward until the belt cut into her stomach. She looked to her right, and saw her father blinking like an owl. Someone was whispering; Job, she thought, praying. Her mouth was dry. Above her, the pilot continued his conversation with the co-pilot, both, seemingly, able to do many things at once.

"It's ice, Hiram. Where else could we have ice?"

"Filter anti-icing?"

"Light's on. Should be OK."

"Water in the system?"

"Doubt it. When did you last do a routine check for water in the tanks?"

"Dunno. Ground fitter did it last servicing I suppose . . ."

"Well, there you are then. Mind you, I think maybe I did hear something, once . . ."

"Hello, Barrow? Barrow, this is . . ." The rest of the conversation was cut off as the engines gave a full-throated roar, the nose of the 'plane angled up slightly once again.

At no time had it felt as though the 'plane were going to crash.

Kate lifted her head out of her lap, so relieved that she felt a giggle rising in her throat. She caught her father's eye and smiled.

Then the engines went dead. One moment they were shouting with their new-found power, the next they were absolutely silent.

"That's right, Barrow, following the pack . . ." The floor canted gently downwards. The wind hissed over the wings. "Emergency landing, Barrow, will advise final position."

"This is not an emergency landing, Hiram; this is a crash!"

The word echoed dully through the quiet cabin. It brought home to each one of them, as even the cessation of the engine-noise had not, the danger they were now in. Up until that moment this movement down at an increasingly steep angle had seemed to be among the fairly normal, unexciting procedures of flying, and much less frightening, for example, than the sudden wrenching tumble into an air-pocket. Only the pilot and the co-pilot, both torn between the advisability of looking at their instruments and the absolute necessity of looking at the speed-blurred rush of green-gold sea and green-white ice which was rearing in front of them, were truly aware of what was happening. As calm as though the aircraft were still flying instead of falling, the pilot adjusted its attitude in the air, his brown eyes flicking over the rushing ocean for somewhere to set them down.

Kate was terrified now. She felt as though she was going to faint, but the position of her body, head on knees, would not let her. She silently raged at the tears in her eyes, at the chain of chances which had put her in this terrible position, at Jon Thompson, at Professor Brownlow, at her father, at herself. She would very much like to have screamed, but she would not let herself. She pressed her forehead against her arms until it really

50

hurt, and recited to herself in the suddenly empty cave of her mind all the swear words she knew.

Simon Quick was sobbing with terror. Had anyone been sitting beside him they would have heard, but Simon didn't care. He was certain he was going to die, and the certainty bore in him an uncontrollably poignant well of self-pity. It was not fair, he thought, why him? God, he prayed, save me. Please. PLEASE. He was running with sweat. He was going to be sick. He wondered whether it would get him in better with God if he offered the others. Take them all, God, but spare me.

Job's prayers were very different. Suddenly, in this moment which was probably his last, the years of Methodist education vanished, and he found himself praying to the old gods, the gods of the high arctic. To Kaila, god of the sky, to hold them up, to Torgasoak, the great spirit who guarded his people to protect them, to Aipalookvik the Destroyer to have mercy.

Warren felt nothing. He could not believe this was happening. Basically he was a mundane and eminently practical man, made totally selfish by the drive of his genius. He had found early that if he camouflaged both his genius and his clear awareness of how to get on in the world behind the carefully assumed character of an absent-minded professor, he could rise quickly and naturally to the positions of responsibility and power he coveted. But now no characterisation could protect him. Or, as an afterthought, his daughter.

Ross felt frustration more than fear. He had faced death before, and faced it down; but he had been in control then where now he was helpless. In many ways it was a cruel test of his courage just to sit here and leave all the responsibility in hands other than his own. He chewed his lips, crushed his head to his right forearm, eased his left arm down beside his left thigh, tensed himself and waited.

Preston might as well have been carved of wax. He had retracted the flaps and undercarriage and now sat, eyes fixed on the spinning needle of the altimeter while the pilot tried to save them. There was nothing else he could do. Even if they had not passed far beyond the ends of his experience and ability, he still would have been too scared to do anything. He just sat, hypnotised as the altimeter clock-face with its functional white numbers, told him the 'plane was less than one hundred feet above the sea while the similar gauge beside it told him the aircraft was still moving at more than one hundred knots.

For the pilot in many ways this was the climax of his life, the moment for which talent, inclination and fate had perfectly tailored him. He had first crash-landed in a Douglas DC3 at Gander during the war and he had force-landed one or two turbo-prop aircraft since, but never a jet. Never on water. And yet he knew well enough what he was doing. With back, neck, shoulders, arms, wrists, hands under rigid control, he was flying a 'plane which could no longer fly; he was keeping aloft a falling object until he could find somewhere to put it down. In his early days, long before he had become a captain, flying had seemingly been the performance of one impossibility after another. He was jerked back through thirty-five years now by this final impossibility and he smiled. They had been good days, those, and this was the last of them, coming out of nowhere in the ice of a north wind. The last of the good days.

They were moving parallel to the edge of the mountainous pack, half a mile now in front of the great whale they had stayed to watch. The ice swept away on his right to the North Pole and beyond, a sharp-edged jumble of blocks reaching more than a hundred feet at their peaks. No chance of landing there . . . His eyes narrowed against the brightness. There! A thousand yards ahead! He might just . . . already he was turning left over the sea, pushing the nose down, the wind lifting the right wing, the 'plane slipping down faster, half-sideways, in a wide arc out – then, sharply, in: into the wind at ninety degrees to his original course, still at one hundred knots, the last turn robbing him of more precious feet. Glance at the altimeter, twenty-five feet and falling. Too little. Christ! They weren't going to make it! The weight of the nose was an awesome pull on the muscles of his back: at these speeds the jet had all the aerodynamic qualities of a brick. He saw the edge of the ice twenty yards ahead, but without even looking he knew there was no more air left under the plane. He opened his mouth to yell, and they hit the ocean still moving at one hundred knots.

What the pilot had seen a thousand yards further back was a tongue of ice thrusting out of the line of the pack. At some earlier time some quirk of wind and tide had bent the ice until it

52

had been thrust up into an unusually long and stable series of hills. When the edge of the pack receded with the summer melting, these hills had remained, and with them a flat platform of ice curved for more than five hundred yards, a little like the blade of a broad knife. He had chosen to try to land on this because it was much flatter than the corrugated surface of the rest of the pack. He had put the nose of the aircraft down, thus gaining enough speed to control at least the beginning of the descent, turned south out over the ocean, then immediately north into the wind, pulling up the nose but maintaining speed, in an attempt to crash-land on the tongue. The 'plane hit the water twenty yards short, bounced forward like a stone skimmed by a boy, throwing up huge curtains of spray and crushed ice.

Kate looked at her father. His head was down on his forearms, pressing them against his knees. She kicked off her shoes and did the same. Sound, movement, water, ice exploded round her. Her body was hurled against the strap.

The 'plane, still in one piece, leaped ten feet in the air, gulped down the twenty yards in an instant, then fell on to the beginning of the great tongue of ice.

The pilot, blinded by the spray streaming down the windscreen, saw only the shapeless hunch of the ice-hills on his left.

Kate's stomach wrenched. Again the explosion of sound and violent movement. Cases from the back of the 'plane hurled forward and burst around her, but nothing heavy hit her. Her knees bludgeoned up with the vibration, knocking her arms away, beating against her forehead with stunning force until her nose began to bleed.

The 'plane was shrieking. It was a truly terrible sound, and it went on and on.

The pilot, still conscious, saw the hills on the port side rushing nearer. He estimated to within a tenth of a second when the wing-tip would touch them, and was tensed to meet the new forces as the aeroplane slewed round.

Abruptly the cabin hurled to the right. Then the fuselage reared up on its tail.

"That's it," thought the pilot as the nose began to rise, crashing up the concave slope of ice as the 'plane slowed, "I've

53

done it." Great pride welled in him. Then the windscreen exploded in against his chest.

The cabin juddered up to the vertical. And the last thing Kate knew was that something had plunged through the wall in front of her like the point of a giant harpoon.

The movement, the sound, everything, stopped.

TWO

THE SOUND OF the crash echoed through the shallow Arctic Ocean, and the great blue whale's hearing had no difficulty in picking it up; but he neither went to investigate nor swam away. He was too tired: simply that. The huge knotted muscles of his back, and the sagging sheets and hawsers in his belly, all sent a dull, persistent message to his brain which it did not recognise as pain. The great flukes of his tail, more than twenty feet across, beat the water only fitfully, leaving him to drift for a moment as he tried to regain his breath. His back broke water again, and he sent a great cloud of steam and water-vapour roaring into the Arctic sky. His jaws fell open, and hundreds of gallons of the krill-thick soup which is arctic water washed over the baleen sieve in his mouth. He pressed it dry with his giant tongue, and swallowed it. His mouth fell open again. His tongue moved. He swallowed. His eyes closed for the first time in nearly fourteen days. He slept.

Fourteen days ago, the blue had been making his leisurely way up through the east Pacific Ocean. He was north of the Murray seascarp, some five hundred miles west of San Francisco, swimming along at three to four knots, diving sometimes to two thousand feet, leaping sometimes completely out of the water, content and at peace. When he heard the screams, songs and clicks which were the voices of other whales, he answered sometimes, and sometimes he did not. Ten years ago he would have been searching for a mate, if he did not already have one; but he was old now, and content to follow his annual odyssey from the arctic to the equator, searching out the krill which he swallowed, a ton in every mouthful.

Then, that day, the day which men called the eighth of June, he heard them: the killers. He identified their cries, twenty-four of them; five close behind, six between him and the shore, and thirteen in an arc to the west closing off the way to the deeps of the central Pacific. At first he was content to raise his speed to a little over ten knots; and by the dawn of the next day he was over the Medocino seascarp, more than two hundred miles north of his original position, and it was there and then he realised that the killers were hunting him.

And they had hunted him ever since.

On the eighteenth of June he had driven his great body into the island-filled shallows of the Aleutian Chain. All that day he worked his way east, playing a deadly game of hide-and-seek with them, but their pattern of gutturals and clicks was well able to distinguish his huge body even among the islands.

Here they had nearly caught him, and in his escape he had seen them for the first time. The leader was huge, longer by a head than any other killer the blue had ever seen; he had two scars on his face: one at the tip of his nose, and the other from his upper lip, along behind his right eye. The second scar pulled the right lip up so that the leader could never properly close his mouth, and the white interlocking teeth were always on display.

He had come upon the group of killers three months earlier as they hunted the reef just south of Midway Island. Come in, wary as a shark out of the black depths to challenge the old bull who had led the pack, and drive him off, trailing blood, to the mercy of the deep. He had selected from among the docile cows one mate, the thirty foot female who was at present at his side, and he had led them east by north towards the American coast.

The pickings were good and they moved slowly, decimating the schools of dolphin along the shipping lanes; hunting seal around Pacific islands and even on the mainland coast; and when there were no large animals, there were always the schools of tuna, and even of mackerel.

During those three months, the killer's mind settled. He returned with ease to his natural lifestyle. He led the pack surely and with confidence, and grew to know the comfort his gentle consort brought. And then, late in the evening of the eighth of June, some fifteen hundred miles west of San Francisco, the leader had picked up a new echo. He had made a short sound which alerted the others to his new, purposeful course, and he had moved off.

During the night they had formed the pattern which held them close to the big blue, and they had begun to follow him properly. They did not move in to the attack for they all knew the power of the great whales, and the first object was to tire it out. So they followed, harried, frightened the blue, making it exert itself to the limit of its abilities during the next ten days as the hunt progressed up the coast of the United States, across the Pacific and among the Aleutian Islands to that first, ill-timed, unsuccessful attack.

Every now and then, when the pack was hungry, one of two hunters went off after seal, sea-lion and walrus, always returning with enough for all. But although they were never starving during this time, the pack were never as full and content as they had been on the sea-lanes of the Pacific. And now, five days later they had driven the blue up through the Bering Sea past St. Laurence Island, through the Bering Straits, into the Chukchi Sea and the Arctic Ocean.

Since mid-afternoon the blue had been still, lying at the edge of the ice, apparently asleep. The leader guided the pack silently closer and closer. He too sensed the aeroplane's crash, ignored it. The water was so thick with krill, that visibility was down to a few feet, but the leader did not want to use his sonar, for fear of arousing their monstrous prey. He left the pack, therefore, and moved forward in the red fog to explore for himself. Inch by inch he moved silently through the living soup, back breaking water occasionally for a quiet breath. Then, unexpectedly, an abrupt current swirled the curtains of krill aside, and there, less than one hundred feet away, was the head of the sleeping giant. The killer paused, and then went back to the pack. Now it was time for the kill.

Counting the calf there were twenty-four killers in the pack. They split into six groups. The mother and one other pregnant female remained well clear with the baby, but close enough for it to see, to learn. This left five fighting groups: Groups One, Two, Four and Five, each of four; Group Three of five. The leader and his mate led Group Five. The five groups silently surrounded the sleeping blue, who was still plainly visible in the krill-free current. He was still asleep, at peace, totally defenceless.

Group One remained behind the whale. Group Two paired off and went to either side of him. Groups Three, Four and Five went to the head. In a few moments they were all in position around the sleeping monster. The leader hovered thirty feet from the immense face, his blood reeling in his veins, hot and terribly alive. His mouth opened and closed and the low sun made his teeth flash like huge candle-flames. He waited. They all waited.

Then the leader's flukes jerked down, up, down, and he was at the giant's throat, sinking his jaws into the blubber. The blue woke in a panic. The teeth in its throat were not dangerous, for its arteries and veins were buried too deep in the fat to be touched by them; but their very presence signalled the gravest danger, and so the blue exploded into a frenzy of terror. Its great tail went up. The hawsers of its belly moved deep under its delicate skin, standing out slightly on either side of its genital pouch. Here Group One centred their attack. Avoiding the downward sweep of the great flukes, they fastened their teeth into the flesh laid open by the blue's panic and as quickly as they could, they tore away huge ragged mouthfuls of blubber laying bare the muscles underneath.

The blue tried to steady himself against the forces unleashed by the movement of his tail, spreading its enormous flippers. Immediately, a pair at each side, Group Two attacked. They bit at the base of each flipper, trying to sever the tendons which made them move.

The blue, in its terror, never came anywhere near to comprehending the almost ritual sequence of moves which were bringing about its downfall; but their logic and their effectiveness were overwhelming. Like picadors in the bullring, Groups One and Two were destroying the sets of muscles which controlled the enemy's most powerful weapons, so the whale could neither run away nor fight back. It was the logic of all types of pack, of wolves biting the legs and shoulders of an elk to stop running and kicking, to make it incapable of tossing those which finally go for the throat. But the ritual here was more complicated and protracted, for its participants were more powerful and intelligent.

With the first two groups fastened in its flesh, the blue whale sounded. It plunged in less than a minute down the six hundred feet to the bottom of the Arctic Ocean. As the floor of the sea rose to meet it, the blue turned on to its left side, crashing its full weight against the thinly sanded rock platform. The terrible power of this landing burst the two killers on its left side like toy balloons. It also crashed the bones in the left flipper to formless splinters.

Above, the leader, who had released his grip on the blue's throat as Group Two went in, probed the dark depths with his sonar, piercing the growing cloud of sand which hid the thrashings of his victim, waiting with groups Three, Four and Five.

After fifteen minutes the blue came up again towards the surface, trailing blood in great streamers from its belly and its crushed flipper.

Then it sounded again, but with so little of its original force that the remaining half of Group Two had no difficulty in swimming away as its right side crashed on to the ocean floor. The flipper was not even damaged, and as the whale rolled over they attacked again.

This time it only stayed down for five minutes, and as it laboured back up to the surface, the five killers in Group Three went into the attack. Swimming at the giant head-on, they fanned out slightly at the last possible moment and fastened themselves to its pendulous lower lip, using their weight and power to force the mouth open. But the blue was not ready for that yet, and, changing the angle of its ascent slightly, it came up with all its force through the ice at the edge of the pack. It was lucky: this section of the pack was still hard as iron, and a razor-sharp edge of ice sliced down one of the males as neatly as some giant fisherman's knife, laying him open from head to tail, gutting him completely and leaving him to tumble down to the foaming water entangled in his own insides.

A third time the blue sounded, and there was no force at all in it now. The great down-sweep of the tail, however, was enough to sunder the tendons in its belly, and Group One's work was done. Without the counter-pull, the hawsers in its back spasmed into knots, pulling the great tail up, breaking the back, tearing open the huge bag of its lower abdomen, letting coil after coil of fat yellow intestine tumble free. Group One remained where they were, feasting greedily.

At the head, Group Four went to work, fastening themselves

to the thin lip of its upper jaw, trying, with Group Three to force its mouth wide. As soon as it felt them there, the blue began to fight towards the surface again, as well as it could. It lay there, a derelict hulk, unable to move, the great sail of the flukes at first erect, like the tail of a scorpion, but slowly toppling as the whale rolled ponderously on to its side.

Group Five went into action even before the great tail settled into the sea. First the leader, then the others in rapid succession threw themselves clear of the water to land, hammer-blows of up to seven tons, on the back then the side of the blue's broad head, roll off, swim away, and start again. Time after time. After half an hour, they had all had enough. The killers in Group Five were all battered and exhausted, and, through the haze of his semi-consciousness, each blow seemed to the blue to be splitting its head open. It was almost time to give up. Almost, but not quite.

The blue allowed its mouth to sag open. At once one of the young bulls in Group Three let go of the lower lip and hurled himself in. Immediately, the trap snapped shut. The young bull's tail just protruded from the working, toothless mouth where he was being slowly crushed to death by the relentless pressure of the great tongue. Minute after minute the others wrestled with the pendent tatters of the lips until eventually, unwillingly, the mouth opened. The young bull floated out, and slowly began to sink. His mate, another member of Group Three, immediately left her post and tried to support his lifeless body. Two others joined her in her endeavours, but even after they had managed to get him to the surface he still did not revive.

The leader, meanwhile, leaped into action, and, with his mate by his side, sped into that enormous living cave. They brushed past fronds of fine white baleen which danced at their passing, and dived hard for the back of the blue's throat. They bit into the root of its tongue on either side, gulping down the aperitif of blood. They tore. They strained. They hauled the great pale blade foot by foot out of the constricted throat. Two more joined them, pulling at the top. Two more came up from the tail, taking hold where they could and heaving back with great lurches of their lithe bodies, squealing with delight. And at last it came free, nearly five tons of it, ripped out in a cloud of bright arterial blood which roared out of the blue's throat as if from a fire-hose, pulsing nearly twenty feet under the water to the beat of its dying heart.

They left it then, alone and dying, forgotten at the scarlet edge of the pack.

They danced away through the red water, playing like children, tearing the rubbery flesh of the tongue as they went, giving a piece to all. And so they feasted, late into the night. After they had eaten, they rested.

The leader withdrew from the rest of the pack, followed by his faithful consort. As the others ate and slept, he kept a lonely vigil, his mind full of memories associated with the heady taste of the whale-tongue meat; memories of the fierce joy bred into him at the anchorage in Oregon, when this same meat had been fed to him as reward for the killing of men. And as the night passed, the longing grew in him, confused with the memory of the last terrible agony in his face, to see again the reaching arms, the kicking legs. To feel again the joy of attack, of destruction, of the killing of men.

As the sun was just about to move up in the heavens signalling the beginning of the new day, his meditations and their rest were disturbed by a great explosion which gave birth to a distant column of fire. And they went to investigate.

THREE

At first, when he had woken, Ross was only aware of anger: it was always like this – you lowered your guard, even to the extent of indulging a frightened girl, and people died. If you became involved with people, you bought grief.

He opened his eyes. He was still sitting on the left-hand side at the back of the 'plane, but his seat had been tipped until his back was horizontal and his legs were in the air. The body of the 'plane rose above him and it was as though he was lying at the bottom of a slim tower, looking up. It took him a moment to realise that the jet was somehow resting on its tail. There was a smell of high octane fuel which was not in itself unpleasant, but the realisation of what it meant, together with one or two less pleasant smells, served to send a shiver down his spine. Thus he discovered he could still move.

Least pleasant of the smells was the sweet, slightly iron smell of blood. Ross turned his head towards the companionway and Job who was opposite. Job lay absolutely still. Ross, his heart thumping with something more than the exertion of lifting his battered torso, looked across, but the blood he could smell so strongly was not Job's. He slumped back with a grunt, and, as he did, he saw it on the top of the seat in front of him, over to the right side of the white headrest: a long glistening red stain; and as he watched, the stain sluggishly attained depth, gathered itself into a drip, and fell towards his eye. He instinctively jerked his head away, and the drip fell clear, landing with a splash beside his right ear. Then he saw a red stain on the back of the seat two in front of his own, and beyond that, on the backs of all the other outside-left seats up the length of the aircraft – up to where the girl had been sitting. His stomach heaved. He breathed deeply. Another drip fell by his ear.

62

Outside the body of the 'plane, the wind hissed. There was a lapping of water. There was a restless clicking and cracking of ice. Inside, suddenly, a groan. Ross's head swung right, pressing his cheek into the cold sticky dampness. Job was moving.

"Job!"

"Aaaah."

"Job?"

"I hurt."

"Me too." He realised as he said it that it was true. His stomach was bruised by the belt, his back was stiff with strain, and his neck felt as if it had been mildly whiplashed. He had bitten his tongue and two teeth were loose. He moved his head, easing his neck and shoulders, and repeated, "Me too."

Job laughed. "It is good hurt: only the quick hurt."

Ross looked up along the broken waterfall of blood. Someone up there didn't hurt. Not in the slightest.

"Sssssssa," Job hissed, "I smell blood."

"You don't say 'Sssa'," Ross told him, beginning to undo his seat-belt, "you say 'Fe Fi Foe Fum'."

"What matter?" asked the Eskimo, beginning to undo his also. "It is still blood." He looked away up the length of the 'plane.

"Is it the girl?" asked Ross.

Job shook his head. "I cannot see."

They slowly untangled themselves from their seat-belts. They might have been two very old men.

"Can you move?" asked Ross after a while.

"Yes, I can move, but where to?"

"We'd better try to get up the length of the 'plane and see if anyone needs help."

"We can try."

Ross reached up and took hold of the back of the seat above him at its outer edge. He began to pull himself free of his own seat. Job was already half out of his, moving more quickly than the big Englishman. Ross wedged his feet against the back and arm of his seat and pushed up. There was nobody in the next pair of seats on his side. He tensed to push up, and his shoulders collided with Job's back. He looked up and back. Job was leaning over Quick.

"How is he?" Suddenly, and with overwhelming force, Ross

63

wanted him to be dead. For five years now he had hidden behind the desk in Washington, hidden in other, darker places. And now, when he had ventured out again, it was only to face the hatred of this one man, reaching out of his very nightmares.

He hadn't heard Job's answer, and asked again, "How is he?"

"He's fine."

Ross shrugged, and continued to climb up the seats, using their backs as a ladder. The higher he climbed, the deeper became the crusted blood on the headrests. He paused when his head was level with the second seat back because a curtain, which had originally blocked off the small entry-compartment, was hanging back down the 'plane, obscuring his view. He was out of breath, dizzy, nauseous. He hung on, trying to regain his breath. Job was behind him.

"Job? What have you done with Simon?"

"What could I do? Leave him to wake up."

"Yes. That's all we can do."

"I'll get rid of the curtain, see what's going on."

Job eased up past him. The curtain moved, strained, reluctantly began to tear. "Doctor Warren seems to be all right," said Job conversationally as he worked on the curtain.

"Yes. Looks like the blood's all coming from his daughter. That's really bad luck. All this way to be . . ." The curtain came away. "Christ."

He still couldn't see much: a hand, dripping blood on to the floor; strands of long gold hair, rust-coloured now, formed into long stiff rats-tails, running with blood.

He tensed himself to pull up . . .

"AAAaaaahhyiuH!"

The door at the top burst open and the co-pilot tumbled the length of the companionway, tearing Ross's precarious hold loose so that they fell together, with sickening force down into the tail. Colin's ears rang. His head throbbed. There were bright lights.

"Colin? Colin!" A distant voice, drawing nearer. Job was there beside him, untangling him from Preston.

"Ouch! No; it's just wrenched a little. I'm OK. What about him?"

"Unconscious. He seems to be all right, though. I wonder

what brought that on? He seemed quite a level-headed young man."

"Well, we'd better get back up and see what's happening," said Ross. "We really can't risk hanging around in here."

"But where else is there to go?" asked Job.

"There's only one place we can go. Out on to the pack. We can't stay here. This 'plane's a bomb with all that fuel around. It's a miracle it hasn't blown up yet; it'll only take a spark or two. God knows when it will go; but I'd rather be out there than in here when it does." He picked himself up laboriously, and swayed for a moment, leaning against the backs of the seats. Another drop of blood fell beside his head. "Right. Up we go again."

As though he was climbing a ladder, he moved up the body of the 'plane. It was several minutes before he was back where he had been when the co-pilot tumbled through the door. The girl's limp hand brushed his shoulder as he tried to place his left foot firmly on the blood-sodden seat below; then, with one galvanic heave he was up, half-bending over her. Her head and torso were thickly crusted with red, but there seemed to be no wound on her. Ross wedged his left arm between the two seats, and felt on her cold neck for a pulse. A wave of relief swept over him as he found it almost at once, strong and regular.

But if Kate was unhurt, then whose blood was this? He looked around, and at once saw the hole in the wall immediately before her. It was not a large hole by any means, and it seemed to be blocked by something; but blood was running out in a steady stream. It had to be the pilot's blood.

"Job?"

"Yes?"

"The girl's all right, but she's covered in blood. We'll have to move her and cover her in something warm."

"Right. On my way up."

Together they lifted Kate out of the seat and lowered her down the 'plane, letting her slide the last foot or two to rest beside the co-pilot.

"Right," said Ross, "I think we'd better cover her up as soon as possible, or she'll be getting pneumonia; but I really must look in the cockpit."

In the back wall of the cockpit was the door which had

slammed shut behind the falling co-pilot. Ross opened this door and heaved himself up. The woodwork creaked. Job held his legs. His head and shoulders erupted into the cockpit. What he could see – the right side – was a shambles: everything clearly useless, broken glass, pieces of facia, wire, unknown equipment, all gleaming painfully in the bludgeoning brightness. Ross blinked, shook his head, slitted his eyes. Through the ruins of the windscreen he could see a hump of snow curling over like a wave about to break down on them; beyond that, gold, almost copper, marked with ghostly stars, the sky. He turned, facing the floor, to look at the left hand seat. His stomach heaved again.

"What is it?" asked Job from immediately below him.

"It's the pilot."

"What about him?"

"He's dead," said a toneless voice below both of them.

The co-pilot was standing in the tail of the 'plane, his hand to his head, looking down at Kate. He asked, "What about Miss Warren? All that blood . . ."

"It's the pilot's," said Job. "She seems to be all right."

"The pilot's? Ed's? How? . . ."

"That thing came right through," said Ross. "Nearly into the cabin here and through her too."

"My God," said the co-pilot, awed.

"What thing?" asked Job.

"Would you tell him?" Ross asked the co-pilot. "You should be able to explain it a little."

"Yes. I can." Preston gathered himself. He had the resilience of youth; the boundless self-confidence whose strength is that it has never been tested; and circumstances had proved it right: he was still alive. So he began to explain as concisely as he could. "Ed kept her under relative control. These things do not glide without power, they fall: but he kept the nose up, which is all you can do. It really was a fine piece of flying. Anybody else would have buried us; you know? But there were hills all along one side, and the left wing touched them. This swung us to the left, with our nose into the hill, and we were still moving at one hundred knots. The nose went straight up in the air . . ." He breathed deeply, his face white.

"On the top of those hills is this overhang, and down from the

66

overhang are huge icicles . . . maybe ten foot, some of them; I don't know . . ."

Job looked at Ross. "Icicles? . . ."

"That's what the man said . . . All right, you've done enough, thank you. Hiram is it? Could you look after Miss Warren and anyone else that wakes up?"

"Hiram Preston. Yes sir, surely."

"Oh, Hiram," Ross turned back, "the radio. Any hope? . . ."

"'Fraid not, but I did get our position off before we came down. They'll be looking for us eventually. If we just stay by the 'plane . . ."

"Isn't it going to be a bit dangerous to stay too close?"

Preston sniffed the air. "My God! The fuel . . . Yes. We'd better get out, if we can. Is the door all right up there?"

"We shouldn't have much trouble," Ross said.

Job thrust his head above the level of the lower wall. A spear of ice came through the windscreen like some great harpoon, and went straight through the pilot, the seat, and the wall behind him. It was covered with blood, which had soaked into the cracks and faults in the slim column, giving it an almost marbled appearance. Job turned his head away.

"That is a terrible way to die!"

Ross said, "Very few ways are nice."

Now they were at the door. Ross turned the emergency handle, and the whole section sprang free, crashing down the wing in a shower of ice-crystals. Ross and Job both tensed at the noise, at the possibility of a spark.

A light breeze came in through the hole. Ross's whole body shook. "Lord," he said, "it's cold."

Job laughed. "Colin, Colin. Here we are in a 'plane that is full of holes in the middle of the ice-pack within spitting distance of the North Pole at what must be nearly midnight. That gentle breeze will have a temperature a good deal less than nought degrees Centrigade. And we are in Washington clothes."

Ross was assailed by a sudden doubt. "Should we leave the door closed and just wait for help?"

"No. I'm an Eskimo. I would much rather freeze than burn. And if we stay in here, we *will* burn; perhaps soon."

"Right. I'll go out and have a look around." He moved

67

forward gingerly to the doorway itself, and looked out. What he saw stopped him dead.

The pack.

The sight of it hurled him back through five years and over the length of the world.

There was a tongue of ice, perhaps five hundred yards long. One side was the chain of sharp ice-hillocks, the other a flat plain stretching roughly two hundred yards to the restless sea. The tongue of ice curved slightly so that the track of the plane-crash, originally a straight line coming up from the distant tip, inevitably came up against the cliffs. The cliffs were transparent green, and eroded above him until they formed an overhang at the top, and from this overhang great fangs of ice bit down at the crystal air. One of them had bitten down at the front of the aircraft, and this not only held the pilot, but also kept the 'plane so steady on its tail. Where the cliffs curved away and down towards the sea, breaking into a series of low, sharp peaks, the steady wind lifted flags and banners of ice-crystals from each crest, and the sun made them burn green and indigo, red and yellow, against the orange ice, the golden sea, and the far, copper sky.

Ross looked down. "No trouble," he called, "the crash brought snow down from the cliff. Easy enough slide down from the wing."

He eased himself carefully out of the door. When his feet felt the front edge of the wing he put his weight on them, let go of the door-frame, wavered precariously on the ice-coated metal, managed to turn his back to the cliffs, sat down, and slid safely to the surface of the ice. Shivering violently now, his shoes instantly soaking, sinking almost to the ankles in the loose snow thrown up by the crash, he looked round.

The first thing he saw was a crate, with markings on the side. For a moment he wondered what it was, and then he heard Quick's bored voice in his memory, as though reading from a list. Tents, canoes, sleeping bags, blankets, cold-weather clothing . . .

Of course. The cargo!

Slipping and sliding on the treacherous surface, he ran round the hump of the port engine to the high silver fin of the tail. Under the wing, as though the jet was trying to hatch them out, were more crates. As he went closer, Ross could see what had happened. Sometime during the wild ride up the tongue of ice, an edge, sharper than the rest, had torn open the belly of the 'plane, and ripped off the loading door. The cargo had come loose and been hurled out. Five crates lay here in an untidy jumble. The rest would be inside: but they were obtainable! And in those crates lay everything they needed to survive. All they had to do was get them out, unpack them, set up camp, and wait to be rescued. It was that easy! Certainly Doctor Warren and Kate should know their way round considering their scientific specialities; and as for Simon and Job, you couldn't wish for better companions under these circumstances! Only the co-pilot, presumably, was not used to being on ice . . .

Exultantly he pounded on the side of the jet. "Job! Job! Come out!"

The pounding echoed in the burst hold, making the wires vibrate, and the fuel-lines tremble. One wire, severed by the crash and swinging in the slight movement of the sound sent a blue spark arcing through the petrol-laden air. The boxes, precariously balanced, shifted a little. The 'plane settled slightly. The wire stopped swinging.

The ice opened at Ross's feet, and he was precipitated across black water. Stretching from the tail, through twenty yards to the sea, was a crack in the ice, its narrow width shining with fuel. Ross caught at the boxes on the far side of the crack, and held on with his right hand, his left slipping uselessly until the black glove was in the water. His feet desperately sought for purchase on the treacherous ice. "Job," he called.

Treacherous. The word ran through his head. In five years away, he had forgotten the one fundamental fact engraved on the mind of every ice-man: the pack is as treacherous as a rabid dog. And as deadly. You usually only got one mistake, and he had just made it. The ice opened wider beneath him, the grin turning to a yawn. If Job didn't hurry, the yawn would widen, the throat swallow, the ice-lips close. In the water in these clothes, he would be lucky to last two minutes. His shoulder cramped viciously, as he knew it would. His belly ached with the strain of holding on. He couldn't last much longer.

"Colin? Where are you?"

69

"Here, Job. Hurry." He was shaking as though in a high fever. There was a bright light in front of his eyes, out of focus, drawing nearer. Abruptly he saw Charlie in the middle of it.

"Charlie," he whispered. "Help me, Charlie." But she just stood and watched. Not helping. As she had always refused to help. Loving a dead brother more than a live husband. All his old futile bitterness flowed back. Just standing away, far away. Not answering his letters. Not coming to see him during those months in hospital, not caring to face him, to have it out with him. Just distantly blaming him for something that Robin had brought on himself. Not giving him a chance. No chance . . .

Inside the 'plane Kate was trying to open her eyes. She raised her eyebrows, straining. Something seemed to move on her forehead, cold and crusted, but still her eyes would not open. Her hands flew to her face by reflex, and felt the sticky mess on her skin. What was wrong? She absolutely refused to panic, rubbed her fingers over her eyes, then her knuckles like a crying child, then the backs and the heels of her hands. And at last the eyelids separated. She blinked.

All she could see was a multicoloured jumble, stretching away half-focussed to grey curves of wall; a movement of her head revealed seats on their backs. Her disorientation was complete. She tried to move and discovered that she was still trembling – not with the effort of remaining calm, but with bitter cold. And she was stiff with bruises.

"It was all over so fast, he didn't even have time to call out." She recognised the co-pilot's voice.

"A terrible way to go. You wouldn't think the ice . . . ." Now her father's voice.

"Daddy?"

"Katherine? Ah, so you're awake, are you?" His voice came from above her head, and she looked up. She had been lying on her back anyway. Now she was looking straight along the body of the aircraft. On her right was the single row of seats, on her left the double row. Her father's head peered from the front seat of the single row. She could have been standing looking down the 'plane at him – the illusion was complete. But she knew she was on her back: her father, the co-pilot one seat above him, the whole 'plane – they were all on their backs.

"We crashed," said her father.

Her face itched. She remembered about her eyes and looked at her hands. Her stomach heaved. Abruptly the co-pilot was out of his seat, climbing down towards her using the sides and backs of the seats like a ladder.

"Take it easy," he said. "The blood's not yours. You're OK. Honest."

She moved, half sat, shuffled across the mess of clothing and wrecked cases until her back was supported by the roof of the cabin. The co-pilot was beside her, pale but calm.

"You're OK," he said again. She looked down at herself. She was totally saturated with blood: skin, hair, clothes – everything. She was very careful not to ask whose blood it was – time enough for that, she thought, when she had herself more in hand. She frowned.

"Yes," said the co-pilot, "they're a mess. You'd better change out of them. Have you anything else?"

"Of course. In my case . . ."

Her voice trailed off. She was sitting on the stuff that had been in her case, that had been in all the cases. She began to look around. He was standing on her favourite negligee. Before she could stop or think, she snapped, "You're standing on my things!"

"Oh. Of course. I'm sorry. I . . ." He blushed like a school-boy and began to climb back up the seats.

Kate, in a rage with herself, clamped her teeth together for a moment very tightly and then said, "Look, look . . . Oh dammit, I've forgotten your name!"

"Hiram, ma'am, Hiram Preston."

"Look, Hiram, I'm sorry. I didn't mean to be rude, I . . ." There were tears running down her cheeks. It was shock she told herself; shock, nothing more. She picked up a towel conveniently to hand and began to wipe the tears away. The rough cloth came away coloured brownish red. She began to scrub harder, choking back sobs, hiding tears, cleaning her face.

As she found her handbag, brushed her hair, changed out of her stiff clothes and into jeans, shirt and heavy Arran pullover, her father and Preston continued to talk.

Halfway down the vertical row of seats on Kate's right, someone else moved. "My God!" said Simon Quick's voice, "what the hell happened?"

Quick had been half-unconscious for some time. Now he had jerked awake. "Oh, my God," he said again. Then he undid his belt, opened it out and painfully began to crawl out of his seat.

Kate at the foot of the gangway combed her hair as she watched him roll out of his seat, grab on to the sides of the seats above him, and climb stiffly through the hole at the front of the 'plane. Suddenly the full uncertainty of their position washed over her. The euphoria caused by the simple fact that she had survived chilled in her. Had she survived to any purpose? Would she – would any of them – last for long on the ice without food or shelter?

"Ye Gods!" she said, her voice shaking with panic, "what on earth are we sitting in here for? What's going on outside?"

"Well . . ." began Hiram.

"Oh never mind!" She began to search through all the jumbled contents of the cases on the floor for anything which would be of immediate use, but there wasn't much. She caught up her dark glasses – those, she thought, would be useful against the painful brightness she could see through the portholes. Gloves, other things. She stuffed them all in her capacious handbag. Then she picked up her father's book *Food In The Arctic*, and held its bulk speculatively in her hand, reading the title for the thousandth time or so. What do I need the book for now? she thought. I've got Daddy in person! She felt excited and began to climb up the seats . . .

Job, coming round the tail as fast as he dared, saw Colin lying there, saw the black wound in the ice running under his friend's stomach, widening inexorably. Colin's right hand was anchored firmly among a jumble of crates; his left was uselessly in the water. Without thought, working from countless experiences of the same nature, the Eskimo ran catfooted forward, grabbed Ross's ankles, and gave a spasmodic heave. Ross was torn back, away from the crates, over the grinning mouth of the ice, and into a heap beside his friend. The green eyes were distant, the face paper-white.

"God," said Ross, "but my arm hurts."

"Of course it does," said Job gently.

After a moment, Ross's face began to clear. "The crates," he said. "They're full of equipment. We can set up a camp!"

Just then Quick's voice came from behind them. "What are

72

you two up to? Stealing the rifles, just to make sure you get through? A bit of food, perhaps, in case it gets short? Oh, I know how you work in these conditions, Colin, old chum, and I'm going to make damn sure that this time if you make it we all make it."

Job took a step towards Ross, fearing an explosion of anger at the younger man's taunts, but suddenly Ross was smiling. "You always were a self-confident boy, Simon; well go ahead: save us."

Quick was for a moment nonplussed by Ross's abrupt change of attitude; but it was plain what needed doing, and so he set about doing it.

"Most of the crates will have their contents stencilled on the side," he said. "Job, what are those?"

"All food."

"A good start. What do we need first?" This to himself, but Ross answered, "Clothes, I should say."

"Right." Quick was too preoccupied with the immediate problem to continue for the moment his feud with Colin. There was still much to be done if they were to survive the bright arctic night. "Clothes and then shelter. The tents were packed to this side, they should be there."

"Perhaps they came out further back down the peninsula," Job.

"Yes; right. We'd better check on that. No, you two had better continue getting the stuff out of there." He banged on the side of the 'plane.

In the hold, the loose wire swung and sparked.

"Co-pilot! What's his name? Preston? Preston! We need you out here."

"Coming." Muffled.

Ross gave Job a grin, and began to move the crates of food away from the wreck. As they moved towards the first low hills of the pack, however, the ice became slushy and rotten. Their feet began to sink deeper and deeper.

"This is no good," said Ross after a few yards. "We'll have to take them round the other side. At least the ice is firm."

Job nodded. They reversed. They had just reached the crack at the 'plane's tail when a much aggrieved Warren came round the port engine.

"What do you mean by leaving us in there like that? Quite a fright I had when I woke up. Nobody much there, only that Preston fellow and Kate all covered in blood. Made me feel quite ill. She's all right though. Anyway, that's not what I wanted to say . . ."

"Dr. Warren, would you excuse us a moment?" Ross's face was pale with the strain of holding the box. He was in some pain. "If we drop this we've lost several day's worth of food . . ."

"Food? You're saving FOOD? What about my equipment? We'll be picked up before we're even hungry, but that equipment is very expensive and would take months to replace! Have you people no sense of priority?"

Preston slid down the wing. Ross had a brainwave. "We think a lot of your equipment fell out as we crashed, Doctor. Would you take Mr. Preston here and look down the ice for more boxes, please?"

Warren stopped dead, turned round, and saw the crate beside the line of the crash. "Jolly good idea."

He trotted off, Preston following. Ross and Job moved the box to safety, and put it down carefully.

"Doctor!" called Ross. Warren stopped and half turned. "Just remember there's nothing under us except seven hundred feet of freezing water; and this ice isn't very thick." He kicked down with his foot: it sank in to the ankle. The doctor waved to show that he understood, and carried on in exactly the same belligerent way. Preston followed behind as though on eggshells in hobnail boots.

Ross and Job went back to where Quick was wrestling with the remaining food boxes. He had moved them back now, and had some access to the open hatchway door. The door was partially blocked with more boxes.

"Took your time," said Quick.

"We met Warren and Preston. Sent them to look down the crash-path for more crates," said Ross.

"Good. Now I don't think we need move the boxes too far; we'll be staying pretty near the 'plane: that's standard procedure in these situations, but I do agree we ought to move them to the other side. This side's very messy."

"Look Simon, I hate to disagree this early . . ."

"Then don't!"

"But I don't think it's too good an idea to stay beside the 'plane. There's a lot of fuel about, and it's just waiting to blow up."

"Nonsense! It hasn't blown up yet. I see no reason to believe it ever will. It's quite steady . . . The engines are off. It's quite safe." He thumped the silver fuselage. The wire swung in the dark hold. The blue spark arced through the shadows and the petrol fumes.

Ross shrugged. He and Job picked up the next case without further comment, but they carried it well clear on the other side.

Warren's voice carried back to them from the distance. "Bloody dynamite in this one!"

Ross shook his head. Job said seriously, "God must love us very dearly: we should be dead ten times over." They went back. As they reached the port engine they heard, "Hey! Mr. Ross; Job."

They turned, and Kate Warren was hanging out of the door, her feet just short of the wing. They went over. "Let go," called Ross, "we'll catch you."

"Right," she said without a second's hesitation, "here I come." She slid down the wing on her stomach and hit both of them surprisingly hard. They all went over on the slippery ice.

Kate sat up first. "You two should really play cricket for England," she said. "They need a couple of fielders like you."

"And what's your sport?" asked Ross, trying to catch his breath. "Weight-lifting? Shot? Heavyweight boxing?"

"If it was," she said as they got to their feet, "I'd thump you first."

Ross noticed she had brushed the stiffness, most of the blood and many of the rats' tails out of her hair, given her face a good scrub and found a pullover somewhere. She had changed into jeans, and with these and the thick pullover she was by far the most suitably dressed of them all. They took her to Simon Quick who was just opening a way into the hold.

"Excellent," he said when he saw her. "You're just the one I need. Slip in this hole like a good girl, and move the boxes from the other side."

"Right-oh," she said, and went forward.

75

She wriggled between the boxes and into the dark hold. She closed her eyes tight, trying to get them used to the darkness; and so she missed the sudden blue light which flashed briefly far above her head. After a few moments, she could see. It was as though she was standing at the bottom of a cluttered chimney. There was no light from above, except from a thin tear in the metal of the fuselage, and the walls seemed to gather around her. She had a moment of claustrophobia, but shook it off. She began to move the crates. They were not heavy, and she soon had them into sufficient order to begin passing them out to Simon Quick. He was sorting them out into piles on the ice, after which Ross and Job carried them well clear of the 'plane.

Preston and the doctor brought one or two more back from further down the ice, the doctor becoming sufficiently hungry to admit that perhaps Ross had a point. At last a tent came out, and the first of the boxes containing clothes.

"Right," said Ross. "Unless we have anyone who fancies hopping around starkers in the snow, we'll put up this tent as a temporary changing room. We'd better do it now before we're entirely incapable."

They were just in time. The cold was draining their vitality, so that even Job's expert hands fumbled over perfectly simple tasks, and it took them a long time to get the tent up. It was a large blunt pyramid, its base eight feet square, six feet in height, Its dark material was heavily insulated against the cold.

Quick said into the dark hold, "Miss Warren?"

Kate said, "Yes?"

"They have a tent up, and we have all the absolute necessities now, I think. Can you see a net anywhere? It's in a bundle, not a box. Orange nylon, like the ropes."

"All right. I'll look."

"Good. Won't be long." When he reached the tent he said, "This is far too far away from the 'plane. You'll have to move it."

"Why take risks?" said Ross, from inside the tent where he and Job were changing. "Anyone who sees the 'plane there will see us here. And here, we're out of danger if it does blow up."

"Blow up! It's not going to blow up! Why should it blow up? It's quite safe. The engines are off, everything. It's quite safe, isn't it? Preston? You tell him!"

76

"Yes, it's quite safe," said the co-pilot –

"There! I said . . ."

" – if you've disconnected the battery."

"The battery? My God – Miss Warren's in there!" Quick snarled. "She's in the hold!"

Ross wriggled out of the tent, still doing up his jacket, pulling up the furlined hood. He went slipping and stumbling over the slippery ice towards the 'plane. The others paused for a moment, then followed him with equal urgency.

As Quick's footsteps sloshed away, Kate had begun to search again among the boxes and crates still piled around her. It was not there. An orange bundle . . . As the 'plane hit, the bundle would be thrown forward. Of course! She looked up to the high far end of the hold. It would have been thrown up there! Probably it had wedged.

On one side of the bottom of the hold, like ivy on a wall, were jumbles of pipes and cables: an easy enough climb if they were firm. She tested them. They were strangely warm, but solid enough. She swung herself off the ground and began to climb, steadily and with ease. At first she tested her footholds, but she became more confident as she got higher. It was only twenty feet or so, after all, and there was plenty to hold on to if her foot slipped. The pipes and wires were hotter up here, but not uncomfortably so: quite the reverse, as her hands had been going numb with the cold. She paused, looked around. It was much darker up here and she could see very little. She climbed a little further, and struck her shoulder against something soft. The net. She pulled at it, but it was caught on something. Pushing it to one side, she went up a little more.

Above the net she could see a flickering blue light. Her mouth tightened. She knew what it was – by God, would she have words with that Simon Quick when she got out. Still, if the 'plane was dangerous, this stuff was better out than in.

The net was simply hooked on to a broken edge of a packing-case which had wedged here. The case contained some of her father's equipment, packed in fibre and woodshavings which were bulging out of the damaged boards.

Kate unhooked the net and let it fall. Then she began to climb down, her eyes now fascinated by the jumping of the blue spark above her head. She had gone perhaps five feet when her

Arran pullover caught against something. She stopped, went up a little, began to undo it. It was only wrapped around a small bracket which had come loose. Only a fibre or two. She carefully unwound the heavy wool, one hand on the pipes and wires. She was still preoccupied with this when her foothold gave. She swung out from the pipes with only her left hand maintaining firm grip. The 'plane moved. The blue light above her became continuous and very much brighter. The warm wire beneath her hand suddenly became hot. A smell of burning filled her head. She choked, began coughing. Her hand began to hurt. The wires quickly became too hot to hold. She knew she would have to let go, and looked down to where the net lay. That was her target. God but it was small! She let go. Her pullover jerked as she fell, tearing free of the bracket. She hit with force, rolled like a parachutist, bounced up as she did so, crashed into the steel wall, and knocked herself out.

Above her, the flex on the shorting wire began to burn. The flame ran up the wire to the packing case to which the net had been attached, and from which bulged woodshavings and woodfibre. The crate instantly caught fire. And the next. In seconds the whole nose of the 'plane was ablaze, the flames running down the outsides of the damaged fuel-pipes looking for a way into the tanks.

By the time Ross got to the hole where the last remaining boxes were, he had to shout to make himself heard above the roar of the flames. "Miss Warren? KATE!"

No answer. He tried to get in, but was too big. The heat was not intense, but the danger was extreme. With almost half of his body in the crack, he could see her lying on her side well out of reach. At first he thought she was dead, but then when some sparks fell by her she moved. "MISS WARREN! KATE! KATHERINE!" No reaction.

Then Preston was at his side. "Here, Mr. Ross. I can get in there."

"Good."

Ross moved. The others were coming. "Get back," he yelled. "You can't help. She's going any minute!"

He went down on his knees as the co-pilot passed the girl's inert body through the narrow gap. Inside the 'plane sparks and pieces of blazing wood were falling like bright snow. Kate stirred as the cold air hit her. "The net," she said, quite distinctly.

"Can you get the net?" Ross yelled, struggling to his feet, and slinging Kate over his right shoulder like a sack of potatoes.

"No sweat," yelled Preston, and pulled it loose.

Then the pair of them were negotiating the crack in the restless ice at the 'plane's tail, and charging clear as fast as they could, each careful of his burden.

Behind them, the flames had not found easy entry to the fuel tanks, but had been forced to spread outside the fuselage before finding abundant petrol. The snow was soaking with it, and flamed easily. The cracks were thick with it and the water blazed. The ice writhed and cracked. The jet became wreathed in pale flames. The roaring was tremendous, the ice shook, over fifty yards away the survivors felt the fierce heat.

Then, at last, with a sullen rumble, the tanks exploded. A column of fire cleft the pale sky. Metal rained all around them, striking no one. A complete wheel bounced nearby with deadly force, then rolled nonchalantly into the water as though propelled by an invisible giant, who stalked the ice, destroying the tent with insolent ease, tumbling the boxes about, beating the people into insensibility. But more than this, he attacked the ice.

The heat of the fire was concentrated along the cracks and weaknesses, into which much of the fuel had drained, and it melted and widened them until only the low ice-hills were holding the tongue of ice in place. The force of the explosion, however, rising as it did under the overhang of the eroded ice-cliffs, blasted thousands of tons of this backbone high into the air. With a rumble that echoed far over the Arctic Ocean, the crest of that frozen wave finally broke like solid surf, and tumbled down for twenty yards either side of where the jet had been. The huge plain of ice rocked slowly, jerked once or twice, then began to move, with all the inexorable grace of an ocean liner, out into the sea. More than twenty acres of ice, varying from inches to many yards in thickness, different from all the other floes only in that it boasted on its mighty surface six immobile bodies, seventeen packing-cases, the wreck of a tent, and one or two pieces of debris, moved out into the Arctic Ocean, further and further away from the rigid safety of the pack.

FOUR

Preston was being shaken.

"Mr. Preston, wake up. Wake up."

English voice. He opened his eyes, shook his head, clearing it of the brightness. The Englishman, Ross, was shaking him, frowning.

"All right," said Preston, "OK." He watched the tall man move towards Warren, next in the ragged line.

"Doctor Warren, are you all right?"

"Yes . . . Yes." The doctor began to shiver.

"We'll have a change of clothes for you in a moment, Doctor," said Ross.

Warren turned his head. The co-pilot, whatever his name was, was picking himself out of the snow. Kate lay beyond him, quite still.

Something welled up into Warren's throat, something which as a scientist he distrusted. The 'plane! It all came back to him. "My instruments," he said.

"Lost, I'm afraid."

Warren looked at all the boxes and crates which had been saved. "Lost? All . . .?"

Ross nodded. He rose and went towards Simon Quick. When Warren was sure Ross was concerned with wakening Quick, the doctor stumbled over to his daughter's inert form.

Quick had been watching Ross move down the line towards him, lying there, conscious but half-stunned. Now Ross knelt, and reached down towards him, the light of the low sun carving out hollows in the blunt hatchet of his face. "Simon . . ."

"Don't you touch me!" he snarled, relishing the pained frown it brought.

He squirmed to his feet and stood over his enemy. His eyes swept over the floe. He caught his breath as panic gripped him. The tongue of ice had broken free: they were drifting, at the mercy of wind and tide. And the others didn't seem to realise the danger. He opened his mouth to speak, to scream, to do something, but a feeling of helplessness swept over him, and he remained quiet after all. What could he say? What could they do? Suddenly he was desperately tired. He suspected they all were, too battered and tired even to care. His shoulders slumped, and he stared dumbly at them. Job was busy among the crates. Warren was half-supporting his daughter. Her hair was cascading on to the ice, catching the crystal light. There came a twisting of lust in his stomach. The other man, Preston, was standing looking helplessly around. It was very cold. There was a slight breeze, and the wind-chill factor lowered the temperature by a further degree for every knot the breeze blew. Only Ross and Job were properly dressed: the rest of them were in imminent danger of freezing. If Ross hadn't woken them, they would all have slept forever. He went over towards Warren and Kate, hearing Ross rise unsteadily on the slippery ice behind him.

"How is she?" he asked the doctor.

"I'm all right," Kate said.

"Good." He switched on his most dazzling smile. "It was very brave of you to go into the 'plane like that: you've probably saved us all."

She smiled back. "Thank you, Mr. Quick."

"Please call me Simon. Well, Doctor, I think we'd all better get changed, or Ross and Job will be the only ones who make it through the night." He made it sound light, like a joke; but he hoped it would draw their attention to the fact that rather than seeing to their safety, Ross had seen first to his own.

"Job, are you sorting out the clothes there?"

Job nodded.

"Good. I'd better give you a hand then. We'll use the tent that's unpacked. It's a bit battered, but it should preserve the proprieties. I'll get it up again." His hands weren't working too well, but he managed without much trouble. The double-layer of material, carefully designed to give maximum protection against cold and wet, had been torn down one side by the force

81

of the explosion and hung a little open. It would do, however, as a changing room; and after that as a store tent.

"I'll just pop in first, if that's all right with everybody, then I can help Job with the crates here," he called.

Job paid no attention to him; Warren, Kate and Preston nodded; Ross had wandered off somewhere.

Quick climbed swiftly into the tent. The hole in the wall let in light as well as cold, and he had no trouble reading the tickets on the bundles of clothes on the floor. One read *Large*; two *Medium*; one *Small*. They had that well enough sorted out, he thought. *Large* for Preston, *Medium* for Warren and himself, *Small* for Kate. He undid the string on the bundle he had chosen for himself, and laid the clothing out: long underwear, carefully quilted; heavy trousers and shirts; thick woollen socks; insulated water-proof overtrousers; an anorak lined with wolf's fur; woollen gloves, sealskin mittens and boots. The clothes were a little loose, but not too bad: the boots at least fitted satisfactorily. He stepped out of the tent, pulled up the furlined hood, and gestured to Miss Warren that she should enter the tent next.

He went to one of the crates on the far side of the tent, and began to open it. It contained sleeping-bags. His hands – warm at last! – mechanically began to unpack the crate. A careful look round revealed that he was alone here. His eyes fastened to the slit down the side of the tent. The wind moved the material, and he caught a glimpse of movement. He bent to pick up another sleeping-bag, eyes riveted. A bare arm moved over the blackness. Abruptly the side of the tent billowed out, and he could see her balancing on one leg, the other raised ready to insert into the quilted long-johns, her body in a delicate curve of hip, back and arms down to the stark white material . . .

"Simon?" Ross was beside him. He knew. Ross knew!

Quick swung towards him, face blazing. "What?"

"Look. I've been looking over this floe. It's huge; maybe twenty acres. It would be better if we moved further down it. It's wider, the ice is thicker, it would be a better place for a camp."

The change of focus temporarily disorientated him. He had not yet got round to thinking about the floe; had not even looked it over to get a full idea of their predicament. It angered him that Ross had had the forethought to spy the land and

82

begin to make a plan. It was what he should have been doing, if he was going to function credibly as leader; instead of standing here trying to get a look at that blonde tart flaunting herself in the tent.

"I see," he said. "Well, I'm glad to see you've been making yourself useful after all. It's not a bad idea; I'll think about it."

He turned away, safe in the knowledge that his outrageous behaviour would disarm Ross.

"Don't be bloody silly, Simon. This is no time to regress to our old fourth-form days. We could die up here; for God's sake try to act like a grown-up!"

"Don't tell me how to behave! Good Christ, I've been on the ice now for ten years. I'm chief of the camp we're going to. I haven't been hiding behind a desk for the last five years; I haven't got eleven deaths on my slate. Where did you get the arrogance to think that I should listen to your advice rather than looking at the problem and making up my own mind?"

His voice had risen, but not in hysteria: in the righteous anger of an offended man who has been grievously misjudged by one who should know better. The others had gathered around now.

Ross gave his lop-sided shrug, and moved off. Job followed him.

Kate came out of the tent. "What was that all about?" she asked.

Warren and Preston looked away.

"It's very simple, Miss Warren; Ross believes we should all do as he says, whether we want to or not. He supposes himself to be so much better equipped to survive than us, that we should consider his words gospel."

"And is he? Is he better equipped to survive?"

"My dear Miss Warren! I understood you had been in cold climates before?"

"So I have. In Iceland and Norway."

"And your father?"

"Of course."

"Mr Preston?"

"Yes; I have been in Greenland and Iceland."

"Well there you are! We all know our way around; why should we take orders from someone who's been sitting behind a desk for the last five years because the last time he was in a position anything like this one, everyone who was with him died?" He could see he had scored a telling point, and was willing to leave it there.

He turned again to the crate of sleeping-bags and a quiet voice interrupted.

"So," said Job, "you all know your way around. You, Doctor Warren, when was the last time you were on the pack?"

He waited a moment or two for an answer.

"Miss Warren?"

"I've never actually . . ."

"Mr. Preston?"

"Me neither."

"Simon; I don't have to ask you. Unless you've been doing it in secret, you have never survived off land either."

"It makes no difference, Job . . ."

"A moment, please, Simon. Let us take it a slightly different way. Look around you, please, and tell me what you see."

Quick, feeling the incentive slipping away, thought desperately, shading his eyes and looking around. "I see the ice, the ice hills, the sea, the sky, the sun . . ."

"Quite right, Simon. There is nothing else *to* see. But it is understanding what you see that counts. When you look around, you must not see sea, ice, hills, sky and sun, but enemies bent entirely upon your destruction."

"Oh. For Heaven's sake!"

"No, Simon . . . Although the sea is seven feet beneath our feet on average, we are in fact only inches above sea-level; and the water is our enemy. This current is cold. It is several degrees below freezing because it is salt. If you have a weak heart the simple shock of falling in means instant death. If you are fit and well, you might last for a couple of minutes."

Kate moved a little closer to her father.

"The sky. The sky is either clear or cloudy. If it is clear, it drives the temperature down; if cloudy, it heralds a storm. The sun. The sun will send you blind if you are not very careful. And the ice. The ice once again is an enemy; perhaps our greatest enemy, because it masquerades as a friend. I have said that it is about seven feet thick. This is the average thickness of a pack. It varies. In many places, on the hills for instance, it is very much thicker; here it may be thinner: it may be only a crust over a hole reaching seven hundred feet down to the bottom of the ocean. You will not be able to tell the difference until it is far too late. It feels as firm as a mountain-side, as safe as the sidewalk; but it is not. When you walk you must never trust it to support you, for as sure as you do so, it will let you down, and you will fall through, drown and die. Remember this: no matter what happens, no matter how good things seem to be, even if there is the promise of imminent rescue, you must think of it as yet another trick of the pack to try and fool you into dropping your guard. Whatever the pack does to us, it is part of its plan for our destruction."

He looked around them. "Now you think I have gone too far. You begin to doubt me. Well; it may sound paranoid, but that is how you must think, or you will surely die."

The Eskimo turned, and walked away from the quiet group, following his friend down the massive tongue of the floe. He soon caught up with Ross, and they walked on in silence for a while. A gentle wind whipped flags and streamers of ice-crystals off the top of the reassuring wall of the ice-hills to shower like tiny diamonds all over them. The floe widened here, and the sea was almost a hundred yards away on their left on the far side of a slightly undulating plain.

"What did they say?" asked Ross after a while.

"They said nothing. They are frightened and confused, Colin; you must give them time."

"I'm not giving them anything! They're no responsibility of mine."

"Colin . . ."

"No, Job. In Antarctica I allowed myself to be swayed by a man whose judgment I didn't trust, and I've been carrying that guilt for five years now. I'm not looking for any more. Eleven people. And Charlie."

He lapsed into a morose silence, and tugged distractedly at the black kid glove which was all he wore, even now, on his left hand.

Job knew better by now than to interrupt, and after a while Ross shook himself out of it.

"Well, what's the next step? I vote we just take a tent and move down here."

"Colin, that is not charitable, wise, or practical. We would only alienate these people; we would be too far away to help them if anything went wrong; we would be so far away the food would be cold when we got it. You know as well as I do that the best chance is if we all stick together."

"The best chance for them, perhaps; but **our** best chance is to stay well clear of them until they have all **managed** to kill each other off, then move in."

"Colin!"

"It's true, and you know it! If we join them, we risk our lives automatically, because if they're not going to take perfectly reasonable advice, then they're going to start having accidents, and we're going to have to start getting them out of whatever they fall into."

"You are right. And can you think of a better reason for going back?"

Then Ross gave a brief bark of laughter. "No, dammit; you're right; I can't." He turned, and started back up the floe. "Come on; let's go and save them from themselves."

There was a spring in his step as he walked that Job, hurrying behind, hadn't seen for years. He felt himself beaming like an idiot and shaking his head, hardly daring to believe the change in his friend engendered by that simple decision.

A few yards further on, Ross stopped and called back over his shoulder. "I smell soup."

Job sniffed the air. "Oxtail!"

"Right!"

They had all changed now, and had set out the boxes in a rough square in preparation for the unpacking and setting up of the camp in the place Simon had suggested. They had opened another crate. This one contained a general survival kit: fishing-tackle, several packs of pressed meat, some cans of soup, can-openers, chocolate, a knife, a compass, de-salinisation unit, sterilisation tablets and a fire-tray. This last was a steel tray on short legs, designed to stand a little above the snow and make it possible to light a fire even on ice. Kate was in charge of this, and was heating one of the tins of soup in an aluminium pot, with six tin mugs waiting to be filled. Ross and Job joined in with a will, unpacking the other crates and beginning to erect the tents. Kate gave them a smile as they

86

arrived. Preston nodded. Warren and Quick carried on working silently.

In all there were seventeen boxes, eight gathered from the ice, and nine brought out of the belly of the 'plane. Of these nine, two each contained two tents with groundsheets, guy-ropes, and pegs; one held six sleeping-bags; one contained twelve blankets; there was a box with two rifles in it, and another of ammunition; two crates of food; the crate they had just opened with the general survival kit; rope; the net, and, caught up in the net's strands, a three-foot six logger's axe. From the ice they had collected one box containing two tents; a crate containing a collapsible canoe; and, of all things, two chemical toilets; a second crate of clothes containing changes in all three sizes; another box of rifles; a crate containing a harpoon-gun and four harpoons; a box of the dynamite and two more crates of food.

They set up the tents in a rough square. The torn tent which they had used as a changing room was to become the storage tent. They piled the crates they were not going to open immediately in and around it, except for the dynamite which they put well away. Then they put the sleeping-bags and blankets in each tent, except the one a little away from the others in which they set up a makeshift latrine.

By the time the soup was cooked, there was nothing to do except open the crates by the storage tent. They all grouped round the fire-tray and swallowed the hot strong soup with great relish.

"I'd better heat up a little water so that you can wash," said Kate: most of them were still covered with blood.

"Good idea," said Ross. "But you'd better make it quick or we'll all be asleep." And it was true. They had all been so dazed with shock and fatigue since they had woken after the explosion, that it was a wonder they had managed to do this much. They were all gazing dully at their cups of soup.

Kate scooped up handfuls of the crystals from the ice, and put them in the pot which had heated the soup. "I hope it'll not be too salty," she said.

"No," said Ross, his eyebrows raised with the effort of thinking, "all the salt leaches out in the first year. It's fresh."

As they sat in the fatigue-stunned silence, mindlessly watch-

87

ing the pale flames consume the planks in the fire-tray, Ross was desperately trying to get his brain to function. It was absolutely necessary they understand something about the position they now found themselves in, with regard to both the floe and the pack as a whole. It was clearly his responsibility to tell them, for he knew most about the pack and he had looked over the floe with the eye of an expert. He had half-heard Job's words on what the pack was, and the dangers of the ice, but Job's love of theatrical expression, the hyperbolic power of his arguments would have out-weighed what Simon and the others thought they understood of the facts.

"Look," he said, his voice rusty with fatigue, and far too loud, "the Arctic is a big place . . ." It sounded flat even to him. Banal. Patronising. Simon Quick smirked. He ploughed on, unwilling to stop. No matter how badly he put them, the facts themselves would – must! – carry some weight. "The area actually inside the Arctic circle is in excess of eight million square miles. That includes a fair amount of land, but the Arctic Ocean itself is so big, it's broken into seas for easier reference. In winter it's almost all frozen. In the summer, the edge of the pack retreats until it gets to its smallest area around August, but it never shrinks much under an area of three million square miles."

He looked around them. Even had they been fully awake, he doubted whether figures of this size would have meant much to them. Perhaps later he would think of some analogy which would make it spring into life. After all, three million square miles of the pack was bigger than the U.S.A. They were all still watching him, their faces blank with fatigue. They didn't really want to know. A great wave of hopelessness broke over him. To his exhausted mind it really seemed then that this was all his fault. Five years earlier he had fought the Queen of Bitches, Antarctica; fought her and won. Since then he had hidden away, safe from ice and snow. But she had not forgiven him, not forgotten. That this was the North Pole, the Arctic, made no difference: it was the work of that terrible enemy which had cost him everything then, and was demanding more now . . .

He frowned. This was rank stupidity. How long had he been wool-gathering? He glanced round them again. Kate at least still looked vaguely expectant, and so he ploughed on.

"The pack is on average seven feet thick, although, as I'm sure you saw, areas which are actually flat, like this piece, are very rare. The problem is, of course, that the pack is never still. It moves in a clockwise direction around the centre point of the Pole. This movement, caused by the action of winds and tides, varies from two to eight miles a day. The forces needed to move something of three million square miles at that sort of speed are naturally enormous, and so, if there is the slightest hesitation or inconsistency in the movement, the pack ice folds, cracks, piles up on itself to heights of well over one hundred feet. This is clearly what has happened to form the hills back there which in turn have formed this floe."

Nobody looked at the green iridescent humps and hollows rising between thirty and fifty feet, only yards away. In the silence the water on the fire began to boil, steam billowing impossibly thick in the dry icy air. Ross persisted. It was important they knew more about the floe.

"The floe we're on is quite a big one, as you can see. In all, I suppose it's about twenty acres, but of course a lot of that is at the edge and so treacherous as to be unapproachable. What we've got then, is this great tongue of ice about five hundred yards long, and at its widest point, two hundred and fifty yards wide. Part of it is the spinal cord of the hills, and the rest, flat plain – as you can see. On the west, the hills slope steeply down into the sea. Some of them overhang on this side, with concave faces so that the summits are highly unstable. You really ought to avoid the hills."

He paused again. He was at the crux of the matter now: safety. How to behave on the floe: how to stand a good chance of staying alive. He decided the best approach would be to suggest modes of conduct as strongly as he could, without forcing them so much that he set people's backs up.

"Apart from about ten acres in the centre of the floe, in this plain, it's all highly dangerous. Even the apparently safe and stable ten acres of the plain here might prove treacherous." He spoke forcefully, they stared dully. "I have said that it should be about seven feet thick. But please remember that even with a thickness of seven feet, the water is still close: the water level is, in fact, little more than a foot beneath you. Please try and remember that no matter how flat and stable and safe the ice may look, there is always the possibility that it may not take your weight. This is not a pavement, a floor. It is a thin layer like glass between you and water so cold it could shock you to death instantly if you fall in. Is that all clear?"

They continued to stare dully at him, saying nothing.

"Now," he continued, a little desperately, "the question of rescue."

That stirred them a little, but not enough to elicit any reply.

"Hiram broadcast the position of the crash on the radio. How much further did we travel before we actually touched down?"

The co-pilot shrugged. "Thousand yards. Two."

"So they will be looking for us within a mile of our present site . . ."

"I thought you said the pack drifted." Simon Quick, belligerent. "And anyway won't the floe move faster than the rest of the pack now it's loose?"

Ross was really too tired for these games. He answered almost spitefully. "Much faster. About ten miles a day. Maybe fifteen."

That shook even Quick. He went white. "You mean that if they don't get here almost immediately, we'll have drifted miles away?"

"Yes."

Their interest was almost tangible now. Their concern.

"But they'll send something immediately, won't they? A 'plane?" Kate asked it. Her gaze shifted from Ross to Preston.

He shrugged again. "Depends what they've got. There're 'planes enough at Barrow I suppose, helicopters." He looked around them, heavy with news. "But when I sent the Mayday, Barrow said the weather was closing in. A storm. I mean they mightn't be able to get anything up immediately . . ."

"A ship," said Kate. "They'll warn shipping."

"That's true, but it will largely be a matter of luck whether or not a ship would see us. They think we're on the pack, you see . . ."

They sat for some while without saying anything more, dipping cloths into the hot water, cleaning themselves, their movements made vague by fatigue, latent shock, stiffness and cold. There was little else to say, after all.

90

As they sat, the wind, pushing gently from the east, catching the hills like sails, and the current thrusting restlessly from the Beaufort Sea effortlessly moved the twenty acres of ice away from the location of Preston's last message. And from Barrow, wrapped at the moment in the worst summer storm in living memory.

The sun was quite high when they collapsed at last into their tents. Ross and Job shared one, Preston and Quick another; Warren and Kate had one each, together, nearest to the sea. The split side of the storage tent billowed lazily in the breeze, the latrine tent flapped and cracked quietly like the sail on a ship.

Ross and Job quickly stripped to their quilted underwear, and, packing their clothes around their sleeping-bags to keep them warm and supple, fell swiftly asleep. Ross's dreams immediately carried him back through five years and over half the world. He began to stir and mutter.

Preston and Quick removed only their boots, and fell asleep immediately. Warren, his boots still firmly in place, didn't even undress or make it into his bag, but wrapped himself in blankets, and dozed off hoping they would be rescued before he ran out of tobacco.

Only Kate, in her underwear, wisely surrounded, like Job and Ross, with her clothing, could not sleep. She blamed herself for their predicament. All along the way, when things had gone wrong, she had been there, at the cause. It had been her idea to look at the pack. Her wish to follow the whale. It was her fault they had crashed here. And later, it had been she who had climbed up a wire she knew was live, causing the short, nearly killing herself, and blowing up the 'plane. They would never be found now, with the 'plane gone. And it was her fault. She was so tired that her normally practical mind accepted the pointless self-accusations, and began to sink deeply into a pit of self-pity.

Abruptly it was all too much for her. She was fourteen again, standing by her mother's grave; and there was only one person to run to. She dressed quickly, and went to his tent. He was sound asleep. She shook him, tears running down her face. "Daddy; Daddy."

He stirred; turned over. His eyes opened; looked at her vaguely. Remained on her face as he frowned. "Who is it?"

It was too painful. With a sob she turned to run from his tent, but his voice came after her. "Katherine; Kate!"

She paused, turned back.

"I couldn't see. I didn't have my glasses on, darling. What was it you wanted, Kate?"

He was sitting there, all rumpled and untidy, peering through his misted spectacles at her. A great warmth welled up in her chest. She reached for him. And then the polar bear came in through the back of the tent.

The bear, a young male just entering his prime, had been hunting the edge of the pack for seal but had found none. Earlier that evening, however, his attention had been caught by the sound of the explosion, and he had gone to investigate. Over a mile downwind he had picked up the smell of the humans, and he would have gone on his way except that he picked up also the smell of the soup. His hungry stomach churning inside him, he had thrown himself into the water at the point where the floe had broken away, and had swum with floundering, rapid strokes to the source of the delicious smell. Silently he had skirted the island of ice, keeping effortlessly in the water, protected from its great cold by his ample layers of fat. He had found a quiet place to land, and had crept up silently on his great fur-covered paws. The smell of humans was very great now, and he moved like a ghost; but a ghost of muscle, teeth and claws. When he saw the tent, he didn't know what to make of it, and so, with all the logic of the wild, he attacked it. He reared up behind it and brought both his great front paws down on it. The short, blunt claws ripped through it like paper. Something in it screamed: he charged.

Kate saw its huge shadow just before it attacked, and she stared, transfixed, through that eternal moment as the shadow fell, and the black talons destroyed the tent-wall. Then, framed in the tatters was the flat, evil head, its eyes ablaze, black lips stretching back from scarlet gums and yellow teeth in a terrible growl.

She screamed, and then she was rolling for the way out, pulling her father with her. He followed her, yelling at the top of his voice. The bear floundered after them with a roar, but it became entangled in the tent and was forced to pause.

At Kate's first scream, Ross sprang awake. He heard the

thunderous roar as he was pulling on his boots, and understood immediately what was happening. "Bear," said Job, also struggling with his boots. Ross nodded and threw himself through the tent-flap. He slewed round in a flurry of ice and took in the scene at a glance.

The bear had risen to its full height, and was tearing the tent away like so much wet tissue-paper. Warren and Kate were running away towards the fire. Quick and Preston came out of their tent, also running.

"The guns," yelled Ross; and the three of them made a dash for the supply tent. They threw boxes and crates hither and thither looking for the three crates, two of guns, one of ammunition.

"Here," yelled Quick. "The carbines." He was tearing at the top. Ross found the ammunition , and smashed the top in with one blow of his left fist. "Neat trick," said Preston, as he opened the second box of rifles. Quick slammed a magazine into one of the carbines just as the bear tore the tent from its face, and charged after Kate and Warren. He aimed and fired. Ice kicked up beside the charging animal, and then the gun jammed.

"Christ!" screamed Quick. Preston was wrestling to load the long, sleek shape of a Weatherby Varintmaster.

Warren tripped over the discarded survival-gear box and fell full-length while something metallic slid from it across the ice towards Kate. He struggled helplessly to rise, slipping on the treacherous ice. The bear caught up with him, and rose above him, ready to strike.

Then Job was there, astride the doctor, whirling a lumber-jack's axe in front of the bear's face. The bear paused, and roared wildly. The axe flashed down, only to be struck aside by a contemptuous blow from the monster's paw. The doctor, on all-fours, was almost at Kate's knees. Job turned to run, and the bear caught him. Ross was running wildly towards them, carrying Quick's useless carbine. Kate brought up the silver object from the general survival box: a Very pistol.

"No," cried Ross. "You'll get Job."

There came a crack from behind him, and a heavy bullet from Preston's Weatherby smashed into the bear's shoulder. Its head came up, great strings of saliva dripping from its jaws. It began to bend Job backwards. The rifle cracked again. Ross saw the bear's flesh jump. It roared. Job was hissing in pain now, as the bear fought to get a crushing grip on him. Ross swung the carbine back over his shoulder like a club, then forward with all his towering strength. The stock landed with a dull thud against its wounded shoulder. The bear hurled the gasping Job away and turned. Ross smashed it over its nose and catfooted away.

CRACK! A hot wind burned past Ross's cheek. The bear paused. Ross turned. Preston, reloading the Weatherby, Quick with a Remington 7MM Magnum. Ross ran. The bear charged. Preston fired again. The bullet mushroomed into the bear's shoulder: it didn't even limp.

Running on all fours, steady on the ice, it was rapidly overtaking Ross. He was at the fire when it caught up with him, rising up to its full ten feet, ready to grasp him. Quick squeezed off another shot: it didn't even bleed.

Ross felt the heat of the metal tray at his back. He swung his left shoulder towards the blaze. The bear shambled forward a few steps. The evil head came down. He was almost overcome by the stench of rotting fish, but his left hand was in the flames now. He drove it into the heart of the fire. Someone was screaming: Kate. He jabbed forward with his right hand. The bear's arms reached for him, the jaws drooled and snapped, inches from his face. Another bullet slammed into it. Ross saw the flesh jump. The report nearly deafened him; point blank. The bear screamed. The enormous cave of its mouth opened, blood red and terribly deep, and he lurched into action.

His left hand, black glove blazing, grasping a piece of red-hot board, reared out of the fire, over his shoulder, and down the bear's throat. Its screams were drowned in the hiss; the smell of fish vanished under the burning. The bear reared up, its jaws snapping shut like a trap on his left arm. Ross was lifted from his feet, and hung for a moment while the jaws champed, then he dropped, and was away, his arm left dangling in the ruins of the sleeve, leaving the agonised bear. The monster, choking, coughing, tearing at the board with its paws, stumbled erect towards the water. The board came free and was flung away. Ross stood by Job, watching as it hurled itself into the sea.

"Who'd have thought a false arm could save your life?" he gasped, folding the tatters of his sleeve away from the twisted metal and torn plastic. The bear floundered through the golden ocean, raising its head every now and then to bleat.

"Hell," said Quick, "that brute'll never die." Then the bear's head suddenly jerked under the surface.

"What . . ." Warren.

The head came up again, screaming.

"Oh God," whispered Kate, turning her face against the nearest shoulder: Ross's. The ocean heaved. The bear's scream choked off as it vanished again. Job's hand was iron on Ross's shoulder. Ross's arm went around Kate. The bear's head reared out of the churning water. A crimson fountain burst from its gaping mouth and arced through fifteen feet of silent air. Then it was gone.

And in the silence two things happened.

The tall triangular fin of a whale broke the surface and powered away; and Job said, "It is the Knucklebones of Sedna. May God protect us now."

FIVE

JOB WOKE FIRST, and lay listening to the sounds which surrounded him: the restless hissing of the ice-crystals in the wind; the sobbing of the wind in the guy-ropes supporting the tent; the occasional crack as a tent-panel flapped like a sail in the wind. The waves lapped at the distant edges of the ice-floe; the water made tinkling sounds like tiny streams moving against the ice beneath his head. And beyond that, deep in the heart of the ocean, squeaks and clicks, gratings and groans, sobbing songs and long bubbling cries. He let their strange, heart-wrenching beauty wash over him for a moment, tempted into memories of childhood and the Hudson Bay. But he knew too well that the cries of the killers could represent a very real danger: if the whales decided there was something on the ice they wanted, they would have no hesitation in smashing the floe to pieces trying to get it. He saw again the head of the bear straining out of the water, the blood curving through the air. The bear, which they had exerted themselves to their utmost to get rid of, destroyed by these monsters in seconds.

Colin stirred, making a morning noise in his throat, half-way between a groan and a snore. He yawned.

"Morning," said Job.

"Morning. Or is it?"

"No. It's afternoon. About one full day since the crash."

"Great." Ross huddled in his sleeping-bag, pulling the blankets up round his ears. Not at his best in the morning. Job smiled.

Ross stirred. "I can still hear them singing down there."

"Yes. We'd better hope they don't think of any reason to return."

"God, yes!"

They lay a little longer in silence. Ross's breathing slowly returned to the deep regularity of sleep. "Colin? Are you asleep?"

Silence.

Job lay back and half-dreamed, half-thought. There was nothing else to do. He was not going to get up until he had to because he would only get bored out there: he was used to having things to do. So were they all, he supposed. Ross certainly; Quick and Warren if he knew anything about how company research stations were run; and the woman, unless universities had changed radically since his day. He really knew nothing about the life of a pilot, but he suspected that that would be pretty busy also. And now they all had nothing to do except wait and hope. Nothing to do . . .

Soon they would talk – reveal too much about themselves and how they felt about each other. Then they would begin to spread out on the floe, wanting to keep clear of each other; but being on their own would be worse than the strains of company and, still nursing their grievances, they would drift back warily, unwillingly, like starving wolves gathering round a fire. And this period would be the most dangerous . . . He had seen it before, the ill-chosen words, the explosion of violence.

The sound of the lumberjack's axe unsteadily wielded added itself to the others in the background of his thoughts. Someone was preparing the fire.

"Is it going yet?" Kate, in the middle distance.

"Not yet." Doctor Warren, close at hand.

The wind made the unsteady roaring sound it makes when fanning flames.

"There." Kate's voice, suddenly close at hand. "Powdered eggs, water for coffee, ham."

"Do the coffee first. I'm freezing."

"You should have taken off your anorak and trousers when you got into your sleeping-bag. I told you."

Silence: the doctor was not used to being told off. Job smiled.

The pots and pans clinked gently against each other. The conversation dried.

Then, "Tell me about Colin Ross," said the woman.

"Tell you what about him?"

"All about him."

"I don't know all about him."

"Oh Daddy! Tell me what you do know. When did you meet him?"

"I can't remember when I met him first. I've known him for years."

"For years? How many?"

"I told you: I can't remember. Oh all right. I met him seven years ago in the South Shetlands near the Antarctic."

"What – "

"Just be quiet and let me tell you! My God, where's your patience, woman? Where was I? Ah yes, the South Shetland Islands. I was doing some research there and Ross was in charge of the camp. And he was the best I ever met."

I hope Simon doesn't hear that, thought Job.

"He had a massive reputation even then. He had worked for the Royal Society, the Royal Geographical Society, all of them . . ."

"But what did he do?"

"Basically, I suppose, he's an organiser. In those days he was what Simon is now. He set up camps and ran them for us scientists. Helped us a lot, too."

"Helped you?"

Pause. "You remember you told me only one man had come within five marks of our results at Oxford in more than ten years?"

"Yes."

"Ross was the man who came that close."

"You mean – my God, I had no idea! But then . . . ."

"What is he doing as organiser instead of researcher? Look at him. Can you really see him sitting around with a microscope?"

"No. Under no circumstances."

"Well, what apparently happened was that he went on a project to some godforsaken spot, and the leader of their expedition was hurt. Ross was the youngest and by far the least experienced, and yet he took over the whole expedition and brought them all safely through. I say that's what apparently happened, because I could never get him to tell me. He doesn't talk about his past at all. Insists on keeping everyone at arm's length. I suppose that's what makes him so good at command decisions: he's never confused by personal feelings. Cold, you

98

know? Strange man. Now I much prefer Simon: not nearly as efficient, not half the man he thinks he is, not a tenth the cold-weather man Ross was, but much more human. Likes a joke; loves a drink; that sort of thing: human."

"You say 'was'."

"What?"

"'Quick isn't the cold-weather man Ross was.'"

"Oh yes, I see. No. This is the first time Ross has been out in five years. I don't know what he's like now. Seems to have gone down hill quite a lot."

"Why?"

Pause.

"Is it something to do with his arm, and his wife, and . . . ?"

"Well yes, I suppose it is."

"Simon told me about the expedition to the South Pole. Is that when he lost his arm?"

"Yes."

"How?"

"You'll have to ask him."

"I think I will."

"He won't tell you."

"I'll risk it. Is that all?"

"No. There was an enquiry of course, when Ross got out of hospital, and it turned pretty nasty, from what I hear. Some of the missing men's stuff was found on Ross, and he was actually accused of taking their food in order to survive himself. But Jeremiah made a death-bed testimony which was made public. Saved Ross's reputation."

"Saved him? You think he was guilty?"

"Well, I don't know. Ross refused to say anything, you see. He's never said anything about it to anyone, as far as I know."

"So everybody thinks he's guilty."

"Many people wonder, yes."

"Then what's he doing with such an important job?"

"I told you, darling; he's a genius. What he doesn't know about surviving in the snow, he can easily guess. He's a very valuable commodity, especially in these days when so much of worth seems to be hidden under snow and ice."

"And yet you don't trust him fully to take charge here?"

"Well, he's been out of the snow for five years. And he hasn't

99

made much of a push. Anyway, it shouldn't be too long now before we're picked up. They talked to the people at Barrow before we crashed. And Simon knows what he's doing . . ."

The conversation outside veered away from Ross as Quick joined the breakfast party.

Ross stirred; and woke. "I smell coffee."

"Just going to get some," said Job. "You'd better hurry, or it'll be cold."

"Just coming."

Ross rolled over, and pulled his shirt towards him. His left arm was wrapped in it. Job bent down to crawl through the wind-proof flap. Ross began to position his arm with dexterous ease. He was humming a tune.

Outside it was still bright, although the sun was low. The four of them were grouped round the fire-tray, seated on the crates, supping steaming coffee. On the pale flames sat a huge pan filled with a mess of ham and reconstituted eggs.

"I know," said Kate as Job eyed it, "it looks terrible, but it'll taste OK, I promise."

"It looks great," said Quick gallantly.

"After more than twenty-four hours without solid food, even my cooking would look good," said Warren. "Coffee?"

Job picked up a cup from the pile of utensils on the lid of one of the food crates. Preston poured. Job drank it. It was hot, and black, and perfect.

"Is Mr. Ross all right?" asked Preston, his face concerned. "After last night . . ."

"He's fine. Just coming." Job stretched, his whole body stiff with bruises from the crushing grip of the polar bear. "If you have any sympathy to spare, save it for me."

"I knew a lady once, who hugged like that," said Warren, relishing the memory. "Ran a house of ill repute in Skagway . . ." Then he remembered he was sitting next to his daughter, and blushed.

Ross came out of the tent.

Kate, her face still warmed by a smile at her father's embarrassment, felt her eyes drawn to the tattered sleeve, the buckled plastic and scarred metal of his arm. The black glove was gone now, and the plastic hand blackened by fire instead. All the unkind thoughts she had felt about Job carrying Ross's bags, helping him with his coat like a servant, came back to mock her. Her eyes went up to his face, and he was smiling at her. She realised she was still smiling about her father: Ross thought she was smiling at him. She felt almost embarrassed, and widened her smile a little.

"Coffee?" asked Preston.

"Please."

His eyes left Kate, who smiled for a moment or two more. Ross pulled up a crate, and sat on it carefully.

"That smells good," he said, gesturing to the pan.

"All right," said Kate, "you don't have to tell me what it looks like. I know."

"I wasn't going to. I've never seen anything that looks like that."

"I have," said Warren, "but only under a microscope."

"Much more of this," said Kate, "and you'll need a microscope to find your share."

"Just like her mother: can't take a joke."

"But I'm sure," said Kate, her voice like honey, "that the ladies of Skagway laugh ever so much."

They all got plates from beside the cups, and ate with spoons. Kate was right: it tasted OK.

They ate in high spirits, as though merely out for a picnic. The evening was clear, deceptively sunny. The heavy clothing kept them warm enough. The sea lapped quietly, distantly. The wind was gentle, playful. The floe was really huge, and the ice lovely. The tall hills towered reliably close at hand, the tongue of ice reached out and out, away from them, substantial, solid, shining, nearly twenty acres of it. The surface of the ocean was dotted with other small floes, all of which were empty and still. In the far distance the pack shone brightly and insubstantially, like the smoke from a green flare. In the high bright sky, a 'plane passed, a tiny flash of intense light and a comet-tail of cloud; the echoes in the silence giving a whisper of its power.

"Tell us about your arm, Colin," said Kate.

Ross, about to drink, looked at her speculatively over the rim of his cup. The old familiar wrench in his belly died almost immediately; the sudden tension around the fire did not emanate from him.

He swallowed. "No," he said.

101

"No. Of course he won't," said Quick, bitterly, but without hysteria. "He doesn't want you to stop smiling at him."

"Simon!" shouted Warren. "How dare you . . ."

"Then," said Kate, loudly, keeping fast hold on the conversation, "perhaps Job will tell us precisely what he meant last night by his reference to Sedna's Knucklebones."

Job shrugged. "It is only a legend of Innuit."

"A legend! Just right! We've nothing to do but unpack things, eat, sleep and get on each other's nerves. A legend would help pass the time."

Job looked around, nervously. "I don't . . ."

"Oh come on, Job," said Warren; "you tell a mean story, you know you do."

Job shrugged again.

"First tell us what Innuit is," said Kate.

"Innuit means 'The People'. It is what we Eskimos call ourselves."

"And the story of Sedna is one of your legends?"

"That is correct. It is the story of how the things in the sea came to be there. Not plants or fish, but creatures, animals."

"Oh, please, tell us," begged Kate, filled with the excitement she had felt when she first saw the pack.

Job looked at Ross, who shrugged his lop-sided shrug, and nodded.

Job nodded back, and began to speak: "Long ago, at the beginning of all, there lived in a hut by the seashore the girl Sedna, her father Angusta, and her great dog. They lived there a life of ease and plenty, for the Inua, that is to say the spirits, of the sea were good to them and the fishes were plentiful and fat. Now as Sedna grew in years, she grew also in beauty and soon the young men would come to her hut with gifts of ivory, bone and amber, with lucky stones and love. And they would say to her; 'Sedna, I bring gifts which took great finding and love which will never die. Come with me now and be my wife.' But Sedna always said to them, 'No.'

"At first she said this because she loved her father more than she loved any of the young men, and she would not be tempted away from him even by fat love-figures carved from the teeth of bears; but later she said, 'No' because she loved to see the longing unfulfilled in their faces and she would wait with

102

excitement to see what wonders they would bring to her the next time they came courting. So the name of Sedna became known through Innuit for her beauty and for her cruelty, and many came to her hopeful but went away from her sad.

"Then one day, as she sat by the seashore, thinking nothing of suitors, and talking with the Inua of the stones, there came towards her a man in a kyak. Such was his paddling that he seemed to come up from the ocean and down from the sky. Such was his beauty that the sun grew dim, for his hair was the silver of dull pearls and his skin was ivory gold. His nose was large, but beautifully shaped, and his eyes were black as the winter's night.

"He called to Sedna saying, 'Sedna, come with me.' And Sedna, looking on him loved him, but she said to him, 'What will you give me as a courting-gift?' And the man with the pearl-grey hair said, 'This will I give you if you will promise to be mine.' He held up for her to see a necklace made of amber beads such as she had never seen before.

"'Then what will you give me as a bridal-gift?' asked greedy Sedna. 'These I will give you as a bridal-gift,' said the man with ivory skin. And he held up for her to see ten fat love-figures made from the teeth of great white bears.

"Then was Sedna tempted to go with him in his silver-sided kyak, and this he saw with his eyes as black as the long winter's night. So he said, 'Fairest Sedna, whose name is known through all the Lands, if you will come with me now to my kingdom over the sea, I will give you these lucky stones which will keep you from all harm.' And he held up two grey stones which danced with magic in his hands, and such was the power of the stones that all the Inua of the stones upon Sedna's beach fell silent.

"Then Sedna called to the beautiful stranger, 'I will come with you.' So he brought his kyak close to the shore, and Sedna went with him.

"Far and far he paddled to his kingdom over the sea, and all the time proud Sedna knelt behind him, counting her amber beads. And so, after many days and nights they came to a rocky shore, black and tall with cliffs.

"'Where is this?' asked Sedna.

"'It is my kingdom,' said her husband.

"'It is a cold, forbidding place,' said Sedna, putting away her fat love-figures made from the teeth of the great white bears.

" 'It is your home,' said her husband.

" 'But where is your hut, my husband, that I might make fire and cook for you?'

"And her husband pointed to a high cliff-ledge and said, 'That is where I make my abode.'

" 'I see no wood to make fire,' she said to her magic stones.

"Then her husband cried in a high strange voice, 'I need no fires, Sedna, my wife, for I eat my fish as I catch them and my feathers keep me warm.' And as he said these words, the beautiful prince rose out of the kyak and spread his wings in the sky, for he had become a fulmar petrel. Then was Sedna torn with sadness and fear, for the beautiful prince she loved was thus revealed to be a Kokksaut: a powerful and terrible spirit he was, who roamed the skies on the wings of a bird and almost never came to land. Then Sedna cried out in her grief. Loud and long she cried, but nobody heard or came. And her spirit husband quartered the sky, searching for distant game.

"Now Sedna's father, who loved his daughter as surely as she loved him, was made most sad and lonely by her absence. So he said to himself, 'I think it strange that Sedna has sent me no word since she went away. I will go and find her myself,' and left his hut and went. Many and many the days and dangers he met, and braved, and left, until one day in the distance he saw a seashore tall with cliffs, and he heard a voice which wept.

" 'It is Sedna,' said Angusta, and he paddled towards his daughter's voice. Sure enough, it was Sedna who cried at the foot of the cliff. But when she saw her father she smiled; and she said to him, 'Take me away now, for I have fallen out of love.' Her father was glad to do so, for his hut was cold without her. So they paddled over the mighty sea, but the Kokksaut who loved Sedna ventured home from his windy roads and saw that his ledge was empty, that she was gone from the foot of the cliffs. And he cried his wild fulmar's cry, and set out in his turn to search. High and high the petrel flew, and he quartered the sea below. After many hours and days he saw the kyak of Angusta with Sedna kneeling in the back. He dived down to the kyak then and cried out, 'Sedna, return.' But Sedna cried, 'You tricked me: I will never return.' Then was the Kokksaut truly enraged, and he cried to the Inua of the ocean who were his cousins, and to the Inua of the winds who were his brothers, and they built up a terrible storm. Angusta's kyak was battered and swamped. The waves fell out of the sky, and they became the black-grey of the magic stones, with teeth the white of the ten fat love-figures; and once in the distance they saw the sun, and it was the colour of clouded amber. So great was the storm that Angusta at last became afraid.

"'Go back to your husband, my daughter,' he cried.

"But she replied, 'I will not return.'

"Then the storm became so terrible that Angusta cried out in fear, for the waves were as light as full grey pearls, and their teeth were ivory-gold. There were rocks both large and beautifully shaped tearing the water like the skins of birds; and, although it was high summer, the day became as dark as the winter's night. And Angusta cried, 'Go back, go back.'

"And Sedna answered, 'No.'

"What the storm became then cannot be told, but it drove the old man mad. He hurled his daughter from the kyak and tried to paddle away. 'Do not leave me, father,' she cried. But her father replied, 'I must.' Then Sedna broke free of the ocean's embrace and caught at the side of the boat. And Angusta, mad, brought the blade of his paddle down on his daughter's hand, and the bones at the tips of her fingers broke away. She grasped again, and her father struck, and the bones of her fingers broke. The third time she tried and her father struck, and her knucklebones broke off.

"Then Sedna sank, and the sea grew calm, and Angusta paddled home. But the Inua of the sea were kind: they gave Sedna a kingdom of her own. She called it Adliden, and rules there now, with Angusta her father and the dog.

"Now the magic of the Inua did not rest there, for the tips of Sedna's fingers became the little seals; the middle bones of her fingers became the deep-sea seals; and the knucklebones of Sedna became the terrible whales."

They sat for a moment in silence.

The wind cried, the water lapped, the ice cracked and roared; and deep in the heart of the ocean they heard the songs of the hunting whales.

"That is what I meant when I said what I said about the Knucklebones of Sedna." There was a pause. "Mind you," he

105

went on matter-of-factly, "the killer isn't even a proper whale; it's the largest of the dolphin family: Orcinus orca; the killer whale. More than thirty feet long, clever as a chimpanzee; the wolf of the sea."

"All right, Job," said Ross, "you've made your point. Now reassure these good people. Tell them there has never been any recorded instance of an attack by killers upon people."

"Wrong," said Quick, enjoying the feeling of scoring over Ross, ignoring his almost imperceptible shake of the head. "Herbert Ponting, in Antarctica. He was with Scott on the *Terra Nova*. Their dogs were on the ice, and a pack of killers was trying to get them. Ponting decided to go over the side and photograph them. They came up through the ice after him. Nearly got him."

"Thank you for the history lesson, Simon," said Ross coldly. "But Ponting was the last man ever to be attacked by the things, and what Simon has just told you took place over sixty years ago."

Quick stirred. "Yes, well; it shows you it can happen."

"Right. But it hardly makes the things super-sharks, does it?"

There was a strained silence. Ross had made his point, but the elation they had been feeling earlier was now replaced by nervousness. The ice cracked sharply. Kate jumped. "They came up through the ice?" she asked quietly.

"Yes, Miss Warren," said Ross, "but it was thin ice; only three feet thick. They can come up through thin ice by smashing it from underneath with their heads. But only thin ice."

They all nodded. Kate smiled at her groundless fears.

"Right," said Quick, "rest-cure over. Let's get back to work. There's quite a bit to do."

They sorted out the food in the chests. It was fairly basic, but it would last.

"We have fishing lines," Preston said. "We can get fish enough I guess."

Ross shook his head regretfully. "Not until those killers move away. They'll scare everything for miles around."

They all looked nervously at the bright water. In the far distance something moved, sending up a thin plume of spray. Then there were more: they seemed to be moving away.

Suddenly there was a splashing roar at the edge of the ice. Kate's hand flew to her mouth: she did not scream. The men jumped up, grabbing at the guns. And out of the water, grunting with the effort, snorting, hissing, cascading golden droplets, came a seal. It was huge, nearly twelve feet long, eight feet in girth. It flopped along the edge of the ice, taking no notice of them, and eventually came to rest well clear of the water's edge. It reared up on its flippers, looked suspiciously round, and lay down and went to sleep.

"Now there," whispered Quick, "is enough fresh meat for quite a while."

"It must weight fifteen hundred pounds," said Preston, an avid hunter. "What a kill. We could do it fine with the Remington and the Weatherby."

"A soft-nosed bullet in the head," agreed Quick, "but we'd have to get close."

"I don't think it would be a good idea to kill it," said Ross.

"Oh come on, Colin. Got a weak stomach?" sneered Quick. "Where will the blood go when you butcher it?"

"Into the sea."

"And in the sea is a pack of killer whales which will be attracted by the blood."

But already Preston was creeping across the ice towards the black-brown mound, his gun slantwise across his chest. Quick moved off after him. Mouth tight, Ross watched from a distance. His eyes flicked out to sea. Six black sail fins were moving towards the ice, moving so fast that little bow waves foamed at the front of their sinister triangles.

"Preston, Preston get back! Simon, SIMON!"

Preston's hand went up and waved: shut up, you'll scare it. Simon turned. Job had run towards him. Now he pointed: the fins were near the ice now, their tips visible even over the fat bulk of the seal.

"Preston," cried Ross, "get back!"

Preston swung round, his face ablaze with rage. The seal, roused now, heaved itself up and turned towards him, mountainous, angry; it bellowed, began to move towards the camp . . .

And the killer came out of nowhere, reaching ten feet across the ice. Huge black flippers holding it steady on a base of fifteen feet from tip to tip, huge black fin flopping over out of the water. The great mouth closing on the flank of the seal, huge teeth, suddenly awash with blood, tearing the hide and blubber like paper, finding purchase in the writhing flesh, pulling . . .

Ross saw the black and white head from a distance, yet even he was shocked by its size. Kate couldn't believe it. Quick nodded with satisfaction: told you so. Kate covered her ears against the seal's terrible cries. Ross put his arm around her. Warren was saying "Jesus, Jesus, Jesus." Job watched, utterly detached, as the seal fought forward a few inches, its hide making a dry ripping sound as it tore. Preston saw a round black eye regarding him coldly; he saw the scars on the killer's snout and cheek. He raised the Remington and fired. He missed.

The killer, its mouth awash with the dizzy heat of the blood, saw the man. It saw him raise the rifle and heard the sound. It saw his arm reach out under the long thing, and remembered the agony and the wild, fierce joy trained into it in Oregon.

All this happened in the second before the seal's grip on the ice broke, and, with a twisting convulsion, the leader tore the fifteen hundred struggling pounds into the ocean.

Warren sank to his knees. He was shaking. Job leaned on the rifle, breathing deeply. Ross looked out to sea, frowning, his arm still round Kate. Preston came stumbling back towards them, white as the snow.

Simon said, "Look." The black sails had come up again; twenty of them, distant, indistinct, merging with the sharp patterns of black and gold the sun made on the water. And as they watched, they began to patrol up and down by the floe, waiting; keeping watch and waiting.

They returned the little way to the camp, and sat in silence round the fire.

"What've we got to fight them with?" asked Preston.

"Fight them?" said Job, almost shocked at the idea.

"Rifles," said Quick.

"Not big enough," said Preston with a shudder.

"Dynamite," said Warren. "We have dynamite."

"And the harpoon gun." Quick.

"They won't attack," said Job, but he didn't seem too certain, "there's only the one recorded . . ."

BOOM.

The ice leaped beneath them: heaved into a cracked hillock twenty feet away. "Christ!" screamed Preston, "they're coming through." They began to scramble to their feet.

CRASH.

The ice hillock burst open. A huge black and white head thrust through, streaming water from its gleaming skin, venting a cloud of breath with a great roar. The unimaginable mouth opened, revealing the huge teeth. The pink-white tongue lolled out. The head swivelled towards them, the liquid black eyes observing. Quick grabbed the Remington and aimed . . .

The immense head lifted lazily, insolently, and slid out of sight. The bullet sped through empty air, and Quick swore. Preston was on his knees by the box of dynamite, his mittens off, tearing at the fastenings with clumsy wool-gloved fingers. Warren was at the crate containing the harpoon-gun. Kate was standing, feet spread in standard two-handed firing position, holding the Very pistol like a handgun. Ross still sat on his box, for once rendered inactive by his great knowledge: killers did not attack people. The occasional skeleton was found in a dead killer's belly, he knew; and he had not been entirely honest about Ponting, but this was something strange, beyond belief. Killers just did not go hunting people.

BOOM.

The ice leaped. The tents reeled. The fire jumped out of the fire-tray and landed in a cloud of sparks: that had been right beneath them.

BOOM.

A lead opened up five yards away, its edges parting spewing black water. Ross sprang to his feet.

"Kate! Not the pistol. Can you use a rifle?"

"Yes."

"Bring the Remington. Job; the Weatherby and shells."

He was off out of the camp, over the twenty yards to the edge of the ice. He slid to a stop well clear of the water as another fin, as tall as he was, parted the water as silent as a knife and dived.

"Look out!"

BOOM.

He fell to his knees. Then Kate was beside him, the slim, Remington 7MM Magnum rifle snug against her shoulder. She searched the molten gold water for the next fin, her eyes narrow.

"Just a sec," she said, lowering the rifle, and she produced a pair of dark glasses from the recesses of her anorak. The rifle came up again.

"Where'd you get those?"

"Handbag."

"Silly question."

"Right."

Job arrived with the Weatherby, and two boxes of bullets.

"Can you see all right, Job?"

"Fine."

"Here comes one," Kate, tensing.

"Just before it dives." Ross, quietly.

"Right . . ." Job. ". . . NOW!"

Both rifles spat together. Two small plumes of water rose on either side of the tall fin.

The fin vanished. They all tensed. Nothing.

"Good. Keep it up." Ross scrambled to his feet, and ran back to the camp. Preston was crouching beside the opened box of dynamite, his hand just reaching towards the brown ranks of sticks, and the coiled fuse. Warren and Quick were lifting the harpoon-gun out of its crate. It would take them some time to set it up. He left them to it, and went back to Preston, who was binding four sticks together.

"That's too much," snapped Ross. But Preston, clutching the bundle feverishly, sped past Ross, grabbing a burning stick from the fire as he went. "Preston!"

"I know what I'm doing . . ."

"I hope the hell you do!"

Preston had reached Kate and Job now, and Ross was following as quickly as he could. Preston jammed the burning stick against the fuse. It spluttered into life. He drew back his arm to throw . . .

BOOM.

The ice heaved. They all went flat. Preston fought to stay erect, his feet slipping and sliding wildly. He fell; the dynamite slipped away from him, hissing on the ice. He began to crawl towards it, his movements desperately fast. The ice rocked again, only slightly in the aftershock of the blow: the dynamite slid back towards him. It was only inches from him, and there wasn't much fuse left. He made a last, convulsive grab at it. His gloved hand closed on it, lost it, closed again. He rolled on his back and threw it.

It curved up into the bright sky, leaving a trail of smoke, turning over and over. Then it began to fall, clear of the ice. Just clear of the ice.

BOOM.

The dynamite exploded. The floe heaved up and up. The four of them began to slide back towards the camp and the hills. The supply tent collapsed. A huge column of water and ice rose majestically and cascaded down upon them. The floe began to tilt the other way. The explosion had filled their ears so they did not hear the great *crack*! as the lead opened by the whales widened and a raft of ice broke away just beside the camp: the raft they were on.

It was Warren who saw what was happening first. With Quick he was running out of the camp with the harpoon-gun. Suddenly, unbelievingly, they were at the edge of the floe. He looked down stupidly at the strangely dark water lapping against the foot-high cliff of ice. He looked up again. It was then he realised. "KATE. KATE!" he yelled.

"*Kate. Kate!*" The sound cut through the roaring in her ears as though from a great distance. She was wet, cold, stunned, lying on the ice; one cheek was numb. She stirred, lifted her head. The world was unsteady. Preston was lying just beside her. She frowned, pulled herself up a little more. Job was picking himself up, going over towards Colin. Beyond them, her father was waving frantically.

Kate's head was clearing now, but the horizon still seemed unsteady. She tried to stand: and she found that the ground was moving beneath her feet. Job was gesturing to her now, and there was great urgency in his voice. "Miss Warren, wake Hiram; bring him."

She stumbled over to Preston and shook him till he stirred. Then suddenly Colin was beside her, a pencil of blood running down from his hairline. His hand slid under her arm. "Leave him."

111

She rose obediently. Job lifted him to his feet, and the four of them went stumbling across the ice.

There was a gap now of a little more than four feet, but even as they arrived at the edge, a quirk in the current began to part the two pieces of ice more rapidly.

"Jump," said Ross to Kate.

She went back and took a run, but the treacherous ice slid beneath her feet, and she began to lose control, her arms waving wildly, her mouth opening to scream. She threw herself forward, into Simon Quick's arms. In the air, over the black, threatening water, her mind was filled with one thought: she had broken the straps on her bra.

And as he caught her, through all the clothes they were wearing, in spite of the tension of the moment, Quick felt the firm fluidity of her breasts.

Preston came across next, still half-unconscious, precipitated by Ross and Job together. Then Job. Then Ross.

Then they all stood and watched as an acre of ice drifted away and began to break up. Ross said, "We can afford to do that maybe fifteen more times, then we run out of ice. And there are still maybe twenty whales."

He turned away from them and walked towards the camp.

"Jesus Christ," said Preston. "I didn't mean; I didn't think . . ."

Kate and Job turned at the same time, and followed Colin. Quick's eyes followed Kate, and then he also went towards the camp.

They were standing in the middle of the small square, beside the fire-tray. They were silently looking at Warren as he finished setting up the harpoon-gun, with Preston helping.

"We'll have to move camp now, Simon," said Ross.

"Right," said Quick, still lost in the sensation of Kate's breasts.

"Right," said Ross. "We'll begin to move the camp down to the middle of the plain down there, where the ice is widest. Job will show you."

"What about the killer whales?" asked Warren.

There was a little silence, then Ross said, "The dynamite seems to have scared them off for the time being, but you're right, we ought to keep a watch. Would you stay by the harpoon-gun? If you see anything, just call out. Don't fire unless you have to. OK?"

"Fine."

So Doctor Warren stood by the harpoon-gun as the others began to move their camp one hundred yards further down the flow. At first, he stood almost at attention behind the gun, his hands on the double grips, his eyes quartering the burning gold sea; but then, as nothing was happening, his mind began to wander.

At the camp, they first set out the net. It was a red-orange nylon net with medium-spaced strands, four hundred square feet of it: a square with twenty-foot sides.' At the corners, and half-way along each side there were guy-ropes which were forty feet long. Using steel pegs where they could, and pieces of board from the crates, they pinned it firmly to the ground, making sure the strands did not become lost beneath the snow and ice-crystals. "There," said Ross when they had finished, "that should stop all this slipping and sliding about. We'll bring down the tents next, and unpack the spares."

Warren took out his pipe, and put a few shreds of his remaining tobacco in it. He was still lost in thought.

They set up the tents between the guy-ropes at the edge of the net, all facing inwards, except the latrine tent which faced the other way. The side of the net facing the nearest shore, the shore opposite the ice-hills, was left empty. On the opposite side to this, under the shadow of the hills, were the two tents shared by Ross and Job, Preston and Quick. On the other two sides, one still looking north towards the pack, the other south towards Alaska, went the three other tents: the latrine on its own, to the south; the supply tent and the Warrens' tent to the north, facing south. In the corner, between the Warrens' tent and that shared between Preston and Quick, stood the fire-tray. They trooped back up to the ice to start on the crates.

Warren's mind had returned from the past, and was foraging ahead now. In front of his blind eyes a thick cloud of smoke hung on the still air. The black and gold curves of the calm sea broke up silently, and began to form spikes; black triangles. He was so preoccupied with his thoughts that he did not see a great black fin break the surface twenty yards away. He did not hear the quiet hiss of the water on the broad, glistening back as the

113

whale drew rapidly nearer. He was not aware that anything at all was wrong until the killer blew. Then the sudden roar, the smell of fish and death whipped him back to the present: he saw the tall column of water-vapour, the huge shoulders powering towards the ice, the turbulence of the working tail, and he aimed, still partly in a dream, and fired. The coiled rope followed the flashing blur of the harpoon in its slight curve into the flesh beside the fin. There was a solid thump! as the arrow went in. The whale slewed round, showing a gaping mouth, a huge black flipper, sending up a cloud of spray, and it began to run hard until it sounded. The rope attached to the harpoon was rushing coil by coil into the ocean, its friction melting a deep groove in the ice.

Warren stood, transfixed, letting the roar of the running rope wash over him, then he yelled, "I got it; I got it!" and he raised his hand and hallooed like a schoolboy playing Indians.

Within seconds all the rope was gone from the coils. It snapped taut with a crack! and hummed with bass overtones. Slowly, incredibly, the floe seemed to swing round. Warren brought his hand down and held the gun tightly, forcing its pointed legs even further into the ice. He glanced over his shoulder: they were labouring up the treacherous ice from the new camp-site.

The angle of the line altered: the whale was coming up again, but there was no slackening on the pull. Warren, his gloved hands tight on the handles of the harpoon-gun, leaned forward, searching the brightness of the water for the first sign of the broad black back. Roaring filled his ears; the sharp percussions and the crackings of ice. He disregarded them, concentrating . . . There it was.

"There she blows!" he yelled. The fierce joy of it possessed him. He was Ahab with two good legs, and this was his Moby Dick! He turned, exultantly to wave to the others, when he was thrown against the gun with vicious force. He lurched forward and back. He turned forward again. Spray lashed up into his face: he was moving very fast. Behind him came a scream: he turned back and saw the widening gap. The ice he stood on had broken away and the whale had pulled him free.

Job watched incredulously as the ice broke, and the fifty square feet that Warren was standing on lurched away into the sea, gathering speed as it went. "JUMP!" he yelled: it was the old man's only chance. He saw Warren turn and look at the foaming water. "JUMP!" he yelled again, but it did no good. The large floe had broken into smaller floes which ground against each other only feet away. Warren's small floe was rocking violently now; as Job watched Warren staggered, and his little floe tilted dangerously. Job stood, bitterly helpless. Around the floe, other fins began to appear, following easily, silently.

Ross took it all in at a glance: the distant floe, the rigid man, the black sails taller than he was. His face twisted and his mind raced: if Warren stayed where he was, he was dead; if he went into the water, he was dead; he had one chance: the smaller floes, spread like stepping-stones out over the water.

"Rifle," snapped Ross. They had not yet moved the rifles down to the new camp-site. Preston passed the Weatherby to Job. He aimed at the killers.

"No: at Warren. Close as you can!" Kate's mouth opened. Ross's hand came down on her shoulder. Job aimed, fired. A little plume of ice puffed up at Warren's feet. "Again," said Ross.

Warren had never been so frightened. He glanced to his side, and the tall black fins seemed to tower above him. He did not dare look down into the rushing water. "God, help me," he said. It was a prayer.

CRACK.

He looked down at his foot, not understanding.

CRACK.

This time he saw the ice kick up into a cloud. "Sweet Jesus, they're shooting at me!" He looked around for somewhere to run. He took one hand off the gun to signal the lunatics. He half turned.

CRACK.

He took a half-step forward: the ice tilted. He looked around wildly, and the next floe was upon him. He went for it, screamed as the cold water closed over his legs, his pipe at last falling into the sea, and then he was scrambling out like a mad man and up on to the ice. The black sails moved silently past.

He pulled himself to his knees and looked over the bright water to where the tiny raft with the harpoon-gun on it finally toppled over and abruptly vanished as the whale sounded again.

He looked back to where the others were, automatically flinching before he realised that the shooting had stopped. He recognised Ross because of the tattered sleeve of his anorak. Ross was beckoning him, urgently. He got up and walked unsteadily over the ice of the floe. At the edge he found the edge of a second, larger floe only five or six feet away. He paused, looking at the unsteady gap, walked back a little, then ran up and jumped. This time he didn't even get his feet wet. The ease of the jump, however, seemed to trigger a reaction to his terrible fear. As he walked across the floe his knees began to quake, and he found he couldn't breathe properly. He fell, picked himself up, fell again. The edge of the ice seemed further away than ever. He began to crawl towards it.

The killer thrust itself out of the water perhaps twenty feet from the crawling man. It rose for over fourteen feet before hooking its flippers on to the edge of the ice, adjusting itself to compensate for the movement of the floe settled into the water under its weight. It breathed out. Warren turned his head at the sound, and what he saw drove him to his feet again. He began to run in earnest. The whale turned its head slightly, and the brightness caught the puckered lines and scars on its face. It watched him with all the detached indifference of a pagan god, then it sank again. Warren gasped and wheezed; his head reeled with the effort of running. He stumbled over the rocking floe. The ice seemed to be breaking up around him. He reeled forward, drunk with panic. The floe lurched again as another of them threw itself out of the water, skidding along the ice, reaching for him with huge teeth. The rifle spoke three times in rapid succession, and gouts of blood blasted loose from the killer's head with a crisp slapping sound. It shivered and sank away. Warren ran on, his legs shaking, making each step an enormous victory of the will. He blotted everything out except the necessity of putting his right foot before his left, his left foot before his right. The floe began to heave again, but he hardly noticed. He lurched from one foot to the next, oblivious of everything, nearer and nearer the edge . . .

CRACK.

Ice kicked up in front of him. The ricochet whined. He froze, confused, jerked out of his nightmare; he looked up. He was only feet from the water. Another step, maybe two, and he would have been in. The edge of the big floe was ten feet away. His legs gave out, and as the floe lurched again, he sat down. He looked stupidly at the gap he could never jump. There was a roar close by him. He looked round. A smaller one, drooling water, teeth like white fingers grasping. He watched it reach over the ice at him, as birds are said to watch snakes, unable to move.

Job jerked up the rifle again: he had changed the Weatherby for the Remington with its big, soft-nosed bullets and magnum power.

The first shot blasted the killer's eye into a bloody cauliflower. It began to slide back, screaming. The top of its head blew open: it became silent.

A rope slashed across Warren's face. He grasped automatically, still watching the dead whale.

"Tie it round you," called Ross's voice. He did as he was told, then he suddenly slammed forward. His shoulder crashed against the ice. He slid forward again. The edge of the ice appeared under his bemused face, passed.

The icy water closed over him.

The shock drove the breath from his lungs.

He blacked out.

SIX

BOOM.

Ross sprang awake. He began to fight with his recalcitrant trousers. He was never at his best first thing in the morning. It felt as though he had grains of salt under his eyelids. He blinked, and pulled grotesque faces trying to clear them. Job was dressed and heading out the tent.

"Coming," said Ross, and also got to his feet, only to stagger and fall as the next whale hurled itself against the underside of the floe.

BOOM!

"Seems to be standing up OK," said Job.

"More than I am, I tell you," said Ross, struggling to get up again.

"Can I help?"

"No. See what's happening outside." Ross was on his knees now, shirt in place, the solid club of his left arm supporting his trousers as he zipped them up with is right hand. Job wriggled out of the tent, and Ross followed him in a very few moments.

BOOM!

Ross came out into the snow and the sun stabbed his eyes with vicious force. "Oh HELL!" he said with feeling, surveying the rest of the party through a burning golden haze. He took a step, and tripped over the net.

"Snow-blind!" said Quick, a world of disgust in his voice. "And only the girl had the sense to wear dark glasses." To her face he called her Miss Warren; behind her back, it was always *the girl*: that was how he actually thought of her – not a person, but as a collection of physical parts which he was finding increasingly attractive. She was not there now because she would not leave her father.

118

They had pulled him out of the water apparently dead, but Ross, Quick, Job and Preston had taken a limb each, and they had run his heavy, inert form down to the new camp-site and in to his tent. There they had stripped off his clothes to Ross's curt directions, and dried him with the rough blankets so energetically that Kate had become almost concerned that they would strip his skin off. But she was well versed in first aid, and of a temperament which was anything but hysterical. As soon as she had seen that everything was well in hand in the tent, she had gone outside to the fire-tray, and begun to heat water gathered carefully in handfuls from between the strands of the net. Then she had cast around for something else to make hot-water bottles out of. The best bet seemed to be the the the one litre glass bottles she found filled with orange juice. She heated them until the juice unfroze, then poured it into every receptacle she could think of rather than waste it. She filled the bottles with hot water individually, wrapped them in blankets and delivered them to Colin. Ross pushed them inside the sleeping-bag with the body, which was rapidly gaining warmth and colour. He had smiled at her. "He's going to be all right."

She had nodded, and brought them all coffee; but they couldn't drink it because of the orange juice frozen in the cups. It had been Job, eminently practical, who had come up with the solution. They had simply emptied the chunks of orange ice in an old box, and kept it outside like ice-lollies in a freezer. Then, as there was nothing else to do for Warren, Ross had begun to make a meal while the rest of them transferred the last of the crates and boxes, and Kate had sat with her father. Then, after a disquietingly short day, they had all gone exhausted to bed.

BOOM!

"Can anyone see as well as usual?" asked Ross.

"Only me, I expect," said Job. "We should have taken precautions earlier."

"Obviously!" snapped Quick.

"No sense fighting," said Preston. "What can we do about it?"

"Make goggles," said Ross, cutting off Quick's angry tirade.

"Yes," said Job, "we'd better do that before we take on the killers again."

"So they made elementary snow-goggles from strips of

119

material cut out of a small anorak that no one was using. They were shaped like rudimentary glasses, with long narrow slits just big enough to see through, but cutting out much of the brightness. And while they were doing this, Job checked on Kate and her father. He seemed to be doing well. Then Ross made coffee.

The whales, unable to break through the thicker ice, seemed to have given up for the time being. Nevertheless, the four men went to the edge of the floe, and looked at the water, and the distant, restless pattern of fins. There seemed to be fewer than earlier, even allowing for the two killed while rescuing Doctor Warren, and the third he had harpooned.

"I've never known them act like this," said Ross.

"I bet it's that big bastard with the scars on his face," said Preston. "I don't know much about these things, but he looked as though he was in charge."

"One with scars on his face?" asked Ross, suddenly interested. "What did it look like? I didn't see it."

"I dunno. I only got a glance at his face when he came up through the ice that time. Ask me, those scars are bullet wounds, not that I'm an expert, mind, but I've seen enough to know."

"Christ!" breathed Quick. "Do you think that could be it, Colin? Is it possible? Could someone have shot that big bastard in the face so that he now has a vendetta against people?"

"I've heard of such things happening to game animals in Africa, when they go rogue, but I've never . . . Anyway, what do we do about it?"

"Do about it? We damn well kill them!"

"That's the problem! Can we? Oh, the guns will take out the smaller ones, if we get enough of the Remington soft-noses into them. But we haven't an unlimited supply."

"The dynamite," said Preston.

"Yes, granted; but it hasn't been an unqualified success so far, has it? And we don't want to run out of ice."

"God!" said Preston, "that's one thing we've plenty of! Look around, there still must be fifteen — twenty acres. And those ice-hills. They'd never come through those."

"Unfortunately," Ross said, "it's not as simple as all that. Those hills are probably weathered down now into a shape completely different to the one they had when they were formed. It is highly probable that all that is holding them upright is the rest of the floe here. Don't you see? If anything happens to the rest of the floe and they break adrift, they'll probably turn upside down!"

"Jesus," said Preston in disgust, "so you mean all we can do is just sit here and wait to be eaten?"

"No. We have to fight," said Ross. "It's just a question of working out how."

"I know how," said Job.

It was his first contribution to a conversation which had grown increasingly loud, but, although he spoke in his usual soft tones, the others turned towards him and listened quietly.

"What we do is this: we make a small raft, perhaps of wood, and we pile it with dynamite, and we float it out to where they are, and then we shoot the dynamite . . ."

"But it must be almost a mile," said Quick. "I'm not that good. Are you?"

"No . . . But Colin is. There are telescopic sights on the Weatherby, and it has the range."

"He could never do it, man . . . his arm!"

"Actually," said Ross. "I'm a better shot now than I ever was, under the right circumstances." He gave a sheepish grin. "It takes out one of the variables, you see. It doesn't shake, so it can make an absolutely rigid tripod for shooting from."

"Can you do it, Colin?" asked Job.

"Well . . . There's only one way to find out, isn't there?"

In the event, they used a piece of ice as their raft, with a plank of wood wedged into it rather like a sail. Around the bottom of the plank they piled ten sticks of dynamite, four of which were attached to a length of fuse wound round and round the plank.

"That way, you see, I only have to hit the plank to set off the fuse," explained Ross as he was working on it.

"Only!" said Preston, shaking his head.

Within half an hour it was ready. They lowered it carefully into the water and gave it a gentle shove, then stood mesmerised for nearly an hour as the gentle breeze took it and moved it slowly away.

Conversation began sporadically, rose in intensity, then

dwindled away as the time passed. When Ross took the gun, there was silence.

The bundle, black against the water, was almost invisible to the naked eye, but it jumped into focus, surprisingly large, as Ross adjusted the telescopic sight. He was kneeling on his right knee, the elbow of his left arm firmly on the lower thigh of his left leg, the stock of the rifle sculptured on his cheek. The black sails passed restlessly between him and his target. He began to build up his concentration, cutting out everything in his immediate surroundings, focussing all of his mind on the bobbing target beyond the precise cross-hairs. He adjusted the sight, hearing the quiet click sound crisply on the air. He regulated his breathing, and held the cross of the hairs just a little above the top of the board when it was vertical. But, of course, it was vertical for only a very few seconds in every minute, for it swung from side to side like a metronome, moved by the waves.

Ross counted silently. "Over one two, Upright one two, Down one two, Upright one two . . ." At least it was regular; or it would be as long as the wind held. This time, then, before the wind could change. His gloved finger began to tighten on the trigger slowly, smoothly: Over one two, Upright one two, Down one two, Up . . .

He felt the fluke of the wind on his cheek, and saw the target hesitate; but it was too late. CRACK! The rifle jumped back against his shoulder. His snow-mask slipped down from his forehead and rested on the cold metal sight. His eye remained pressed against the rubber eyepiece, watching as the wood jumped just an inch or two left of centre, and the fuse exploded into action. Job's hand came down on his shoulder and gripped. Preston breathed out loudly: "Hot Damn!" Simon Quick nodded.

The fuse did not follow its spiral course as it burned. Once it had caught, all the carefully wrapped strands ignited together, and the top of the plank burst into flame. The single strand running down to the four sticks burned swiftly, which was as well, because as soon as the fuse began to burn, the black sails all vanished in golden swirls of water.

BOOM!

A great column of water and ice hurled into the sky as though there was some unimaginable cetecean blowing there. A cold, wet wind blew counter to the gentle breeze for a second, carrying with it the aftersounds of the explosion as the column began to tumble back into the water.

Kate came running over the rocking ice. "What was that?"

"Ross scaring off the whales," said Preston with satisfaction. She stood, watching the distant column as the waves broke over the edge of the floe, sending shallow washes of icy water around their feet. Ross lofted the Weatherby with one hand to his shoulder again, and searched the gleaming water for the tell-tale fins.

Nothing.

"I think we may have managed it," he said.

He turned, scanning to the south with the gun-sight. In the far distance the sun caught fine colunns of water-spray and vapour moving away.

"We've done it!" His voice was exultant. The others danced and capered and cheered. A distant voice demanded, "What's all this then?" And Warren, fully dressed and as belligerent as ever, barrelled across the ice towards them, stopping only to slip an arm round Kate as she ran over to him.

"Well," he said as they told him, "I think that calls for a little something. I for one am famished!" And so, lacking alcohol, they celebrated with ham, powdered eggs and beans. Preston saved his ham.

"Don't you like the ham?" Kate asked him.

He winked. "There's lines and hooks in that box we opened first. I'm going to try to catch some fresh fish for supper."

"Good idea!" said Simon Quick. "We'll not have much else to do now until we get picked up."

"How long d'you think that'll take?" asked the doctor.

Quick shrugged. "They got a message off before we came down. Someone should be looking for us."

"Will we have drifted far?" asked Kate.

"Up to thirty miles a day," said Ross.

"How long have we been adrift, then?"

They all looked at Job, who looked at the declining sun. "Three days."

"Three days!" said Preston, surprised. "It hasn't seemed that long."

"Well, it's about sixty hours since we crashed; and we've been sleeping for at least half of that."

"That's nearly a hundred miles away from where we crashed!" Preston gasped. "And heading for Russian waters . . ."

They were all quiet after that, and sat sipping their coffee thoughtfully.

Preston was the first to move. He left his plate on the ground, and went across to the supply tent. "I'd better get things set up before the bait freezes solid," he said cheerfully, waving the heavy green line, and the assortment of hooks.

He found he was quite excited at the prospect of doing some fishing, even if it was only dangling ham in the ocean on the end of a hand-line. Neither Ross nor Job told him that the chances of him catching anything were minimal; he knew it anyway, but he didn't care. The thought of sitting in the camp with nothing to do was irksome, but the idea of sitting doing nothing while holding a line in the water was considered by millions of people to be a most acceptable occupation.

He checked the tackle: a dozen hooks of different sizes, all covered in tiny spines the better to hold in a fish's mouth; and the line itself made of braided nylon coloured green and with a breaking-strain of at least two hundred and fifty pounds. It was by no means the kit for a sportsman: there was no subtlety in it, no art. The fish, once it became hooked on the deadly spines, really stood no chance whatsoever. And that, of course, was the whole object. This kit was not designed to give people sport, but to keep them alive.

Preston expertly looped a weight on to the end of the green line, attached three hooks of different sizes to the first eighteen inches of the tackle, biggest at the bottom and graduating up, and slipped his firm chunks of ham over their nickel-gleaming spined curves.

"Right." He picked up a small box and the axe, and went up the floe towards the old camp-site. "Wish me luck," he called over his shoulder.

"Break a hook," called Ross.

"Be careful," called Kate.

He waved his left hand carefully, avoiding the hooks which dangled from it.

At the top of the floe, where the camp had stood, there were holes enough for all of them to fish through. He chose one carefully, although he was completely ignorant of the correct things to look for. He pulled a box up, sat down with the line in his hand, and then fed it carefully into the black-green depths at his feet. There was one hundred and fifty yards of it, and he let out half its length, watching it dreamily as it angled down, pulled away by the drag as the currents moved the floe faster than they could move fine line and dead weights. Lacking a rod, he rested his arm on his knee so that it reached over the hole. At first he had worn only his woollen gloves, but his hands soon became cold so that he put his mittens back on. The line was difficult to hold with his hands covered by the heavy sealskin, so he wrapped it round his wrist a couple of times, then he just sat and dreamed, not really expecting to catch anything at all.

There was much to dream about. Through the narrow slits in his mask, his surroundings were still staggeringly beautiful. The flat green ocean stretched all around him, calm and quiet, its steady colour interrupted only by the mottlings of the floes and the cloudshadows, and the burning gilt of sunshine. It reached to the far horizons, to the fine green-smoke line of the pack far to the north, to the great smooth arc to east and south where the horizon was lost in a still gold mist, and the pale gold sky faded into the pale gold sea somewhere near Alaska . . .

The jerk on his line was so unexpected that at first he didn't believe it; but he automatically jerked back, wrapped the extra loop of line around his wrist, and half rose, his arm still straight like a rod, resting with its elbow on his left knee. The second jerk on the line was so strong that it broke his arm at the elbow like a dry stick, dislocated his shoulder, and slammed his collar-bone into his jaw with such force that he was stunned. The ruined lever of his arm slid off the fulcrum of his leg, and, as he pitched forward, vanished into the hole in the ice. His hand opened, but the line was wrapped round his wrist, and its strength was more than one-and-a-half times his own body weight. He looked at the ice under his face. He opened his mouth to do or say something and suddenly the ice under him was mottled red-brown. He tasted iron at the back of his throat. Oh damn, he thought, I've bitten my tongue. The line jerked again. Agony blazed down his left side. He began to cry out, but the sounds were swallowed in a silver muffler of bubbles as the water closed over his face. The line angled away, pulling his body down into the hole until his hips wedged, and his legs waved in the air. His eyes, ears, temples, and especially his teeth ached fiercely in the icy water.

He found himself able to distinguish only huge, seemingly formless shapes, until something suddenly hurled towards him, becoming clearer as it neared. When he saw what it was, he sucked in breath to scream with, but there was only water to fill his lungs.

"Christ!" yelled Ross, and was up and running across the net before the others had a chance even to react. He had glanced up just in time to see Preston's torso disappear and his legs rear into the air, kicking wildly. He tripped on the guy-ropes of the supply tent, fell heavily, pulled himself to his feet, and pounded across the treacherous ice with Job and Kate close behind him.

Preston's legs were still kicking as he slewed to a halt in a cloud of crystals. He leaned forward, his face turned away from the drumming heels, and with his one good arm hugged the ankles and shins to his chest. He spread his legs and heaved with all the strength of his thighs and back. Job and Kate stood on either side of the hole, ready to take Preston's arms and lift him clear of the water as soon as his body came free. As he heaved again, Preston came free, surprisingly easily. Kate's eyes went down, and her body automatically tensed to help the drowning man, then she was on her knees retching helplessly on to the ice. Ross looked wildly at Job, and took a step backwards. Job's face was oily white and twisted with horror. Ross took another step back, and the legs slipped from his grip; then he too looked down.

Above the hips which had wedged in the ice there was nothing. It was as though Preston had been hacked in half by a chain-saw at the waist. The legs lay in a great thin puddle of blood, still kicking.

The water in the fishing-hole parted. "Back!" screamed Ross, and the other two hurled themselves away.

Infinitely slowly, and with surprisingly little sound, the ice parted and the great black and white head reared up, streaming water. The huge mouth, twisted with scars, gaped open. The pink carpet of the tongue lolled out, collected Preston's legs as though they had been cheese-straws, closed with a stomach-wrenching crunch, and sank from sight, the booted feet sticking out from between the teeth where the lips did not close.

The three of them were still kneeling, frozen with horror, staring into the dark hole when the other two arrived.

"What happened?" snapped Quick.

"The killers . . ." Ross's voice was not working properly.

Kate was still trying to be sick on the ice, but there was nothing left in her heaving stomach but bitter bile. Warren went and knelt beside her. Job was taking great draughts of air, gasping and choking.

"The killer took him," he said.

"The killer? But I thought . . . Ross said . . . they've gone. Sweet Jesus, they've gone!" And as Quick said it, surprisingly close at hand, terrifyingly loud, came the roar of a breathing whale. They all swung round. It was at the edge of the floe, no more than thirty feet away, its flippers holding it erect as it watched them. The mouth opened, the tongue lolled out, the eight-inch teeth burned in the sunlight. The white chin glistened defencelessly, and none of them had a rifle.

"Damn you!" shouted Ross, and he was up on his feet and charging towards it. He caught up a lump of ice as he ran, he hurled it and missed. The whale lowered its head, slid back a little and waited. Its head alone was larger than the man, but Ross didn't hesitate. He hurled himself at it, left arm raised. The whale waited, unaccountably, unbelievably, until he reached it. His left arm came down like an axe, crashing on to its scarred nose. He raised his arm to strike again. Forty feet away, the killer's tail slammed down. The huge body lurched forward. The mouth, opening, slammed into Ross's stomach and hurled him backwards to sprawl helplessly on the ice. The huge head rose above him, mouth gaping.

Job and Kate moved together, running towards it, hurling chunks of ice. It paused, hesitated, slid back out of sight into the quiet ocean. Kate and Job took an arm and picked him up.

"Very brave!" sneered Quick. "I suppose you're going to tell us you've driven them off again!"

"For Christ's sake, Simon!" snapped Kate, "Will you grow up!"

His face worked. He turned away. To say that he was motivated only by hate for Ross and lust for Kate would be a gross oversimplification. Like many people, his ability to convince himself that he was the true hero of every situation he was involved in, and to explain his mistakes and meannesses to his own satisfaction, was almost infinite. He saw nothing wrong with his regard for the girl, and was only surprised that she did not obviously return it. Could she fancy that cripple Ross? No. She was only sorry for him. And now they were all on Ross's side, in spite of the fact that it was all his fault; he had said the whales were gone; he hadn't stopped Preston fishing. They ought to be chucking the big murdering sod off the ice, not nursing him. God; when would they learn? How many more of them would go the way of Robin and Charlie before they realised Ross was quite unable to lead anyone anywhere other than to hell?

Out of a mist, surprisingly close, there loomed an iceberg. He remained lost in his thoughts for a moment. Then his mouth opened. It was a huge berg, looking like a million tons of glass, towering hundreds of feet into the air, sculpted by wind and weather into buttes, cliffs, ice-pebble beaches . . . He looked towards the others, still grouped round Ross. None of them had seen. He felt the great bubble of excitement building up inside him. If he could get them off this melting death-trap and on to that . . . IF he could . . . Why, it was like getting out of a leaking lifeboat and into a drifting battleship.

He looked up at it again: a huge standard mesa-type iceberg, flat-topped, steep-sided, doubtlessly spawned by some glacier on the north coast of Greenland. He had some experience of icebergs, enough to know that the ice beneath the water would be plunging to untold depths into the ocean, in strengths and thicknesses which would reduce even the power of the killer whales to less than nothing . . . He walked back towards the huddled group.

Ross was sitting up when he reached them, regaining his breath. Kate glanced up at Quick, wondering briefly at the change in his face, from the thunderous frown he had been wearing moments earlier. He was smiling now, and his eyes were sparkling even behind the slit-eyed mask.

"Colin," he said, "I think I can save us . . ." He beamed round them all. "If you'll just look out to sea, you will see the answer to all our problems." He gestured towards the iceberg as though he had personally arranged it.

They all looked up. It was still several miles away, but it towered like a glass mountain, floating nearer as they watched. "I'd like to see those damn whales getting up through that!" he said.

Ross nodded: Simon was right. If they could get on to that, they would be safe from the sea and clearly visible to rescuers. "All right, Simon. That's a great idea . . ."

But even as he spoke, there came a sound like a muffled explosion, followed by a rumble which made their teeth rattle in their heads and a towering cliff on the approaching berg slowly crumbled and hurled thousands of tons of ice and snow into the foaming water. The berg rocked form side to side with the shock, becoming almost completely lost in a fog of disturbed ice-crystals and spray. They sat, bemused by the scale of the thing, while the waves spread towards them as though a gigantic stone had been hurled into the ocean. The floe was too big to ride over them like a boat, and so they broke, several feet high, against the ice, sending a shallow wash of freezing foam over the surface towards them.

The echoes of the rumble died like distant thunder. The foam halted, receded. Quick, not knowing what to say, was silent. Ross got to his feet with a great deal of agility. "Right. We'd better get back to the camp. We have to think this thing out."

"What is there to think about?" demanded Quick, trying not to sound aggrieved.

"We'll find that out," said Ross. He turned to Job. "Where's the Weatherby?"

"In the supply tent. Why?"

Ross shook his head, and led the way back to the camp. Quick remained where he was while the others followed Ross. He looked bitterly towards the berg. That bloody great lump of ice had somehow let him down, had let Ross take the initiative. It never occurred to him that Ross had taken the initiative because he knew what he was talking about. Still – ever hopeful – the idea *was* good: even if the berg did lose a cliff or two, it was still safer than the floe. He turned and hurried to the camp, still hoping to take the lead again.

They were all standing at the edge of the ice nearest the

camp, gathered around Ross, who was examining the iceberg through the Weatherby's telescopic sight.

"Well," demanded Quick, "what do you see?"

Ross moved the sight methodically up and down the towering cliffs, narrowing his eye against the golden blaze from the reflecting slopes, methodically probing the green crystal shadows where it seemed as though the berg's very soul was visible. It was almost like looking at a huge wave held at the moment of breaking, composed for ever of white, suncolours, lucent water-shades. But it was not the beauty of the thing which claimed Ross's attention. The gun moved carefully. Slowly. The urgency of his quiet scrutiny communicated itself to the others so that even Quick stood silent, and waited. Then the gun stopped moving, and Ross's breath hissed. At a slight angle to them, a heavy buttress pushed out of the sheer wall, creating a broad shadow. The Weatherby's sight brought this deep green cliff terrifyingly close, and plainly revealed its depths. Ross looked in the deeps of the iceberg, and saw there the tell-tale mottlings which warned of different thicknesses of ice behind the cliff, of huge caves deep in it structure. And through this cliff moved bright veins, gathering to opaqueness at one point after another, then spreading like the webs of giant spiders. The whole cliff was covered in cracks, as though someone had attacked it with a giant sledge-hammer.

"It's a Ghost," said Ross, looking at Job.

"God be merciful," whispered Job.

"What do you mean, a Ghost?" asked Quick possessively. "For God's sake . . ."

"Come back to the camp, Simon; I'll tell you."

"No damn it, explain here . . ."

But Ross had already turned towards the camp and walked off. Quick looked at the iceberg, frowning, not understanding. A Ghost Berg: he had heard the phrase . . . He also turned, and followed.

"You all know how icebergs are formed, how they break free from the' ends of glaciers that debouch into the sea, and float away like giant ice-cubes." They all nodded. Quick sat down, prepared to disbelieve every word.

"Many of these bergs float south into the North Atlantic; some get into the North Pacific. In the big oceans, they tend to

130

move farther south until they hit warm current, and then they melt." Ross looked round. His audience's attention was not riveted to him: they knew all this. But they were still listening, so he proceeded.

"Icebergs that remain in the Arctic Ocean can act slightly differently. They often melt much more slowly, for a start. And they come in for severe weathering. The effect of this weathering every now and then is to produce what is called a Ghost Berg. A Ghost Berg is a berg that has been floating around up here for so long that the wind and rain have worked down cracks in the ice, widening them, hollowing them out, making fissures and caves. And if it becomes hollow, it becomes highly unstable. You saw that cliff fall. If that is a Ghost Berg, the whole mass of the upper terraces could go in the same way."

"What sets them off?" asked Kate.

"Almost anything; but most often, noise."

"Noise?"

"Yes. When the ice begins to hollow out, it goes into great caves; now these caves, like most caves, can act like echo-chambers so that any noise becomes multiplied to such an extent that its vibrations can cause the walls of the caves to fracture or shatter. And if that happens, the whole lot comes down. Maybe fifty thousand tons of it."

They looked at the berg now with trepidation.

"You said 'if that is a Ghost Berg'. Don't you know for certain?" asked Quick.

"I know the whole wall facing us is fractured, and in a dangerously unstable state; and that the terracing behind it is full of caves," said Ross equably. "I notice that it is rapidly overhauling us, blown, I assume, by the wind which you will have noticed has shifted back to the east. This to my mind hints that the upper terraces, although broad and massive enough to catch this wind, and act as an effective sail, are not heavy enough to impede the movement of the berg as a whole."

"But what if you're wrong? What if it is just the nearest cliff that's dangerous? Can we afford to throw away the potential safety of moving on to the berg? I mean, if we stay here, we could all go the way of poor old Preston." He spoke of it as though it was some distant event whose importance had been sapped by the passing of a long period of time.

131

"I suppose we could try to bring the risky terracing down and see what happens," said Ross. "But if we're going to try it, we'd better do it before it gets too near, because if anything goes wrong, if the cliffs all go, and the upper terracing comes down, the berg will upend. The whole thing will turn over."

They went over to the point at which Ross had examined the iceberg with the telescopic sight on the Weatherby, which he still carried in his right hand. As they watched him, he went down on one knee, and took up the position he had assumed to shoot at the dynamite. The rifle gave its whiplash crack once, twice, three times.

Ross watched the tiny plumes appear low on the cliff in the sight. His keen ears caught the strange echoes: as though the sound of the rifle were being reproduced, increasingly loud, in an electronic synthesiser. He scanned the face of the cliff anxiously. A powdering of crystals sprang out of the ice wall as though someone had dusted it with caster-sugar. The sounds continued to grow. Something moved. He slammed the guard of the sight against his eyebrow. A concave face low on the cliff wall had suddenly become convex.

"There it . . ." His voice was lost in the roar. It was as though an express train was charging at full throttle out of the tunnels of the ice. The whole cliff began to slide, bulging at the bottom, descending with stately grace at the top, into the exploding cloud of crystals and spray.

"BACK!" yelled Ross. Already the first waves were boiling out towards them, walls of white foam throwing up great gouts of spume. They all scrambled to their feet, and ran as best they could to the camp.

"DOWN!"

Nobody needed to be told twice. They all threw themselves on to the net, and hung on for dear life. The floe, large as it was, rose steeply. And this was just as well, for had the waves swept on unchecked they might have washed the whole camp away. As it was, the storage tent collapsed, hot ash spilled from the fire-tray; the ice beneath them cracked and groaned as though it was in pain; and long after the waves had all passed, they lay too stunned to move.

After a while, Ross spoke. "I really think," he said, almost apologetically, "that it would be better if we all stayed here."

He heaved himself up. The berg was looming dangerously close now. He could see the foam as the small waves broke against its huge underwater reaches. It would pass, he thought, a couple of hundred yards north of them: too close for comfort. "We'd better make as little noise as possible," he continued, "and it would be better if we didn't move around too much."

Even Quick was more than content to stay where he was, clutching at the bright orange strands of the net. He licked his dry lips, and looked at the looming berg, his mind far too busy for comfort, seeing what would happen if it went now: the great waves, ten times higher than the ones they had just suffered, would sweep over them, tearing their hands from the net, sweeping them into the water to drown. To drown if they were lucky; a sudden vision of the killers reared in front of his eyes, tight-closed as they were. The huge black and white faces, the monstrous teeth.

BOOM! The ice leaped.

"Oh sweet Jesus," he whispered. The berg loomed so large, its shadow ate at the whiteness of the floe. Another killer hurled itself at the floe.

BOOM!

Just beyond the perimeter of the camp, the ice heaved up into the familiar blister.

"What do we do?" asked Quick, his voice, grotesquely quiet, spiralling out of control.

"Pray," said Ross, and under the brisk monosyllable, came the double click as he opened and closed the breech of the Weatherby.

"Colin! You'll bring the berg down!" gasped Kate.

"I don't think so. Not if I space the shots carefully."

BOOM!

The blister of cracked ice burst. A familiar black and white head rose, beautifully marked and deadly: a young male. Ross shot it under the chin: a fountain of blood blasted out of the top of its head. The mouth opened and closed. The tongue worked. It hesitated for several moments, while echoes of the shot grew and receded, before sinking slowly out of sight. But even before the water had closed over it, and while the last high sounds were hanging threateningly in the air, another one exploded through the thinner ice to the north of the camp, and another.

133

"Shoot!" screamed Quick.

"I can't! Not until the echo dies!"

"I don't think the bullets you have in there have enough stopping-power," said Job quietly. "You'll be better with the Remington and the hollow-pointed stuff."

"Right," said Ross, squeezing off a shot at last at the larger of the two on the ice. The bullet went into the top of its head, glanced off the heavy skull, and did little damage. The whale screamed. The echo grew and lingered, like a chord struck on the piano with the loud pedal down.

Job was up and running for the supply tent. He had just reached it when two whales drove up together against the thick ice beneath his feet with a terrifying explosion of sound. He fell to his knees, his eyes drawn anxiously to the huge cliffs of the berg with their dusting of ice-crystals glistening like a cloud of caster-sugar. His gaze followed the crags up and up until he could feel the skin roll at the back of his neck. A great gout of snow fell off the heights of the nearest terrace as though an invisible shovel of mammoth proportions had hurled it over. Job watched as it fell down the dizzy cliffs and rumbled ominously into the water. The cliff stayed up.

The ice beneath him crashed and heaved again, smashing him out of his reverie. He reached into the tent, and took out the Remington. He slammed the breech open: it was ready to fire. He clicked the safety off, and began to run back across the ice. The high whip-crack of the Weatherby came again. The echoes began to grow. Again he glanced up at the berg, looming over them, seeming to give off a cold wind all of its own, so close now that when it heaved back, its underwater masses rose to grind against the northernmost reaches of the floe. The echoes of the Weatherby seemed to grow inside Job's head, the sounding caves of ice were so near. He could see the webs of cracks on the glistening buttresses and towers.

BOOM!

The ice between the camp and the sea exploded again. Another head thrust into the light. Job slammed the Remington to his shoulder . . .

"JOB! NO!"

. . . and fired. The heavy, soft-nosed bullet destroyed the whale's face. The echoes roared in the ice, working with those from the Weatherby so that the very air seemed to shake. Snow from the upper terraces fell through two hundred feet and more to thunder on to the floe itself. The sound roared and shuddered through its cycles, growing and dying. And the berg did not fall. But the whales, unafraid of the guns, were forced to withdraw to protect their delicate ears. Silence grew slowly, and remained.

"Christ!" Warren.

"That berg's more solid than I thought." Ross.

"Only just!" Job.

"But enough!" Quick. "Don't you see? If we're careful and fairly quiet, we could be all right on there!"

Silence.

"Christ, Colin; look around you! This is the thickest part of the floe, and they're coming right through as though it was bloody tissue-paper! What chance will we stand later, tomorrow, when it's even thinner?"

A freak of wind and the berg caught the sound, demanding, *"Thinner – thinner – thinner – thinner?"* into silence.

Ross looked up at it. The slight friction as the underwater portion of the berg ground against the floe seemed to have slowed the speed of its passage, and turned it slightly. A perfect beach leading by gentle gradients up to an eminently suitable platform presented itself. Less than fifty yards away. Ross nodded, and the attempt was on.

Strangely, as though they had discussed it quite fully, each knew what to do. Kate got the longest roll of rope. Warren took both the guns. Job and Quick tore the crate containing the collapsible canoe open. Ross went up to the top of the hills at the north point of the floe. The canoe was big enough to take two men. It was made of canvas on steel box-struts and collapsed into three sections. It had paddles. They put it together quickly and efficiently as though fully practised.

"Give me the rifle just in case," Quick said, "and a couple of good strong pegs. I'll take the rope over and anchor it. Then we can ferry the stuff across fairly quickly. OK?"

"OK," said Ross.

Quick took the Remington and the pegs, and climbed aboard. He felt good. He knew about boats the way Ross knew ice. He was at home here; knew what he was about. He began to paddle strongly; easily. The berg had moved away with surprising speed: they would have to work fast. He dug the paddle in deeper, surged out of the shadow of the iceberg. He had come about fifty yards. The nylon rope was not too heavy a drag because it floated. He slitted his eyes even behind the mask because of the sudden return to the golden brightness. Nor far now . . .

"SIMON!" Colin's voice, surprisingly clear. Urgent. He looked back. The rope snapped taut, hurled him forward: Job had stopped paying out. Now he was pulling in feverishly. The stern, sharp as the bow, creamed through the water. Quick knelt in the waist of the boat, looking wildly round. Then, in the distance, he saw them: five huge fins in arrow formation, coming in at impossible speed.

"Mother of God!" He was tearing off his mittens, reaching for the Remington. Knees spread, moving from the waist, he arced the barrel over the ocean, searching. He was back into the shadow now. So slow . . . so slow . . .

The first one erupted yards away, forced up by the submarine reaches of the berg. He swung on to it, jerked the trigger: missed. Slammed another into the breech. Tightened his finger again, but it was gone. The echoes of the first shot roared around him, hurting his ears. Idiot. How many in the magazine for Christ's sake? Don't waste them! Wait! Wait till you see the whites of their eyes.

He was still speeding backwards when the next killer hurled himself out of the black water. He fired once, saw the roof of its mouth explode. Its body twisted in the air and crashed down beside him, the top of its head burst like a bag. He swung back. They were coming up beside the boat. CRACK. CRACK. A black and white head flew to pieces. They would be coming up under the boat. He leaned over the side, disregarding the dangerous list, peering into the depths. There! A black and white form streaking up. He aimed at random, and fired three times. Black and green streamers sprang from its head.

CRACK! CRACK! CRACK! Out of sequence. Setting up overtones so deep they made his eyeballs tremble in his head; so powerful he could feel them as he breathed. So high they were like nails driven into his ears. And beneath it all, swelling as though out of a tunnel, the terrible roar of collapsing terraces.

136

He swung back to look at the berg. As he watched, the colour of the nearest cliffs became lighter and lighter. Great cracks shot up the towering faces like lightning. Monstrous boulders sprang free and began to tumble. The whole outline of the huge berg lost definition, and began to fall. The sound was unbelievable: nearly fifty thousand tons of ice exploded into boulders and rushed into the water. The boat ground silently into the ice of the floe behind him. Quick reeled out of it. Ross and Job chucked the rope into it, lifted it, and ran for the distant camp. Spray rained down on them all, engulfing them. Quick turned back and watched.

The great foaming column of water tumbled back. The sea reeling, tearing hither and thither, trying to cover the great wound. The huge waves speeding away to the west, twenty, thirty feet high. The foam spreading calmly. Then, slowly, unbelievably, with all the inevitable majesty of a rocket rearing against the sky, the edge of the berg which had been held under the water by the weight of the terraces, shrugged the wild sea aside and rose, foot after foot, yard after yard, its shadow spreading like oil over the water, over the floe. Water cascaded down its crystal sides. The great point reaching up: two hundred feet high.

Now the column of ice reeled, more than half out of the water. The rate of its great leap began to falter. It began to turn in the air. Finally it began to fall.

A column of spray roared up into the sky. The waves began to form in their circles, fifty feet high, and move out at high speed. They hit the floe, exploded against the solid wall of the ice-hills, reared them up, forced them back. The floe seemed to slam into the air, the whole range of the ice-hills rocking up and back along the line of the crash. Such was the noise that the cracking of the ice was lost. The hills closed down on the ice like ragged crystal jaws folding shut, then opening again.

It was long after the silence returned that they realised the noise had stopped, and they were safe. Ross rose first, and looked around. One by one the others rose with him, and stood looking, silently. There was nothing to say. Half an hour earlier, they had been in the middle of a floe of nearly twenty acres. And now it was mostly gone: the ice-hills, all except one; the old campsite; the southern point where the 'plane had

137

bounced on to the floe; all smashed loose, and floating in the jumble of restless ice all around them.

As they watched, the last sight of the berg faded into the golden mist. It had reduced their refuge by nearly two thirds, from the size of a modest farm to the size of a large garden; and now it left them as it had come, suddenly, silently.

SEVEN

i

THE SOUNDS ECHOING in the caverns of the iceberg moved through the water five times faster than they moved through the air and the killers had begun to run even before Quick's boat had been hauled up on to the floe. They did not all run in the same direction, but split up and scattered. They did not run as a unit because they knew as well as the men on the floe the danger, and did not pause to organise. The leader and his consort ran side by side, great boulders of ice plunging deep into the water around them like unimaginable hailstones, spurting bubbles, turning over and over, crashing against other boulders coming sluggishly upwards, crunching, crying, ringing.

The current caused by the iceberg's massive rush towards the air plunged them willy-nilly deep in the black heart of the ocean. The female, injured, hurled down like a dummy, trailing bubbles. The leader followed her, only partly in control of his headlong rush. Blood streamed from his mate, but was whipped away by the terrible currents like smoke in a hurricane. Powerless as leaves in autumn they tumbled into the deep, until the solid shelf of the bottom rose to meet them and the turbulence rushed them towards the surface again. Then, abruptly, it was over.

The leader slowly regained absolute control of his progress, and caught up with his wounded mate. Carefully, he angled his vital body against her still flank and began to push her away from the danger and towards the surface. As he moved he sent out urgent cries, but it was many minutes before any of his pack came to their aid. Even then he would not relinquish her completely to their care, not accept their help himself. Another large male supported her on the other side, and more rapidly now, they lifted her towards the air. Most of the rest of the pack returned and grouped solicitously around them, rising rapidly ahead of them to smash away the half-frozen debris of ice which now covered the ocean, so that they could breathe.

For several hours they lay on the surface, breathing deeply, recovering, beginning to shrug off the weariness and move more freely – all except the leader's consort who lay still, not obviously wounded, nor bleeding any more, but badly stunned by a heavy blow to her head, the back of which was swollen and horribly discoloured by a great bruise. No more of the group joined them. Now there were only twelve of them: not a large pack, but still a formidable force. The leader carefully positioned his mate across his broad forehead so that she could still breathe, and began to move with her: temporarily heading south away from the ice-pack.

ii

Back on the floe, the hours dragged interminably by in a haze of shock for all of them. Even Ross and Job were deeply shaken by their narrow escape, and depressed by the greatly increased danger of their new situation. For now a gentle wind came creeping from the west and moved over the floe, shifting crystals like sandgrains, pushing the temperature down even further, bringing the sounds of restless ice and quiet water. The wind had been blowing for some time, but the ice-hills had functioned as a barrier against it and kept it from the floe itself.

Ross, his face towards the soft, damp chill of it, found ice-crystals drifting against his feet like tiny sand-dunes. Through the angled slits of his mask he saw the bright solidity of the floe stretch only a few yards away before the equally bright liquidity of the sea replaced it. He looked at it, feeling a great hollowness form inside him. Briefly he saw the inside of his chest like a huge limestone cave wooded with stalactites, running with fear. It was not an image he liked. Fear was not an emotion which he relished. But he knew it well enough.

He slapped the white crystals from his clothes and looked

about. The fear in his belly and chest did not ease with what he saw: it would now take him, at most, five minutes to walk from one end of the floe to the other – always assuming he was willing to go anywhere near the actual edges of the ice, marked as they were by deep cracks and tell-tale patches of lucent green where the ice was very thin. The remnant of the floe was roughly square, each side being some two hundred yards long. It was quite flat, the surface at the most a foot above sea-level, except for the last remnant of the ice-hills, a low protuberance rising perhaps ten feet into the air, and at the moment acting like the prow of their tiny ship. And it was tiny. Looking around, Ross automatically stepped back towards the centre of the floe. The removal of the ice-hills enabled him to see all around, and his mind reeled. There was nothing except the bright ocean stretching away seemingly forever. He slowly turned through 360 degrees until he was facing the small ice-hillock prow again. There was nothing. And the more he looked the smaller the floe seemed to become; the larger became the cave of fear inside him. He realised there was sweat under his mask. He was terrified.

"Christ!" said Job. It was not blasphemy. Ross glanced down at him. The Eskimo was on one knee, his narrow eyes busy among the bright floes. He was looking for the whales. Ross had also probed the ocean, but there was nothing to be seen.

"It's so *small*," whispered Kate, her voice broken by awe.

"Still bigger than the *Queen Elizabeth*," said Ross, bracingly.

"Of course the floe looks small," said Job quickly. "But it's big enough to last for weeks."

Nobody said anything. Doctor Warren looked around. He sniffed deeply, filling his lungs to capacity. "Ah," he said, "good sea air. Always gives me an appetite."

"Don't we ever do anything but eat and sleep?" snarled Quick.

"Yes! We survive!" snapped back Kate.

"What else is there to do?" asked Job quietly. He immediately wished he had said nothing, for the simple fact became immediately obvious – there was nothing else to do: nothing at all. In the silence that followed, the crystals scratched quietly; the waves lapped; the ice cracked like rifle shots; the orange net shifted, tautened, flapped; the tents hollowed and puffed: the wind, pushed out of North Russia, flowed over them like an icy, invisible river.

Kate's eyes swept over her companions, cold as the wind, suddenly seeing clearly – ill-shaven, dirty, hollow-eyed, desperate. There were new lines between Simon's blond eyebrows. His hair was a birdsnest, the gold stubble on his cheeks blurred the lines of his jaw, making his chin suddenly look weak. And the mask. He looked dangerous, desperate, frightening. Job looked better, but his hair was an oily mess; his solid cheeks were rough, his smooth skin also marked with new lines. Her father's face had aged. There was desperation in it too, now, deepening creases between mouth and chin; turning lips down, furrowing forehead. His mask, so much bigger than Simon's, hid his eyes completely, but she knew they would also be desperate. And she thought she understood. His fear would not be for himself, but for his work.

And Colin, withdrawn now into some secret thoughts of his own, his expression closed, masked eyes distant. His face seemed to have filled out strangely. Not that it was any less hollow or lined than Quick's or her father's; it was just that the wildness added by the thick black stubble reaching down his neck into the fur collar, the tumbled hair, the thin pinched nostrils, the snow-tan, the hard, desperate line of his mouth turned up at the corners into a slight smile, deepened the face, made it more memorable, gave it more power. Her eyes drifted down his huge frame, sliding away from the wreck of his left arm towards his right. She was suddenly struck by the size of his right hand, curled loosely in the woollen glove outside the mitten. How much strength, she thought, lay in that huge square hand. Her eyes moved up to his face again, but it was still distant.

Anyway, she thought, I'm probably no picture myself. She could imagine it well enough: her hair, deep gold now because of the dirt and grease, would frame her thinning face in rats-tails. She shifted. Her whole body itched: what she would give for a bath! And never, ever again, would she go out without a little perfume!

"Food," she said.

The word brought Ross back. He had, suddenly, and for no

142

apparent reason, found his mind filled with thoughts of Charlie. He nodded. "Good," he said.

"Christ!" hissed Quick, full of disgust, hopelessness.

Ross suddenly became aware of the aura of desperation coming from the man. All that huge nervous energy was somehow going wrong. Shorting out. Going to explode. Why?

"We must do something," cried Quick. "Something. Anything. This is bloody ridiculous. Sitting drinking tea while we die. For Christ's sake," he became enormously persuasive, "can't you see it? We can't just sit here waiting. We must – we can't just . . ."

Colin understood him then very well: he understood the public school training which had made Simon a leader, training him up through from prefect to school prefect and head of house. Under any pressure, everything in Simon's upbringing demanded that he take charge; everything in the traditions he had been raised in demanded he succeed. But now there was nowhere to lead them to; and the only success would be if they remained where they were, on the ice, alive. In fact, of course, Ross was no more capable of truly summing up the twisted assortment of strengths and weaknesses which drove Simon Quick than he was capable of seeing through to the true depths of the ice on which he was standing. Not that there was anything obscure about the next step that Simon's mind took, it was just that Ross really knew nothing about the true way the younger man saw him.

Simon's eyes swept over them all: the fat old man not even paying attention, the rat-tailed tart staring at him. Job, even fatter than the old man. And Ross. His mind automatically blamed Ross for everything. It was Ross's fault. And he would get him. In time, somehow, for it all, he would get him.

"Well," he said. "Perhaps this once – a little food mightn't be a bad idea." And he smiled.

Warren had hardly been listening to any of this. He was a mild agoraphobic, and he had been totally absorbed in controlling the fear which had welled up inside his stocky body at the terrible sight which surrounded him: over a thousand square miles of nothing. The ice, clacking, cracking, echoing, glistening away to impossible distances, mocked him. His fear was nothing to do with his daughter, nothing to do with his work.

143

All his life, even in the far-flung corners of the world where he had pursued his research, had been spent in the small safe boxes of his laboratories. How he ached for them now, the solid walls hidden by ranks and rows of equipment.

He turned desperately, and saw the tents. The tents! Walls, confined spaces. Salvation. Sanity. He began to stumble towards them, over the orange net, driven by the pain in his belly towards the latrine tent. Kate called something to him, reached out, but he could not stop now. Could not. He stumbled on to the side of the tent, flung it open, crawled in. Laced the flap shut behind him. Stripped down his trousers. Nearly threw up. Shivered. Let the proximity of the walls calm him.

"Sweet Christ," he muttered, wiping his mouth, "you're a grown man. Get a hold of yourself!"

Job saw the way Kate's hand fell after her father had pushed rudely past her, and compassion moved his face into a slow, unaccustomed frown. He started forward towards her, but Colin pre-empted him, sliding a comforting arm round her sagging shoulders. They walked towards the orange net and set about picking up the fire-tray and relighting the fire. The Eskimo's eyes moved back to the golden sea. None of the others had said anything since Hiram Preston's terrible death, but he assumed that their minds were, like his own, still full of it. It seemed distant now, for so much had happened since, but he could still see the horror of those madly twitching legs heaving out of the water with nothing above them except the dark empty cave of a belly from which all the intestines had been torn. And that huge insolent head coming back up to collect them.

He was deeply disturbed by the fact that no words had been said over the poor boy's body. As Kate had guessed within minutes of their first meeting, he was a deeply religious man. Religion had been drummed into him at the Methodist school he had attended on the shores of the Hudson Bay as a boy, and another religion by his grandfather in their village. Now he stood between two worlds, torn between gods. He didn't know whom to pray to for salvation: to the Methodist God of houses and cities, or the gods of the wilderness who had protected Innuit from time immemorial. The words for the boy should be Christian at least; but his prayers for them and for their salvation might be better addressed to Aipalookvik the Render and Destroyer, god of the Icebergs and the deep waters; or perhaps to Torgasoak, protector of Innuit, of the People.

He walked slowly away towards the top of the floe, as near as he dared to the edge beyond which the old camp had been sited, where Hiram Preston had been torn in two. As he moved, he cried in a deep voice which echoed hollowly over the lapping ocean: "I would not have you ignorant, brethren, concerning them which are asleep, that ye sorrow not, even as others which have no hope." He had come near the edge now and, although there was more than a yard of ice ahead of him, it was dangerously cracked and far too unstable to be trusted with his weight. He stopped, threw wide his arms and declaimed over the sea, closing his mind to the terrible memory of Hiram's death, of the stark thrust of his spine pushing out of the thick cut muscles of his back, of the fat white worm of his spinal cord . . .

"O Lord Jesus, who by thy burial did sanctify an earthly sepulchre; vouchsafe, we beseech thee, to bless and hallow this grave, that it may be a peaceful resting place for the body of thy servant; through thy mercy." He closed his eyes, opened them slowly and gazed over the golden-green ocean, as though expecting to see Preston himself walking on the water there. Then he turned and went back: there was nowhere else to go.

Warren came out of the latrine tent, pale, shaken, shamefaced but calm. The size of the ocean sent a shiver through him, but he controlled his panic and went towards Ross and Kate who had a fire burning on the tray. Quick stook a short distance off, separate. Kate glanced up, and even though her face was half-hidden by the ridiculous rounds of her dark glasses, he could see hostility in it. A stab of anger went through him – after all, he couldn't help his fear. She turned, and spoke quietly to Ross. Warren realised that he had driven his daughter into Ross's arms. Unreasoning jealousy rose in him as Ross asked, "Are you all right?"

"Of course I am!" He snapped it out pettishly. Quick looked across speculatively. Ross frowned, not understanding. Warren felt that the big man was patronising him, and stumped past him towards the fire. He stood belligerently over Kate, willing her to look up at him.

When she did, drawing back her hair out of her eyes, he said,

"I'm sorry baby, I . . ." It was difficult to say more. He was ashamed of the weakness. He gestured at the ocean, the ice, the distances. "Agoraphobia." The one word explained it all.

"Oh, Daddy." She was on her feet. She came to him and hugged him.

"Are you all right now?" asked Ross quietly. Warren felt as though Ross had been eavesdropping, and said nothing.

"We'll go inside the tent," said Quick understandingly. "Then you'll feel better."

It was a good idea on the face of it. Certainly it helped Warren, but in the confined space the five of them crowded uncomfortably together and the atmosphere of hostility became almost tangible. To begin with there was an uneasy silence. "Is anyone hungry?" asked Kate. They all shook their heads.

The human body gives off approximately as much heat as a two-bar electrical fire. The heavily insulated tent, designed to hold three people, rapidly became warm. Job was the first to undo his heavy outer jacket and strip it off. The others silently followed suit, Job helping Ross whose great frame and club-like left arm made him unwieldy in the cramped conditions. Quick, sitting close to Kate, suddenly became aware of her as she moved. Even the heavy vest and tightly buttoned red-checked shirt could not conceal the fact that she had been unable to replace her broken brassière. Quick froze, fascinated by her breasts as they moved beneath the heavy layers of cloth. He stared unashamedly until she looked up. They had taken their masks and glasses off in the mellow shadow of the tent and their gazes met. It was too late for Quick to disguise the lust in his own, and her blue eyes raked him like claws. He shifted, blushing. Another element was added abruptly to the strain of the atmosphere in the tent. With her eyes coldly on Quick, Kate leaned her back against her father's still shoulder, lifted her buttocks, pulled down the sealskin overtrousers, and kicked them off.

"For Christ's sake . . ." he muttered, and wrenched his eyes away. He found that he was trembling.

Kate knew very well what was in Quick's mind. It made her angry. What the hell did he think she was? She couldn't help being a woman, and wrapped up as she was, she was hardly anybody's pin-up; and yet at the least thing, his pale eyes kindled and stripped away every layer she was wearing. Well sod him! she thought viciously. Her eyes flashed around to the others: Ross and Job were concerned with Ross's jacket, her father was thinking of something else. Quick looked back at her, and she automatically looked down to check that all her buttons were done up.

She lost her temper. "Mr. Quick. If you can't think of anything else to look at, at least put your mask back on so I can't see your eyes!"

All their eyes swivelled to Quick who went red with embarrassment and rage. His mouth opened and closed, but he said nothing. He half rose, jostling Job, and began to make for the way out.

"Oh for Heaven's sake, man," snapped Ross, his temper at last in shreds, "sit down and act your age. It's not her fault she's a woman, or that her bra's broken." He tried to get Quick to sit down.

"Keep your hands off me!"

"Sit down, Simon."

Quick slumped back to the other side of Job, and remained where he was, his face twisted. "I'll get you for that . . ."

"Oh for God's sake shut up, Simon."

"You can't order me about! I'm not one of your team! You're not going to leave *me* to die!" In two deft bounds, Quick's mind was back to the inevitable plaint.

"Let it rest!" snapped Ross.

"No, I will not let it rest!" Quick gasped for breath, his self-control completely gone, looking for any weapon, finding only one sharp enough, two-edged but sharp. "That's what Charlie said. But I wouldn't." His mind worked feverishly, fabricating a story, which would wound his enemy deeply. "'Let it rest' she would say, stupid cow that she was, 'Let it rest'."

"Simon . . ." a cry of agony, hardly Ross's voice at all.

Quick pressed his words in like a stiletto. "You could have had her back if you'd come to her."

"I called. I came round. She wouldn't see me! I was in hospital for four months. I came as soon . . ."

Ross's reaction so far had been pained confusion. He cast

about like a blind bear poked by spears. Quick pushed his spear again . . .

"Four months. That was when she went off the pills on to the dope! She was waiting to hear from you."

"But I wrote!"

"I took the letters, you bastard. I still have them . . ."

It was too much. Ross hurled himself across Job, the iron club of his left hand crashing on to the ground with such force that the ice beneath the heavy canvas groundsheet was hollowed. Quick, yelling, rolled clear. Ross swung again, screaming, "You bastard, it was you, you . . ."

"I did it for my brother's sake. You killed him!"

"NO!" There was absolute certainty in the word.

Job had Ross now, holding him still. He twisted. "Can't you see what he did? While I was in hospital he poisoned her mind against me . . ."

"Don't be bloody silly," jeered Quick. "I didn't need to touch her mind! You killed her brother. You did it!"

"No, I did not! He bloody killed himself. And you know it."

"I know it?" Still jeering.

"Of course you do, but you can't accept the fact that your bloody heroic brother made a mistake, so you blame me. And you made Charlie blame me. You did that. You drove her out of her mind with it. You killed Charlie, but you can't face that either, so you blame me for that as well. You make me sick."

Quick's eyes blazed. "What do you know about it? Were you there? Did you see? What the fuck do you know?"

"I know. As clearly as you know I killed your stupid bloody brother, I know."

Quick leaned forward. Ross shrugged Job away, and they met in the middle of the tent on their knees, punching, clawing like animals . . .

BOOM!

The whale struck exactly under the tent, guided in by their noise. The shock threw them all flat.

BOOM!

With hardly a pause the killer struck again, driving the ice beneath the tent into a small cracked hillock. The canvas floor rose with the blow. For a moment they were rendered helpless

148

by the unexpected power of it, then Job, nearest the exit, cried, "Out! Quickly!" and threw the flap open.

Warren crawled through the gap into the bright sunlight. Kate followed, hissing as her bare hands disappeared into the ice-crystals to the wrist. She half turned to say something, but Job shouldered her aside as he too tumbled out. She staggered a step or two over the ice, suddenly freezing as the gentle wind cut through her shirt and vest. "Job," she gasped, "the gloves, jackets . . ."

"Yes . . ." he turned, still on his knees. Ross was half out of the tent behind him. "Colin, the clothes!"

"Hell!" Ross paused, half in, half out of the tent. His head and shoulders disappeared again.

BOOM!

As Ross's head reappeared in the tent, the floor was hurled up again by another blow from the killer's massive head. Quick actually flew into the air and crashed against Ross's massive shoulder. "Simon, the clothes. Quickly!"

The floor, terrifyingly, was beginning to sink beneath them as the broken ice fell away, removing the last barrier between them and the whale except for less than a quarter of an inch of canvas.

Ross's eyes swept over Quick. He had never seen anyone looking so scared. Simon's face was frozen into a rictus of terror, eyes bulging, lips curled back, skin utterly white, throat working convulsively. "Simon," he repeated urgently, "the clothes – we'll all freeze!"

Incredibly, Quick understood what was required of him. He looked among the jumble of stuff under him, summoning reserves from God alone knew where to cut through the crippling panic which threatened to hold him immoblie while he died. "Right," he gasped. Had Colin heard? Did he know how calm he was now under pressure? Abruptly, he became light-headed with his own heroism.

BOOM!

The floor slammed up into Quick's face and chest, lifting him into the air again. When he landed, the canvas sagged under his weight and water began to seep through.

He was never able to recall with any clarity what he did next, or whether he did it because of panic or clear-headedness. Still

149

in his sealskin trousers whick kept most of the water out, he slopped about in the bottom of the tent, passing up to Ross the mittens, gloves, jackets, trousers, the sleeping-bags and blankets, the face-masks and even Kate's glasses before the whale struck again.

Ross clumsily thrust the articles past his own massive chest on to the snow outside, where Job picked them up and threw them in the general direction of Kate and Warren.

"That's the lot," gasped Simon, and began to get up. The floor of the tent was now three feet below the level of the door. Ross reached down to give Simon a hand as he reached his feet. Simon took a step forward, and the canvas, put under a strain far beyond its designed strength, began to tear along the edge of the ice below Ross.

"Simon." The hand reached out imperatively towards him. The green crystal shone through a rent suddenly two feet wide. He could feel the floor sinking beneath him. "COME ON!"

Simon looked away from that terrible mouth fanged with ice. He held his hand out, took a step. The floor ripped again by another two feet.

Then their hands met. Ross, rolling back out through the door, jerked Quick after him one-armed, to lie on his stomach, his legs hanging down over the edge of the ice.

Incredibly – to himself at least – he still did not panic. He refused, consciously and absolutely, to acknowledge the picture which rose unbidden to his mind of the killer coming up again, mouth agape to tear away the floor of the tent and take his legs. Ross still held his hand in an iron grip. Once again their arms were at full stretch, and Ross, with a guttural grunt, jerked him free.

Then, with a great roar, even as Quick's feet kicked clear, the whale's head filled the tent, stretching the reinforced canvas, tearing the whole thing up into the air: five feet, ten feet. They staggered back across the net. The tent shook, billowed, began to come to pieces in the air.

"Guns!" yelled Ross. Job ran; Quick followed, still full of his heady courage.

The tent fell away revealing the great glistening black and white cone of the head, face unmarked, teeth gleaming. It was a young male. It looked at them, then sank a little.

150

"Hurry!" yelled Ross.

From the storage tent, the heavy Remington spoke. The side of the whale's head split. It lurched forward on to the net, teeth snapping. The Remington spoke again. The top of its head seemed to explode as the heavy bullet, flattened by the impact, glanced off the top of its thick skull. It sank back, and vanished into the black water.

They stood, silently, listening as the whale sobbed quietly beneath them. The water in the hole where the tent had been began to freeze.

"He won't be back," said Job, lowering the rifle.

Kate said bitterly, "One tent gone and all of us nearly killed, just because of you two . . ." She swung on them both, blazingly angry. "Well you can damn well settle your differences later when we're all on dry land! Do what you want then! I don't give a damn if you beat each other's stupid heads to pulp then, but we'll all die if you keep this lunacy going much longer!"

Ross looked back at her levelly, meeting her hot eyes with his own until her gaze switched to Quick. But Quick, buoyed up by the strength given to him by his courage under pressure, also looked back without wilting until she swung on her heel, swept up her jacket, trousers and glasses and headed for her father's tent. The others began to follow her. Quick's eyes were drawn to the angry swing of her buttocks, loosely outlined by the heavy denim of her jeans. Suddenly he felt sick, and yet oddly at peace. He picked up the coat he had saved, one of the sleeping-bags he had saved. He had saved them: jackets, gloves, trousers, sleeping-bags, masks, all. He had saved them. He hummed as he followed the others.

In Kate's tent they sat down again, silently.

"Right," said Kate, "we'd better have this out. Colin, tell us what happened."

"But . . ." began Quick.

"Shut up, Simon; you'll get your chance later. Colin, will you please tell us about Antarctica?" Kate's voice held rock-hard authority.

Ross looked at her. Blue eyes, still warm, met cold green in another level stare. This time Ross looked away. He looked down and nodded. He held up his hands, one blackened, blistered, twisted, part-melted, glistening with metal pins, struts, and strings; the other a great square, blunt fingered, thick knuckled, black haired. He studied it for a moment, remembering.

And then he told them.

EIGHT

Ross STUDIED THE flesh of his two hands as he held them up towards the faint warmth of the stove. How white and thin they looked, the black hair on their backs made deeper, thicker, by the whiteness of the skin. They looked almost skeletal, the fingers thin, knuckles bulging unnaturally. He couldn't keep them still. Half cold, half the pain of his split nails. The nail on each of his index-fingers was split to the quick. The nails on the other fingers were long – there had been no real chance to cut them since the team had started back from the South Pole – but they were strangely clean. Ross knew about city dirt which collected under the nails from grubby handles on street-doors, dirty trains, black newsprint, but here there was no dirt at all. He had been pulling a sledge day after day for longer than he could clearly remember, unable to wash properly, unable to shave, sometimes too tired to even eat, and yet he had perfectly clean fingernails. He studied them in silent, stupid wonder. They were so perfectly clean.

Outside, the storm raged as it had been raging for over a week, pinning them, helpless, to the unforgiving ice, as another storm had pinned Scott and his men more than half a century before, almost in the same place. Scott. It all came back to Scott.

When they had put it to him so long ago, so far away, it had all seemed so easy: do what Scott had done, but come out alive. Walk to the Pole, using ponies, only a few dogs, and men; walk to the Pole, and walk back. December and January had passed as they walked in, February and much of March as they walked out. At least they had lost none of the men: Scott had lost Evans and Oates by the time the storm had pinned him down a few miles from here. Scott, Wilson and Bowers had lasted ten days.

Ross, Jeremiah, Quick, Smith and McCann had been here for ten days. They had food, drink, heat still, but the magic ten days was up. The Antarctic was not going to let them go: they must move or die. Ross knew it, Jeremiah knew it, Captain Robin Quick knew it: Smith and McCann seemed to know nothing. Even after the long rest – if the endless war against cold and wet could be called a rest – they were dull-eyed and uncaring. Left to themselves, they would do nothing. And Camp 13 was twenty miles away on Scott's route towards Cape Evans: four days' walk. Ross looked up from his shaking hands, his clean fingernails.

"You'll never make it, Robin," he said. "Not four days. Not in this."

Quick looked over at him. The argument had been the same for over a week, while they had waited for one of two things: the end of the storm, or the arrival of help. The one thing they had over Scott was the fact that a fully motorised rescue team was looking for them. The problem was that the rescue could not follow the route up from Cape Evans: it would be coming over from Edward VII Peninsula, 450 miles to the east. And it was impossible, of course, that help could come on foot over that distance in ten days.

Before they had started out, Ross had made contingency for just such an emergency as this. Job was at Amundsen's old base, where they had helicopters. And even if the weather closed in, and the helicopters were grounded, Job would still come to get them out. But when they had sent emergency signals on their radio, they had received no acknowledgment . . . Quick had agreed to wait ten days before making an attempt with his team for Camp 13. The ten days were up, and there was still no sign of Job.

"We've got to try," said Robin.

Ross smiled, and winced as his cold-split lip opened again. He sucked the lip – the lower – into his mouth: he must not let the blood freeze on his face. It turned his smile into a grimace, but Robin understood. They had had it all out before, going through the gamut of outrage, anger, acceptance. Ross was the leader, but he was a civilian: Robin, a captain in the Army, and

Smith and McCann, a sergeant and a corporal, did not have to obey him. Even the best teams can come to a leadership crisis: Amundsen had had his crisis before he left for the Pole, and had changed his final team: Ross was having his leadership crisis at a less convenient time, and he could only give in. Robin and he had known each other for most of their lives; Ross was married to Charlie, Robin's sister – and he knew now that there was nothing more he could say, nothing he could do, to stop Robin taking Smith and McCann away towards Camp 13. And of course Robin might be right: the three Army men might be the ones to take the story of their attempt back to the rest of the world.

"Think again, Robin."

"I'll sleep on it, Colin."

Ross shrugged his shoulders. The ice on his heavy anorak grated at the joints. The wind howled with vicious force, making the canvas of the tent flap, starring the slick ice of the sagging walls, sending it tinkling to the ground. Ross felt his body begin to shudder spasmodically. He moved his toes in his boots, exploring the unyielding solidity of the toecaps, relieved that he could feel anything through the pins-and-needles of his cramped legs.

"You will never make it, Captain." Jeremiah.

"I didn't know you were taking sides in this, Jeremiah."

"I do not like to see men going to their death, Captain."

Ross shook his head wearily. "Leave it, Jeremiah." His eyes rested on his old friend's face, on the red-rimmed eyes in their deep black sockets which shifted restlessly, and never met his own; on the high, skull-like cheekbones mottled white with frostbite, the hollow, hopeless face lined and cracked like an old oil painting, the thin split mouth, blood-caked for all the sucking of lips. And Smith and McCann looked even worse: there was a look of utter defeat, almost of death on their ice-pinched features. They had given up already.

Quick knew this, and it was part of his desperation: a natural leader, he had felt keenly the pressures of taking orders, even from his closest friend, and now that things had gone so badly wrong, he had to make a move away from Colin to try to save his two men. Yet he was well aware that in doing so he was giving in to a selfish feeling which bordered on cowardice: he was not man enough, he thought, to trust the ultimate responsibility to his friend, even though he knew that Colin was a better cold-weather man than he could ever hope to be. That was what lay at the root of it, he knew; and this was his last chance to prove himself. He had to grasp it, live or die.

But Jeremiah was speaking again. "Even Scott could not make it, Captain. Even Scott, and he had Wilson and Bowers. Great men all, and fighters to the end." He shook his head. His eyes moved to the huge Scot, McCann, and the wiry Cockney, Smith.

"Smith!" he rapped out.

After a moment, Smith replied in a dull, dead voice, "Sir?"

"Why are you here, Smith?" Jeremiah asked.

"Orders, sir."

"Where would you like to be?"

"Home, sir, wiv the old lady. By the fire. Home." His eyes moved round the cramped tent, not really seeing anything. "God, I wish I was at home and out of this. Well out."

"Will you get home?"

"Nah. No way. It's all up, innit?"

Jeremiah looked at Robin Quick. There was no need for him to say more. Quick hated him then, hated all his calm acceptance which was so different from the hopeless collapse of his own men. For all he sat there half asleep, unmoved by it all, the Eskimo would fight to the last fibre of his being, and would fight beside Colin in a way Quick could never do. The captain made a brief guttural sound which was lost in the relentless cacophony of the wind, and turned away.

After a while, Ross switched off the pressure lamp. They went into a bottomless pit of black exhaustion. Outside, the storm screamed like a wounded giant, rolling madly on the ice, tearing at the heavy sky with wild fingers, drumming its thunderous heels on the frail, frozen tent, and crying tears of ice, gnashing its iron teeth, bleeding in fountains, and whirlwinds, and deadly drifts of snow.

When Ross woke up, they were gone. They had taken, as had been agreed, almost all the supplies out of the tent, leaving only the lamp and the stove, with enough food to last a few more days if Ross and Jeremiah chose to wait. Quick had also left a letter, written in a scrawl horribly different from his usual neat copperplate script:

Colin,
I have to take this chance: it is the only chance we have to save something from all this. If you do not make it, we might: and vice-versa. It is a hellish way to part after so many years, I know, and I can only explain it in that terrible old cliché we have laughed at so often in Western films: I have to do what I have to do. That's all there is to it. I think I see a chance where you see none, and I have to grasp it because I see no hope in waiting for Job. God help whichever one of us is wrong.
If we are both lucky, I will see you at Evans or Edward VII, and we will laugh about this.
If you do not make it, I will look after your affairs as though you were my brother.
If I do not make it, look after Charlie and young Simon. See to Mrs. Smith, and McCann's mother in Greenock.
God help us all,
Robin.

With it was a short note:

To Whom It May Concern,
I hereby relieve Colin Ross of all responsibility for anything that might happen to myself, Sergeant Albert Smith and Corporal Hamish McCann, in that by leaving this place at this time we have contravened the orders of Mr. Ross, the leader of this expedition, and have disregarded his advice.

It was signed by Robin, Smith and McCann. Beside the note, they had left some keepsakes, unimportant trinkets to go to their families if the worst should happen.
There were tears in Ross's eyes as he looked at Jeremiah.
"He did it. I never really thought he would."
"When you looked at him you saw only your friend. You did not see the desperate man."
"Desperate? What about, for heaven's sake?"

Jeremiah's gesture took in the tent, the storm, the glaciers, the plateau, the Pole itself.

"What shall I tell them?"

"You are so sure you will tell anyone anything?"

Ross's head came up. His eyes were as cold as the ice. "I have never doubted," he said.

"You should have looked at Quick like that more often."

"But perhaps he also saw only a friend."

Jeremiah nodded: it was undoubtedly true. He saw another man to the man Quick had seen. That much was obvious, otherwise Quick would still be here.

Jeremiah never doubted that Colin at least would come out alive. And he had another advantage over Quick: even if their radio messages had not been received, they were so long over-due that he knew for certain that Job would come. Jeremiah had an immense respect for his younger brother; and he knew that not even the worst the white south could do would stop him.

"Do we sit and wait for Job?" he asked.

Ross was lost in thought. There was silence except for the wind and the ice falling in the restless tent. Then Ross said, "No. We go out and find him." Jeremiah said nothing. After a little while Ross continued, "He's coming in due east from here; or rather, he is if he picked up our last message. If he didn't, then he's coming in due east from our last transmission received at Edward. If that's happened we're dead anyway, so we might as well take the chance." He was arguing with himself, still uncertain. He stared at the flickering blue flame of the paraffin stove, and it was that which finally made his mind up for him, for, as he watched, it changed colour, flared and died. "My God, they've taken the paraffin."

They both stared, unbelieving, at the dead stove. As always, a pot of hot water stood on it, steaming slightly. Jeremiah reached quickly, and moved this precious thing to safety as Ross reached for the stove, and wrenched it open. It was dry. Empty. Drained. Quick, or Smith, or McCann, had carefully removed the paraffin to add to the life-saving store the three of them had taken with them to Camp 13. The act of a man terrified for his life. The most terrible thing a man could do out here. The ultimate crime: the theft of fire; the theft of heat; the theft of life. Without warmth they were dead. Without warmth a terrible race began between many forms of death. First, the slow, sleepy death by cold, dulling the mind, freezing the heart to sleep. Then there was thirst, for without heat, there was only ice to drink: ice so cold it froze to the lips, blistering them with an agony of frostbite until the face could stand no more. And hunger, for the food would be frozen like the water, and even if forced past the lips, it would freeze to the inside of the mouth and tongue, and the teeth, trying to chew it, would break before the ice broke.

All these spectres came in to replace Quick, Smith and McCann in the crowded cold of the tent, and Ross regarded them with sombre eyes. Then he turned to Jeremiah, and he said: "OK. We go."

As soon as he came to his decision, they began to move. Jeremiah took meat, cooked but half-frozen, and put it in the hot water. When it was warm, he put it in a vacuum flask to stop it freezing again. Then he made soup from the now lukewarm water. He put it in another flask: there were two pints of it. Ross collected everything that he could fit into two knapsacks. He put one or two of the personal effects left by the others into his pockets, but he put the letters into his knapsack. When they had finished tidying up, they heaved up their knapsacks and Jeremiah forced his way out into the night. Ross went to turn the lamp off, but he stopped, and checked his watch. He had to fold the top of his mitten forward, the sleeves of his anorak, his heavy woollens, his shirt, his thermal underwear back, the top of his underglove forward. It was 9.30 am. Then he turned out the light, and crawled out after Jeremiah.

Inside the tent, the storm had seemed to be a terrible thing. Out here, the wind took Ross as he lurched to his feet, and sent him staggering until he slipped and fell. Jeremiah's hands found him and helped him up, but he could hardly see Jeremiah, only feet away at the other end of the strong, steady arms. The freezing snow cut the whole world down to little more than the size of his head. When he looked down, his body became vague below his waist; the feet, with their heavy snowshoes, were totally invisible. He took out his luminous compass, but he had to press his wool-covered nose hard against its glass before he could see what it was reading. When he was facing due east, the wind was coming from his rear, due west.

"Sledges?" he screamed, out of curiosity. Jeremiah shook his head. Ross never discovered whether this meant none had been taken, none had been left, or he didn't know.

Walking with the wind was easier than walking against it, but only just. They still staggered, hunched forward, almost completely blinded by the solid white fog. They went shoulder to shoulder then, the snow drifting against their backs, crystals flying in flags and pennants from their heads into the clearer air a little in front of them. They stumbled on, their feet sinking into the shallow snow, slithering on the treacherous ice; they fell, got up, walked, fell, got up. The sweat beaded their goggles, and froze on the glass. The fur around the edges of their hoods became spiky with ice. Soon they were as white as the snow itself, two silent shapes moving slowly over the uneven ice, doggedly, relentlessly. In the first six hours they covered perhaps three miles.

Six hours. Robbed by the snow of anything to relate their progress to, they soon slipped deep inside themselves, and the boredom of simply walking, seeing nothing, saying nothing, began to eat at their sense of time. But their bodies were not so easily tricked. After three hours, at lunchtime, their bellies began to demand food. Ross let it last for as long as he dared, until he genuinely thought he was becoming faint with hunger; after six hours they stopped to eat.

They crouched shoulder to shoulder at a slight angle which protected the food from the wind. They opened the Thermos flask with the soup. This was not an easy task. They had to open one of the knapsacks, select the flask, remove it, close the knapsack, buckle it shut, take the flask, unscrew the cup-top, unscrew the stopper, pour out the soup, drink it, turn-about from the cup, re-seal the stopper, replace the cup, and put it all away. All this they had to do with a wind whose temperature was well below freezing, gusting to seventy miles an hour, without being able to remove their mittens for fear of frostbite, having to ease their balaclavas down from their noses and over their mouths to sip at the soup held uneasily with both hands, being careful, in spite of their shivering, to spill none of it in case

160

it froze on their face-masks and gave the terrible cold access to their mouths, cheeks and chins.

After they had eaten half the soup, they began to move on again. The wind began to slacken now, and the walking became easier. Inch by inch, the whirling white curtain of the snow fell back. They began to make better time. They could make more of a guess as to how they were doing now, and the walking became relatively pleasant. Time slipped by almost unnoticed as they plodded on. The wind died completely within the next three hours, and suddenly the cloud vanished also, revealing an ice-blue sky and the afterglow of sunset.

They decided to eat the meat now. They had stopped anyway to go through the complex procedures of relieving themselves. The meat was slimy and cold, but they ate it with relish. They were tired; they had walked all day, for nearly ten hours.

"Better keep moving," said Ross, his voice gravelly with fatigue. Jeremiah nodded, pulling his face-mask back up over his nose. His breath rose white on the still air, and hovered in a cloud about his head.

The clear weather was a mixed blessing, for the clear sky sent the temperature a further twenty degrees below zero. The ice on their clothes grated and flaked as they rose and began to move. The sky began to darken slowly, and the two of them followed their hunched shadows into the gathering dusk.

During the next hours, the quiet became almost as great a strain as the wind had been. In the strange twilight which never seemed to fade they shuffled on. Ahead of them, the stars began to twinkle. Ross kept consulting his compass, checking its unreliable readings against the constellations of the southern sky.

Time passed out of time. Each man had withdrawn into himself again; tapping deep sources of will and energy; a primeval urge to survive in spite of all. Ross's lips moved as he walked, singing old marching songs with a steady relentless rhythm to which he moved his tired legs over and over again. A strange euphoria began to take hold of his mind. Pain receded by degrees until it became a distant thing. He became exultant, high, confident.

He cried out, "Do your worst, you Queen of Bitches. I'm ready for you." And the Queen of Bitches took him at his word.

Jeremiah, at Ross's side, saw it clearly coming, now out of the east, luminous, dead grey, reaching its unimaginable head to where the stars had been, tearing the horizons with its claws, galloping over the ice with terrible sinuous ease. He saw its ears flatten back amongst the clouds, he saw the wells of its eyes which were as black as the skies before stars, he saw the great hammock of its belly sweeping aside the snow, he saw the black of its lips writhe back to reveal its lightning teeth, and he heard its thunder-roar in the moment before it gulped them into the chaos of itself. Jeremiah saw all this, and screamed. His fists beat upon Ross's invisible shoulders.

"It is the Bear," he cried, again and again. But Ross did not hear. He stood, horrified, dumbfounded by the power of the thing he had summoned out of the icy night.

A great anger welled up in him, tore him inside as the terrible Bear tore him outside; an anger that called upon him to howl at the wind, strike at the snow with his fists, smash all the iron ice with his head, curse with most terrible curses the Queen of Bitches, and God. The wind screamed at him; he took no notice, but walked on. The wind, finding its armament of snow too slight a thing to stop him, tore the frozen crystals from the grasping fingers of the ice, and hurled them into his face, like knives; he took no notice, but walked on. The wind bided its time before unleashing its greatest weapon, and meanwhile folded Jeremiah into its cloak of invisibility; noticing this, Ross stopped, and the two men tied themselves together with a length of rope, then leaning into the full power of the wind, they stumbled forwards, first one in the lead, then the other.

Thus they went through many more hours while three great witches danced around them. The great witch Night covered them with darkness and fatigue; the great witch Winter crept south early to weave her chill spells and lend her weapons to the third – Antarctica, first witch here, whose cold is greater than Winter's cold, who for more than a month in each year refuses to surrender to Night. And as they wandered among the trains of her frozen skirts, the witch Antarctica looked down over the shoulder of her wild white Bear, and plotted their destruction. If he closed his gravelled eyes, Ross could see her: Antarctica, Ice Maiden, Snow Queen, Queen of Bitches, watching him.

So midnight passed unnoticed. They had been walking for

162

nearly sixteen hours with hardly a break. They had covered less than six miles.

Jeremiah was in the lead when the white Bear played its next great trick. The green ice hid its terrible nakedness under the blankets of snow which made even their legs invisible to the two men. In this way, with deadly cunning, it prepared its weapons.

Ross, his anger cooling now, and thickening to despair, walked in a waking dream, followed only the steady pull of the rope held taut by his friend walking far beyond the limits of his weary vision. Suddenly it jerked him off his feet, and pulled him rolling over the ice. He screamed and spread his four limbs, seeking purchase, trying to stop. The rope pulled him forward relentlessly. He closed his eyes and dug the heels of his hands and the toes of his boots into the slick ice. The movement slowed. The rope was no longer pulling him. He stopped, and lay, breathless, on his face for several minutes before he pulled himself on to his hands and knees and crawled forward. He came to the edge of the crevasse. The rope had worn a deep friction-groove into the green translucent lip, and had frozen fast as soon as the movement had stopped. He looked, stunned, down into the Queen of Bitches' trap. He could just see Jeremiah, caught between the jaws. "Jeremiah?" he called, but no sound came. Jeremiah did not move.

It was several minutes before he thought of pulling on the rope. When he heaved, however, his friend's unconscious body moved easily. But moving it and lifting it were two entirely different things. Ross soon found that his arms were unequal to the task, so he carefully untied the end around his waist, took hold of it below the edge of ice, below where it was frozen immovably into the lip, and, using the whole strength of his body, he began to move back. The wind in his face, traitor to the witches, helped him a little; the ice sent enough unevennesses to give him purchase, and inch by inch was Jeremiah raised. But the pressure on the rope made it eat again into the ice-rim, so that after a while Ross could not move back any further. Leaning back, tensing his shoulders, pulling with all his might, hand over hand he went up the rope again to the edge of the crevasse. Jeremiah was hanging almost a foot inside the ice, but the rope was so far into the edge that Ross had to wrap what slack he could around his waist, kneel carefully, and lift the dead-weight into his arms. Then he untied the other end of the rope from around Jeremiah's waist. Both ends of the rope were now frozen into the ice, far beyond the ability of the exhausted Ross to move them, and so he left it where it was. Through the heavy cold-weather clothes, Ross could make no guess as to how badly Jeremiah was hurt. The only thing he was certain of was that his left leg was broken below the knee. As he tried to straighten this leg, Jeremiah stirred and groaned.

"Jeremiah? Jeremiah, can you hear me? We have to move. Can you move?"

"Colin? I've broken my leg, I think."

"I know. Do you think you can move?"

"I don't know. You'll have to help me stand."

They struggled unsteadily to their feet. Jeremiah's left arm gripped Ross's shoulders. Ross's right arm grasped his friend's waist. They moved down the side of the crevasse, with the wind coming from their sides.

"It's too slow. You'll have to leave me."

"No."

"Colin, we'll both die."

"The hell we will."

"Leave me, Colin. Go on by yourself."

"No." They came to the end of the crevasse, and pushed once more into the teeth of the white Bear.

And hours began to pass again. The going got easier after they discarded Jeremiah's knapsack. They did not talk, each man preoccupied with his own agony. Ross felt his right side becoming warm where Jeremiah's body pressed against him, but the uneven pressure on his shoulder of the crippled man's limping gait soon attained the heights of agony. The arm gripping Jeremiah itself began to cramp. Ross's shoulder began to fight to tear away from his neck, and as the dawn glimmered far away in front of them, he found himself crying out at every step as the claws of the white Bear tore down the length of his back.

As Night deserted the unholy Trinity, the storm seemed to ease a little; and even the Queen of Bitches seemed to be content with what she had done.

"Not dead yet," said Ross.

"Leave me," said Jeremiah.

164

"I'll put you down for a bit," said Ross, "and we'll finish the soup and meat. Breakfast's the most important meal of the day, my old mother always says."

"Especially for condemned men," agreed Jeremiah.

"Don't come to me for sympathy," said Ross, easing him to the ground, "I'd swap your leg for my back any day."

He straightened, and stretched luxuriously, feeling his muscles exult in their freedom. Jeremiah looked up at him: he could only see a vague shape above the legs: the white Bear had not eased that much. And a plan took shape in the cripple's mind. He began to look for his opportunity, and it came at once. "You get the stuff out," said Ross. "I'll be back in a minute." He vanished into the swirling snow, leaving Jeremiah with the knapsack. Ross only took four or five steps away, then he turned his back to the wind, lifted the front of his anorak, eased the front of his heavy trousers carefully almost to his knees, took one mitten in his teeth, undid the zip in his second pair of trousers, opened his thermal underwear, relieved himself, and went through the reverse procedure. As he had left his mitten off, he checked the time: it was just after five o'clock. He turned, and followed his fading tracks back over the five steps, and Jeremiah was gone. The knapsack was there, but Jeremiah was not.

"JEREMIAH? JEREMIAH!" He did not think to look for tracks until it was almost too late, then he snatched up the knapsack and stumbled after his friend. Jeremiah had not gone far: there was little purchase on the ice now that most of the snow had been lifted by the wind, and ten minutes furious scrabblings with his desperate hands had dragged his heavy body only a few yards. But such was the concentration of effort needed to move at all that he did not notice that his friend had caught him until he found himself pushing against Ross's unyielding legs. Then, robbed even of Oates' terrible glory, he began to cry with the pain and frustration.

Ross fed him gently with one of the strips of meat, and half of the now-cold soup. "I can't go on," he said. "Leave me here. I am dead already: look." He gestured at the leg, and Ross looked. From ankle to crutch it was frozen solid, held immobile in a cast of ice made from blood and urine. "Even if you take me back, what will be the use? I will have no legs, no manhood, the white Bear has taken both. Let me lie here and die."

165

"I can't," said Ross. "I'm sorry, Jeremiah, but I can't."
There were tears freezing on the white mask of his face. His eyes
were mad with desperation.

"What choice do you have? I can no longer walk. What can
you do?"

"I'll bloody well show you what I can do."

Ross emptied the remaining knapsack, containing the letters, on to the ground, and began to tear feverishly at the seams.
When they broke on the two sides, he had a canvas flap hanging
down. He laid the knapsack on the ground, and moved
Jeremiah on to it. The Eskimo's buttocks just rested on the flap.
Ross tied his shoulders into the frame with the last of their rope,
and went around to his head. Then he took the straps in his left
hand and stood. Jeremiah found himself sitting on the improvised sledge, the weight of his torso leaning back against the
pull of his friend's arm. And so they began again.

Ross walked on in a nightmare. The great Ice Barrier reared
up in front of him, and the Queen of Bitches sat on top of it
saying, "Climb this, Colin, and I'll let you go. Climb up to me
and I will let you sleep." And he shouted at her, raved, stooped
down as he stumbled towards her and gathered up chunks of ice
to throw into the leering face. And she clapped her frozen hands
and laughed.

Then abruptly she disappeared, and he saw Job. He ran
towards his friend, crying out, "Job Job Job." He ran so fast the
straps on the knapsack-sledge broke and Jeremiah slumped on
to the ice. "Job Job Job Job . . ." Ross ran towards the broad
dependable figure. Nearer, nearer . . . And he too vanished.
Ross stopped, unbelieving. "Job?" No answer. "JOB?"
Nothing. Ross fell to his knees and wept.

When he looked up, there was the great Ice Barrier stretching up into the morning, and she looked down at him and said,
"Climb this, Colin, and I'll let you go . . ." He went back to
Jeremiah, and looked at what he had done to the sledge. Try as
he might, his icy mitten would take no purchase on the frozen
tatters of the straps. Time and time again the ice-crusted
leather slipped off the stiff webbing and Colin hurled face-down
in the snow. During the next half-hour they hardly moved any
distance. Each time Colin's hand slipped and he fell forward,
Jeremiah fell back, wrenching his frozen legs and screaming. It

166

was no good, he could no longer move the makeshift sled in this way.

He never knew just when he decided to try it without the mitten and glove, but he would always remember what a fair trade it seemed to be: a hand for a friend. There was so little chance for them now that it didn't really matter much. He looked at the still body of his friend for a moment, then he slowly took off his left mitten, and his underglove. He looked at his white, clean left hand.

"Come on then old son," he said to Jeremiah, and he wrapped the stiff broken straps around his hand, and started forward into the storm. There were no hallucinations now, only the cold-pains in his fingers. Even his relatively warm right hand ached in sympathy with his tortured left. The cold ate at the joints of the fingers and thumb. His hand seemed to swell with the pain. It crept into his palm. All the joints inside his hand ached and burned. It was as though the hand to the wrist was in boiling water. Before the first hour was up, he was screaming as he walked. The cold-pains began to creep up his forearm. In his mind he could see the warm blood flowing down past his shoulder into the increasing cold of his arm. He began to feel his veins full of blood returning like ice. His mind reeled away from the terrible thing he was doing to himself, and the fantasies began to return. People he knew. Job again, crying out, and, disregarded, vanishing. Robin Quick, stumbling at his shoulder crying, "I'm dying, Colin; carry me too. For God's sake, Colin ..." Ross paid him no attention, and he wandered away in the half-light.

"Colin? Colin." Now Charlie called to him. She stood a little way from him, clad from neck to knee in a grey fur coat. Something inside him tore loose and ran across the snow towards her. Ross stumbled on, watching his own shoulders recede towards her. His phantom reached her. Ross screamed, and fell to his knees. The movement nearly cracked his frozen shoulder. But then his phantom self was back, looking down at him, and screaming, "Get up you son of a bitch. Get up and walk or I'll leave you here, I swear I will; I'll leave you here and you'll lie forever." "NO," screamed Ross, looking up along the length of his dream-like self like a whipped dog, without dignity, without pride, without will. "Up, you lazy bleeder, up," screamed the phantom. Ross's lips moved silently as the ghost of himself shouted, echoing the words as though learning them by heart. "Your eyeballs'll be as hard as marbles. Your lungs'll fill with ice."

And Ross's voice broke into a sob as he himself screamed, "Oh get up." And he got up.

He curled his right arm over his eyes to keep the snow from his goggles, and, dragging the dead-weight of Jeremiah forward, he moved again into the throat of the storm.

His shoulder ached, and his whole left side was a mass of tiny blood-vessels packed with freezing blood. He wanted to sleep. God, how he wanted to sleep. It was hopeless anyway.

The figures started coming back again. Job appeared suddenly. "Colin, thank God . . ."

Ross swept back his right arm, and walked on. But Job did not disappear.

Ross's arm swept down, connected solidly: Job fell down, and Ross fell over him.

Ross had been walking for twenty-eight hours. He had covered less than ten miles. He fell over Job and tumbled into a well of delirium four months deep.

NINE

i

IT HAD DONE no good, of course, telling them the story. He had not expected it to: Simon hadn't believed it, Kate hadn't understood, Warren hadn't cared and Job already knew. A waste of time, an unnecessary and bitter humiliation with nothing settled, nothing solved, nothing exorcised.

After a while he got up and went out. As soon as he was out of the tent he had narrowed his eyes automatically and cursed under his breath – he had forgotten his face-mask. But then he noticed that he didn't need it; the power of the sunlight had decreased radically while he had been stumbling through his story. Suddenly the gold all round had turned to blood. The sea, the floes, the ice itself were a deep, shifting shade of red. He glanced up at the sun. It was hanging low in the sky coloured dull orange. And the sky to the south was no longer blue – it was khaki-grey, shading down to nicotine-brown where the horizon should have been. Then he realised what it was: a fogbank.

His mind raced. There was only one cause for a fogbank as high, as solid and as well-defined as this one: a warm current, its surface evaporating into the icy air. A warm current.

Even as he stood there, gazing at the silent white wall, they were swept into it.

Job's head appeared through the tent-flap. The Eskimo paused, looked around, and crawled out.

"Bad," he said.

"Oh, I don't know . . ."

The fog swirled, thickened, thinned in its own mysterious dance, blanketed them completely. The others came out and stared, bewildered. In moments the size of their world had shrunk from thousands of square miles of sea and ice to a few square yards. Instinctively they drew together into a huddle as though they now had less space to occupy. In moments they were all beaded with droplets of water.

"There's nothing we can do," said Job, his voice strangely hushed.

Simon looked around wildly. "But the fucking ice is going to melt!"

Job shrugged, and repeated, "There's nothing we can do."

"If we wait long enough, we can swim," said Kate, with a wry smile.

"Oh, we'll have drifted to the Shetland Islands long before that!" sneered Quick.

So, tired out in any case, they went to bed, Kate and her father sharing one tent, Simon moving in with Ross and Job in the other.

As he composed himself for sleep, Job heard the song of a killer calling to the pack, and, distantly, a reply.

There was a scratch at the tent-flap.

"Yes?" called Quick, waking instantly, and Kate stuck her head in.

"Breakfast?" she asked.

"Great," said Quick. "Bacon, eggs, fried bread, sausages, toast, coffee. Porridge. Please."

"Coffee I can manage. Anything else you'd better find for yourself. It's all in the supply tent. Somewhere."

"I'll go and look," he said, cheerfully amenable. "I've got a good idea where most things are."

"Good," she said, pleased and mildly surprised by the new face of the little man.

Quick himself would have been hard-put to explain his light mood. He began to dress.

"Mind where you're putting your goddamned elbows," snarled Ross, still half asleep.

Job, awake now also, shook his head. Quick was still smiling when he stumbled out into the fog.

One of the things which was affecting Colin's mood was his left arm. It had now been several days since he had removed the false limb for any length of time, and it was chafing painfully against the bruised areas where the arm itself and the straps had cut into him when the polar bear had lifted him off his feet. He waited, therefore, until Job had also left the tent, then he stripped off his vest and unstrapped the length of plastic and steel. He briefly examined the slightly crusted welts across the pale expanse of his chest, shrugged his lop-sided shrug and got dressed without it.

When he came a little self-consciously out of the tent some time later, Job and Kate were sitting beside the fire-tray. Of Simon and Doc. Warren there was no sign. Kate's eyes swept briefly over him, pausing on his left arm with its empty sleeve neatly folded and tucked into his pocket; her eyebrows rose a little, and she smiled. It was a warm smile which seduced a fleeting grin out of him. The air was heavy with the smell of cooking and the tang of coffee. Ross's mood lightened a little.

"Morning," he said.

"Morning," she said in the same tone.

"Where are Simon and your father?"

"Gone off somewhere." She gestured into the fog.

He frowned fleetingly and glanced at Job who shrugged and said, "They'll be careful."

"They'd better be. God knows what it's like out there."

"They've taken the axe," Kate said.

"Oh great," said Ross. "That'll help. We'll just have to hope Nootaikok is in a good mood."

"Who is Nootaikok?" asked Kate.

"Ask Job later. He'll tell you about them all."

"Anyway," said Kate, concentrating on the business in hand, "do you want some breakfast or not?"

He realised how hungry he was, and sat down beside her. "Love some. What have we got?" With a gleeful flourish she produced a plate covered by another, and handed them to him. They were hot. He balanced them on his knees and slipped the top plate off.

Bacon, sausages, re-constituted eggs, baked beans.

"Simon wanted porridge," she said, "but we couldn't find it. That tent's a shambles."

"Yes. It's about time we tidied it up, sorted it out. We should have done it ages ago, but . . ."

The little silence contained much that words might have

rendered imprecise – the fact that the final sorting of the supplies would be an acceptance of the fact that they no longer hoped for early rescue. And rescue had been on all their minds. Hope was necessary to their continued existence, and it was necessary to keep it alive: they were all adults, they all knew it, they all worked at keeping it alive.

"Well," said Colin, as he finished his breakfast and his third cup of coffee, "I'll see about sorting out the tent then. Heavens knows how long this'll last for." He looked at Job in half-enquiry.

"Not for long," said Job. "There will be a breeze soon."

Ross nodded. "Well, I might as well do it in the meantime. Anyone looking for us in this'll be hard-put to see their noses, let alone the floe."

"How do you know things like that, Job?" asked Kate, fascinated. "About the weather – some sort of collective Eskimo knowledge passed from father to son down the years?"

"Not really. I just know the High Arctic, that's all."

"Even after a lapse of five years?"

"What?"

"Well," she gestured at the shrinking shape of Ross's back, "I thought you two . . ."

"Oh, I see. You think I have been in Washington with Colin. No. Colin and I haven't worked together since . . . well, since Jeremiah died."

"Oh."

"No. I live up here. I've a wife and family in Togiak. Couple of hundred miles south-west of Anchorage."

"Oh I see. How old are the children? How many? What are their names?"

"Four boys: Matthew, Mark, Luke and John. Matthew's the eldest, he's ten; Mark and Luke are eight; John's two."

"What happens if you have another? I mean there aren't any Gospels left."

Job smiled. "We'll start on the disciples – Peter, James, Thomas, the rest."

"Well, what do you do if you don't work with Colin?"

"Oh, I work in the field, like Simon, a bit."

There was a silence, then Job continued. "It's funny, really. Mary didn't want me to come out on this one. Well, it's my

172

summer holiday: I thought that's why she was so upset. And," his eyes slid away from her and his voice dropped, "she's a little jealous of Colin. But perhaps she knew more than she said. She can smell trouble the way I can smell a wind . . ." He lapsed into silence again.

"What do you usually do for your summer holidays, then?" she asked him next.

Job smiled broadly. "Took them to Florida last year." He laughed. "My God, they hated it! All except Disney World – the boys loved that, so did Mary and I, I must admit; but the rest! It was so hot! And the people! Mind you, it's hardly surprising; no one could believe it. I mean, a family of honest-to-God Eskimos in Florida!" He chuckled. "No, we usually just stay where we are. I paint the house, do odd jobs, you know? Mary's a school-teacher, so she's got good long holidays. We could go away more often, I suppose. Maybe Europe. We could visit Colin, he asks us often enough, but . . . Maybe next year . . ."

Kate remembered something Colin had said at breakfast. "Who is Nootaikok?"

"Lord of the Icebergs. He is one of the gods."

"What gods?"

"The gods of this, of the frozen north, of the High Arctic, of Innuit." His hand and arm took in the ice, the snow, the pack, the permafrost and midnight sun . . .

Kate caught enough in his gesture to feel the interest stir in her. She asked him to explain, and he smiled and told her of the Inua, the Spirits. The Inua were everywhere, he said, and fell into the three main types, the Evil, the Indifferent, and the Good. The Evil were headed by the great spirit Aipalookvik the Destroyer who had great jaws which rend and tear. And with him were such spirits as Paija, the huge woman with one leg who prowled the winter nights and killed with a look; and Wenigo who haunted the dark pine forests, feeding on the unwary. And there were those like Aulanerk who struggled beneath the sea thus causing the waves and Nootaikok the spirit of the Icebergs, who were neither good nor evil. And there were the Good Spirits, like Anglooklik the Great Seal, Aumanit the Great Whale. And the greatest of all these was Torgasoak the Great Spirit, the Good Being.

173

"Don't tell me," said Kate, "Torgasoak is a big bear or something."

"No," said Job . . . "He's a big man and he's only got one arm."

Kate opened her mouth to reply, and then the screams began.

ii

Doctor Warren had convinced himself that he was genuinely interested in the rust-red stain he had spotted on the ice ahead. He was only interested, however, because he had nothing else to do. Certainly there was no premium in doing any work here, not that there was actually the equipment to do any real work with – but he was bored.

"I say," he called to Simon, "there's some plankton frozen into that hill; I'm sure of it."

"Oh. Right."

The fog eddied and swirled around them, constantly changing the quality of the light by its varying thicknesses. One moment the hill would be vaguely visible, the next a hand held at arm's length invisible.

After they had been walking for two minutes or so, the ice beneath their feet began to hunch up, and the restless sound of the ocean moved more forcefully through the heavy fog as the warm waves lapped at the little cliff of ice.

"Here we are then," said the doctor cheerfully. "I think it's somewhere up towards the top here."

Close-to, it was a hill of some substance rising twenty feet above them to a little plateau then falling nearly thirty feet sheer to the sea with only a little ledge some six feet down from the top to break the sheer cliff.

Simon was at the top several minutes before the doctor, and he spent the time in exploring the little platform he found there. It was only about six feet by six, and, with the fog at that moment close around him he did not venture too near to the seaward side, but sure enough, on the crest of the upslope there was the tip of a rust-red stain stretching down one side. He knelt to examine it and chipped a bit free with his axe. The stain

174

went down into the ice far beneath the sliver he had broken free. He held it up awkwardly in his mitten and looked through it at the sky. As he did so, the first intimation of a wind disturbed the fog and the sky brightened.

The doctor puffed up beside him. "Let's have a look."

He knelt beside the younger man and quickly uncovered his hands. Simon handed him the piece he had cut, and he studied it for a moment.

"By Jove, you know this *is* interesting . . ." He became quite animated. "You can see how it might have happened, can't you? I dare say it's not an uncommon occurrence. A cloud of krill very near the surface, snap icing, and there you are. But this is something else again! Unless my eyesight's even worse than I thought, this stuff isn't surface krill at all, it's from the Deep Scatter Layer."

"What's that?"

"The Deep Scatter Layer? Oh, it's found in most oceans. It's a layer several hundred feet down unusually rich in marine life which rises and falls depending on the height of the sun during the day. At midday, it's at its deepest; but it rises during the night. I suppose the Deep Scatter Layer in the Arctic Ocean would be a pretty shallow one; the ocean itself is only a little more than six hundred feet deep in most places."

He began to follow the stain along the edge of the little platform towards the seaward-facing cliff. "Yes. It goes right across. Now I wonder if this ice has just been stood on its end, or has been forced up as a whole? I mean, if this cliff is a section straight down through the cloud of krill it could be a fascinating study."

The wind stirred the fog fitfully, stripping it away for several hundred yards on the seaward side. Quick rested his shoulder against the axe-handle and sat, gazing out over the dull grey water.

He was hypnotised by the movement of the grey sea and the bedraggled-looking floes that filled it like pieces of white bread cast out for giant ducks. The doctor scrabbled to the very edge of the cliff looking down towards the sea. He was on hands and knees, looking over at the stain as it receded down the sheer face.

"I say, I think it goes green down there. That would be

something! Banded by colour!" He leaned further out, straining for a clear view of the striations stretching down six feet to the little ledge. Another inch. Another.

"Hey, Simon, hold my feet would you?" The doctor half turned his head to look up at Simon, and his glasses fell off. As they fell, he instinctively grabbed for them, losing his grip on the ice, and tumbling out, one hand straight in front of him reaching over the sea, the other behind him clutching at the ice. His body rolled over to the right. His left hand gripped. He dangled with his back to the ice, right arm still out, as his feet sought the ledge. He was aware of a great roaring. He was trying to turn and face the ice, so he could get his toes in the ledge and grip with both hands. His half-blind eyes swept the ocean and the fog, unable to distinguish between them, but he saw the great torpedo shape which suddenly thrust its black and white length into the air before him.

Simon Quick jerked out of his reverie as the doctor called for him to hold his feet. He turned in time to see the old man hanging over the cliff, backside in the air. And then, with horrifying suddenness he was gone. Simon was on his feet in an instant and had covered the distance in two strides. The old man was hanging by his left hand, his right hand thrust out as though trying to grasp the fog, his heels drumming against the ice.

Then the whale exploded out of the water, hurling itself up through twenty feet, turning until the liquid-pitch eye could see them clearly.

Quick froze.

The whale's mouth opened. Its teeth were dull yellow. As it began to fall back into the water, Quick began to move again. He fell to his knees at the edge, one leg on either side of the twisted left hand. He leaned down, his eyes busy on the slate water, grasped the old man's wrist and pulled. The doctor was still trying to turn round and grasp the edge with his right hand. Quick heaved again but the old man remained where he was. "My hand," he cried, "Simon, my hand!"

Quick looked down between his knees. Warren's left hand was frozen fast in the snow.

"Jesus H . . ." He was up again and running for the axe.

The doctor had found the ledge with his heels now, and was

able to get some of the pressure off the twisted wrist. His eyes were full of tears, so he was doubly blind. His mouth was open, gasping in the icy, fog-laden air.

Simon swung the axe up. "It'll be all right," he said, "hang on." But the old man didn't hear. He swung the axe down. As he did so, the ocean exploded up, and the whale reared into the air, mouth agape. Simon's concentration faltered. The axe wavered by six inches and took the old man's fingers off at the knuckles. The hand sprang free, spraying blood. Simon watched, unable to move, as the old man toppled forward, head-first, into the mouth of the whale. He just had time to scream. The whale, with the doctor's legs sticking grotesquely from its mouth, fell back. The water closed.

Simon dumbly swung the axe again, this time true. The edge of ice split away and fell, taking the doctor's fingers with it. He sank to his knees and leaned against the axe, still trying to believe it.

Then Ross was beside him, and Job.

"What . . ." began Ross.

"What happened?" screamed Kate, coming up over the crest at a rush. Ross caught her arm and swung her round bodily away from the edge.

"He went over. He dropped his glasses and went over. He caught the edge, but the killer . . . I . . . he was reaching out, with his hand. He couldn't see. He was reaching out, and the whale . . ."

Job picked him up. Ross took Kate and led her stiff body down the hill.

Kate was numb. She couldn't believe it. She felt no pain, no grief. She didn't even feel sick. She felt nothing. She couldn't believe it.

Job held Simon as he vomited over the edge of the crystal cliff. The wind came more firmly stripping away the fog. The sea brightened and began to ripple. At the bottom of the crystal cliff a small piece of ice turned. Buried in it, almost as white as the ice itself, were four fingers neatly severed just above the knuckle. Job shivered and almost vomited himself. A deep superstitious fear swept over him.

He watched the white fingers for a moment more until the water closed over them.

177

TEN

i

DURING THE FIRST hour after the doctor's death, a steady wind rolled away the heavy bank of fog, but while the floe had been covered, the weather had undergone a radical change. In place of the high bright blue of the sky, there was now a low ceiling of fat grey clouds pressing down against the sea and moving restlessly towards the west. The blinding power of the light was gone, and instead there was a heavy, threatening gloom. The sky was reflected in the oily grey of the ocean which lifted itself into sullen waves under the persistent prompting of the wind. The grey sky and the grey sea stretched to a vague grey horizon, and only the ice had life. The floes, their crystal interfaces seeming to multiply what little light there was, continued to glow with the blue of a paraffin flame, making it seem as though they contained some individual form of energy which lit them like cold neon. Even under the surface of the sea they burned mysteriously.

The dark clouds closed against the dark ocean. As though a plug had been pulled from the lower sky, thin trails swirled in a whirlpool in the air thousands of miles across. The storm continued to follow its sluggish course west. Four days ago it had closed Barrow Field for seventy-two hours, now it was raging over the Bering Strait, its leading edges already disturbing Russian airspace.

They sat in the gloom of the tent, silent for more than an hour, each a prey to thoughts they dared not entrust to the others.

Job thought of the white fingers floating on the grey-green sea, imbedded in a shard of ice. He had realised quickly enough that they had to be the doctor's fingers, and yet the deep dread they bore in him had not abated. He attacked the superstition of such dread from the levels of his Methodist education, and yet he could not break its power over him. He forced his mind on to thoughts of his wife and children, of his home in Togiak. But the fingers rose unbidden to his mind again; nails pale; joints swollen; the knuckles seemingly burst open like over-ripe plums; the stubs of bone. He flooded his mind with memories again, like a child who has had a nightmare thinking of nice things in the dark. His preoccupation was so deep that he was blind to the gathering shadows, deaf to the freshening wind, unaware of the change in the weather.

Simon Quick thought of nothing. Over and over to himself he was saying, "I am thinking of nothing, I am thinking of nothing. There is nothing for me to think about." It seemed to him quite logical and acceptable that he should think like this. It seemed to him the best way to stop himself cracking up.

Colin watched Simon's face, pale in the shadows and drawn with strain. His lips were moving with repetitive monotony as he whispered something to himself over and over. The whites of his eyes gleamed restlessly as they shifted aimlessly, seeing nothing. Colin couldn't think of anything to say. The old weary self-recrimination washed over him. He could almost hear the Queen of Bitches, Antarctica, giggling insanely as her claws closed around him once more, destroying his companions as she had five years ago. His mind ran back along the familiar nightmare's lines so that he too was unaware of the change in the weather outside.

Kate was more or less asleep. The shock made her mind blank, but snatches of memory flashed up before her tightly closed eyes like the trailer in a cinema for some coming attraction. Her mother's funeral, the pages from *Time*, from the London *Sunday Times*, the airport at Anchorage as her father had given that great whoop of joy. Silently she began to cry.

Quietly at first, the wind sang in the tent-ropes, stirring the orange net, blowing sparks in clouds from the smouldering fire on its steel tray. The waves began to break on the edges of the floe as the grey ocean became more choppy. Flashes of white broke the water's monotony as white horses formed and

179

foamed. The floe, small enough now to answer to the ocean's dictates, began to rock gently as the long combers following the outskirts of the storm moved regularly under it. In the supply tent, tins began to chime against each other, the silver harpoons rolled from side to side. The clouds seemed to graze the tops of the floes. The day assumed all the dark claustrophobic solidity of a cave.

One or two heavy drops of warm rain dashed themselves against the coldly glowing ice.

"Have we any aspirin?" asked Kate suddenly.

"Aspirin?" Ross was jerked out of his thoughts. He shook his head to clear it.

"I have a bitch of a headache." The word made the small hairs on Ross's back and neck stir.

"I don't know," he said. "We should have some in the supply tent. There was a first aid box . . . Simon? Simon!"

"Yes?" Dully.

"Simon, have we any aspirin?"

"Aspirin? For Christ's sake! Yes, I suppose so. In the first aid box. It's in the supply tent." Glad of something to do, he began to move stiffly. "I'll get some." He stood up and staggered slightly as the floe moved. "What the hell . . . ?"

Very slowly they began to realise that the weather had undergone a radical change. Simon pushed the tent-flap open and went out, his eyes automatically screwed up against the light; but it was almost as dark outside as it had been in the tent. The wind freshened against his face, warm and wet. He began to walk to the supply tent, his progress slowed by the restless movement of the orange net. He looked up quickly at the swirling clouds, and a volley of raindrops fell into his eyes. He hunched his shoulders without thinking any more about it and went after the aspirin for Kate.

In the tent, Ross asked Kate, "How do you feel?"

"A bit better . . ." She was surprised to discover it was true.

"Just the headache?"

"A bit queasy." She sounded a little preoccupied.

"I hope it's nothing you ate . . ."

She realised that some of her panic had been caused by the fact that she had really expected to come to pieces herself now that her father was no longer there. But she wasn't. She was

180

OK. She was going to be OK. "Hey! No aspersions against my cooking!"

Ross began to laugh. It wasn't much as witty repartee went, but it meant she was going to be OK. She sketched a smile in reply.

The floe gave a little lurch as two waves passed too close.

Job looked up, blinking his long eyes, disturbed more by the movement than the laughter. He glanced around the dark tent and frowned. After Ross's laugh there came a little silence broken by the sinister song of the wind, the restless lapping of the waves, the fading roar of the blown fire. One section of the tent flapped and strained like a sail. The two men glanced at each other, and seemed to realise the danger as their eyes met. Then they were scrambling for the opening, bursting out on hands and knees into the black cavernous day as the first serious shower of warm rain slashed out of the sky.

The floe was still the size of Wembley stadium; large enough to make their camp on the lower half look small; still large enough to make anyone feel safe. But Ross and Job knew well enough that no matter how long and wide it was, the important questions were how thick was it and how stable? If there was any serious rough weather, this seemingly solid refuge would shatter like a car-windscreen in a crash. And even if it held together against the waves, the current and the rain would both be melting it until it was unsafe to walk anywhere – and when Sedna's knucklebones returned, thought Job, there would be nothing to stop them coming through. His eyes automatically swept over the all-too-close ocean, but there was nothing to see through the rain except the black clouds, the black and white sea and the restless floes with their ghostly cold blue light shining steadily.

"The wood!" yelled Ross over the first serious gust of wind. "We must keep it dry!" Job nodded. Without fire they could not cook; they couldn't even melt the ice for water. They could be in bad trouble without fire. Bad trouble! That's what we're in now, he thought. If the wind freshened, if the waves rose, if the rain lasted for any length of time they were dead.

The squall eased slightly. Ross had a bundle of wood under his arm and was stumbling back to the tent. Simon Quick came out of the supply tent with the aspirin. They collided. The wood

181

went all over the place. Colin swung round, eyes blazing. "You clumsy sod! For Christ's sake . . ."

But Quick just pushed past him and crawled into the tent, Kate's aspirins held safe. Job helped Ross pick up the wood again, but he took it himself this time, and shoved his way into the tent with it. Quick was kneeling beside Kate, giving her the tablets.

"Time enough for that later," snapped the Eskimo. "We've got to get all this stuff in out of the wet."

The supply tent was by no means waterproof. If everything in it got wet, and the temperature dropped again after the storm, most of it would become covered in ice, unusable. Not just the food, but the first aid equipment, the guns, everything. Job's mind refused to start an exact catalogue: there simply wasn't time. He grabbed Simon by the shoulder and bundled him out into the rain. After a few moments Kate, who had caught the urgency of Job's words if not the exact tenor of his thoughts, also came out.

Suddenly there was a sound like the high registers in thunder. Ross was thrown down as the ice heaved. Inches below him was a crack in the ice, running straight through the camp. There was a brief silence, and then the cracking began in earnest. Like a cube brought out of the freezer and plunged into a warm drink, the floe was cracking apart. Beneath the camp the orange net flexed, tautened, twisted. The edges of the crack beneath him ground together quietly like teeth. The roaring quickened.

For half an hour they moved the articles most at risk out of the supply tent into the nearest of the undamaged tents: the latrine tent.

The wind continued to rise until a good deal of spray was mixed with the heavy rain. The waves began to break over the floe and wash across the ice towards the camp. The edges of the crack beneath the net ground restlessly, growling like an angry lion. The sides of the tents billowed and flapped until it seemed as though they would split. The tents themselves bent and flexed as the gusts swirled. The ropes tautened, loosened, howled through whole octaves and keys. Ripples of water washed about their ankles, broke against the reinforced canvas, froze in smooth blisters over the pegs holding tents, nets. The fire-tray shifted, began to tilt.

182

Water slicked Ross's oily hair to his head and face. It ran into his collar, into his cuffs, into his boots. It got in his eyes and his mouth. It dripped from his chin. He looked, half blind, around the camp, searching for anything else that should be moved out of the wet. The others were already stumbling back to the tent. He bent his head, hunched his shoulders, and began to follow them. Then a movement caught his eye. He looked up. What was it? Everything was still – straining to burst into a frenzy of movement – but still. His eyes swept over the camp, checking. The four tents, the net, the fire-tray. His eyes swept on, then jerked back. The fire-tray! He began to run.

It lifted gently, easily, like a leaf. The front legs came free, the back legs folded and collapsed. The ashes hissed on the wet. It stood on its end for a second then turned faced down, kicked up, began to roll.

Ross was running at full tilt now, and even over the wind he could hear the ice crack at each footfall. He leaped over the black wound of the crack and pounded on. The tray was beyond the edge of the net now, bouncing over the ice faster and faster. Ross dashed over the floe, boots sinking to the ankle, rotten ice clinging like mud; he was almost up with it now, a few more steps. He was reaching out, leaning far forward, hand grasping. He had it!

The ice gave.

One minute he was running, the next on his right knee with his left leg vanished to mid thigh. But he had the fire-tray. He looked down bemused, a dull ache starting in his hip where he had wrenched it. He felt his boot fill with water.

"Damn!"

He began to get up, pulling the left leg gingerly through the sopping mess of white crystals. He used the edge of the tray as a crutch, keeping his balance as he straightened his right leg. The ice clung. Suddenly, unbidden, the memory of Hiram Preston rose in his mind. What if that bastard of a whale was down there now? He felt a tug at his foot. In fact what he felt was an edge of ice catching the top of his boot, but he didn't know what it was so he straightened his right leg convulsively. The boot came off.

Ross looked for a moment at the sopping trouser-leg, the dripping sock. "Fuck!"

He began to hop back to the camp.

Kate, thrusting her head out of the tent to see what was holding him up, saw him coming through the rain, his left leg held up ridiculously, left sleeve flapping like a banner in the wind, right arm holding the fire-tray, thrust out for balance. In a brief lull in the wind she heard what he was saying and she began to laugh. She fell back into the tent, tears of mirth running down her face, and Simon also had a look.

When Ross crawled through the tent-flap, his mood was not lightened by the hilarity that met his entrance; but he was by no means a naturally bad-tempered man, and in fact was a good deal relieved to see the improvement half an hour's hard work and a little laughter had worked on both Kate and Simon. Even in spite of the crack beneath the camp's netting.

Only Job was quiet. He had not yet been able to shrug off his feeling of depression, and he saw nothing to laugh at either in Ross's accident nor in their present predicament. Quite apart from the question of how the ice would stand up to the battering it was receiving, they were all damp, and Ross, his leg soaked, a definite candidate for frostbite.

"We'd better get these wet things off," he said, and began to strip off his anorak, shirts, boots and jeans. Ross nodded, and began first with his right boot, overtrousers and jeans. Simon and Kate stared at this grotesque strip-tease for a moment, and then the obvious good sense of it struck them. Their outer clothes were soaked; their underwear damp. It was obviously necessary to dry off as best they could or the cold would set in with deadly effect. Kate moved first, stripping off her dripping anorak, her wringing pullover, her wet shirt. She started to undo her trousers when she saw that Simon was staring at her, wide-eyed. She moved her trousers to her knees with a wriggle of her hips and sat, her body completely disguised under the shapeless white sagging of her quilted combinations. From neck to ankles she might have been dressed in a loosely-fitting boiler-suit.

"What the hell's the matter with you, Simon?" she said. "Have you never seen a girl in her underwear?"

Simon choked. "Underwear!" he said. "Christ!" He began to laugh again; Ross joined in, then Job, and, last, Kate herself. For some reason it struck them all as exquisitely funny and the crisis passed as they sat chuckling a little, chatting easily to each other while the temperature in the tent rose and their clothes began to dry.

Outside also, things were getting better. The storm-clouds thinned, the wind fell, the rain stopped, the sea quietened. The sun did not return, however, for a heavy layer of nimbus cloud continued to blanket the sky and colour the ocean dull lead. The floe slowly stopped rocking. The waves no longer broke over the edge of the ice, but a good deal of water continued to slop about on the surface of the floe, freezing slowly on any protuberances, slicking over any unevennesses, bringing the crystals to a slippery, solid sheen. Even the net seemed to be half buried in grey glass.

They kept up the chat for nearly two hours. Only Job, although he pretended to be as involved as the others, was aware of the returning calm outside, and he quietly, but deeply and sincerely, thanked Kaila, God of the Sky, for not sending too great a wind, Nipello the rain for not being too warm, Hiko the ice for being so strong for so long.

At last they began to run out of energy.

"What we need is some coffee," said Kate.

"Right," said Simon. "And maybe something to eat, eh?"

"Good idea," said Colin. "We'll be warm enough in jeans and pullovers if we hurry." He looked at Job who nodded. They put them on quickly and slid out. Ross remembered his boot.

"Get me another boot!" he yelled, and as he waited, he took the opportunity to strap his left arm back on.

"OK," Kate replied, and began to slither across to the other undamaged tent. There were spare dry clothes in one of the bundles they had transferred. She opened it, and pulled out a roll of large clothing, sorted out the boots, and stumbled back. Halfway across the orange net, she slid to a halt. Something caught her attention. She narrowed her eyes and looked away to the south. Something was moving out there in the flat grey water. She frowned. Fear reared in her. It's them! she thought. The whales.

She began to run towards the tent, where Colin was, suddenly very cold indeed. Simon was on one knee, putting the fire-tray back up.

"Simon," she gasped. "It's them . . ."

"What?"

But she had crouched down and thrust head and shoulders through the flap. She almost threw the boot at Colin. "It's them," she shouted. "They're back!"

"Oh Christ!" He was scrambling on to his knees, pulling on his pullover.

Job pushed roughly past both of them and stumbled out on to the ice.

"Are you sure?" asked Colin.

"I don't know. Something. Oh, Colin. Why?" There were tears in her eyes. Colin straightened his back, put his arm around her shoulders.

"It'll be all right," he promised. "Quiet now. It'll be all right."

She pressed her face against his chest, eyes tight closed, trying to control her fear, her weakness. After a few moments she pulled away, angry with herself, and crawled across to one corner of the tent.

Ross went out and stood beside Job. The dark sky and the dark sea seemed to press one against the other. Visibility was bad. In the distance there was a brownish mass moving sluggishly towards them. He looked at Job, who was preoccupied with looking at the distant creatures.

Over the water came a faint sound like the ringing of bells. The light caught yellow tusks as one of the creatures heaved itself on to a small floe. Simon and Kate came out of the tent and stood by them. The sound of bells, a strangely resonant two-tone honking, grew louder.

"Odobendiae," said Job.

"For Christ's sake, Job," snapped Kate, "will you stop speaking bloody Eskimo."

"It's Latin," said Job, spectacularly unmoved by Kate's anger. "They're walruses."

"Oh," said Simon, "is that all?"

ii

In fact there were nearly two hundred walruses. A month earlier, as part of a huge herd nearly two thousand in number,

186

they had drifted through the Bering Straits, carried north past St. Lawrence Island by the great spring current to their breeding grounds in the High Arctic. Every year they moved south in the autumn as the pack froze down to the south of Alaska. For the winter months they lived on the islands and coasts of the Bering Sea kept free of ice by the warm currents which swirled north along the edges of the continents. In April they began to move, and in the early days of May began to ride the currents up to their food-rich arctic breeding grounds.

Generally they had an easy life, rarely straying out of the shallow water which supported the small shellfish on which they fed. Never very active, they lazed in the sun, protected from the intense cold by their massive layers of fat. When they were hungry they swam to the ocean floor, stirred up the pebbles and sand with their tusks, eating huge amounts of the creatures which they disturbed. In winter, this particular herd lived in the general area of the Aleutian Islands; in May they ran up through the Bering Straits to the rich banks off the north of the Chukotskiy Peninsula, the eastern point of Russia. This particular summer, as they were on their way past St. Lawrence Island, the Eskimoes from Gambell town on the north coast had come out after them in unusual force in their umiaks, or large open boats, each man armed with three or four powerful hunting rifles, and began a slaughter which had panicked the herd. Every year for possibly ten centuries the Eskimo had come against the walrus, but this year for some reason, the herd panicked. Perhaps the Eskimo were unusually numerous, unusually accurate; perhaps the walrus were more easily scared than of old. Whatever the reason, this particular herd, made up mostly of young family units, began to run north at unusual speed, tending to the east, towards Alaska as opposed to Chukotskiy, leaving behind nearly one hundred young females stripped of skin and tusks, their flesh hacked into round chunks, their intestines hanging in the sun to dry. Gambell town would make it safely through the rest of the year, and some of its citizens might even make a profit. The herd, however, had followed the coast of Alaska until they had uneasily joined the breeding rookeries on the North Alaskan coast.

They had remained there for little longer than a fortnight when the storm had hit. Storms are not unusual in the High

Arctic even in summer, but this one was of rare ferocity. Coming from the east along the coast from the Beaufort Sea it swept huge chunks of ice before it. The walrus herd, unhappy with the unfamiliar breeding grounds, had been easily disturbed, and had plunged as a body, more than a thousand of them, into the wild water. The massive waves, throwing chunks of ice around like unbelievable jugglers, split up the herd into several smaller units. The smallest of these new herds was driven far north, out of the storm, on to the edge of the pack-ice. They had waited until the storm had passed, and then were forced to move, for they were in an area of water more than three hundred feet deep and they could no longer dive to the bottom for their food.

There was much of the summer left and so they struck south west, following the drift, to their usual breeding ground on the Chukotskiy Peninsula.

The herd, consisting of many family units, and a number of old females past the age of breeding, was led by a vanguard of old males, also without mates. The unusual activity, the great distances they had been forced to swim, and the lack of food had all contributed to a general weakening of the whole herd. They were near their destination now, however, and they were swimming with the last of their strength in order to reach it as soon as possible. Their usual policy was to ride slowly on the floes, piled in ungainly hills of maroon flesh, but at the moment, hungry and still in deep water, they were swimming just below the surface with easy sideways swipes of their rear flippers, as fast as they were able.

The group of old males led the herd; every now and then one of them would hook his great straight tusks into the edge of a floe and haul himself on to the ice for a breather and a look round. Immediately behind the old males came the family units, the young calves, very tired now, riding on their mothers' backs. To the rear came the old females, performing the functions of a rear-guard, although there was nothing in the ocean near enough to pose a serious threat.

The tension on the floe, tightened briefly by Kate's panic, relaxed again. Job was disturbed to see the walrus herd so far from their accustomed breeding ground, but he said nothing to the others. As the herd came closer, they were able to distinguish individuals. The old bull who rose most often on to the many small floes which lay scattered on the flat grey ocean, whom they could recognise easily by the fact that his right tusk was broken off about a foot shorter than his left, seemed to be the leader of the herd. Several younger males, two with only one tusk, also rose occasionally. Only one female, an old cow whose tusks curved so much that they crossed against her massive chest, was in evidence, and they did not see her clearly in the distance until the old bull with his uneven tusks was well past them.

"Are they dangerous?" asked Kate, surprised by their bulk. They were nearly fifteen feet long, able, when they sat on the ice, to raise their heads more than six feet in the air.

"Probably not," answered Job, "at least not if we keep clear of them. They're strange animals; slow, lazy, very hard to kill."

"Could we kill one? For food?" asked Simon.

Job shrugged. "We could kill one, I suppose. A couple of shots from the Remington should do it, but the rest of the herd might well attack us if we did; and even if we managed to kill it and get it up on the ice, we haven't any knives sharp enough to butcher it. They have incredibly tough hide, and their blubber's five or six inches thick."

The bell-like sounds had been growing louder as the herd neared, and they were joined now by the slapping and squealing sounds with which the walrus explored their environment and performed their elementary communications. Their heads were big, but the bones were so thick that their brains were very small.

Kate, entranced by the grace which the water lent to these bulky, seemingly ungainly animals, went as near to the edge as she dared and strained to see more clearly.

They were anything up to fifteen feet in length, and so fat as to be almost ten feet in girth. Their blubber gathered up above their faces in thick cowls. Their heads sat squarely on their powerful shoulders, the shoulders faded to narrow hips and truncated rear flippers without shape or semblance of frame, bone, even muscle. And yet there was muscle beneath the maroon velvet of the skin, beneath the six solid inches of blubber, muscle in those massive shoulders which ran directly over the tiny neck to the back of the massive, thick-boned head, muscle in that huge barrel chest which could pull down those tusks with terrible force.

189

Even as she considered the members of the first section of the herd, Kate heard a sudden roar from behind her at the far end of the floe. She turned, surprised. Beyond the camp, at the edge of the floe, nearly thirty yards away, the leader of the walrus herd had reared out of the water. He had swum back from his position at the front of the herd to explore the floe. Now he hooked his tusks into the soft ice and dragged his great bulk forward until his front flippers could grasp and pull him further forward. He lumbered, streaming, on to the blue-flame ice, and paused, his breath coming in great clouds. He faintly discerned the shapes on the far end of the ice so he roared a challenge and drew himself up to full height.

Kate drew a little nearer to Ross, just in case there was any danger, but the old bull only looked at them, flaring its nostrils to their scent. Shortsighted even in water, it was almost blind in the air, but its nose was keen enough. Satisfied that there was no threat, it roared again, turned, gave out the two-note bell-like tone, and dived into the water. They stood at the edge of the ice then, and watched as the rest of the herd pushed slowly past into the flat grey expanse of the western ocean, moving darkly among the bright ice-floes.

Job had the Remington now. Ross went over to him. The quiet after the animal carillon carried their voices quite clearly.

"Job, what's wrong? Why the rifle?"

"In case he wanted to stay."

"What?"

"They ride on floes; rest on them, in piles. It's the way they move."

"What are you talking about, Job?"

"Don't you see? There must be nearly two hundred of them. If even half of them came up here they'd tear the floe to pieces, smash it up, coming up through, piling up. They'd destroy us! And this is the only big floe for miles."

There was a little silence, then Simon said, "Well, it's just as well they've gone!"

They automatically looked at the vanishing herd. And as they did so, two of the walruses suddenly hurled completely out of the water, rushing maybe ten feet into the air, bursting like paper bags.

Kate screamed. Simon went towards her. Job and Ross knew

190

what had happened and stood silently side by side, their eyes narrowing, searching the churning water.

Beyond the herd they saw them, an arrow-head formation of black sail fins.

And then the walruses turned and, floundered wildly through the water, tearing each other, screaming with panic, started coming back with all the slow, terrible destructive force of a tidal wave.

iii

The leader had been travelling at more than thirty knots when he hit the first walrus, and, although in the water his vast body had no weight, the force of his charge was enough to hurl his target, itself weighing more than a ton, nearly ten feet into the air. In the time-honoured mode of complete surprise, he hurled suddenly up out of the dark depths, from the quarter where attack was least expected. As a vehicle travelling at a similar speed will destroy much of anybody it hits, so the whale destroyed the walrus: it was dead even before its body started falling; and even before the massive corpse hit the water again, three more of its companions were similarly destroyed.

Walrus did not normally form a large part of the whales' diet, for they could be fearsome enemies when roused; but the mothers with their calves were too great a temptation to resist. The whales struck at the vulnerable centre of the herd, but the old bulls in the lead and the cows at the rear were on to the attack almost instantly, swimming with surprising speed against their black and white enemies, heads back and tusks held out like three-foot spears before them. Without fear or hesitation, twenty in all swam into the carnage to do battle, twenty more covered the retreat of the panicking families.

Most at risk among the whales were the young males whose excitement dulled their caution. Several of them were feeding voraciously upon the slowly sinking body of a particularly heavy female which the leader had chosen as his first target. Among those was a male less than five years old, and this was his first major attack against a walrus herd. He knew that caution was needed, for he had seen during his youth what walrus were capable of doing, but in the excitement for a few fatal seconds he forgot. Oblivious to all else he tore great mouthfuls of blubber and meat from the shoulder of the dead victim, and wolfed them down, holding himself steady, with flippers spread and the great flukes of his tail moving sluggishly, as he guided his body down after his falling feast.

He was attacked by two old male walruses at once, and destroyed almost before he had had a chance to react. The first walrus plunged its tusks into the bulging muscles of his neck just behind his sleek head. With all the force in its massive chest the walrus drove its tusks more than two feet into the whale's flesh, then it wrenched them sideways, tearing them free, and breaking its enemy's neck. The other swam up under the sleek belly and used its great blunt ivory daggers to equal effect, disembowelling the whale with one massive jerk of its neck.

Others of the whales were in no better case. Although the slaughter of the walruses continued, there were casualties among the attackers also. Here, one tusk – the other was a broken stump barely protruding from the mouth – was driven down with such force that it split a sleek black head; there, two bodies slowly sank, the tusks of the dead walrus impaling the throat of a dead whale. For all the great maroon bodies torn and bleeding, there was a considerable toll of ragged slashes on harlequin faces, flanks, backs. Even the leader was held at bay by three old cows whose curving tusks cost him more scars on his head, before he broke the resolve of one, and the two who still could do so, then joined the slow, bloody retreat.

He tasted the diluted blood on the broad blade of his tongue and screamed with delight. Gaining speed, he was quickly back in the midst of the mêlée, whirling, diving, jumping, snapping, tearing and rending with the rest. The old bull with his slightly broken left tusk turned to meet him as he came. It had already crippled two whales and killed a third, using knowledge hammered past the thick bones of its head by a long full life in the Arctic; and as it saw the great bulk of its new adversary loom among the blood-thick foam it turned from the body of its last victim, pulling its long tusk from eyesocket and brain with a convulsive heave of its whole body.

For a moment they paused, circling around each other, then

the leader attacked. The old bull jerked its head back in its time-honoured gesture of attack and defence. The leader swirled clear just in time to avoid the downward slash, but the charge that followed it caught him unawares, and the full force of the walrus's huge body concentrated behind the heavy bones of its skull crashed with sickening force into his ribs. The air exploded from his lungs. He fought his way to the surface, dazed and sickened by the terrible force of the blow. For those moments he was totally defenceless. The old bull flipped over on to its back and swam up beneath its enemy, already jerking its tusks from side to side in anticipation of the disembowelling movement it would perform as it sank them into the leader's unprotected belly. But the leader was not wholly unprotected. His consort, not far away, saw the danger clearly enough, and, with a great scream, she threw herself through the water between the walrus and her mate, totally unconcerned by the danger to herself.

But even before she came anywhere near the walrus, she was hurled aside by a young male who also dashed to the rescue. And to his death. Concerned only with protecting the leader he gave no thought to protecting himself, and it was into his belly the tusks were thrust. A great cloud of bubbles and blood exploded out of him as the ivory spears wrenched to one side, and he turned slowly on to his back, rigid and dying as his intestines were torn out.

The old bull turned to meet the big female as she followed up her attack, still fighting to give her mate time to recover; but before the battle was truly joined the leader had returned. The mate held back on his cry of command, and the leaders of the two battling herds closed again. Once again the old bull pulled its head back and charged at the leader, tusks out-thrust; again the leader swirled aside at the last moment before the longer tusk cut into his flesh, but this time he twisted his body through an extra few degrees so the walrus's head rushed under his belly, and only its shoulder hit the white flesh. The leader whirled round, mouth agape, but the walrus had turned also, half on its back, tusks still thrust out. The leader went for the old bull's rear flippers, but they were jerked beyond his reach, and the blunt broken tusk scraped the length of his back without doing any damage.

Once again they faced each other, a little more than five yards apart. Oblivious of the battle still raging around them they held themselves motionless in the water, each waiting for the other to make the first move; then they began to close. The walrus reared its head back again, staring over the great bridge of its nose. The killer put his sleek head down and thrust his body forward at increasing speed, stretching forward, his mouth opening, seemingly going for the throat. At the last moment the walrus, its nerve broken, brought its chin down to protect its chest and neck from the killer's teeth. The killer, shifting his attack, opened his mouth delicately, and caught hold of the walrus's upper lip, pulled up by the movement of its head down through the water. It was the walrus's only weak spot, and the leader had caught it perfectly. With a great wrench of his long, sleek body, he dragged the old bull's head down further and, keeping clear of the wildly slashing tusks, he dragged the walrus into the depths. The old bull's breath, already short, ran out in the next few moments, and long before the leader felt the need to breathe, the walrus had ceased to struggle and the last silver bubbles of its breath were struggling towards the surface.

Almost as slowly, the leader followed them up.

What had been a battle was now a rout. Thirty of the walruses were dead or too badly wounded to swim, for the loss of five whales. The family units, their flanks and rear protected by the remnants of the old males and females who had borne the brunt of the killers' attacks, were in full flight towards the only protection which offered – that of the floe. The whales, their killing instincts still fully aroused and, if anything, extended by the ten or fifteen bloody minutes of the battle, were in full and wild pursuit. The grey water all along the east side of the floe was alive with screaming brown and maroon heads with their dully flashing tusks. All were heading through the steel-grey foam towards the safety of the ice.

The leader, seeing all of this, and as yet unaware of the fact that the survivors of his early attacks were still on the floe, gave a great cry and thrust himself back into the attack.

He had swum perhaps five yards before the first shots rang out.

iv

"Good Christ, they're coming back!" yelled Simon Quick. He ran to the edge of the ice overlooking the churning water and turned unsteadily on the ice. "They're coming back!"

Job's lips moved silently as he watched the first moments of the attack. He was a religious man, and he was not about to call Quick to order for calling upon his God. His own prayers, however, were addressed to an older, wilder deity – Aipalookvik the Destroyer. But Innuit are a practical race, and he knew well enough that prayers unsupported by action weigh little with any god; so, with the words still moving his lips, he turned towards the supply tent and the rifles.

Kate, not understanding the implication of what she saw, asked Job what he was doing.

"I've told you. They'll tear the floe apart, destroy us. We must keep them off." And he was gone.

She turned to Ross, who was rushing towards the sleeping tent where the clothes were. "Colin, are we really – "

She was going to ask were they really going to kill these poor creatures caught between two forces they did not understand. Ross answered her question before she had even formed it.

"Yes. We have to. Job's right – they'll bury us. We have to keep them off. . . Now come and get the warm clothes: this may be a long job. Hurry!"

He turned and gestured to Simon who began to stumble towards them. They waited a moment, and when he arrived, the three of them set off together towards the tent and the warm damp clothes.

While they were dressing, Job was busy in the second tent where they had moved the guns during the rainstorm. He made sure the Remington and the Weatherby were fully loaded, and put aside twenty more shells for each; then he started work on the carbines, making sure the action was free, whispering a prayer to Kaila, great God of the sky, and another to Torgasoak, tall one-armed protector of Innuit, that the mechanisms would function properly in the cold. Then he laid out the magazines ready. There were five guns in all. Many less than they needed. As he was making his preparations, his mind sped

195

through the possibilities. Obviously, even if the automatic carbines worked perfectly, they would be unable to keep all the walruses from coming on to the ice, so they would need something for close fighting. He sorted out the three silver gleaming harpoons and laid them beside the guns. And they could use the axe as well, he thought. If the carbines jammed they would need to use the axe, the harpoons, anything.

God help them if the carbines seized.

Ross, Kate and Simon were dressed in moments, and were rushing back across the net towards the tent as Job came out through the flap, a rifle in each hand.

"Get the carbines. I'll dress," he said to Ross, and was off at an easy surefooted lope.

"Get the carbines." Ross passed the terse order on to Kate and Simon, then he was heading for the other supply tent with its gaping side. Simon paused, frowning, but Kate obeyed immediately and without thought.

"Come on, Simon," she yelled over her shoulder, and he followed.

In the supply tent, Colin was moving the pieces of the boat around, looking for a coil of rope. Most of the rope was being used to hold the net in place, and the floe together, forty-foot strands of it radiating from the corners and sides of the orange square. But he came out with the last heavy coil hung over his shoulder. The rifles were leaning against the side of the tent where Job was changing. Simon had two of the carbines, Kate one and the ammunition. Ross shrugged the rope on to the ground with a crisp smack.

"Cut two forty-foot pieces," he said, and went back into the tent for the harpoons.

Again it was Kate who reacted first. She put the carbines and the ammunition beside the rifles and hefted the axe. It took her a couple of minutes to unravel the jumble of forty feet and measure it by eye against the twenty foot sides of the net. She was cutting the second length when Job came out of the tent.

"What are you doing?" he yelled, at the top of his voice, over the cacophony of screams, groans, grunts and cries coming from the terrified walrus herd.

"Cutting rope, Colin said."

Ross came out of the storage tent, the harpoons glistening

196

under his arm. "Good," he said. "Now three twenty-foot pieces." Kate began to measure and cut.

"Do we have time for this?" asked Job, lifting his hand and gesturing towards the red-foaming battleground which was surging towards them like an avalanche.

"Got to," said Ross. "We'll use the long bits round our waists. I'll take Kate, you take Simon. That way anyone who gets in trouble will get help."

Job nodded. He was about to ask why Kate wasn't his partner – she wouldn't be much help to Colin if he went down, but she might be able to at least pull his own lighter body to safety – when he saw Simon Quick and realised the two at either end of a rope would have to act as a team or they wouldn't stand a chance. Ross and Kate stood side by side tying the rope round their waists. Job watched them move smoothly and in unison. Unnoticed during the last few days, something of central importance had sprung up between them, and it was as though they had been working together all their lives. He wondered if they realised yet that they were tied together by much more than the rope.

He turned and picked up the end of his own rope. Simon was already tying his end in place. Ross glanced up at Kate, who was tugging the knot round her bulky waist. Her teeth flashed in a lean smile.

Job went back to the tent-side and got the Weatherby and a carbine. He handed the latter to Quick, who made a negative gesture with his hand and went and got the Remington. Job shrugged and gave him the shells from his pocket. They stood between the camp and the sea, on the eastern edge of the floe, the rope between them in coils on the ice.

Colin took a carbine and five clips of bullets. Kate did the same. On the way past the fire, he picked up the axe and slipped it through the rope around his waist. Kate picked up a harpoon and one of the shorter pieces of rope. She tied the rope to the end of the harpoon, and looped it ready to go over her wrist when she needed to use the silver spear. Colin loped off until the rope grew taut. Then they moved together towards the northern edge of the floe.

Out on the ocean, terrifyingly close, was the wildly screaming crescent of the walrus herd. There were more than a hundred and seventy of them in all, not counting the young, and they were swimming with slow, unshakeable, terrifying purpose towards the floe. Suddenly, behind them, a great black and white shape reared up out of the water, a great scream echoed even through the terrible noise, and the killer hurled itself forward.

They opened up. Ross, on one knee, had the carbine on automatic and was spraying the walruses, trying to turn them. Job, however, was shooting deliberately, like a marksman, with the Weatherby. After each whipcrack of his rifle, a head would sprout a brief aura of red, and begin to sink. Simon was doing the same with the Remington, but there were fewer red auras, fewer deaths. Kate put her carbine on single-shot and began to shoot smoothly and accurately.

The herd hesitated. One or two turned, only to turn back again. Ross snapped the carbine off automatic and threw away the first empty clip. It took him several moments to fit the second, and he cursed Simon under his breath – he had practised with enough rifles to be able to shoot and re-load them as smoothly and easily as a man with two hands, but this carbine was different. Eventually he held it upside down under his left arm and wedged the curving clip in with his right hand.

When he brought it up again the walruses were very much closer. He glanced down at Kate. She was standing, legs spread, torso turned a little, mittens hanging like spare hands, leaning into her shots like a professional. He nodded, smiled, slammed his own carbine back to his shoulder. He squeezed off short bursts of three or four bullets at a time. He swung his sights down the lines of bobbing heads, squeezing the trigger and passing on, each target exploding into a shapeless mess, tusks falling like trees. He threw away his second clip and his mind came out of the gun for long enough to realise there were tears on his face. He felt sick. Great God, this was a terrible thing they were doing. Had they the right, even in these circumstances, to slaughter these strange, ungainly, oddly beautiful animals? His conscience doubted, but his hands did not. Even as he wondered, his body without pause or hesitation turned the carbine upside down and re-loaded it. By the time his mind came to a pause in its train of thought, the stock of the

198

carbine was at the shoulder again and his right forefinger had squeezed the trigger.

Kate's mind was a blank. She had never killed anything, nor ever wanted to. She felt guilty even about her anger against the whales. And yet, there she was, shooting like a seasoned warrior. Why was she doing it? To survive? To protect herself? *To protect Colin?* The thought hit her right between the eyes. Her faced jerked towards him; his jerked towards her, and their eyes met.

The walrus exploded out of the water and slammed its tusks into the ice with the force of a pile-driver three feet from Kate's right boot. She screamed, stumbled back, fell. Colin, swinging smoothly from the waist, blew its head open. Kate picked herself up, and went back into the war. She put the rifle to her shoulder again, but she had to point it almost straight down before she found anything to shoot at. The walruses were there beneath her feet! Panic ran up her spine.

The rope jerked at her waist. Colin was falling back; she went with him. One moment there was just one walrus at the edge of the ice, its corpse like a lone sentinel frozen into position; then, all at once, there were twenty, and the floe was juddering as they erupted in unison and crashed their huge tusks into the ice. The sound was terrifying. Colin had the rifle at his hip and was spraying them wildly with bullets. She swung herself back to the hulking maroon-brown wall with the great yellow-white bars of the tusks. Many of them were on the move, humping forward, raising their tusks to drive them in again, their great flippers gripping the ice, pulling them forward.

The first row of walruses were still half in and half out of the water – many of them slowed down by gunshot wounds – when a second row arrived and, totally panicked, hurled themselves up out of the water, and – as there was no clear ice – drove their tusks into the backs of the creatures before them. Then they too began to hump forward as fast as they could.

Ross and Kate froze. The second row hauled themselves over the first – and just as they did so a third arrived and also drove their tusks indiscriminately into ice and quivering flesh before they humped up out of the sea. The noise grew, as the outer row screamed in panic, and the inner two – those still alive – screamed in agony.

199

By the time Colin and Kate started firing again there were more than fifty walruses on the ice before them, lumbering forward in confusion, but with terrible purpose.

Simon and Job were more fortunate. The beginning of that small hill from which Doctor Warren had fallen swept down along their edge of the floe, not only giving them an excellent vantage point to shoot from, but also presenting the walruses with a crystal wall which they had no chance of climbing. As soon as they began to come up where Colin was at the north of the floe, Job fell back to cover the other edges of the ice, but Simon, carried away with bloodlust, did not notice the Eskimo's movement, and would not answer the urgent tugs on the rope round his waist. Perhaps they could have stopped them coming up at the bottom of the floe if Quick had moved faster; perhaps not. In any case, by the time they got to the south of the tents, what was happening on the north of the floe in front of Colin and Kate was happening there, within ten yards of the camp.

Colin was still cursing Simon for taking the Remington, as he wedged the carbine under the club of his left arm and began fitting the clip. It wouldn't go in! He breathed three times deeply and began again. When the rope jerked, the long shape of the gun went skidding away over the ice, and the clip arced away through the air. He knew better than to look at Kate. He swung towards the walruses and saw a bull charging, tusks on a level with his chest, ready to tear him to pieces. The bull was perhaps seventeen feet long. It stood more than six feet from flippers to head. Its tusks were four feet long. It weighed a little less than two tons, and it was going to kill him.

His mind shifted smoothly into top gear. He jerked the axe from the rope belt round his waist, and began to run forward towards the walrus. At the last moment before the dripping tusks tore him open, he dived to one side, feet skidding crazily on the ice, swung round, and buried the axe in its neck with all the strength in his arm, shoulder and back, intending to sever the spine between its shoulders and head. But the ice, treacherous under his boots, spoiled his aim, and the deadly blade turned in his hands and smashed into its shoulder, doing little damage. Ross jerked it free as the creature turned and charged again. This time he did not throw himself aside. The axe was four feet long; his arm well over two feet long – he had two more feet of reach than the walrus's tusks. He met the charge head on, bringing the axe down between its eyes with almost insane force, screaming as he did so. The bull collapsed on the spot, its tusks driving again into the ice, inches from his boots. He jerked the haft of the axe, but the blade remained buried in the walrus's massive forehead. He jerked it again. Nothing.

He went back to the end of the haft to exert the maximum amount of leverage. The cliff of walruses nearly ten feet high hulked unsteadily over him. He stooped to tug at the axe again.

The first of the killers hurled itself out of the water on to the pile of walruses, snapping and tearing. The floe rocked and settled further. Ross's feet skidded again and he fell. Kate was back thirty feet from him, keeping the rope taut, and she was pulled on to her knees as he fell, but, with the genius which comes to some people under pressure, she drove the carbine into the soft floe, belayed the rope round it and held it firm with her full weight. Ross stopped sliding. The killer fell back into the water.

Colin's feet were only a couple of yards away from the mountain of walruses. He twisted, found his footing, grabbed the axe and hauled himself erect. The steel head came free. He began to move.

The leader and his consort hurled themselves out of the water now, followed by more of the pack. They landed on the screaming pile of walruses snapping, chewing, tearing.

Ross suddenly found himself up to his knees in water. He began to run towards Kate. Behind him, the unsteady wall of walruses broke like a wave, tumbling forward, burying the body of the old bull.

Ross ran on but he was suddenly running up hill.

And there was a sound like thunder. The rope snapped taut. The gun tore out of the ground and sailed away over the ice. Kate saw the ice just beyond her feet rear up into a cliff, the rope at her waist leading up, over its crystal edge.

The floe had cracked in two, and Colin was on the other half.

The rope round her waist snapped taut, almost lifting her off the ice, the loop ripping up her back until it caught under her arms. She stood up, moving her body carefully because it felt as if the rope had stripped off most of the skin between waist and neck. Thank God, she thought, I wasn't facing the other way.

201

Abruptly the rope loosened, and as Kate looked across the five feet of agitated water, there was Colin standing unsteadily fighting for his balance. Kate began to run backwards tightening the rope. He jumped. The axe flew out of his hand. The rope snapped taut, he lurched forward in the air. She fell. He crashed into the ice thirty feet away from her just at the new edge of the floe.

As their half of the floe had lurched in the water, Job and Simon were hurled down on the net and a wave of icy water washed up among the advancing walruses. The killers had been following the main body of the herd, so there were none down here as yet, and Simon and Job had had no trouble in controlling the sluggish advance of the great maroon creatures. There were maybe twenty left out of the first surge. The ice was now the colour of beech-leaves in autumn and was littered with the great still sacks of their corpses.

But the floe's sudden lurch had a disastrous effect on Simon, for, as he stumbled on the net and fell, he sent the Remington tumbling end over end towards the water. The wave which swept up among the corpses at the edge of the ice took the sleek rifle lovingly and sucked it into the ocean.

"Oh, for fuck's sake," said Simon. He picked himself up wearily, slipped his mittens back over his hands and picked up one of the harpoons. He began to tie the rope to the end so that he wouldn't lose it.

Job continued firing at the advancing walruses. Until he turned and saw the walrus which, unnoticed by either of them, had broken through the rotten ice between the camp and the hill, its approach covered by the shadow of the second empty sleeping tent, hulking towards Simon, burst through the tent, totally destroying it, and rushed towards Simon's back. "Simon!" screamed Job now, but his voice was lost. He jerked the Weatherby up to his shoulder and shot the monster in the head, but the light high velocity bullet simply glanced off the huge tough bony dome of its skull. This was a job for the Remington, but the Remington was gone. Job ran forward as fast as he could. Simon was still tying the rope to the harpoon, blissfully unaware. Job stopped and squeezed off another shot. The top of the creature's head seemed to vanish, but still its advance did not stop.

Job was only feet away now. Pulled the trigger. The gun jammed. He reversed it in his hands, holding it by the barrel, swinging the stock up like a club, running forward as the walrus swung its head back, the rolls of fat behind its stub of a neck bulging, for the killing stroke.

At last Simon heard something over the wild noise and turned.

Job brought the gun down on the bloody crown of the creature's head, just as its tusks began to tear down. The stock splintered. The jar of the stroke numbed Job's whole body. The walrus turned, its stroke uncompleted, the tusks still inches from Simon's chest, and bellowed. Job stumbled back and fell, helpless. The walrus began to move towards him, still screaming; blood poured down its face, ran down its tusks and chest in a sluggish stream. Job floundered backwards, looking for something, anything, to protect himself with – but knowing there was nothing.

Simon discovered he was still holding the harpoon, and before his mind could react to the situation, his body was in fluid motion. The walrus, in turning its head towards Job, had exposed its throat to Simon, and, the harpoon, seemingly of its own accord, reached across the few feet which separated the man from the beast.

As though it had always been there, a silver shaft suddenly sprang from the walrus's flopping maroon throat. Job stopped moving and looked at it, astounded. The walrus tried to turn its head back, but Simon threw himself forward, taking the harpoon under his right arm, and he twisted it deeper with all his wiry strength, until his chest was hard against the monster's shoulder. The walrus tried to bellow again, and a great gout of blood came from its mouth. The flippers slipped. The head dropped. The tusks buried themselves in the ice on either side of Job's ankles.

Ross was still lying stunned on the edge of the floe when another walrus exploded out of the water, hooked itself on to the ice two feet from him and began to lurch forward, bellowing indignantly. He considered moving, but remotely as in a dream. Really it wasn't worth the trouble.

And then Kate was there, wielding the axe caught up off the ice where he had dropped it. He didn't see what she did, but suddenly the walrus was no longer there. Kate was.

"Colin!" Her face was flushed and swollen by the force she had to put into her voice to make it even faintly audible to him, even though she was kneeling over him.

He began to pick himself up. She got up and helped him climb to his feet. For a moment there was a silence. The sea was still, innocent even of the black sail fins. Most of the dead walruses had sunk from sight. Those still alive were under the floe. Ross and Kate might have been a pair of lovers at the seaside, her shoulders tucked so tightly under his right arm, their heads so close together, their breath mingling in a pale tower above them.

Sluggishly at first, and then with increasing force the surviving walruses began to climb on to the other floe. By the time Ross and Kate thought to move they were piled in an untidy maroon heap slashed with dull yellow of the tusks. They were no longer screaming and over the silent sea came only the occasional ding-dong! of the two-tone bell call.

Ross and Kate turned and began to walk back, tired eyes on stumbling feet. With the other floe there so available and so obviously safe, their own refuge was now safe in turn. They had gone only two steps when Kate stubbed her foot on something sticking out of the ice. They stared at it dully. It was a steel peg. There was an orange rope tied to it. And forty feet from the peg the net began.

There were only a hundred and fifty feet of floe left. They stood, frozen by the realisation.

They had been fighting the walruses for more than an hour and, in that they were still alive, they had won. But they had lost so much of the floe that the piece they were on could only just contain their camp. And they had lost most of their stores also. Only those items they had moved into the dry were still undamaged, with the pieces of the boat, and the dynamite. They had lost all the guns. They had lost the will to fight any more; they had almost lost the will to live.

V

As the leader came under the humans' floe, he almost casually

204

took a final bull walrus floating vertically, its head above the water. They had had a good killing. They had taken more than fifty prime walruses, not counting the babies, for the cost of seven whales in all. The leader was deeply content, for, on top of all this, there were still the humans . . .

He had joined in the fighting with the rest of the pack, and had done more than his fair share of the killing, but at the same time, he had been intensely aware of their presence above the thin layer of ice. At first there had been the shots, then the occasional distinctive tones of their voices easily distinguished from the other sounds of the battle. The old uncontrolled excitement burned in him. As the slaughter slowly stopped, he sent out excited cries to the others of the pack, but only his mate and one young male answered. Confused, he circled both floes until, away to the west, he heard the cries of the rest of them.

He went once more round the floe, took the last walrus, and followed.

Five miles to the west, a quarter of an hour later, he caught up with them. An older male was in the lead, moving sluggishly along. The leader joined him, swimming slower and slower until they all stopped. For the next few hours they remained there, playing gently sleepy games, dozing, recovering.

Then, as the sun began to climb invisibly behind the dull curtain of the clouds, the leader gave a brief signal, and began to swim east again, back to the floe.

He had swum for several minutes before he had realised only his mate and the one young bull were following.

Confused, he turned back, and the rest of the pack were waiting, where he had left them. He made the sound of command again, and this time they began to follow him slowly. It took them nearly an hour to come anywhere near the floe, and when they did, the pack faltered again and stopped.

The leader swam among them, ordering, nudging, threatening, but to no avail. They would move no further. He swam on ahead of them again; and, again, only the young male and his mate would follow.

He swam round and round the sullen collection of silent whales. There were still ten of them, with the calf, more than enough to destroy the humans now the floe was so small, the ice so thin. If they would attack with him now, it would be over in a matter of moments. With increasing desperation he swam round them, but they would go no further. They were sated. And they did not share his conditioned joy in killing humans.

For a moment he was tempted to stay with them, but he had lived alone at the anchorage for so long that the ties of his kind were not strong in him. Certainly they were nowhere near as strong as the need to feel the heady excitement of the kill. So he swam round them one last time, and then headed purposefully east. His consort and the young bull followed.

The rest of the pack waited until the three had faded from sight in the rich water, and then began to move slowly south, following their new leader, one or two of them sending out locational calls in case the true leader should want to return to them later, when he had done what he had to do.

ELEVEN

Simon lifted his hands until they rested against the cold flesh of the dead walrus and pushed himself upright. The spear came out from under his right arm, and vibrated slightly in the monster's throat. Simon looked around. It was all much the same as it had been before the walruses came, heavy grey sky pressing on the leaden sea, only the floes having brightness or colour. And the other floe, bearing the surviving walruses, was already some five hundred yards away to the right, caught in a chance current, and dwindling as he watched.

His tired eyes swept over the wreck of their own refuge. There were twenty corpses still lying around the camp, twenty-one counting the one he was standing beside. Only the latrine-cum-storage tent and the tent originally occupied by Ross and Job were still standing.

Where his own original tent had been there was a round black hole, with a spider's web of crack radiating from it. And there was another hole behind him, beyond this walrus. What was left of the floe was now a rough oblong – seventy yards by fifty – and already punched with two holes. Quick shivered.

Still, they couldn't just stand around till they froze to death, could they? It was obvious that if they were to save anything from the destroyed storage tent, they should start work at once. Of the tent itself there was no sign, but the pieces of the boat, disassembled and stored in case it got blown away during the storm, lay around seemingly undamaged. The box of dynamite stood on its end on the badly cracked and uneasily shifting pieces of ice at the edge of the hole. Broken crates and burst tins, chunks of orange ice and broken glass littered the immediate area.

"God, what a mess."

His tired voice was surprisingly loud over the quiet champing and lapping sounds coming from the two holes. He brought up his right hand to scratch the itchy stubble of his chin, only to find it caked with blood on the palm, down to the end of the heavy mitten. He turned it over with a grimace of disgust and rubbed his face with the back of his hand. He looked down at himself. Not too bad – blood on his anorak and overtrousers, but not much. He walked over to Job. The Eskimo was lying flat on his back and so still that for a moment of panic Simon thought he was dead. His hood was up, protecting his head from the cold, and his legs and boots were badly covered with the walrus's blood. Simon went down on one knee and shook him.

Job stirred and snored, turned a little and settled back to sleep. Simon felt relief sweep over him, and with it an insane desire to laugh.

"Job! Job, wake up you lazy bastard! This is no time for forty winks." He thumped the Eskimo's shoulder, and was rewarded by a grunt.

"Ye Gods!" He leaned forward and shook him with all his might. Job's head rolled from side to side. His eyes opened, dark and distant, and closed once more. Simon began to get worried again. He dragged Job's inert body out from under the walrus's head, and half propped him against the tent-side. Job's eyes opened again, this time with some sign of returning intelligence. Simon left him as he began to stir and went over to Ross and Kate.

"Fire," he said.

"What?"

"We must build up a fire. Quickly. There's dry wood in the tent."

"Yes. Of course!" Colin felt a stab of impatience with Simon, then he realised the little man was thinking more clearly than he. Job would be all right when he warmed up a bit. He turned to Kate. "Make some coffee," he said.

"We'll have trouble getting water." She gestured at the blood-dabbled ice.

"Sod it. Blood'll probably do us good."

"If you say so." She began to dig.

Colin got up and went over to the latrine tent which was now doubling as a store. He got out two half-pound tins of ham, several cans of beans, and dried egg powder and went back to the fire with a big pot. Warm drink, some food, medicine – he shifted, feeling the sticking of his shirt warning of bleeding on his ribs – and sleep. That was what they all needed.

Before they started the cooking, they put Job inside the tent, took off his anorak, boots and overtrousers, and wrapped him in blankets and sleeping-bags. Then they went outside again. Kate began to make the coffee, Colin dumped his big pot on the flames. They heated the ham in two solid chunks, poured on the beans, waited until they began to bubble, then added the egg. In all it took perhaps half an hour, and during this time they all chatted amiably, their differences for once forgotten.

They ate. Fortunately the plates were among the things they had moved to safety, for the set which they had kept by the fire-tray had been destroyed during the attack by the walruses. Conversation over the meal was sporadic.

Then Kate got up and went into the tent. The Eskimo had been allowed to sleep long enough. "Job? Food's ready."

He stirred. "My God," he said, mildly surprised, "we're still alive."

"That's right," she said.

"I really didn't think we'd make it."

"But we did."

He nodded. It felt very good. Simply being alive felt very good indeed. He smiled.

"How long has it been now?" she asked.

"I don't know. Five days. Maybe more."

"Five days. It feels longer."

"Maybe."

She heard the roar of the fire outside and the quiet tones of the conversation between Colin and Simon. It seemed so normal. So matter of fact and natural. They might have been here for ever. They might be here for ever. The prospect, nebulous, improbable, didn't frighten Kate at all. Strangely, she felt deeply content. It was as though something had promised her that she would come through all right, unscathed.

"Job?"

"Yes?"

"Is that why you stay with him, because he reminds you of this one-armed god?"

Job gave a half-laugh. "Partly. I suppose you could say so."

"Only partly?" She did not mean to be rude, or to be patronising towards Job's beliefs, but she wanted to know. She was deeply interested.

"What do you want me to say? It is a childish coincidence that he resembles Torgasoak, true; and yet . . ." He thought for a while, trying to define his almost religious regard for his friend, trying to put it in a way she would understand. "Among Innuit," he said quietly, dreamily, "there is a belief that a man can only become a shaman, a truly powerful person, a man who can control the Inua and communicate with the gods, in only one way. He must be eaten by the white Bear and survive."

"And Colin had his arm chewed by the polar bear on the first night . . ."

He laughed. "Yes, there is that, but no, it's not what I meant. It was what Jeremiah told me of the Antarctic. The storm there, when it came in its final stage came as a white bear. There was no doubt in his mind, you see, and he placed certainty in my mind also."

"He loved Colin Ross, too."

"Oh no. Jeremiah hated him during those last few days. I have never seen such hatred in a man." Job shook his head.

Kate's head snapped back, her eyes wide, searching Job's calm face. "He hated him? But why? I mean, Colin saved him . . ."

"Yes. That was it, you see. Jeremiah wanted to die in the cold. You don't understand . . ." He paused again, thinking carefully. "Jeremiah knew he was dead when he broke his leg. There was no chance of surviving after that. For a while he might live, but he would never walk, he would never know a woman. And he was a proud man, Jeremiah, he would take nothing from anyone. He hated a debt, and he died owing Colin an arm, owing him a life he didn't even want."

"But his testimony saved Colin's reputation."

"True. He was never a small-minded man, my brother. He would not strike back like that. If he could not do it man to man, he would leave it to spirits more powerful than he."

"And you? How do you feel about it?"

"There is a death joining us. I will stay with him and help him if he needs helping, until the debt is paid."

"But you haven't been near him in five years!"

"We have been close enough." There was silence. Suddenly Job seemed to her to have become a strangely sinister figure. She remembered the fear his quiet voice had engendered in her on the 'plane when she had first met him. The basic fundamental pattern of his and Colin's relationship as she saw it had been upset, and she was by no means certain whose side the debt was on; whether Job felt he owed Colin a life, or whether he expected to take one.

Kate frowned, trying to understand. Anywhere else, with any other people involved, it would be too ridiculous for words; and yet she found she could believe it of the strange, silent Eskimo torn between two fundamentally opposing cultures, full of strange mystical beliefs which seemed to make so much sense up here in this nightmare environment.

"But you think he's one of these shamans?"

"I don't know. What I believe is of no importance. Jeremiah believed. I said I would be here at an ending. I swore. I will be here."

"An ending?" She didn't really want to know, but she had to ask.

"Yes. I swore. Until an ending: his or mine. It is necessary for Jeremiah."

"Do you really believe all of this?" Her voice was strident.

"It is of no importance." His voice was weary. He had fallen into the trap he feared for the others. He had revealed too much of himself to this girl. He could not stay with her any longer, now that she knew so much, for she would try to find out more, and God alone knew where that might lead. He pulled himself to his feet, put on his anorak, overtrousers and boots, and went outside.

For several moments, Kate waited, her mind trying to fathom it, a strange sense of unreality making her doubt everything about her. Then she got up and followed him outside.

Colin and Simon were crouched over the fire-tray, and Job was picking up stuff from around the wreck of the storage tent, putting the tins he had collected into the latrine-cum-storage tent.

"More coffee?" asked Colin.

"Long as it's hot," she said absently.

For a while they remained as they were, the two men bending assiduously over the fire, the girl reserved, distant, watching the Eskimo with narrowed eyes. Then Colin asked, "What is it, Kate?"

"Umm? Oh. Nothing." She frowned, angry with herself – no sooner had she decided it would be unwise to dig further into what Job had told her than she was making it quite obvious that there was something wrong. She joined them and, much to his relief, took the pot away from Colin, who went to help Job.

"What's the matter with Kate?" he asked, quietly, in case his voice carried.

"She asked too many questions."

"And you answered them?"

"Yes."

"Was that wise, Job?"

"It was not wise, no."

They took the last of the tins into the new storage tent with its untidy pile of boxes and its single evil-smelling chemical toilet. There was no more to be said, so they silently cleared the glass and the orange ice off the floe and dumped it all into the quietly slopping hole around which it lay.

"It won't take much more," said Ross, looking around at the remains of the floe.

"No," said Job. "Three days if the weather holds, and if the killers stay away."

"Will they?"

"Who knows? Perhaps Jeremiah has the ear of Aipalookvik after all."

Ross gave a half smile. "No. He'll wait to settle his own debts later. If this is anyone's work, it's Hers." He gestured south over half the world.

"Perhaps." It was Job's turn to smile.

It may be that they were both a little mad, talking of dead men and continents as though they had power and could order events. But neither thought himself or the other even slightly insane.

"Come and get it, Job," yelled Kate.

When Job was finished he wandered off alone again. The rest of them cleared away, washed up and went to bed. By the time Job came back over the restless ice and climbed quietly into the tent, they were all sound asleep. For a while he lay in his sleeping-bag, cramped uneasily between Ross and Simon, his eyes still full of the dead grey of sky and sea, the livid blue of the floes; his mind restless with the problems his talk with Kate had thrown up. How much did he owe to the memory of a dead brother, how much to a religion he only half believed? He was still wondering when he too fell asleep.

They all slept peacefully for nearly six hours. Job tossed and turned a little at first, and Kate moaned when she lay on her back; but Simon and Colin slept like the dead, undisturbed by memories or dreams. Far above them the clouds began to thin out, and the day, tending towards evening, silently brightened. The sea remained quiet, disturbed only slightly by a gentle breeze freshening from the east. The floes stirred restlessly, brightening with the sky, champing quietly one against the other. A flock of birds flew high swift towards Alaska, disturbing the air with only one or two cries and a distant humming of wings, and the ocean answered with its own quiet songs – the cries of three hunting whales.

Job never knew precisely why he woke then, but suddenly he found himself sitting up straight, tense with some unremembered fear. He looked around the tent. The rest were quietly asleep. He lay down again, but he could not get his eyes to close. In any case he needed to go to the toilet. He rose silently, went to the tent-flap and let himself out. There was a wind. The sky looked quite promising. He stretched until his bones cracked, and then went over the gently shifting net towards the latrine-tent.

Simon woke as Job left the tent. He rolled over, and without thinking he too stretched. His right elbow dug into Colin's ribs and his feet thumped squarely into Kate's stomach.

"Oops. Sorry. Forgot we were so crowded."

Silence. After a while Simon too got up and crawled out. Kate turned over and gasped as her raw back bore her weight. Colin sat up, moving his shoulders stiffly. She watched him through half-closed eyes. He straightened up very gingerly indeed, opened his shirt, glanced suspiciously at her apparently sleeping face, and pulled up his undershirt. His flesh was deeply bruised.

"Oh Colin!" She sat up, quite vexed with his childishness. "You need some ointment on those, and bandages."

"I thought you were asleep!" He sounded almost sulky.

"Well I'm not! Let me have a look at you." She rolled out of her sleeping bag and crawled across the tent towards him. He remained as he was, watching her as she moved. "Come on," she snapped, at her most businesslike, "let's have it off."

His eyes opened wide. "I hope the others can't hear . . ."

"You know very well what I mean!" She felt herself blushing, and covered her confusion by rummaging in one corner for the first aid box, and extracting from it a tin of ointment and bandages.

"You'll have to help," he said.

His vest had become entangled with his left arm. Briskly she undid the straps on his chest and removed both.

"There. Now, let's have a look at you." There were welts up his back from the rope, and she dabbed them liberally with the purple ointment. His ribs and chest were another matter, however. On his right side, running from under his arm down to the arch of his solar plexus was a great crusted bruise.

"That's nasty," she said, reaching for the iodine, keeping her voice very practical indeed because of the tightness in her chest. "This might sting a little," she said.

It burned like a hot poker and he winced. Above it, from collar-bone to nipple was another wound, equally bad. She poured iodine over that too, swabbing carefully, acutely aware of how the silky fur on his chest rubbed against her fingers, her palms, the sides and backs of her hands.

She glanced up, and his deep green eyes were searching her face. She suddenly thought of the first time she had seen those eyes. How cold they had seemed to be then. How warm they seemed now.

"I'd better bandage you," she said. He nodded. She got the roll of white material out and held one end high on his chest. His hand came up to hold it for her, and covered her hand for a moment.

"Thank you," she said stupidly.

"That's OK."

She rolled the bandage round and round him as he leaned forward, sideways and back to facilitate the operation. They were both intensely aware of the small, unavoidable bodily contacts of the operation. Her hands against his chest, arm, back; his hand against her arm. Their thighs touching – even through six layers of material. Arms touching. Her hair in his face, on his shoulder. Her breath against his neck; his against hers. Her breasts against his chest, shoulders, arm. His chest, shoulder, arm against her breasts.

"There," she said after a while. She was breathing deeply and could not disguise the fact.

"Got a safety pin?" he asked.

"Oh. Yes."

She turned to get it, and the skin on her back stretched into scalding pain. When she turned back she was pale and there were tears in her eyes. He took the pin without comment and fixed the bandage comfortably.

"Now you," he said.

"What did you say?" she gasped.

"Now you. Take off your shirt and vest."

"Colin. I . . ."

He picked up the ointment. "What do you want? A chaperone? Hurry." His eyebrows met briefly in a frown, then he was smiling. "I'll be gentle, I promise."

"That's a line I've heard before." She undid the shirt. She tried to do it quickly, unconcernedly, in a matter of fact way, but it still felt like a strip-tease. She glanced up. He was reading the instructions on the tin of ointment. As her eyes flicked down again, his flicked up. She took the bottom of the vest and pulled it out of the top of her jeans and sealskin overtrousers, loosened it gingerly at the back, crossed her arms and pulled it up in one fluid, unintentionally erotic movement. By the time she had got her head untangled from the warm material, he was reading the instructions on the tin again.

"You'll have those off by heart soon," she said, relaxing her shoulders and crossing her hands in her lap. His eyes did not meet hers directly, they paused at chest level for a moment, then moved up.

"If you would lean forward . . ." He held up his arms, the left ending just below the shoulder. She leaned to the left until her shoulder rested against his chest. The ointment was cold, and stung. She hollowed her back automatically and crushed her breasts against him. She froze, intensely aware of the contact.

"I'm sorry," he said. "Did that sting?"

215

"No. Cold," she said.

She bowed her back again, and he rubbed gently. Because there was nowhere else she could put them with any degree of comfort, she put her arms lightly round his waist. His hand on her back felt very good indeed. Her eyes half closed. There was a little smile on her face. She moved her cheek unconsciously against him like a child seeking assurances. She lost all sense of time, but it seemed a very long while before the hand stopped caressing her back and Colin said, "All right. Finished."

Obediently she sat up, returning her hands to her lap like a schoolgirl. They looked at each other. Her arms came sinuously around his neck and held him in an iron grip as their lips crushed together.

Then Simon Quick erupted through the tent flap screaming, "Colin. Jesus, Colin, they're back! They're out here now going round and round the floe!"

For a moment after Simon's head withdrew from the tent, Colin and Kate stared at each other, the desire slowly draining from their faces. Outside, Simon called again, "Colin!"

Colin began to dress, Kate content to help him strap on his arm before pulling on her own vest, so that while she was pulling on her grubby Arran pullover he was already on his way out on to the floe.

The desire which had come upon her with such unexpected but devastating force was gone now, replaced by an empty feeling which at first she thought was remorse, but which she soon realised was in fact a mixture of anger and fear. Anger at having been interrupted so soon; fear that they might never have another chance. She dragged on her gloves and mittens, pulled back the flap and crawled out.

The three men were standing on the corner of the floe where the split brought about by the walruses joined the line cut by the 'plane crash which had broken when the ghost berg fell. The obvious place for them to have stood was on the low hill, but the whole area beyond the camp, still a good thirty yards to the sea, was hopelessly rotten – so much so that two of the great walrus corpses had silently sunk through the ice while they had slept. The hole in the rotten ice made by the walrus Job and Simon had killed seemed to be growing.

Kate went over towards the three men and joined their line.

216

She thrust her hands deep in the pocked of her anorak. They struck against the Very pistol. It was the closest thing to a gun that they had left. She had better look after it, she thought. Heaven knew when they would need it – what they might need it for. She narrowed her eyes and looked over the water. The backs of the ripples were almost white; the sea regaining its infinitely burnished mirror-surface between the burning floes.

"There," said Job.

He was pointing. Kate followed the line of his arm with her eyes and there, surprisingly close, were the three great black sails moving easily round the floe. As she watched, three clouds of breath exploded up as though at the same signal.

"What are they doing?" Simon.

"Swimming round us." Job.

"I can see that! What are they doing?"

"That's all they're doing." Colin.

"Why?"

"Perhaps they're waiting for the others." Job.

"Oh, Christ. You really think so?" Simon.

"Who knows?" Colin.

"Are they really *that* intelligent?" Simon.

"Yes." Colin.

"Oh Christ."

Silence.

"What'll we do then?" asked Kate, conversationally.

"What *can* we do?" snapped Simon.

"Kill them," she said.

"How?"

The sixty-four thousand dollar question.

"What've we got?" she asked, turning. Colin said nothing, but he was turning with her, going back to the camp.

"What've we got for what?" Simon called after them.

"To kill them with," she yelled back.

"Three harpoons," said Colin.

"The axe, if you're going in that close."

"Right."

"The dynamite, of course. Is there any way we can use the bullets? I mean we've got no rifles, but we've got some ammo left."

"I don't know. We'd have to think."

217

"It's as well you're a fast thinker."

He gave a half-grunt, half-laugh. "Get the harpoons and the axe, would you? I'll try and think up something for the bullets."

The harpoons were lying in various places about the camp. No one had collected them since the fight with the walruses. The axe was back by the fire. She took them to Colin who was on his knees by the latrine tent.

"Excellent," he said, and held up a red and white striped bundle.. "Cut that, please." She cut it carefully with the axe. "Thanks."

"What is it?"

"What I've thought up." He was pushing the red and white bundle into an empty baked beans tin. "All we need now is some way to aim it."

Kate saw that he had simply taken half a dozen rounds of the Remington ammunition, wrapped them in quick burning fuse, and wedged them in the tin. An inch of the fuse stuck out of the middle.

"Right," she said. "Something long. That thing'll be dangerous."

"Yes. The original two-edged sword."

"A good name. But how *do* we aim it? I mean, it's far too dangerous just to throw it. God knows which way round it'll land."

"I know, I know." His eyes were busy. "Gottit. Get me a mug."

"A mug?"

"Just do it."

They were using tin mugs, of about average size, enamelled dark blue. Strong but light. She brought one. The tin just wedged into it, and when it was in it was tight. They tied it by the handle to the end of a three-foot piece of plank.

"There," said Colin when they'd finished. "The tin'll come to bits, the mug'll split, the handle will definitely come off and the rope will break anyway, but not until after the bullets start to go off."

"It'll never take over from the A-bomb."

He looked at her very seriously. "If you have to use it, 'light the red touch paper, and . . .'"

"I know, 'stand well back'."

218

"No. Run like hell."

"Right."

Simon came up to them, gasping. He had run from the edge of the ice in less than ten seconds.

"They've gone," he said. "They've dived. Job thinks they're coming in . . ."

BOOM!

The floe jumped, water slopped out of the long crack under the net. The corpses of the walruses stirred. Job arrived.

BOOM!

The second blow was only an echo of the first, but the rotten ice to the south humped up, and the biggest of the killers came through, water streaming from its scarred face, breath exploding in a cloud behind it. The ice heaved and creaked ominously. The whale looked around balefully, then sank slowly. The body of the walrus nearest the hole slowly rolled over, apparently of its own volition, and vanished as the ice at the edge of the hole cracked and gave way beneath its bulk.

Then the three sails were back in formation, going silently round the floe.

"The dynamite," said Job. "It's our only chance now."

"Cutting our own throats," Colin warned.

"What else is there?" asked Simon.

"Nothing," said Kate.

"So that's that, then," said Job. "Where is it?"

"Here." Colin hefted the box over out of the shadow of the latrine tent, and snapped it open.

For a few moments they were silent, working quietly as a team, Kate holding the axe, Colin cutting short lengths of fuse, Job and Simon handling the dynamite like experts, fusing the stubby sticks and standing them up well clear of the box in its detachable tin lid. After they had done half a dozen, Job said, "Right."

"Six enough?" asked Simon.

"I hope so."

"The floe won't stand any more," said Colin as he got up, but he took up the box as well as the lid.

"If it stands these," said Job.

Skirting the hole where the supply tent had been, they went out over the one hundred feet to the edge of the floe. This section, which had been the eastern edge of the floe, seemed to be the most solid platform still available to them. Colin put down the lid, and then the box with the fuse a little way from it – just in case.

For several moments they stood in silence, searching the quiet sea for the black fins. They each had a box of matches, but only Job and Simon held sticks of dynamite. The minutes stretched on to agonising length. They all began to shift uneasily from foot to foot as the tension became harder to bear. At last Kate turned to Ross and said, "Colin . . ."

"There!" he snapped, pointing. At some distance, perhaps two hundred yards, the three fins silently pushed into the air, like the thorns of some huge rose. Again in unison came the three blasts of air puffing into clouds as the sound came.

Job had his fuse alight. Simon's match blew out. He fumbled, trying to light another. Job took a little run and hurled the stick with all his great strength. It curved up into the air, turning end over end, spitting venomously against the dull sky, and began to fall, far too short. It exploded too soon, a yard above the surface, sending back a wave of air, but hardly disturbing the water. Simon got his fuse burning and turned towards the water, but the whales had vanished. He paused.

"Just throw it," said Colin conversationally.

"What? Oh." He hurled it as far as he could, a long low throw, the dynamite vanishing under the surface before it exploded. They didn't have long to wait, however, before the surface heaved up into a brief powerful column which lingered in the air as the waves washed towards the floe.

"That wasn't very good," said Colin.

"Well, I . . ." Simon, angrily defensive.

"No, Simon, not you. The whole thing. Look. Kate and I will light the matches, or, better still, Kate, get some torches from the fire, would you?" She nodded and was on the way. "Then we'll hold the torches and you two can light and throw more easily. OK?"

"Fine," said Job.

Simon nodded.

BOOM!

The floe heaved. They all staggered with the shock. Two of the whales came through the rotten ice among the walrus

220

corpses to the south of the camp. Simon was in action before anyone could stop him. This time his matches did not fail and the short fuse sputtered into life. Ross reached for the dynamite but Simon had turned and hurled it impulsively at the two distant killers.

The stick of explosive curled lazily up into the air over the camp, hissing its bright yellow flame, spitting its cloud of sparks, leaving pale trails of its progress on the eyes of the men who watched it. Ross yelled, "Kate!"

Kate looked up from the fire, and saw it beginning to fall, well clear of the camp now, towards the ice. She saw the heads of the two whales vanish as they jerked under the water. She dived for cover, rolling well clear of the hot tray with its dangerous pile of smouldering sticks to where the tent might afford a little protection.

The stick of dynamite fell through the lower air on to the thin tongue of solid ice between the two holes lately occupied by the killers. When it hit, it skidded along the smooth surface until it wedged itself under the bulk of the largest of the dead walruses.

Then it exploded.

The walrus vanished into the air in a red-brown column.

The sound washed over the floe with the wind, tearing at the tents, taking a great cloud of sparks from the fire-tray. It knocked the breath out of Kate's body, and she lay stunned for a moment. The three men looked through narrowed eyes, Job and Simon at the south of the floe, Colin at Kate. She began to pick herself up . . . and was thrown flat again. There was a grating, slopping sound which seemed to fill the air. The floe heaved and rocked. A curtain of spray roared up through the crack under the tent. The lines holding the net in place, holding the camp together, groaned and stretched. The orange square twisted out of shape, then slowly re-formed.

The hill to the south-west of the floe began to fall over.

The force of the explosion, though not particularly great, was strengthened immeasurably by the body of the walrus which sent almost all of its power down into the ice. The ice here to the south, and in an arc right up to the west of the camp was soft and rotten. The force of the explosion was sufficient to make it break as far as the ice-hill, and the forces set up as that began to move were enough to do the rest. The sections of the floe to the

221

south and west of the camp slowly detached themselves and began to move away. The ice-hill, with nothing to balance its overhang, slowly toppled over and vanished into the water.

The floe was now shaped like a bullet with its blunt tip facing west. It was one hundred and fifty feet long and one hundred feet wide, held together by the firmly anchored net. The camp took up almost the whole of it, with its forty-foot long ropes stretching very nearly to the water in all directions. At the two northern corners of the net there were holes where two tents had stood.

"Jesus Christ," whispered Simon, pale and shaking.

"Where are they?" demanded Job. Wherever they came through now it could only spell disaster.

"Kate?" yelled Colin.

"OK." She picked herself up again. Colin felt better.

"What do we do now?" asked Simon.

"Kill them," said Colin. "It's still all we can do. Before they kill us."

"Which they'll have no trouble at all doing now," said Job, going to the very edge of the water and looking out, hefting a stick of dynamite from hand to hand. "Where are they?" he asked again.

Simon stood at the edge of the hole where the supply tent had been, looking down into the black depths. He felt sick, and this was better than hiding in the latrine tent. The wave of nausea passed and he lifted his head. In the distance, something moved. "There," he said.

"Where?" Job. He and Colin swung round.

"There." Simon pointed. His arm stretching over the hole.

And the whale came up through the small ring of water, reaching – as it had seen the leader do – for the reaching arm. The breadth of its flippers foiled it, however, for they crashed into the ice before it had completed its attack. Its great yellow teeth snapped on empty air. Simon, screaming, went over backwards. The killer lunged again. Simon rolled backwards, just clear of the white chin.

Colin, grabbing one of the silver spears, pounding back again. He came to a halt beside the whale, looking for a weak spot. The killer was too preoccupied with Simon as he scrabbled frantically away on all fours across the ice to be aware of

222

him. Not the head – it was covered with bone of far too great a thickness to be vulnerable. Not the eyes, he couldn't get to them. The back of the neck then. Of course!

The whale lunged again, silently. The silence was terrifying. The ice heaved. Colin staggered, but did not fall. He went round to the back of the hole, and his eyes narrowed, looking for the dimple of its blow-hole.

The whale, thwarted for the moment, began to sink down, its blow-hole gaping as it breathed in. Ross struck with all of his terrible strength and the first two feet of the spear vanished into the body of the killer. It reared back immediately, its mouth wide, its eyes mad with agony. Ross rolled free as the harpoon sang in the air while the killer writhed. Choking on its own blood, it tried to jerk its head free, but the steel sticking solidly out of its back wedged against the ice and would not let it free. Its mouth opening and closing, it lashed madly from side to side, hurled itself forward until its flippers crashed into the ice, jerked itself back, tearing at the brittle floe with all the power in its lithe twenty-eight foot body.

Fascinated, sickened, but unable to look away, Simon and Colin watched the killer in its terrible agony as it tried uselessly to break free, its efforts gradually weakening until it quietened down, blood boiling slowly from its head and its mouth. Then it gave one last terrible, convulsive heave, and lay still.

Colin went over to Simon and picked him up. They turned and looked over the camp. Kate was on her knees by the fire. Beyond her Job was kneeling at the very edge of the ice, holding his dynamite, looking out to sea. Fifty yards away were the two black sails, coming in to see what all the noise was about.

Without looking back, Job said, "Light." His voice was almost a whisper. If I can light this, he was thinking, I can kill them both now. The fins moved in. "Light!" cried Job again. Softly. Urgently.

But Ross was watching the two containers of dynamite behind Job's back, slowly settling out of sight. "My God, the floe's breaking up!" he cried, throwing himself forward on to the suddenly soggy ice. "Job! It's breaking up!"

The last convulsive shudder by the dying whale had done it. There came a series of sharp, defined reports as though someone were practising small-arms fire. The two black fins, one of them even taller than Ross, began to move nearer.

"Job!" Ross flung out his arm, and the Eskimo, turning at last and seeing the danger, also reached out to his fullest extent. Their hands almost met. There were only inches between them. And so they stayed for interminable seconds, frozen, reaching but not touching. Then a vagary of the current swirled the two pieces of the floe apart and Ross watched, prone on the sodden ice, as his friend, spreadeagled on a raft hardly bigger than himself, was turned away and away by the black spite of the Arctic Ocean.

"Job!" he cried. Then Simon was there with twenty feet of rope from one of the harpoons. He hurled it: Job came up on his knees on the rocking raft to catch it, but it was too short. The long rope was on the far side of the camp, beside the sleeping tent, where Kate had left it during the walrus attack. "Get the long rope," snapped Ross.

Simon ran past the whale and leaped over the crack wildly. Then he had the rope and was running back, arms reaching out with it, over the unsteady crack, past the whale . . .

The whale saw the reaching arms again, and it had learned its brief and bloody lesson too well to let Simon past. It gave one last convulsive leap forward over the ice. Its flippers tore free at last, but its high fin, only a few feet further down its body, caught in its turn. Those few feet were enough. The blunt snout crashed into Simon's side, knocking him off his feet. He rolled free, gasping for breath. The jaws snapped at him, only inches away. All self-control gone, he brought the coil of rope over his shoulder and struck at the whale with the heavy coils. The whale caught the rope, jerked it out of his hand, snapped its fifty interlocking teeth shut, cutting the rope to pieces. It lunged forward again.

"*Simon*," screamed Colin.

But Kate was there. She had caught up Colin's roughly improvised weapon of bullets by its length of wood, and touched the inch of fuse to the fire. It blazed into life. She ran forward, holding the piece of plank at full arm's length in front of her until it wedged into the whale's throat. Just as she did so, the first round exploded, and the recoil nearly tore her hand off. The whale jerked back and went rigid. Kate carried on run-

224

ning. Behind her, the makeshift weapon tore itself apart as the rest of the magnum shells detonated, blasting through the whale, ripping away the whole top of its head. With the last of the rope still caught up in what was left of its jaws, the whale sank silently through the hole, leaving only a long streak of rust behind it on the ice.

Kate fell on her knees beside Colin and looked out with him over the quiet sea at Job kneeling on his little raft of ice.

At least the other two killers had gone for the time being. "There's nothing we can do," she said.

He swung round to face her. His eyes were dark, his face thin, desperate, his lips chapped, there was a cold-sore she hadn't noticed at the corner of his mouth. "Don't you see . . ." he cried. There were tears in his eyes. His hand moved to dash them away before they froze on his cheeks. "He is my friend."

She repeated, gently, as if to a backward child, "There is nothing you can do."

"There must be something . . ."

"Ross." Simon. "He's waving."

Ross slewed round, still on his knees. Kate moved closer to him. Job was a black silhouette against the sea.

"What've we got?" asked Colin.

"Nothing."

"Dynamite . . ."

"It's gone," she whispered.

Colin sat back on his heels. There was nothing they could do. A little wind blew in his eyes. He brushed away the tears again. Then, over the sea, came a faint sound. Job was waving his arms.

"C-o-l-i-n!" shouted Job. He waved his arms slowly, carefully, the ice rocking beneath his knees at even this slight movement, the icy water slopping against his sealskin boots and trousers. Distantly, Colin raised his hand. Job continued to wave both hands, the dynamite forgotten in his left mittened fist. He had nothing to say except Colin's name, no idea except to show that he was as yet all right; and so he waved, and so the ice-raft rocked.

Ripples spread in circles, blue-grey and black. Job's eyes followed them thoughtfully as they moved towards him, until they became two solid black shapes, graceful as arrow-heads, sharp as knives. Spray roared into the air. The whales began to circle.

Job began to pray. To what gods?

The fins disappeared.

Job cheered and waved his arms. Ross waved back, waved and waved. Job raised his arms, paused: something . . .

A gentle wind was pushing him in the back. The raft began to move towards the floe. Little waves washed over the blunt ice and lapped at his knees. It was moving! With infinite care, he climbed to his feet. Upright he would make a better sail, if only the wind would keep blowing. The figures on the floe became clearer, began to assume depth, colour . . .

Job's heart beat at the back of his throat. He stood unsteadily, legs spread, arms spread, riding the wind.

A minute passed. Another. Drawing themselves out to terrible length.

"NOT FAR," Colin called.

"NOT FAR," answered Job.

The wind faltered. Job looked up. The clouds were thinning. A change in the weather. Perhaps it will get warmer, he thought, shivering in his wet clothes.

"It's going to break," he called, for want of anything better to say.

"What?"

"The weather, it's going to . . ."

The ocean leapt behind him, drew itself up, bucketed aside. The killer rose, foot after foot, to the height of a second-storey window, blocking out nearly half of the sky. Yard after yard of it: scarred face, black liquid eyes, white cliff of belly, up and up until the flippers reached over the far edges of the tiny raft, reached, hooked, held. Job staggered back until his shoulders were against the snow-white belly, and the whale held him erect. He found he was screaming a name. "AIPALOOK-VIK!" Great God of Innuit The People: the Spirit under the Iceberg, Teeth of the North Wind, He who Bites and Destroys.

The killer Aipalookvik cradled the Eskimo against its chest almost protectively, moving its great tail to hold the tiny raft steady, to prevent it sinking under its great weight. Job waited dumbly for the end: against a god what else is there to do?

226

As he waited, the killer Aipalookvik, Biter and Destroyer, gave a strange low loving call.

The water parted scant yards from Job. The black point of the mate's fin, the black sail, the black shoulder, came . . . and her face, out of the water, mouth agape, hurling the ocean aside. Job's mind raced into prayer. "O Lord, out of the depths." His lips screamed wordlessly and she was upon him, flipped half on her side, her jaws closing round his legs.

Oh Lord, out of the depths . . . Job felt her teeth grate on his bones. She backed away. His trousers flapped in rags against the bloody ruin below his waist. He did not look down. Oh Lord, out of the depths . . . said his mind; *"COLIN!"* he screamed.

Colin, seeing him like that, saw Jeremiah five years earlier, asking to be left to die. He assumed that Job was demanding the same thing – to die well.

Perhaps he was.

"THE DYNAMITE," screamed Colin. "JOB, THE DYNAMITE."

Job held the stick, fused and ready to light, in his left hand. He fumbled for a match. His eyes went up, he could see Colin's face looking as though it were carved of bone. He turned his face away, lit the match, sheltered from the wind by the bulk of the whale. The fuse hissed into life, spitting fire . . .

And the mate came at Job again, her mouth opening like a mantrap at his knees. He saw the teeth, the water flowing past them in little red eddies, pink waterfalls; he saw the great pink-white blade of her tongue working, the crimson shadows of her throat. He fell forward, thrusting out his arm, and she took it, hand with its spitting bundle, shoulder, deep into her mouth.

The flame of the fuse seared her: she jerked back, snapping shut her teeth. They almost met across his upper arm, and as she slid back whimpering, left the flesh stripped away from shoulder to elbow. The muscled walls of the arteries spasmed shut, the length of the bone shone yellow-white.

Job tore himself back from the terrible sight, and the joint of his elbow, still between her teeth, severed with the strain. The white stick of his humerus stood out from the ruin of his shoulder as he staggered back, on his knees now. His shoulder slammed into the rigid flipper of Aipalookvik for the last time, and toppled forward drunkenly towards the waiting mouth of the killer's mate.

"Oh Lord," he said. "Out of the Depths I cry to Thee . . ."

And the dynamite exploded.

On the floe they froze; Kate, her arm round Colin's shoulders, Simon, his legs wide, his mouth open, the piece of rope caught up as Job began to come back on the wind still in his hands. The red mushroom of mist fell back into the sea, and there was nothing there.

"By God he did it," said Simon.

"What did he say?" asked Colin. "What did he say?"

Kate had only half heard herself, but she told Colin. "The debt. He said you were free."

TWELVE

i

THE KILLER WHALE in which Job had seen the great God
Aipalookvik heaved his forty-foot length through the dull
water, back breaking the surface so that he could gasp air into
his blast-damaged lungs. A beard of blood clung to his chin and
upper chest where his delicate skin had been ruptured by
hundreds of shards of bone sent howling like shrapnel on the
first wind of the blast, from his consort's massive skull and Job's
upper torso. He was lucky that his wounds did not extend any
further up his white cheeks, for had they done so, his eyes would
have been destroyed.

For some minutes after the explosion, the leader had rolled
around near the surface fighting for breath, his mind in confusion. One moment his ultimate lesson was proceeding perfectly
as he held the man still so that his consort could learn the joy of
killing humans; then the sea had hurled itself into his face, into
his lungs, seemingly into his mind. As soon as he was out of
danger himself, he started to look for his beautiful sleek black
and white mate, calling to her with the strange, sad, haunting
tones of their language, but there had been no reply. His sonar
had found no shape he could recognise as hers in the quiet
water, and even when his eyes found her, he did not recognise
the truncated mess of her body at all.

Now, instinctively, he was swimming south. The rest of his
pack were down here somewhere he knew, and although his
ears, damaged like his lungs by the blast, had not yet cleared
sufficiently for him to hear the directional and locational cries
they were still periodically giving, he knew where they had been
before the final attack had started, and that was close enough.
He needed the reassurance of his fellows.

During the next half-hour his strength began to return and his head began to clear. A new sense of purpose began to direct his movements as he swam. Suddenly, with a great wrench which seemed to swing the whole length of his body all at once to the north, he turned and went back.

ii

Ross was the first to get up. As soon as she felt him begin to move, Kate took her arm from round his shoulders and let him stand on his own. Her heart was thudding uncomfortably, not only at the horror of Job's death but also in fear at how it might affect her man. She looked past Colin's legs to Simon. He dropped the rope he was holding and turned.

"Christ, Colin, I . . ." But there was nothing he could say.

Ross gave his strange lop-sided shrug, turned and walked away towards the camp. Fifteen strides of his long legs took him to the net, five more to the fire-tray on the far side of the camp. Beyond him stretched a half-circle of ice ten strides in radius. Then the grey ocean began. Thoughtlessly holding his right hand in the warmth over the smouldering fire, Colin studied the hazy grey horizon. He didn't know what to do or say. He didn't even have any feelings to analyse, nothing inside him at all to advise him whether to weep or sing. Jesus, he thought, oh Jesus. There was nothing he could do; nothing left to be done; nothing left. He closed his eyes and Job's face was there.

Pain flared up his arm, and he took his hand out of the fire. The shock of the burn, however, proved therapeutic and he straightened, jerked a little out of the grief. He thrust his burning glove into the pocket of his anorak and turned. Kate was just behind him, picking her way carefully over the restless jaws of the crack under the net. She sniffed, crinkling her nose.

"Something's burning."

"My glove. My hand. It's all right."

"You might have burned yourself badly. Let's have a look at it."

"Oh no. Look what happened the last time you said anything like that. My mother warned me against girls like you."

She smiled automatically. Then replied, trying to keep it

light, "That's funny, my mother told me about men like you."

Suddenly she remembered her mother – for the first time in many years without a twinge of regret – not as a faded face in the huge bed, but as a humorous tough-minded beauty, taking her young daughter by the hand and saying, *"You'll know him when you see him, Kate, and when you see him . . ."*

"She told me to grab hold and never let go." Perhaps she should have blushed, being so brazen. A week ago she probably would have done so.

"Did she now? What a wise old lady. The doctor never talked of her."

Thinking about her father didn't hurt too much either. "She's been dead for nearly ten years."

"I'll have to introduce you to mine, then. It sounds as though they would have got along."

"I didn't know you had a mother!" She had never thought of Colin as having any family. Right from the beginning he seemed to exist on his own, like a phenomenon of nature.

"Oh yes. And a father too. It's not unusual, you know."

"No. I know. I mean I never thought of you as having a family."

"Oh yes. No brothers or sisters, but cousins and cousins' children. I'm an adopted uncle about twenty times over."

Glad to have got him talking, she sat down beside the fire-tray and scooped up some ice to make coffee. "Coffee, Simon?"

"Yes." From the edge of the ice.

"Tell me about your parents," she invited. "From what Job told me, I'd thought of you as just living all the time in Washington all on your own, never having anyone . . ."

"Oh no. Nothing like that. I don't even live in Washington. I'm a Scot. I was raised in the Highlands, just north of Inverness, where my parents still live. Father was a gillie – a gamekeeper – on an estate up there, but he's retired now."

"Do you see them often?"

"Oh, I go back for Christmas, Hogmanay. I'm useful for the First Foot, you see, being tall and dark."

"God, yes. I can just see you looming out of the night armed with coal, demanding a dram."

"Aye, well." Suddenly, for no apparent reason, his English accent wavered and the ghost of a broad Highland Scots moved

231

in his words. A shiver went up Kate's spine again, as had happened when she first heard his deep bass voice.

"You said you don't live in Washington."

"That's right. I work there. Squat there . . ."

"Where do you live then?"

"In London."

"You live in London?" Her voice betrayed her surprise. She had expected him to say he lived somewhere in the United States.

"That's right. I commute from London to Washington on a, well, roughly a monthly basis."

"Why do you live in London?"

"Because I like it."

"You like living in London? But you were brought up in the mountains, and you spend a good deal of your working life in wildernesses like this! It doesn't make sense."

"Yes it does. You just don't know enough about me. You see, I love the theatre, cinema, all that; I can't get enough of it. It started at school, I suppose, in Edinburgh. I mean, I'd grown up in the wilds. I knew a fair amount about red deer, grouse, salmon, trout, and suddenly there I was in Edinburgh and it was all totally different. It . . . I don't know . . . it caught me, somehow. And then there was Oxford, of course."

At that moment the water boiled. Simon came over for his coffee, but he didn't stay long; he just cast a speculative look at the two of them from under lowered eyebrows and then drifted away again, the steaming mug cupped between his mittened hands.

The time slipped by unnoticed as Kate worked quietly and with surprising success at keeping Colin's mind on the distant past, eliciting a surprising number of stories about his undergraduate days at Oxford.

But then the stories began to take a darker turn as they jumped forward into the more recent past. Again, an unsuspected side to him began to emerge as he told of drowning his sorrows in London, Paris, Rome; carrying his nebulous but terribly weighty sense of guilt everywhere with him. The names of several women appeared and disappeared in his disjointed narrative and found she herself wondering what they were like – Marie-France, Laura, Isabella, the others . . .

"COLIN!"

Quick came tearing past the latrine-cum-supply tent, stumbling over the tent-pegs, sliding on the ice. His face was white.

"Colin. It's back. It's out there now!"

Ross looked up. As though a switch had been thrown deep inside him, the growing love he had felt for Kate turned to a cold, terrible hatred. Abruptly he saw Job again, trapped against that immense chest, hemmed in by the white-sided flippers. "Right," he said. "Let's get the bastard."

"Get it? For Christ's sake how do we do that? We'll be lucky if it doesn't get us!"

But Ross wasn't listening. His cold eyes were sweeping over what was left of the floe trying to catalogue everything they had which could be used as a weapon. There was very little: two harpoons; one axe; fire, perhaps. A little ammunition. He thought of making more bombs with the bullets and then he remembered that they had lost the fuse with the dynamite.

So that was it: hand to hand. God, he thought, if only they had something which would hold it still for a few minutes while they got at it with the harpoons and the axe. He looked down, kicking snow aimlessly over a thick orange strand. What they really needed, he decided, was a net.

A net!

It came to him in a great flash. The net! And, even before the details were clear in his mind, he was moving.

"Simon. Put the boat together. Load up the lifejackets."

"The boat!" Quick's eyes swept disbelievingly over the collapsible dinghy lying in a jumble beside the hole where the old supply tent had stood. "Colin, you're not thinking of going out after the thing!"

But Ross had already caught up the axe, and was using it to loosen the pegs at the ends of the ropes holding the net in place. These pegs were now inches from the water, and as he worked on them, his gaze probed the water restlessly for any sign of his enemy. He was muttering to himself, "Just a few more minutes, Aipalookvik, you bastard; just hold off a few more minutes."

Eight ropes held the net in position, one going out from each corner, one from the centre of each side. He began by loosening the pegs on the three ropes pointing east. Then he loosened the one pointing south, his boots several inches deep in water. He searched the placid water before looking down to start work. The hairs on his neck were erect with the tension. It was all very well muttering to the whale that it ought to wait, but he would be in dire trouble if it wasn't in a listening mood. Between each stroke he looked up, sweat running on his face. As soon as the peg sprang free, he was off at a brisk jog to the next one, the first of the three on the round bows of their ice-ship. Four to go.

Once again he paused and surveyed the deceptively quiet sea. He was at the end of the net now. He began to chop at the ice. Again, between strokes he searched the water with keen eyes, but nothing moved except the grey waves and the restless blue floes.

He moved up the net and chopped the next peg free as well. When he had done so he turned and began to walk casually back up the floe. Only two pegs at opposite sides remained, with the few pegs in the edge of the net itself, holding the floe tenuously in one piece.

"Simon," he called, "are you sure you saw anything?"

Quick looked up from fastening the last section of the boat in place and glanced over at Ross. He saw the tall man walking towards him slowly, silhouetted against the grey sea. And then, improbably, a black spike began to grow out of the top of his head. Quick gaped. What was happening?

And then he realised. "BEHIND YOU!"

Ross hurled himself forward at the cry, not looking round. The sound of the whale coming up after him deafened him. Something crashed into his back and hurled him forward. He slithered up the slope which suddenly appeared as the whale put its weight on the smaller section of the floe. Ross found the edge of the net under his hand and pulled himself up. The whale was three-quarters out of the water, raised on spread flippers, its gaping mouth just over a yard from Ross's legs. He saw that great black and white face, scarred on nose and cheek, its chin spotted and swollen, as he twisted his right hand over his head, thrust the club of his left arm under the fire-tray, steadied it with his right, and hurled it with all his might. It struck the whale's scarred nose and exploded in sparks all over its face. The whale screamed and jerked back. The ice slopped down in the water, but the few pegs around the edges of the net held and the halves of the floe remained bound together.

"Jesus H. Christ!" said Ross, slumping back, gasping for breath.

"Colin! Are you all right?" Kate came on to her knees beside him.

"Yes. I'm fine. It was close though. That canny bastard almost had me!" His eyes were blazing, his face white and drawn with hate under the heavy black bristles of his thickening beard. He rolled over and climbed to his feet only to find himself face to face with an equally enraged Simon.

"You fucking idiot," screamed the little man. "You threw the fire at it. We'll all freeze."

"Man, dear! Unless we get that beast up here and kill it now we won't get a chance to freeze! Anyway, with the tent, the sleeping bags and blankets, we'll be able to keep warm even if we can't think of a way to light another fire."

"Quick calmed a little. "So, all right," he said. "Let's hear your plan."

"OK," said Ross seriously. "Look. All we've got are the harpoons and the axe. What we have to do is get the killer somewhere where we can hold it still for long enough to give us a chance to use them."

"Great idea!" sneered Quick. "How do you suggest we do that?"

"We use the net."

"How?" Kate.

"You remember when Simon and I had that fight in the tent?" He gestured towards the hole in the ice where the whale had come through. "The killer zeroed in on the noise, right?"

"Yes."

"Well, we do the same thing here. If we have a mock fight, make lots of noise and yelling right by the crack, we might be able to lure it up into the net. Then, while it's trying to get free, we'll hack it to pieces."

"Oh, great!" said Quick. "And what do we do when it wrecks the floe?"

"If we're quick it won't get the chance! Don't you see? I've loosened all the pegs but two. It should just tear the net away from the ice and tangle it round itself. If we're quick we can kill it before it does any damage." He turned away to pick up the axe again, but he had only taken two steps before something hit him solidly in the back.

"What?" He turned, going down on one knee. Quick was dancing up and down on the net beside the crack. "Simon, for Christ's sake, what . . .?"

"I thought you wanted to fight!"

"Simon!"

"Well, don't just kneel there! Come here and fight!"

"My God," said Ross in disgust and got up. He turned his back on Quick again and began wearily to walk towards the axe. He had made three steps before Simon's shoulder smashed into his back again and he went sprawling. It was then, with the stupid pointlessness of it welling bitterly in his throat, that he lost his temper. He came up off the ice hair wild, face bone white, eyes blazing with the cold light that animated the floes. "All right, you stupid bastard," he breathed, and he began to walk across the ice. Quick danced away, still jeering, arms hanging loosely at his sides, mittens bulky like boxing gloves.

Away to the south the black thorn of the killer's fin split the water silently and began to circle the floe.

Kate turned, mouth open, a harpoon in each hand as the two men closed and stared at each other for a moment over the restless crack.

"Look," said Quick, stepping forward, hand held out, "I'll tell you what . . ." His smile spread, boyish, rueful. His hand had almost touched Ross's shoulder. He came up on his toes ready to kick his lifelong enemy in the crotch.

Ross's right foot lashed out, the boot crashing into Simon's leg a quarter of an inch below the kneecap. Simon screamed. Ross's leg bent, following the blow up the thigh to bring his knee into Simon's groin. The younger man came forward, his face falling hard on to Ross's fist. The nose bruised, nearly shattered. Simon fell down the left side of Ross's body, convulsed into a ball.

Kate dropped the harpoons.

Ross kicked out for Simon's head, but his boot skidded off the heavy parka shoulder. Simon rolled away, pushing with his clenched legs, his clenched fists. Ross came after him, over the crack, one step, two . . . Then Simon hurled himself back, crashing into Colin's legs and sending him sprawling. Ross landed awkwardly, throwing out his left arm as though it could support him, and it twisted against the stump with enough force to send his senses reeling.

The pair of them fought their way to their feet, and Kate, her temper gone, screaming at them in a rage to match their own, came running across the ice and tried to grab Simon's shoulder. He shrugged her off and dived forward so that Ross and he rolled, linked together, knees crashing against thighs, heads driven into faces.

Simon tore off mitten and glove between Ross's back and the ice, and made talons of his fingers to gouge his enemy's eyes. Ross jerked his face away, three deep grooves raked down his cheek. He let go and rolled away. He forced himself on to his knees. Quick did the same.

"For God's sake," said Kate.

Ross wiped his face, and stood up. Simon stood up, paused a moment, and came shambling forward again. They met like ocean and shore, Ross's fist knocked aside and going over Simon's shoulder, their faces colliding, shoulders, chests, bellies.

Kate looked for some way to part these two men who had suddenly, unaccountably, turned into wild animals.

Simon's left fist was delivering short, deadly jabs below Ross's belt. He swung his right in a haymaker into Ross's ribs. Ross's right did the same, again and again. His knee came up once more. His head tore back and crashed forward into Simon's face. Simon staggered back. As he came forward again, Ross took a step to one side and tripped him as he blundered past.

"Had enough?" Colin gasped.

"Yes," screamed Kate. "For God's sake, stop it, the pair of you. The killer's vanished. Christ alone knows what it's up to."

But Simon was up again, and he charged forward, swinging wildly. "I'm going to kill you, Colin!" he said thickly, through swollen lips. "Kill you!"

Kate went for him, her hands in claws. He caught her with one hand, and hurled her behind him on to the smaller section of the floe. She landed awkwardly, slipped and fell, striking her head. She tried to rise, but passed out.

Colin fell back, rolling free of the net, his boot slopping water. He began to get up again.

Simon swung his heavy boot back to kick him in the face. The bitterness which had festered in him for so many years had complete control now, and his bruised and swollen face twisted out of all recognition. He had won. If the first kick did not kill Ross, the second would. He swung his foot forward with all of his wiry strength . . .

And the whale came up, exactly as Colin had foretold that it would, through the crack in the floe and into the net.

The net reared under the men, hurling both of them back one on top of the other, on to the larger section of the floe. The whale froze for a second as the net closed around its head, then it lashed from side to side in a frenzy of movement. The floe heaved and bucked as it tried to free itself.

Simon, trying to reach the harpoons, was thrown to the ground. He struggled to get up, but he couldn't make it. Colin rolled over and got on to all fours, but he couldn't make it either.

"For God's sake," he screamed.

The whale lunged up into the air. The net tore completely free of the ice and closed entirely round it. The two pieces of the floe began to drift apart. The net was held only by the two long ropes, one to each section of ice. The whale, seeing freedom as the crack opened, lunged forward. Simon was on his hands and knees now, the two silver spears just in front of him. Their fight was forgotten. He grabbed one and, rolling on his back, handed it to Colin.

Colin struggled on to his knees, and, using the harpoon as a support, he dragged himself on to his feet and staggered forward. Still half dazed by the fight, he staggered forward until the ice ended under his feet, then he looked up and saw how terribly wrong everything had gone.

From just beside his unsteady feet one of the two ropes stretched to the edge of the net forty feet away. Five yards to the right the other half of the floe was being pulled by forty feet of orange rope. The two pieces of rope joined on the net wrapped around the whale's head. All of it, the ice, the rope, the net, the whale, were moving through the water at an increasing speed. Waves beat against the thin ice, which began to break up.

238

"Sweet Christ!" he cried. He turned back to Simon, and opened his mouth to yell, when the peg beside his knees tore loose. The rope whipped away howling madly in the air.

The movement of the floe slowed, its angle settled back to the horizontal. Colin watched as what was left of the smaller part of the floe drew away at a speed of perhaps a knot, drawn forward by the wildly swimming whale.

He walked back over the ice towards Simon and the wreck of the camp. The canoe lay on its side, the yellow lifejackets lolling out of it, beside the hole where the old supply tent had stood. The latrine tent was in ruins.

And that was all there was.

Colin shook his head. "It'll never get free of that. I think we've won," he said.

But Simon was looking at the small floe following the whale across the grey sea. Colin's face abruptly echoed the panic in Simon's, and he swung round, his right hand coming up over his eyes. The labouring whale was by no means distant, and the small floe was still quite close. Colin's eyes swept over the flat surface on the piece which the whale was still pulling.

And even as he looked at the tilting, rocking floe, he saw Kate slowly kneel up on its unsteady surface, and begin to wave wildly at him, her hair blowing in the slight wind.

iii

Abruptly Colin was in motion, running over that part of the floe remaining to them.

"Hurry, Simon. The boat. Help me with the boat. We have to go now or we'll never catch up." Simon stood up and looked at him unbelievingly. "Help me, damn you, Simon! We can't just leave her there. We can't just let her die. We have to go after her."

That was as far as Ross's mind had got. But Simon was thinking more clearly. "We'll have to kill the whale," he said. "It's no use just getting her into the boat: the whale'll simply eat that too. We have to kill that thing. That's what we have to do."

Ross paused. Then he stopped and picked up the deadly

silver-steel spears and straightened. He nodded. "Yes," he said. "We're going to have to kill the whale. Coming?"

Simon gave a massive shrug, and his bruise-puffed face twisted. "Well," he said, "you can't bloody do it on your own, can you?"

While Ross checked the seals and fastenings on all the sections of the small craft, Simon slipped on his bright yellow cork-lined lifejacket and laced it tight. Then he stowed the two harpoons with their bright orange ropes still tied to their ends.

They each took a side by the bows, gripped firmly, lifted the sharp-pointed hull a little off the ice at the front and ran it forward to the edge of the floe. As they arrived at the sea they swung the first third of the seven-foot canoe into the water. Colin jumped in and went down on his knees in the bows. He was already holding a paddle steadying the frail craft as Simon gave it a push forward, climbed in and knelt down himself.

"Go," he said, grasping the other paddle in his right hand and plunging it into the water as Colin dipped his. On alternate sides they drove the paddles, Simon swinging his body with practised ease, Colin moving with an ungainly but dogged power. The canoe sped over the quiet water at surprising speed until the first waves generated by the churning whale slapped against the pointed bows and water began to wash into the light shell.

"Take me near the floe," yelled Ross.

Simon nodded, and put in two strokes on the same side. "Stop paddling," he snapped. "You're more of a hindrance than a help. You just get ready for your battle. I'll get you there!"

With some relief Colin stowed his oar and got out the harpoons, hefting them in his hand, measuring the change in balance brought about by the attachment of the ropes, testing the fine-honed sharpness of their points.

When he looked up, they were very near to the other floe. Kate, unable to stand on the madly rocking surface, crawled over on to the very edge, water from the uneven bow-waves slopping over her knees. "Colin," she cried.

"Closer," he shouted to Simon. Simon glanced at the edge of the ice, the water folding itself into waves and eddies beneath it, narrowed his eyes, and edged the canoe another foot towards the side of the floe. Then he hunched forward a little more and settled down to the deep rhythmic thrusting of the paddle which would keep them up with the whale for hour after hour if necessary.

"I'm going to kill it, then come back for you," Colin yelled to Kate.

"Be careful."

"Too right I will."

There was nothing more to say. Colin brought his hand down on Simon's smoothly working shoulder. "Right," he said. "Let's get the bastard."

"Aye, aye, Captain Ahab," said Simon and pulled on away from the floe. Ross picked up the harpoons again and balanced them, lost in concentration, his shoulders tense, hulking like some great figurehead over the front of the tiny boat.

They were closing in.

Simon felt good. He felt like singing he was so excited. He suddenly realised that he was not in the slightest afraid, and he laughed to himself. He had taken charge of the boat in the emergency, and before that he had fought with the great Ross and got him at his mercy. All his life, it seemed, he had been working towards this moment.

The killer, lost in a panic at the burning strength of the net around its head, was running, with all its massive strength, on the surface. As soon as the net had closed around it, the whale had been hurled back in its memory to the moment when, as a calf, running in a small family unit with its parents in the south Pacific near Antarctica, it had been captured. They had used nets on it then too, wrapping its sensitive young body in the strong strands, dragging it out of the water and into the boat, away from everything it knew and loved, and into a strange, terrifying world.

But now its panic was coming under control. It had not been dragged, helpless, out of the water. It still had a chance to escape. As it swam, it tore at the strands tight across its face and mouth, and began to free itself from the net.

Ross knelt, rigid, as the great fin loomed up, almost near enough to touch. He had to tilt his head back a little to see its curved rose-thorn point, nearly a yard above his head. Then he was looking down, through the thin covering of water which

241

hissed and writhed over the black bulge of the killer's back.

"Closer!" he yelled. "Give me another ten feet." The monster seemed to be moving faster now. But they were inching up. He was over the net now. He glanced up. Only a yard or so away the back of its head rose like a wet rock out of the churning sea; its blow-hole opening and closing as it gasped in air.

"A yard," he screamed. "Give me a yard!"

Simon paddled harder, the strokes beginning to knot his back and shoulders as he thrust the canoe through the water. Colin took the first harpoon. He should have attached the twenty-foot length of orange rope to the hook at the front of the canoe but he forgot. They were coming in on the whale's right, on their left. He would have to stab it down across his chest. They would have to be very, very close. He licked his lips and was surprised by the sharp taste of salt on his tongue. His face and the front of his anorak were running with spray.

"Closer," he yelled.

The black, orange-squared hump was under the bows now, rising out of the water less than a foot from the left side of the boat. Colin leaned over to his left, harpoon poised over his head, breath held in excitement and against the warm stench of the whale breathing.

Simon, watching, guiding the boat up against the whale's head, terribly aware of the huge black sail of its fin a little behind his shoulder, screamed, "Now!" and Colin's hand began to travel down.

At Simon's cry, as though it understood, the whale's head lashed to the right, striking solidly against the side of the boat.

Colin stabbed out to his left as the boat wallowed right, out from under him. The harpoon came down behind the blow-hole, into the breadth of the monster's neck. For a terrifying moment, Colin hung over the ocean, his one hand gripped wildly on the solid column of the buried harpoon, legs in the rocking boat, the full weight of his massive body trying to hurl him down into the churning ocean. He looked down the length of the silver shaft as though in a dream to where it ended, not in a barbed point, but in a dimple of sleek black flesh which rapidly became a pool of blood. With his full weight resting on it the harpoon slipped even deeper, trembling under his hand as

242

it rubbed against the hard muscles deep in the whale's body, seeming to give off a tone like a tuning-fork. Ross pushed away from it, throwing himself back into the boat.

As soon as the great sail of the fin changed its attitude, Simon hurled the boat, made ungainly by the heaving weight of Colin in the bows, away to his right – and it was as well he did so, for the whale on its way down took the opportunity to strike at them with the breadth of its tail – which was almost twice the size of the boat. The great tail lashed down a scant yard away, missing them completely but nearly swamping them as it hit the water.

For a second they sat still in the wildly bobbing boat, Ross slowly straightening, wiping his mouth with the back of his hand; Simon sitting gasping for breath as though he were drowning.

The line hissed down into the water, until its end disappeared overboard. Colin cursed, then saw it didn't matter. The floe, still moving sluggishly forward, tilted and began to turn round and round, like a very slow spinning top.

"Right," said Simon, and he began to paddle easily away from the floe.

"Simon! Where the hell are you going?"

"About a hundred feet away from the floe. At least a hundred feet away. Further."

Colin still didn't see.

"Look. The killer's attached to the floe, right? It can't dive more than forty to sixty feet. It'll never drag that much ice down with it. It has to stay within sixty feet of the floe. So, if we go within sixty feet of the floe, then we're in the killer's ground. It'll come straight up through the bottom of the boat and tear us to shreds. See?"

Colin nodded.

"If, however," Simon was lecturing now, as though to a backward child, "we stay clear, it will run out of air and – "

"Simon! MOVE!" It was already coming up at them out of the shadows; magnified by the tricks of the water it seemed much closer than it really was, wrapped in the net like a drowned man. Horrible, unearthly. The silver column of the harpoon gleaming behind its head.

In a flash Simon was paddling again at top speed. The whale altered its angle of attack, trying to come up under the boat.

243

"Faster!" screamed Colin, craning back, still seeing it.

"Is it still coming?" gasped Simon.

"Believe me! You want it to bite you in the arse?"

Simon hurled the canoe wildly through the water, panic lending him strength.

At the last moment the net jerked the killer out of its angle of attack, and it hurled out of the water scant feet behind them, its scream of rage exploding over the air. The jerk on the rope pulled it back like a leashed dog. Kate was thrown flat on her back. The whale slammed into the water, floundering for a moment.

"TURN!" yelled Ross, up on his knees at full stretch, the second harpoon up, the white throat and belly just out of reach. "HURRY!"

Shaking his head like a wounded bear, Simon hurled the light craft round and back into the attack as the killer thrashed helplessly. For a second, the boat ground against the heaving side. Ross hurled the spear with all his massive strength.

As it felt the cold steel in its belly, the killer wrenched all the muscles from chin to tail. The great flukes slammed into something with jarring force. It twisted again and tried to dive.

As though in a dream, Kate, sitting up, saw the tiny canoe turn in and vanish behind the black bulk of its side as Colin drove his arm down. Then suddenly, incredibly, the canoe reappeared, broken, turning, flying. Colin seemed to take off and tumble like an acrobat through the air. Of Simon there was no sign. "Colin!" screamed Kate, dragging herself to her knees. "Colin!" The whale floundered and heaved, tangled in the rope now, as well as the net, trying to dive. The ocean closed its grey jaws, and suddenly there was nothing there.

Colin hit the water with stunning force. He knew he had at most two and a half minutes before his heart gave up the unequal struggle against the cold. The floe was fifty feet away. He struck out for it. His face seemed to be burning, his hand swelling with the cold. Every joint ached with it, every muscle throbbed and became numb. He kicked his legs with panic force, gasping air and water in equal amounts. Hair in his eyes. The ocean fought him every inch of the way. It flooded his boots, made his clothes like lead, it tore at every part of him with icy claws.

"It's all right," whispered the Queen of Bitches in his mind. "Just go to sleep. It's all right. Go to sleep. Go to sleep."

He was, in fact, almost asleep when he hit the floe, and it required every ounce of his strength, coupled with Kate's, to get him out of the water and on to the ice. He began to shiver uncontrollably.

Kate looked down at the blue pinched face. My God, she thought, what do I do now?

Suddenly his eyes were open and he was struggling to sit up. "Must keep moving," he said.

"Where's Simon?"

"Gone. They've both . . ."

And then the whale exploded out of the water again and began to run towards them, humping itself out of the ocean, fin high, head still wrapped in the net. The killer, badly wounded, surged towards them with powerful inevitability. Kate's hand dived into the pocket of her anorak. Then she was holding the Very pistol, pointing at the black mountain of the whale's head, waiting for it to raise its face a little so that the shot would do more than just bounce off.

The whale's head was perhaps twenty feet away. Her finger tightened on the trigger.

"No!" Colin's hand crashed up under her arms. The gun wrenched into the air, exploding into life, sending a red flare curving up to blaze into life above the fogbank gathering to the south.

"Look!" He pointed. Incredibly, unimaginably, something was moving on the killer's back.

Simon was dead and he knew it. Unlike Colin, he had not been thrown clear by the blow of the killer's tail. Instead he had become entangled in the net, dragged down when the killer dived, for two and a half minutes of pure agony crushed against its side as it struggled under the water, trying to tear the spear from its belly, and then returned to the surface to breathe. Simon, too, had breathed, and was breathing still. But he had been in the water for more than three minutes. He couldn't feel his legs. His hands burned with unbearable agony. The only thing keeping him alive was the faint warmth of the killer's flesh against his body.

Something solid struck him across the forehead, and when he

245

automatically reached up to ward off another blow, it slapped snugly into his hand – the handle of the axe. He looked at it stupidly for a second, then he began to laugh.

"Right, you bastard," he said, and he began to heave himself up the killer's shoulder, twisting the axe-head free as he did so.

The killer felt something moving on its back. It panicked. Terrified, it began to run, hurling itself through the ocean at top speed until the solid drag of the floe sixty feet behind it slowed it down again.

With massive, dogged, insane concentration, Simon pulled himself on to the killer's back until he half knelt, half sat astride the monster's shoulders, his back against the firm base of the huge black sail of the fin. Every joint screaming with the movement, he closed his fists on the axe handle and raised the long wooden shaft as high as he could and held it there for a moment.

Then, "DIE!" he screamed, and he brought the steel blade down in a glittering arc into the side of the killer's head. The red and grey metal disappeared into the killer's flesh. Simon felt it grate against the shattered bone. He pulled it free again. Moving like a clockwork toy, he jerked it up again, and down. Up and down. Up and down.

The killer, goaded to new heights of strength by the terrible pain, hurled itself with incredible power against the restraint of the shrieking rope.

On the floe, Colin, his trembling forgotten, was pushing his left hand with all his strength down on the peg holding the rope, right hand round Kate's shoulders. But the killer's last, terrible lunge was too much. Colin felt the ice crumble under his false hand, and the sharp steel peg jerked free. The rope howled as it whipped through the air, its steel-weighted end cracking like a pistol-shot.

Simon, his sanity completely gone, had the axe raised for another massive blow, when the whale lurched free. His body, twisting to keep its balance, swung away from the fin, and suddenly, incredibly, something was whirling round it. Simon looked down. An orange snake closed on his chest, covering the yellow of his lifejacket with magic coils. It was as well he could not feel his body then, for his back was broken and his ribs crushed. He tried to breathe but something slammed into him.

He stared down dazedly. One moment there were only the magical orange circles climbing up from his waist, and then next there were two inches of steel peg sticking out in front of his lifejacket.

"S-I-M-O-N . . ." The echoes of Colin's cry echoed over the ocean, curiously deadened by the looming bulk of the fog. But Simon wouldn't hear. Colin straightened, and watched the tall black thorn of the killer's sail disappearing like the conning-tower of a sinking submarine.

Kate stood up beside him and narrowed her eyes, but there was nothing to see except the thickening billows of the fog; the flat grey sea; the sky, light grey cumulus-clouds beginning to break, revealing a thin spread of cirrus; the restless floes . . . Their own floe, the size of a small room now — fifteen feet by twenty — shifted restlessly, water slopping over it. She spun round, eyes searching in panic. But there was nothing to see. She went to Colin who was standing, also silent, looking around. They slid their arms around each other and looked out as though there was something to look at in the billowing fog, but there was nothing.

Nothing at all.

iv

Colin Ross was dying. He lay, still wrapped in his freezing clothes, with his dark head cradled in Kate's lap. He could not feel his legs. It required all his strength of will to stop his massive body convulsing with the cold as both heat and life drained out of him. Otherwise the energy used by the muscles as they tightened and relaxed would set up a strain on his heart that it would not be able to bear for very long. He gave himself an hour at the outside. Kate knew as well as he did what was happening, but neither of them mentioned it. They spoke quietly, contentedly of small, unimportant things, like husband and wife at the fireside during a long winter evening.

But then, gradually, as the fog thickened around them in warm clouds, out of the heart of it, quiet at first – unnoticed by either of them – but growing louder, there came a faint, almost subliminal throbbing.

Suddenly Colin's eyes sprang open. "Listen," he said.

The throbbing had grown almost solid. The fog seemed to shake with it, the ice to tremble.

"What is it?" whispered Kate, awed by the power of the sound.

"It's an engine. A ship!" He heaved himself up on to his knees. The fog swirled around them, shaking with the sound.

And then abruptly there was silence.

"Where is it? Sweet Jesus, where is it?" Colin was searching the fog with almost insane eyes, but all he could see were vague and shifting shadows, looming huge but insubstantial.

"Help!" he yelled, his voice pitifully weak.

"There!" cried Kate, pointing. Something was moving in the lower skirts of the fog. They strained to see more clearly, calling out as loud as they could, "HERE! HERE! HELP!"

But what they could see moving were ten tall black thorn-shaped fins. The pack was back.

Ross fell to his knees, his spirit very nearly broken, and Kate knelt beside him, holding his shoulders, tears streaming down her face as the black sails began to circle the tiny floe.

Unable to speak, they watched as they formed an arrow and began to close in on them, towering out of the water. Shuffling stiffly, the two humans turned round and round, their eyes fixed hopelessly upon the whales. In the tense quiet the ocean lapped against the tiny fragment of ice, the water hissed and bubbled as the fins moved closer. The floe began to rock as the huge bodies brushed against it. There were ten in all, their fins varying from four feet to nearly seven feet high.

The hope which had bubbled in them at the sound of the ship's engines drained away. It seemed to both of them that they had been fools to think they might survive. Like children lost in the dark they clung to each other, and waited for the inevitable end as the arrow-head formation of the killers moved away, becoming vague in the mist, only to turn and begin to build up speed in an attacking run at them.

Now that it no longer mattered, Ross relaxed and his great frame convulsed. Every muscle began to jerk with wrenching force. His teeth crashed together. Kate hugged him harder,

248

wrapped both arms round him with all her strength, stroked his writhing shoulder muscles. "It's all right," she whispered, "it's all right, Colin."

The fins sank out of sight, several yards out. Colin tensed his massive frame for the shock. His right arm, round Kate's waist, all but cracked her ribs.

Nothing happened.

Then the killers surfaced. Kate and Colin jerked round in unison, just in time to see the formation of the fins break up and vanish silently behind them. And out of the silence came a new sound: the powerful buzz of an outboard motor.

Neither of them moved or spoke, as though this were some strange magic which they could destroy by an unwise act or word. They simply knelt side by side on the ice, searching the shifting fog with wild eyes.

Ross saw it first, and told Kate by tightening his right arm again, and lifting the slightly bent club of his left arm. While silently, behind them, the fins reappeared and held still as the pack watched.

Out of the fog a tall shape took form. For a terrible moment they thought it was a fin of a whale for it was of equal size, but a fluke in the wind cleared the fog a little, and a tall, broad-shouldered man was revealed. He was clean-shaven, with short dark hair sticking out from the tight hood of his bright yellow anorak. He was standing erect, legs slightly parted, in the bows of a fat little inflatable. He had a long boat-hook held in the navy-prescribed fashion across his chest, parallel to the surface of the water.

"*Kto vi?*" called the man. He had a deep resonant voice. The rest of the rubber boat gathered itself out of the mist. There were four more men seated in it, all staring suspiciously at them past the legs of the man in front. "*Kto vi?*" he repeated. The boat slowed.

"What?" called Colin. His voice was faint, broken.

"*Kto vi? Vi otkuda?*" The boat stopped and bobbed uneasily.

"What is he saying?" whispered Colin to Kate.

"I don't know!"

There was a little silence before the man in the boat, clearly confused, tried again. "*Kto vi? Vi otkuda? Vi nachoditis v sovjetskich vodach.*"

249

The word *sovjetskich* slowly sank into Ross's cold-fuddled brain. "Of course!" he said. "They're Russian! Soviet!"

"Russian?" Kate's face was blank with astonishment.

"Yes. We must have drifted into Russian waters."

The man in the bows of the boat, only twenty feet away now, looked back over his shoulder, then he repeated "*Vi nachoditis v sovjetskich vodach.*"

"English!" Ross pointed to himself, to Kate. "We're English. Do any of you speak English?"

The man in the bows made a gesture. The boat turned a little. It looked as though they were going away again. Then, suddenly, there was a plump, deep-chested young man standing by the man in the bows. He turned his head towards them, light catching his glasses, glistening in the fog-droplets on his short dark brown beard. "I speak," he yelled. He had a light, baritone voice. "*Menya zovut* Pjotr Picatel." he gestured to himself and repeated, "Pjotr Picatel."

"Well, how do you do Pjotr? It's nice to meet you. Now can you get us off the fucking ice?" Colin was in an agony of impatience. Surely they could sort all this out later, on their ship, in the warm.

"Please," cried Pjotr "Not fast. You listen. *Eto vtoroi ofitser* . . . ah . . . this second officer, Sergei Antonovich Ivanov̄." He gestured towards the tall man holding the boat-hook. "He ask questions. You listen. I translate. OK?" He beamed.

"*Kto vi?*" snapped the second officer.

"Who you?" yelled Pjotr Picatel, cheerfully butchering the grammar of a language he did not fully understand.

"Colin Ross. Kate Warren."

"*Vi otkuda?*"

"Whence you?"

"We were wrecked east of here. 'Plane crash."

"*Skolko vremeni vi uzhye na Idu?*"

"How long on ice?"

"A week."

"*Yeshyour ostavshiyis v zhivich?*"

"Any survivors more?"

"There were four more. They're dead. And we'll be dead too if you don't bloody hurry up!"

Pjotr Picatel obviously translated all of this when he whis-

250

pered to the second officer, because Sergei Antonovich shrugged and said, "*Nash vrach budyet vas osmatrivat.*"

"Our doctor examine you," said Pjotr, grinning cheerfully. "We take you on ship now."

The buzz of the idling engines snarled a little louder. The boat moved slowly forward until the fat black rubber bows nestled against the ice. Kate and Colin picked themselves up stiffly, and, suddenly very weak indeed, staggered towards the boat. Pjotr Picatel leaped on to the ice and stood, holding one end of the boat-hook in his left hand keeping the boat in place, ready to help them on board. The second officer held the other end of the boat-hook. Another of the crew was shaking out heavy grey blankets, ready to wrap them round their frozen shoulders.

Kate went first, stepping carefully over the plump bulge of rubber on to the slatted wooden grating in the bottom of the boat. The second officer helped her aboard. The other sailor wrapped the heavy blanket round her and courteously turned to support her down the fifteen feet of the boat's length to a seat. Her knees gave out. Two more crewmen leaped up to help her. Only the man controlling the outboard motor did not move.

"Now, Ross," said Pjotr, his right arm thrown back invitingly.

Colin glanced round what was left of the floe. It had served them well after all; it would have supported all of them, had they survived. Suddenly it was like leaving an old friend. His eyes flicked over the mottled white, slightly uneven surface, then up into the fog as though he expected to see the other five of them there: the pilot, Hiram, Warren, Job and Simon. And indeed there was something . . .

"LOOK OUT!" he pointed.

The ten fins cut the water, one, nearly seven feet high with a great bite taken out of it. With steady, silent power, they were coming towards the boat. Pjotr let go of the boat-hook and the boat surged back away from the ice. The ten fins closed, the water folding back from their leading edges. Then they began to sink. In perfect arrow formation they dived under the boat, surfaced on the far side, and vanished into the fog.

"*Delfin kasatke,*" Pjotr Picatel said in a conversational tone. "Killer whales."

"I know what they are," snapped Ross, and, turning to face the Russian he stumbled. Pjotr Picatel was not a tall man – he stood perhaps five feet ten – but he was solid as a rock. He caught Colin and held his weight without flinching. The boat began to move back in.

"How did you find us?"

"*Signalu raketi* . . . we see your flare above fog."

The boat was close to the ice now. The second officer leaned forward, holding out the boat-hook towards Pjotr's reaching arm . . .

Something burst out of the water between the flat black rubber bows and the ice. Slowly turning over in the quiet, dark water was Simon Quick, buoyed up by his yellow lifejacket, the axe still clutched in his dead hands, the rope still wrapped around his waist, its end still firmly anchored by the steel peg buried in his chest.

Desperately, Colin tried to fight free of Pjotr's arm, no clear idea in his mind other than to try to tempt the killer away from the boat, before it rose up the fifty feet of rope which would separate it from Simon's corpse. "What are you doing?" the Russian shouted.

An answer exploded out of the ocean like doom.

Although it had been terribly wounded, the whale had not died. Simon had struck six blows in all before the steel peg had slammed into his heart, but such was the structure of the killer's skull that they had not killed it immediately. At the back of its head there were two huge reservoirs which contained large quantities of blood, designed to keep its brain supplied with oxygen during long dives. The blows from the axe had cut through the outer walls of bone on each side, partially rupturing each reservoir, but never entering the brain cavity itself. So the killer, dazed, had swum into the depths of the sea, dragging the assorted jumble of net, ropes and corpse behind it.

The sound of the ship, and the cries of the returning pack had roused it, and, bleeding sluggishly, slowly dying, it had begun to search for them. It hadn't found them. Instead it heard the sound of an outboard motor, and everything became clear. The memory of its trainer rose in the killer's mind. It swam, as it had been trained to do, towards the sound of the outboard motor. Up through the warm water out of the dark it swam, increasingly excited. The tone of the outboard motor varied as the boat manoeuvred. Like a flock of unimaginable birds, the pack passed over its head, but the killer was no longer interested in them, and didn't even alter its slow and dogged progress.

As the surface came nearer, it saw the hull of the rubber boat, it saw the edge of the ice. Then it saw the arms reaching between the two. It convulsed the aching, terribly wounded length of its body into one last galvanic attack. Wrenching the harpoon in its belly, screaming with agony and joy, the great whale lashed its tail up, down and streaked up through the water.

It missed the Russian, took Ross's outstretched arm, and tore him up off the ice. Kate had seen Simon's corpse and knew as well as Colin what it meant. Leaping unsteadily down the length of the boat, she had grabbed the boat-hook from the second officer. Her plan was very simple: as the killer came up, she would drive the boat-hook right through its eye.

When it came up out of the ocean, the net wrapped around its neck, like an orange ruff, its black and white face ruined by great welts where the orange strands had pulled against the skin, the scars on its nose and cheek livid, blood streaming in thick strands like hair from the back of its head, Kate stabbed with all of her strength for the eye above the corner of its massive jaw.

As she did so, its teeth closed on Ross's left arm and its head jerked, unexpectedly moving the liquid tar disc of her target. The point of the boat-hook bit down into its cheek six inches too far back, and tore down the side of its head, ripping bright pink flesh open to the bone until the first strand of the net stopped its progress just at the back of the killer's head.

The handle of the boat-hook slammed up into Kate's armpit, hurling her into the air.

Colin felt the straps crushing his chest as his arm began to tear free. He was hanging at an angle across the thing's face, looking down. Past the great white curve of its chin and neck he could see the sleek wall of its chest where Job had been held prisoner, and lower, on the white bulge of its belly, the stark steel column of the harpoon. It was incredible that the thing was still alive.

The whale's head was thirty feet in the air when Colin Ross's arm tore off.

Kate, still hanging on to the twisting column of the boat-hook, writhed and kicked against the killer's side, and her wild movement wrenched at her improvised harpoon. The point of the boat-hook, still angled down into the muscles of the monstrous neck, tore up again, moving like a lever against the fulcrum of the net's first strands. It slid through the crushed bone splintered by Simon's axe, and tore through the light cartilage into the brain itself. Blood gushed down her face. She let go and fell free.

The killer went rigid as the hook broke into its head, and it began to topple like a falling tree. The crewman at the outboard motor in the rubber boat had reacted well when the whale had come up under the bows, and had slammed the engine into reverse, backing off.

The great wave thrown up as the killer hit the water swamped it, slopping also over Colin Ross as he lay where he had landed in the centre of the floe.

The water closed over Kate's head and she sank, trying to kick off her boots, and working to strip off her bulky, heavy clothes. But by the time she had wriggled out of her over-trousers, she had run out of air. She was terribly tired, and her struggles were growing weak as her head burst free of the water. Two minutes . . . Thankfully she gasped down breath after breath, then she tried to strike out towards the floe. It was no more than twenty feet away – but her arms would not work properly and her legs felt like dead weights dragging her down. The water closed over her head again, and she struggled to the surface in panic. God help me, she thought, I'm going to drown.

On the floe, something moved. To Kate's mind what she saw then was a natural part of this terrible, final nightmare. The shape on the ice pulled itself slowly erect. It had no left arm, only the ragged banner of a sleeve flapping in the wind. Its right arm was huge as it reached out its great square hand, blindly groping in the icy air. As it rose to its full height on the rocking ice-raft, the sun broke through the clouds somewhere far beyond the fogbank, colouring everything a strange greenish-yellow and lighting the fires in the blue ice just beyond her reach. The monstrous shape on the floe staggered forward on stiff legs, the light behind it flaming grotesquely upon the wild tumbled mass of black hair which fell forward concealing its face, making its body a hard black silhouette, casting a giant shadow on the fog, on the blue-flame ice, on the restless green water.

As the shadow covered her head, Kate began to go down for the last time. Suddenly, incredibly, her feet thumped into a solid base. Without thinking she kicked up towards the surface, but something held her legs. Confused, she looked down and saw a black shape hulking beneath her. She saw what it was and almost screamed. She looked up wildly, fighting against the horror, and at the distant edge of her vision she saw the shadow move on the surface as her monster toppled forward, arm reaching, into the ocean.

Colin's numbed legs had saved him, bending automatically into the perfect parachutist's landing roll. Then he heard Kate screaming and began to drag himself towards the sound. After a few agonising feet he realised the sounds had choked into silence. He began to get up, his face pressed against the ice, humping his backside ridiculously into the air, pushing with his arm until he was on his knees. He made it to his feet and staggered stiff-legged over the last few feet to the water. He began to topple forward. As he did so he saw the sharp black tip of the killer's fin rising slowly out of the dark, still ocean. His head broke free of the water, eyes closed, he gasped in a breath and sank again. Something gently thumped him in the stomach. He opened his eyes and the killer was there, its mouth opening in a great tooth-lined cavern. Oh, my God, he thought. His legs swept in; his arms reached up over the snout, out of the water, trying to find something to hang on to, something by which he could pull himself out of the killer's mouth, pictures flashing in his mind of Preston's legs, Job's white-bone arm. But of course there was nothing there to hold on to and he began to slip inch by inch down the monster's throat . . .

Then, suddenly, something grasped him by the wrist and hauled him free. Beside the killer's head, floating in the dinghy, hanging on to the net, were Sergei Antonovich Ivanov, and Pjotr Picatel. Pjotr's hand slapped against the monster's white cheek.

"Dead," he said.

They began to laugh. But Colin's terrible fear was not lessened by the fact that he was safe. He looked down at the men, and they quietened. "Kate?" he said. He handled the word as someone handles a thing that he fears will give him pain. The Russians looked at one another, not understanding. Suddenly, agonisingly, he was certain she was dead. "Kate," yelled Ross, as though the sound of the word, if it were loud enough, could call her back out of the depths of the ocean.

"It's all right Colin, I'm up here." He looked up, straining his neck. On the monster's back, leaning against the fin where Simon had sat with the axe, she was sitting. Her feet dangled down the net. One hand raised to pull her hair back from her face. The other bent across her chest, easing her left shoulder. She was shivering convulsively, but she smiled at him. He smiled at her.

"Someone have one hell a fight!" said Pjotr, slapping the whale again, higher this time, just below where the stub of the boat-hook stood out like a bolt from its neck. He gestured to the net, the harpoons.

"Us," said Ross. "We did it . . ."

He thought of them all then. He thought of the pilot keeping the 'plane aloft against all odds until he could land safely; of Hiram Preston pushing into the blizzard of fire inside the torn cargo-hold to save Kate; of old Doc Warren, legs spread, leaning forward over the harpoon-gun, ready to send a silver-steel spear through anything that threatened them; of Simon, seated upon the killer's back swinging the axe like a lunatic; of Job, of his massive strength, of his weaknesses, of his friendship, of no single thing that he had done, but all he had meant, all he had been, all he still was, somewhere. His eyes, moving up, met Kate's again, and they smiled at each other, silent among the laughing Russians. Not needing to speak, not even needing to touch; tied even more deeply than Job had suspected.

"Just us," he said again. "Just friends and enemies; just us and . . ." He searched for a word that would encapsulate it all, the crash, the explosion, the ice, the water, the fog, the rain, the bitterness, the strife, the nightmare, the bear, the iceberg, the walrus and the whales . . . "just we seven and the pack."

"That is a story you must tell!" said Pjotr.

"Yes," said Colin, "yes it is."